The
LOST
LIBRARY

A. M. Dean is a leading authority on ancient cultures and the history of religious belief, whose expertise in late antiquity has earned him posts at some of the world's most prestigious universities. An abiding interest in the human tendency towards conspiracies, together with a commanding grasp of the genuinely mysterious contexts of real history, inspire the breadth and focus of his creative works. *The Lost Library* is his first novel.

The

LOST
LIBRARY

A. M. DEAN

PAN BOOKS

First published 2012 by Pan Books
an imprint of Pan Macmillan, a division of Macmillan Publishers Limited
Pan Macmillan, 20 New Wharf Road, London N1 9RR
Basingstoke and Oxford
Associated companies throughout the world
www.panmacmillan.com

ISBN 978-1-4472-0951-5

3 5 7 9 8 6 4

A CIP catalogue record for this book is available from
the British Library.

Map artwork © Raymond Turvey

Typeset by Ellipsis Digital Limited, Glasgow
Printed and bound by CPI Group (UK) Ltd, Croydon, CR0 4YY

The

LOST
LIBRARY

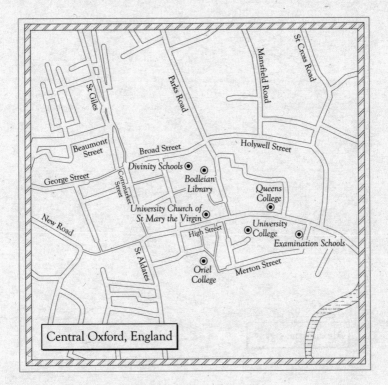

St Cross Road

Mansfield Road

Parks Road

St Giles

Beaumont
Street

Broad Street

Holywell Street

Divinity Schools

Bodleian
Library

Queens
College

George Street

Cornmarket
Street

New Road

University Church of
St Mary the Virgin

University
College

High Street

Examination Schools

St Aldates

Merton Street

Oriel
College

Central Oxford, England

Alexandria, Egypt

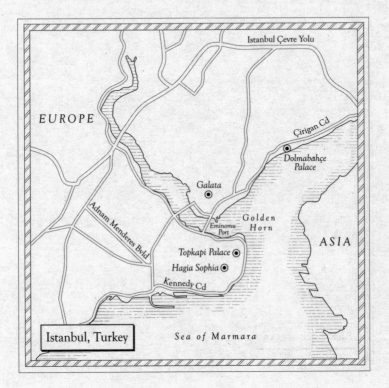

EUROPE

Istanbul Çevre Yolu

Çirigan Cd

Dolmabahçe
Palace

Galata

Golden
Horn

Eminomu
Port

ASIA

Adnam Menderes Bvld

Topkapi Palace

Hagia Sophia

Kennedy Cd

Sea of Marmara

Istanbul, Turkey

Tuesday

PROLOGUE

The bullet that had pierced his lung remained lodged in his chest, but the old man no longer felt its pain. That pain had become focus, even as the edges of his vision began to blur.

This had been expected. Arno Holmstrand had known they were coming – the events of the past week had left little room for doubt. He was ready. He had had to rush the preparations, but they were now done. The stage was set and he had accomplished what was required. All that remained was to complete this final task, and then pray his efforts did not fail.

He collapsed into the rough leather chair behind his desk. The mahogany surface before him seemed to glimmer, reflecting a dim lamplight through the dark office – an odd beauty, in such a moment.

He reached his hands out to the book laid open on the wooden surface, and for an instant the searing pain in his chest returned. If it was needed, it served as a final reminder: there was no way out – only to finish. He concentrated his

3

attention, set his gaze on the volume and counted off three pages. With all the energy he could muster, he tore them from the book.

Footsteps sounded in the corridor, bringing renewed focus. Arno took up a gilded silver lighter, a gift from his service as best man at a student's wedding many years ago, and produced a flame. Holding the pages over a small wastebasket at his feet, he nudged the flame to the paper. A moment later it was alight. Releasing the pages into the bin, watching them crumple and yield to the orange flames, he drew back into his chair.

The final act was accomplished. Arno folded his hands together, interlaced his fingers and watched as the door to his office burst open. The man that faced him held a steeled expression, devoid of recognizable emotion. Smoothing a black leather jacket that traced the contours of a muscular physique, he quickly surveyed the room, glanced at the small fire in the bin and aimed a pistol squarely at the elderly man behind the desk.

Arno looked up, bringing his eyes directly to his adversary's.

'I have been expecting you.' His words were calm, tinged with a reassuring sense of authority. In the doorway, the man with the gun did not flinch. Though seconds ago he had been running, his breathing steadied now into a metered rhythm.

Arno removed the mock familiarity from his voice, now fully business.

'You have found me. That is more than most. But it ends here.'

The younger man gazed at Arno curiously, his pace momentarily halted. The old man's self-assurance was not expected, not in this moment. This moment was his defeat. Yet there he sat, discomfortingly calm.

The intruder took a steady, deep breath. Then, without blinking, he fired two shots in quick succession, both into Arno's chest.

The darkness of the room swelled. Arno Holmstrand watched as the intruder's form faded and swirled, and then seemed to retreat. The darkness grew.

And then there was nothing.

14 minutes later – Oxford, England
Wednesday morning, 5.29 a.m. GMT

The ancient church's clock tower loomed over the city, which in typical routine was beginning to come to life below. A few lights dotted the rooms of the colleges surrounding the square, and delivery vans manoeuvred the High Street, feeding its shops for the business of the day ahead. The moon sat low in the sky, the sun's first light still hidden by the night.

At precisely 5.30, the immense iron hand of the clock clicked forward to its mark. Behind the metal faceplate, a small wooden dowel, deliberately inserted into the ancient gears, snapped in two. The cord to which it was tied lost its tension, and the package it had held suspended high above the tower's base began its carefully coordinated fall.

One hundred and twenty-four spiralling stone steps below,

at the foot of the thirteenth-century tower, the package slammed into its thick, stone foundations. The blasting cap mounted on its outer edge buckled at the jolt, producing its precisely directed ignition charge. Before it had fully caught its colour, the bundle of C4 burst to life, exploding with an unrestrained fury.

In an immense ball of fire, the ancient church crumbled.

Wednesday

CHAPTER 1

Minnesota – 9.05 a.m. CST

The day that would change Professor Emily Wess's life began unassumingly enough. There had been no signs of tragedy, no particular notes of urgency, in the way she had begun the same morning routine she kept every day during term time. She had taken her morning run, taught her morning class, bought her morning coffee; and yet, even as the same heavy autumnal air she breathed each morning on the Carleton College campus filled her nostrils, something felt amiss. Something shivered at the surface of her skin as she walked from classroom to office, even before it could be fully defined. The day had an abnormal shape, an unusual feel that she could not quite pinpoint.

'Good morning, everyone.' She turned out of the central corridor of Leighton Hall's third-floor complex, home of the Department of Religion, through the door leading into her office. Hers was one of a group of offices collected together around a small, common space through an otherwise un-assuming door – a 'pod', as the Minnesotan dialect insisted

9

on having it. Four others had offices in the pod, and they, together with another colleague, stood in one of its corners as Emily entered.

She smiled, but the small company was entirely absorbed in a hushed conversation. A 'hello' emerged back from some-where in their huddle an unusually long moment after her greeting, but no face turned to greet Emily. It was in that moment that she became conscious of an odd atmosphere present throughout the morning, which until then hadn't grabbed her full attention – a strange quiet in the halls, diverted gazes and concerned expressions on the faces of her colleagues.

Fishing her keys from her bag, Emily stopped at a row of mailboxes and emptied the contents of her own into the crook of her arm: the junk mail of two weeks, which she'd wilfully allowed to accumulate. Taken in every day, the dross was simply too much to bear.

Behind her, the muffled voices of her colleagues continued. She glanced over her shoulder as she fitted a small key into her office door.

'One of the janitors found him this morning.' Emily picked up a soft voice, deliberately hushed.

'It just doesn't seem possible,' came another. 'I had coffee with him only yesterday.'

Maggie Larson, the Christian Ethics professor from whom the last remark had come, had a sober look on her face.

No, Emily thought to herself, looking closer. *She looks upset.* Her curiosity piqued when she realized even this wasn't the right word. *No, she looks frightened.*

Emily stopped her key mid-rotation in the lock and turned fully back toward her colleagues. Something was absorbing their focus – something that didn't look, or sound, good.

'Sorry, I don't meant to be rude, but what's going on?' she said as she took a step towards them. The strange tension in the air increased with each word, but Emily was unsure how otherwise to interject herself into their conversation without knowing any of its details. Or even its focus.

The others, however, didn't intend to keep her wondering. 'You must not have heard,' one colleague answered. Aileen Merrin was full professor in New Testament. She'd also been a member of the appointments committee that had hired Emily when she had applied for her post nearly two years ago, and Emily had retained an in-built fondness for her ever since. She hoped that, when the day came, she looked as good in silver hair as Aileen.

'Evidently not.' Emily took a sip from a paper cup filled with cold coffee. Over an hour old, it was no longer pleasant to drink, but the act of raising the cup to her lips helped to break up the awkwardness of the moment with something a bit more normal. 'Heard what?'

'You know Arno Holmstrand, in History?'

'Of course,' Emily answered. The history department's flagship professor was known to everyone. Even if Emily hadn't been a dual-departmental appointment, serving in both history and religion, she still would have known of the college's most eminent and famous scholar. 'Has he discovered another lost manuscript? Or been expelled from another Middle Eastern country for breaking the rules of his archaeological dig?' It seemed that every time Emily heard Holmstrand's name mentioned, it was in the context of some major discovery or academic adventure. 'He hasn't bankrupted the college on one of his trips, has he?'

'No, he hasn't.' Aileen suddenly looked uncomfortable. Her voice shifted to a whisper. 'He's dead.'

'Dead!' Emily brought herself fully into the huddled group with a small shove, jolted by the news. 'What are you talking about? When? How?'

'Last night. They think he was killed, here on campus.'

'They don't think, they know,' Jim Reynolds, a Protestant Reformation specialist, interjected. 'He was murdered. Three gunshots, centre-mass – that's what I heard. Right at his desk. Like some professional job.'

The odd shivers formerly running down Emily's skin were now replaced by fully fledged goosebumps. A murder on the Carleton College campus was unheard of. But the murder of a colleague . . . the news had the effect of blending shock with genuine fear.

'He was chased down the hallway,' Aileen added. 'There's blood outside his office. I haven't seen inside.' Her voice faltered. She looked at Emily. 'Haven't you noticed the police around campus?'

Emily was numbed by the news. She had seen police cruisers when she had parked her car before her morning lecture, but had not given them much thought. Law enforcement was not an entirely unusual presence on a college campus.

'I – I had no idea what it was about.' Emily paused. 'Why Arno?' She couldn't fathom what else to ask.

'That's not the question that worries me.' The voice this time, timid and fearful, came from Emily's fellow religious historian, Emma Ericksen.

'Then what is?' Emily asked her.

'The question that worries me is, if one of our colleagues has been attacked and killed right here on campus, then who's next?'

CHAPTER 2

Washington DC – 9.06 a.m. EST

Outside the conference room marked '26H', D. Burton Gifford passed his leather briefcase to a lackey and gave him a look that made it clear he wanted to be alone following the conclusion of their morning meeting. Standing aside as the other men filtered out of the room and down the corridor to the exit, he ignored the numerous 'No Smoking' signs, extracted an unfiltered Pall Mall from a case in his breast pocket and lit up. He had worked on the president's foreign policy advisory committee for the two years that the great man had been in power, a loyal supporter of the president's work in the Middle East, even if the man in charge didn't share his desire to be more aggressive, more of a dealer, in the post-war reconstruction work there. He had become one of the commander-in-chief's most influential advisors, shaping policy as well as ensuring the president always knew his friends from his enemies. Gifford's background was in business, and business was nothing if not a world of networks. He liked to think that the president was connected, or not connected, due to his wisdom and influence. And he was not entirely wrong. He was the man with the connections; the president was the moral voice that only chose the right ones.

In the shadows, a man called Cole stood motionless, his unseen face bearing an expression of loathing toward the portly, arrogant power-broker, who lived up to every stereotype of the fat cat, domineering man of influence. Bloated physically as well as in his arrogance, Gifford was oblivious to everything that he did not deem relevant to his own designs.

It was a flaw for which he would pay, today.

Gifford took a long drag from his cigarette in the empty corridor, the half-smoked butt dangling from his lips as he used his hands to straighten his jacket. Taking advantage of this distraction as well as his vulnerable body position, Cole chose that moment to step out of the office across the hall, and in a single, smooth motion grabbed the fat man by his wrists and forced him back into the conference room.

'What the hell are you doing?' Gifford demanded, taken aback, the cigarette falling from his lips.

'Be silent, and this will all go more easily,' Cole answered. He kept Gifford in an arm lock with his left hand while he eased closed the door behind him with his right. 'Now sit down.' He thrust the man into one of the recently vacated leather chairs surrounding the long conference table.

Gifford was indignant. The insubordinate man had not only manhandled him, but also twisted his wrist in the process. He pulled his hands before his chest, fuming as he rubbed away the soreness. He was already ranting as he began to swivel his chair towards his attacker. 'I'll have you know, young man, that I'm not an individual who sits back and idly accepts this kind of—'

He cut off his rant mid-sentence as his chair completed its turn and his eyes came to rest on Cole's hands. Calmly turning the silencer the final few twists to fasten it to his .357 SIG Glock 32, Cole replied without so much as looking up.

'I know precisely who you are, Mr Gifford. Who you are is why I am here.'

Gifford's condescending rage was now gone, entirely replaced by helpless terror. His eyes would not move from the gun. 'What . . . what do you want?'

'This moment,' Cole answered, clicking the silencer into its locked position and switching off the safety from the Glock's trigger. 'This moment is exactly what I want.'

'I don't understand,' Gifford spat, horrified, instinctively pushing back into his chair as if hoping to find there some retreat from the threat before him. 'What do you want *from me?*'

'That's just it,' Cole replied. 'I don't want anything. This is not an interrogation, or a kidnapping.'

'Then what is it?!'

Cole finally looked up, squarely into D. Burton Gifford's wide, terrified eyes. 'It is the end.'

'I . . . don't understand.'

'No,' Cole answered. 'I don't imagine you do.'

Any further conversation was cut short by the three bullets he fired into Gifford's heart, his right shoulder comfortably absorbing the familiar report of the small gun's discharge and the long room only slightly echoing the soft 'pings' muffled by the silencer.

Gifford gaped in disbelief at the slight whiff of smoke drifting up from the gun barrel that had just delivered its charge through his upper body. As the blood poured out of his heart and seeped from the wounds in his chest and back, he fell into the chair.

Cole watched as the man breathed his last and slumped forward into the darkness.

CHAPTER 3

'Do they know who shot him?' The hesitating pull of Emily's words betrayed her own discomfort. She still could not fathom why anyone would want to kill Arno Holmstrand. The man was without question the college's most famous public face, but he was also ancient, from Emily's perspective – well into his seventies. Essentially a quiet, if eccentric, old man. Emily didn't know him well. They had met a few times, and Arno had occasionally muttered strange comments about Emily's research – the expected right of any old professor to balk at the work of his juniors – but that had been the extent of their relationship. They were associates, not friends.

This, however, did little to ease the shock. A death on campus, much less a murder, was no ordinary news. And Emily couldn't help but feel a certain attachment to Holmstrand, even if it was largely through reputation and professional appreciation rather than personal interaction.

'No idea,' Jim Reynolds answered. 'The investigators are

in his building now. Whole wing's blocked off. Will be all day.'

Emily impulsively took another sip from her coffee, but this time the gesture of bringing the cup to her mouth felt forced and obvious, almost disrespectful, as if utterly too normal an act to be done in the face of such news.

'I can't believe this has happened here.' Maggie Larson's fear still showed. 'If someone was willing to go after him . . .' She allowed her words to trail off. Her unspoken statement was made for them all: with a colleague murdered, everyone felt unsafe.

A long silence fell over the group, brought to an end only by the ringing of the office bell sounding behind their heads. The day's next session of classes was about to begin and worried glances passed between them as they departed for their classrooms and obligations. As they made to go their separate ways, Emily felt an uncomfortable compunction. Was it acceptable just to leave, to go about business as usual after a conversation about a dead colleague? Surely, something needed to be said, something at least to acknowledge the emotion of the situation.

'I'm, well . . . I'm sorry to hear about Arno.' It was all she could come up with. She was surprised at the degree of loss she felt. The emotional reaction she was experiencing would have been more expected in response to the death of a close friend – something Arno Holmstrand had never been.

Aileen gave her a soft smile and departed the pod. Emily, struggling with her shock, walked back to her office, unlocked the door and entered the tiny room. It was amazing how quickly the focus of a day could change, how consuming a tragic act could be. Until the moment she had heard about Arno's death, her focus had been on another realm entirely – on visions of an impending reunion with the man she loved. The final Wednesday before an extended Thanksgiving weekend meant only a single lecture, first thing in the morning. The remainder of the day, if Emily had her way, would be spent in the successive steps of a much anticipated journey that led from Minneapolis to Chicago and a holiday weekend with her fiancé, Michael. They had met four years ago, on Thanksgiving itself – he an English man studying on his home turf, she an over-eager Master's student doing research abroad, attempting to share the significance of the great American tradition with the old colonial overlords – and the day had remained theirs ever since.

But that blissful detachment had met a sudden end. Emily's heart was now racing, her adrenaline on the increase since she'd learned news of the death in her halls.

Still, she forced down her discomfort and switched on the computer at her desk. The work of the day could not halt entirely, whatever the shock. Unbending her arm, Emily allowed the mail she'd gathered from her box to fall onto the surface of the desk.

Her mind still swimming with thoughts of murder and loss, she did not at first notice the small yellow envelope nestled between two brightly coloured flyers. Her eyes did not catch the elegant, strange penmanship on its exterior, or the lack of postage, or the absence of a return address. It slipped, unnoticed, past her gaze and into the mix of all the rest.

CHAPTER 4

Two small holes pierced the leather of the old chair, marking the fatal shots that had taken Arno Holmstrand's life. They were centre-mass, no more than an inch apart: tell-tale signs of a professional. The body now removed, the detective was able to ascertain trajectory from the distinct tunnels the bullets had left in the chair's padding. The assassin had stood in the doorway, no more than five foot seven in height. The victim had been seated, facing his assailant.

Detective Al Johnson watched as the crime scene unit went about its work. A thin pair of tweezers, grasped deftly in the latex-gloved hands of hands of a man who had obviously done this before, extracted a bullet from one of the holes in the chair. Perhaps a .38, Al considered, though he was hardly prepared to insist on the point. That was the territory of the techies in ballistics. Enough for him that it was clearly a handgun, clearly an assassination, clearly a professional job.

Things he had seen before.

The body had been taken to the morgue earlier in the morning. Three gunshot wounds in total, with the hole in the elderly man's right side having come first, likely outside the office. Johnson peered at the trail of blood leading into the room. The coroner suspected the first wound would have been fatal on its own, but the victim had lived long enough to stumble through the door – the detective raised himself from his crouch, moved to retrace the hypothetical steps – through the door and to the desk. For what? There was a phone on the desk, but no sign that it had been touched, and 911 had received no call until the next morning, when a janitor had discovered the scene.

Another evidence technician dusted for prints on the door-frame. A third mirrored his partner's activities at the desk. Two uniforms were taking photos, Johnson's partner interviewed night staff in the hallway, and at least six other people milled about the room. Not for the first time, Al marvelled at just how bustling with life a murder scene could be. It was one of the strange paradoxes of the job.

Al stepped closer to the desk. It looked like he imagined an old professor's desk should look: green-shaded lamp, brass pen holder, faded paper blotter, and a computer that appeared as if it had been out of date since the day it was built. A leather tray contained old letters, each opened meticulously with an ivory letter opener, since laid across them.

Ivory opener, ivory tower . . . there was the making of a cultural statement here.

At the centre of the desk was a large, hardcover book,

filled with photographs. It lay open, somewhere near its middle. The detective moved closer, and lightly ran his gloved hand over the surface pages. Beneath the powdered latex, his calloused fingers stopped at the touch of unexpectedly rough edges. The binding at the book's centre concealed a small ruffle of jagged remnants, where a number of pages had evidently been torn out.

A flash caught his attention as a young member of the Crime Scene Unit snapped a photograph of the book, together with Al's hand.

Al imagined the scene: *A man, shot in the chest, scrambles back to his office, to tear a few pages out of a book.* It made little sense. But then, murders rarely did.

Another photo, the camera this time aimed at his feet. Al looked down at a wastebasket, filled with blackened remains. Kneeling next to it, a slick younger man in a tailored suit flicked through the charred remnants.

A nice suit, Al mused, his annoyance immediate. *An agency boy – just what we need.*

He wasn't one for Hollywood blockbusters, but the one thing the movies always got right was the hassle that arose any time multiple law enforcement agencies vied for jurisdiction over a case. And detectives in the local squads never wore nice suits. He didn't know where the younger man was from, but whatever the answer to that question was, it was going to be damned frustrating.

'Do history professors always burn their trash?' the younger man asked, without looking up.

'You got me, kid.'

The suit flinched visibly at this last word, evidently displeased at being reminded of his youth. He rose slowly, forcing himself to reclaim his composure.

'It's not much. Just a few pages curled together. Burned in one go, I would guess.'

Al motioned to the open book on the desk.

'Some pages were torn out here.' He indicated the tattered edges that remained in the volume. 'From the page numbers before and after, it looks like three are missing.'

'That's about what we've got here,' confirmed the younger man, indicating the charred sheets in the bin.

'I don't get it,' Al said. 'The old man is shot in the hallway, but manages to stumble his way back into his office, to his desk. There's a phone right in front of him, but he doesn't pick it up. Doesn't call for help. Paper and pens all around, but he doesn't jot down a note. Instead, he opens up some picture book, rips out a few pages, and burns them. It doesn't fit.'

The younger man did not reply. Picking up the book, he examined it with an intensity that went beyond the frustration Al was feeling. He looked – angry.

'Look, kid,' Al said, 'I didn't get your name. I haven't seen you around before. You been in the Cities long?' Most detectives in the Twin Cities of Minneapolis and St Paul, the hub of local law enforcement for the southern part of the state, had at least a passing familiarity with one another.

'I'm not local.' The words came as a complete statement. The young man offered nothing further, nor did he give any sign of wishing to continue with such professional pleasantries. The book turned over again in his hands, and his eyes rested on the blackened paper in the bin.

Al was not quite as ready to let the matter rest.

'Not local? You State? What's State doing here?' *This is clearly a local case. Damned State Police.*

The younger man did not answer, ignoring Al's persistence, but at last set the book back on the desk. Straightening his suit, he turned to the detective with an air of office efficiency. For the first time in their conversation, he looked directly into Al's eyes.

'I'm sorry. I've got enough for my report. Nice to have met you, Detective.'

'Your report?' The dismissive remark was almost too much. A book and a bit of burnt paper were materially significant, but hardly enough for a report. Al looked around the room at the flutter of activity – sampling fingerprints, bloodstains, spatter patterns, footprints. All *that* would make a report. And yet the younger man had seemed to ignore it all, his attention solely on the desk and the charred paper in the wastebasket. As if the rest of the crime scene was non-existent.

It wasn't normal investigative behaviour, even for a state squad.

He turned back to the unknown agent, a sarcastic rebuff at the ready, but found himself standing alone.

CHAPTER 5

'The question that worries me is, if one of our colleagues has been attacked and killed right here on campus, then who's next?'

Her colleagues having gone off to teach their classes, Emily was left alone in her office to ponder the strange contours of their conversation. Emma Ericksen's words lingered in Emily's mind. It was not just the unanswerable questions associated with Arno Holmstrand's murder that contributed to the uncomfortable fear she felt – it was also the ominous presence of death itself. There had been a murder, of a peer, mere yards from her own office. Was there a wider danger? Were they all at risk?

Am I? Even as it came, Emily pushed away the thought. Making the situation personal was irrational and would only feed her fear. She would have to fight her wandering mind with activity: work, and the few tasks that remained to be done before she could depart the campus for her trip to Michael's.

She looked down to the pile of mail she'd retrieved from

her box – at present, the most immediate distraction from her troubling thoughts. Junk, junk, junk. Emily had developed a reputation for being bad at collecting her mail, and this was why. Nearly two weeks' worth in hand, and almost all of it garbage. An envelope from a publisher, advertising a book she almost certainly would never read. A circular about animal rights awareness – an exact copy of the circular she'd received on the subject the week before, and the week before that. A memo indicating that she'd been given a new code for the departmental copy machine, which the office secretary announced with the same air of impending seriousness and importance that might accompany being given launch codes to the nation's nuclear reserve. An academic's life might be intellectually engaging, but filled with raw excitement it was not. Emily flicked the memo, along with the other papers, into the bin.

Beneath it lay a single yellow envelope, crafted of textured, clearly expensive paper. Emily's name was neatly written on the front, and there was no return address or postage.

Something about it caught Emily's eye. She noted the elegant handwriting in which her name was penned. The flowing lettering was in brown ink, bearing the unmistakable wells and arcs of having been delivered from a fountain pen. Emily turned the envelope over and paused at the blank surface. No postage, no indication of a sender. Someone had dropped this into her box by hand. Perhaps it was an invitation to some party or event, though from the look of the envelope it would be of a slightly higher class than she was used to.

She finessed her little finger through the flap to pry the envelope open, and a single sheet of paper, folded once over the middle, fell into her lap.

She unfolded the page. If first impressions set a stage, Emily thought, this note wished it to be an extravagant set. The paper was fine, obviously expensive, a soft cream in colour, and – if she wasn't mistaken – scented slightly with cedar wood.

What she saw at the top of the page caused her stomach to tighten. In embossed type, raised smartly above the sheen of the page, ran a clear letterhead:

FROM THE DESK OF PROFESSOR ARNO HOLMSTRAND,
BA, MA, D.PHIL, PH.D., OBE

Arno Holmstrand, the man murdered the night before. The great professor.

The dead professor.

What came next snapped her to full attention.

'Dear Emily,' the note began, written in the same elegant script, with the same brown ink as the envelope. 'My death has surely preceded this letter.'

CHAPTER 6

Dear Emily,

My death has surely preceded this letter. I write it in full knowledge that this is coming, and in the yet surer knowledge that you will play an important role in what comes next.

There is something I must leave you to discover, Emily. Something that puts all my other work in a shadow, into the dustbin of insignificance.

I know the location of a library. Of The Library. The Library built by a king familiar to your own research, Emily. The Library of Alexandria.

It exists, as does the Society that accompanies it. Neither is lost.

There is far more at stake than just an archaeological curiosity. When you receive this, I will have been killed for it.

This knowledge cannot be abandoned, Emily. Your help is now required. There is a telephone number printed on the back of this page. Finish reading, and dial it. I promise you, things will become clearer soon.

We did not know each other well, Emily. I regret that fact. But you must be certain that I write you in sincerity and urgency.

> Respectfully,
>
> Arno

CHAPTER 7

New York – 10.35 a.m. EST (9.35 a.m. CST)

The Secretary picked up the phone before it had completed its first ring.

'Yes?'

'It's done. Just as you instructed.' The voice on the other end of the line spoke in straight, cold tones.

'The Keeper is dead?'

'I saw to it myself. Last night. The police found him today.'

The Secretary sat back in his chair. A sense of satisfaction and power swept over him. A noble aim had been met, and the future of their project preserved. Few men in history had attempted what they were attempting. Fewer had met their aims. But they would succeed, and as the progress of the last week showed, there were none who would be able to stand in their way. The Secretary ran his fingers through his silver hair.

'He knew we were coming,' the other man voiced.

That was to be expected. Termination of the Assistant the week before had been a public affair. It had been impossible to avoid. A Washington DC patents clerk isn't shot in his office without the media catching wind. But then, the Council's aim had not been to conceal the termination. Such murders would simply be reported as murders to most, but to the people their moves were targeting, they would be seen as messages. Warnings.

'That is irrelevant,' the Secretary responded, 'as long as you've done your work. Apart from the source, whom you'll deal with shortly, he was the last man who had access to the list.'

The leak of the list had been inexcusable. Everything they had worked to bring together had been put at risk by something as unassuming as a list of names. A list that included names that no one could know. On that secrecy – that anonymity – their whole plan rested. Yet somehow the list had been compromised. The only response had been to act and eradicate those who had seen it. The Keeper and his Assistant were men whose lives had an undeniable value to him, but that value was outweighed by the risks.

The Secretary had become so absorbed in his thoughts that at first he didn't notice the silence that met him from the other end of the line. All at once, however, it set off an alarm. Snapping out of his reverie, he leaned forward.

'What is it? What went wrong?'

'The fact that he knew we were coming – it might be more relevant than you think.'

The Secretary winced. He was not a man who enjoyed surprises. He leaned forward further, pressing the receiver into his cheek.

'Do tell.'

'He got to his office before I could finish him off. Something struck me as not quite right at the time, but I couldn't linger. When I went back this morning to follow up, my suspicion was confirmed.'

'Continue,' the Secretary demanded, retaining a practised calm. He had decades of experience in receiving bad news. Composure in difficulty, he had always known, was important. A good leader was at his most ferocious, his most fearful, when he was most at calm.

'There was a book on his desk,' the Friend said. 'Three of the pages were gone – torn out. I found them burnt in the trash next to his chair.' He paused, allowing the Secretary to digest the details. He did not expect or await a response. That was not how their relationship worked. He was expected to say what was required. If more was wanted, the Secretary would ask.

The older man mulled over the strange report. So, there was something the Keeper didn't want his assassin to see. Even in death, he was determined to foil them.

The Secretary spoke his next words as much as a threat as a question.

'Did you get details on the book?'

'Of course, sir.'

He forced his shoulder muscles to relax. The Friend was trained well.

'I want details on my desk in half an hour. Get them to me on your way to Washington.' The chase was not going to end like this. 'And get me a copy of that book.'

CHAPTER 8

The news contained in the red file folder in his hands was disturbing, but hardly more thorough than what the blonde woman behind the scrolling ticker-tape feed at the CNN news desk was reporting on the television across his office. He'd muted the television a few minutes ago, before his aide had entered the room. The anchorwoman had said her piece on the explosion in the United Kingdom, and a circling helicopter kept an aerial video feed of the wreckage live on the screen, but apart from the time of the explosion and a visual survey of the extent of the damage, little else was known at this stage in the investigation. A great old church, a landmark of English heritage, had been destroyed in a bomb blast in the early morning. There were no reported casualties, save for sentimentalism and historical legacies.

'Has anyone claimed responsibility?' he asked.

'No, Mr Hines,' replied his aide.

Jefferson clenched his jaw at the young man's lack of

deference. The failure to refer to him by his office was, he knew, entirely intentional.

'The CIA is following the British SIS in trolling sources, but so far, not even the usual crazies are scrambling for the credit.'

Hines took in the information, or, rather, the lack of information. Terrorist bombings were usually followed by torrential streams of groups claiming responsibility and seeking the publicity that came from an attack on the Great Western Beast. There were exceptions, of course, and they were frequent enough to keep the lack of claims on the present case from sounding too many alarm bells, but it was still an interesting silence.

'Has there been any formal response from the British government?'

'Only that they are shocked and horrified, working with due diligence, intending to bring the culprits of this heinous crime to justice, et cetera, et cetera.' Mitch Forrester fluttered his fingers in a gesture indicating the essential meaninglessness of such standard responses. He had worked in Hines's office only six months, yet he passed along the comments with an air of having heard all this before.

Hines suddenly couldn't stop himself from asking the question.

'How old are you, Mitch?'

The question caught his aide off guard.

'Excuse me?'

'Your age. How old are you?'

The younger Forrester looked at him strangely, his usual

veiled contempt combined with a puzzled confusion. Had they been alone, he might have responded with an open display of the loathing he was feeling, but he was only too aware of the presence of another man in Hines's office – someone who sat in the corner, silently. Someone he did not wish to see his full impertinence.

'Twenty-six,' he finally answered.

'Twenty-six,' Hines repeated. He let out a sigh at the depressingly low number. Had he been so headstrong when he was that age? He'd had more than that many years again since, and he had always been an ambitious man, but he couldn't believe he'd ever been as impetuous as the youth that stood before him.

'I'm not sure I see why that's releva—'

'It isn't, it isn't,' Hines cut him off, waving his hand to dismiss the tangent. He paused a moment. 'Is there anything else?'

'Nothing yet,' Forrester answered curtly. 'As soon as we receive anything, I'll let you know. Sir.' He let the pause before his final word accentuate his unhappiness with the way he had been treated. Yet, with all the egotism of youth, he still stood, waiting for acknowledgement. Hines, however, simply gazed past him at the video feed on the television. Realizing at last that he was getting nothing else, the aide turned and left the room.

Hines waited a full thirty seconds in silence before he turned his head to the man sat in the far corner of his office. Though he had long since reconciled himself with the service that these men did for the organization, he still felt a tinge of nervousness whenever he was actually alone with one of them. His role in the organization had always been diplomatic, professional. He had never been one of the wet men – those who did the necessary dirty work. It was a vile dimension of their cause, but essential. Though many in the world would consider him to be an individual of great influence, Jefferson Hines knew that the man sat a few feet from his desk represented a power far greater than any he would ever possess.

'Do you think it's connected?' he finally asked, motioning towards the file on his desk and then to the muted television display. 'Connected to the mission?'

'Of course.' Both men knew not to speak of the plan in any other terms than simply 'the mission'. In this city, and in this office, the walls most certainly had ears. 'But do not let it sway you. We will stay the course.'

Hines wasn't satisfied.

'This was never discussed. Marlake, Gifford . . . the rest – *that* was the plan. What the hell is going on in England?'

The other man sat upright as Hines spoke. He cast him a glare that allowed no room for doubt as to his meaning: *shut up*. Names were not to be mentioned.

Hines took in the glance and its message, rattling his fingers across his desk, half in annoyance, half out of nervousness.

'Tell me we were anticipating responses like this,' he said. 'Tell me this doesn't come as a surprise.'

If the other man felt any hesitation before his response, he did not show it. He bore the air of a man who wished to exude confidence, and who wanted his interlocutor to remain strong and steadfast.

'Our plans are secure. So let us deal with our side of the business, and you deal with yours. Then, we all win.' He gave his words a moment to linger in the heavy air between them. 'Don't lose sight of where you're going.'

Despite his innate fear of the man, Hines took comfort from his apparent certainty. Exhaling a long breath, he straightened his composure. Statesmen were meant to be strong, and he would rise to the task.

'Good. Then I suppose I'll speak to you tomorrow?'

The other man nodded, rising from his chair.

'Indeed you will, Mr Vice President.'

CHAPTER 9

Minnesota – 9.45 a.m. CST

Emily stared at the letter in her hands. It shook, and she became aware of her trembling. She re-read it a second, a third, a fourth time. And then again. Only minutes before, she had learned that Arno Holmstrand had been killed, and now she held in her hands a letter penned by the very man. Penned before his death. Knowing he was going to die.

More than that, Emily thought. *Knowing he was going to be murdered*. That fact made a sizeable difference.

In that knowledge, Arno Holmstrand had written to Emily Wess. A giant, writing to a peon, in the last moments of life. She could not fathom why. Whatever Holmstrand may have found, why was he involving her? It was a question made all the more pressing by the direct connection of the letter and its author's death. It seemed entirely within the realm of possibility that the knowledge to which the letter referred had led to Holmstrand's murder. He suggested as much in his own hand. It did not seem at all unlikely, then, that in possessing it now, Emily's own life was suddenly at risk. Her stomach turned at the thought, and at the reality of what she held in her hands.

She turned over the letter, and her eyes passed quickly to the telephone number penned there, written in clear numerals in the centre of the page. The letter instructed that Emily was to call the number, though it gave no indication of who might answer. Yet as her eyes scanned the number, her body froze. She stared in shock and confusion at the ten digits written in brown ink on the dead man's stationery.

It was a number she knew only too well.

Though she normally dialled it through a pre-set contact setting on her phone, she still recognized the digits for what they were. There was no way she could not.

Picking up her office phone, Emily dialled each number on the sheet in slow succession. *Maybe I'm wrong*, she thought to herself, knowing she wasn't. *I'm just flustered. My thoughts are confused from the shock of the news.* But she knew it was a lie.

Her breath tensed as the line rang. She knew inside that the moment it connected, the morning's events were going to take on a whole new tone.

An instant later, that moment came. As the line connected, a familiar intake of breath on the other end served as the preamble for a greeting, coming from a voice who already knew who was calling.

'Em!'

The British lilt to Michael Torrance's voice was unmissable. With an exuberance to match her confusion, Emily Wess's fiancé greeted the love of his life.

CHAPTER 10

'Mike?' Emily answered, her heart thumping. Their connection by phone, having its source in Arno Holmstrand's cryptic letter, heaped confusion on confusion.

'Where are you?' Michael's voice was filled with energy.

'I'm still in my office,' Emily responded. 'I haven't left for the airport.' She wasn't sure how to carry on with the only thought on her mind. Bluntness, she at last decided, was the best approach. 'Something's happened here on campus.'

Michael was suddenly serious, the transition instantaneous.

'What do you mean? Is it serious? Are you okay?' His tone betrayed a protective panic, and Emily realized she had begun badly.

'No, no, it's nothing like that. I'm fine.' She heard a sigh of relief from Michael's end of the phone. Though they were both formidable characters, Michael's protective impulse was strong. 'But something really strange is going on over here. You wouldn't believe it if I told you.'

'Try me,' he offered.

'A man died here last night,' Emily continued. 'Do you remember the famous professor, here on campus? Arno Holmstrand?'

'The one you didn't stop talking about for a year? Yes, Em, I remember him.' Following their habit of communicating largely by teasing, he had made a sport of goading Emily for what he had called the 'school-girlish infatuation' she had developed when the legendary figure had come to her campus. He'd confessed later that if her star-struck enthusiasm hadn't been so endearing, he might have thought she had eyes for another man.

'That's the one.' She swallowed. 'He was killed yesterday.'

'Killed?'

'In his office. Shot three times.' She paused, unconsciously adding to the dramatic note of her words.

'My God, Emily, I'm so sorry.' Michael's consoling words were compassionate, but there was something hesitating in them. Something more than masculine, protective worry pulled at his attention.

'It's not like I really knew him,' Emily replied. There was a touch of the disingenuous about her response. She hadn't known Arno, but she had known *of* him, had admired him, had followed him. And she felt his loss, however she portrayed it across the phone.

'Still, even so. ' Michael's mind raced ahead. 'Who shot him?'

'No one knows. The investigation is going on now. There are police all over campus. They say it looked like a professional job. It sounds almost like an assassination.' Emily took a long breath and swallowed hard. 'And the whole thing gets stranger.' She waited a moment for Michael to probe, to question, but he remained silent, so she continued. 'This morning, I found a letter in my office. Hand-written, hand-delivered. From Arno Holmstrand.' Emily steadied her voice. 'The letter, Mike . . . it's about his death. He wrote it before he was killed, knowing that he would be.'

Silence continued to meet her from the other end of the line.

'And here's the part you're really not going to believe. His letter gave me instructions to dial a phone number he'd written on the back, with no name attached to it. I did. And here I am, talking to you.'

At last, Michael spoke.

'Actually, Em, I find everything you've just said entirely believable.'

She started. 'Really?'

'Really. Because I got in from my morning run twenty minutes ago, and inside my door was an envelope. It's yellow and has my name written on it in brown ink.'

Emily froze, unsure of how to make sense out of what she was hearing.

'It can't be.'

'It is,' Michael interjected. 'And the letter inside is from Arno Holmstrand.'

Emily's disbelief was now almost uncontained.

'What does it say?'

'Not a great deal,' Michael answered. She could hear him flick open a sheet of paper as he made to read the letter.

'*Dear Michael, Emily will call this morning. Wait by the phone. Open the second envelope and read it to her when she rings.*'

'Second envelope?' The confusion of the morning's events was mounting by the second.

'Inside the first, with this little letter, there's a second envelope. With your name written on it,' Michael confirmed. 'Why is he writing to you? And via me? How are we involved in his life?'

'I have no idea, Mike. I'm still trying to work that out.' She paused. 'The second envelope . . . did you open it?' Emily was wholly on edge at her desk.

'Of course I opened it!' he answered. 'Do you think I was just going to twiddle my thumbs and sit on it?' Despite the tension of the moment, Emily couldn't resist a slight smile. Michael's usual exuberance hadn't been erased by the strange events.

'And?'

'And you may not be coming to Chicago.' He paused, and this time the dramatic silence was entirely intentional. 'There's a printout of an e-ticket inside. Holmstrand has booked you on a flight to London. Tonight.'

Emily was dumbfounded.

'London?'

Michael's mental stride was now sweeping. He moved past her confusion.

'What's your office fax number, Em?'

She blinked her eyes to bring herself back into the moment, and rattled off the number for the fax machine in the departmental office.

'Why do you want it?' she finally asked.

'Because in this second envelope, apart from the ticket, there are also two sheets of paper. My scanner's broken so I can't email you a copy. But you're definitely going to want to see what he's left waiting for you.'

CHAPTER 11

Ten minutes later, Emily stood anxiously next to the fax machine in the office of the Religion Department, a few doors down from her own office. The dedicated fax line didn't have an audible ring, so she stood near the machine, waiting for it to spring to life and deliver digital copies of the two pages Michael had promised he would send in the next few minutes.

Seated across a worktable were two fellow religion professors. Predictably, they were discussing Holmstrand.

'No, it's three,' Bill Preslin, one of the faculty's Hebrew scholars, corrected the other man. 'You forgot Saudi Arabia.'

'Really? I had no idea.' The other man was David Welsh, the department's specialist in South American religions. Emily moved to the table and sat down. She could watch the fax machine from there.

'Do you mind if I join you?' she asked. 'I assume you're talking about Arno. I still can't believe it.'

'Neither can we,' Preslin answered with a welcoming nod.

'But dramatic events are hardly foreign to Arno Holmstrand. He's the only academic I know who's been placed on terrorist watch lists in three countries based on the amount of time he spent in the Middle East. America, Great Britain and Saudi Arabia all consider him a "person of interest".'

'And the Dean's office got a nice little phone call from the Department of Homeland Security when he came here, wanting to know whether we knew about his "interesting background",' Welsh added.

'We told them we did,' continued Preslin, who had served two terms in the bureaucratic wing of the college before being returned to a predominantly teaching role. 'But we added that the man had received honorary citizenship in five countries, an OBE from the Queen of England and honorary degrees from seven different universities.'

Emily rattled off in her mind the names she knew from the immense publicity that had surrounded Holmstrand's appointment. The degrees lining his office walls came from Stanford, Notre Dame, Cambridge, Oxford, Edinburgh, the Sorbonne and the University of Egypt. And those were only the ones Holmstrand had mentioned when asked. There was likely a litany of others.

'But the government didn't seem to think that mattered,' Preslin continued. 'And no matter how many times we told them his work in the Middle East was archaeological, they kept coming back to the point. You'd think "archaeological dig" was code for "terrorist camp" in government vocabulary.'

'Hey, maybe it is,' Welsh added. The two men shared a dark chuckle.

'How did we ever get him to come here?' Emily asked, interrupting the temporary frivolity. She was still a little too struck by the news to be light-hearted, even if it was in friendly tribute.

'We didn't,' Welsh answered. 'We may be a top tier institution, but nobody's on Holmstrand's playing field. He came because he wanted to come. It was his own proposal. Said he wanted some peace and calm after all his adventures, and to get back to his small-town roots. Carleton appealed, and he wrote to us. Even offered to take a bottom-rung salary, as he obviously wasn't in it for the money.'

'No, I wouldn't have thought so,' Emily said. She allowed a moment of silence to pass. The contents of Arno's letter wouldn't leave her mind.

'Do you know if Holmstrand ever had anything to do with the Library of Alexandria?' she finally asked, unable to contain her pressing curiosity.

The looks that came back from her two colleagues were puzzled. It was not a direction either had expected the conversation to take.

'The ancient one? The lost library? What do you mean?'

'I'm not sure. I know he was heavily involved in all things Egyptian. But did he research the Library of Alexandria in particular? Study it? Write about it?'

Preslin rubbed his chin. 'Not that I know of,' he replied. 'But the man did publish almost thirty books. Who knows? Maybe he did.'

As he spoke, the fax machine sprang into activity with an abrupt collection of whirs and clicks. Emily stood up from her seat and walked over to the small table on which it sat.

'One thing I do know,' Welsh noted. 'He discovered things wherever he went. And as you say, he spent a lot of time in Egypt. So maybe there's some connection, if you're interested to look into it. But whatever his interests were, they're sure finished now.' It wasn't quite top-shelf dark humour, but it was accurate.

A moment later, a sheet of paper began to pulse through the fax machine's tray. As a second sheet drew into the feeder, Emily pulled the first from the slowly spinning roller and drew it up to eye level.

Though the quality was rough and the background of the letter slightly grey due to the fax machine's black and white scanning of what Emily suspected was the yellowish colouring of the original letter, its contents were still clearly legible. As Emily read, her whole body tensed.

Dear Emily,

You've come this far, now you must go further. What I wrote before, what I revealed to you, I wrote in deadly serious-ness. The Library exists, together with the Society that guards and keeps it, but with my death that existence is threatened. Let my death be your warning: what I have had, what you must find, is something others want, and for which they are willing to do anything.

There is little time. My death marks the beginning of the journey you must now make. Enclosed is a ticket. You must go to Oxford at once, and alone. What you must find, I cannot write here. Despite all my efforts, I cannot be certain you will find this information before they do. Use that historical mind of yours, Emily. I'm certain you will put the pieces together.

You must. There is more at stake than you can yet possibly know. You must find <u>our library</u>.

> *God keep you, Emily.*
> *Respectfully,*
> *Arno*

CHAPTER 12

The tension with which Emily held the page was almost enough to tear it.

She picked up the second sheet of paper as it emerged from the fax. Her mind puzzled over the strange collection of materials it contained. A single line of text was followed by a strange and unfamiliar crest. Below it, three phrases, showing no obvious relation to one another, were listed.

Two for Oxford, and one thereafter.

University's Church, oldest of them all
To pray, between two Queens
Fifteen, if by morning

Emily stared at the cryptic sheet, utterly baffled. It looked for all the world like a set of . . . clues.

Her silent confusion over the strange page was broken only when she heard Welsh approach. He had observed Emily's intense gaze as the papers emerged from the fax, and had decided to see what was attracting her attention so completely. As Emily heard him draw near, she clutched the papers to her chest.

'Come on, what's with the sudden shift in your attention?' he asked. 'What have you got? Is everything okay?'

'It's nothing,' Emily repeated. 'I don't know.' The last comment, at least, was entirely truthful. Feeling her pulse continue to rise, Emily felt suddenly uncomfortable in the presence of her colleagues. Should their eyes see this? Without knowing quite why, she craved privacy.

'Sorry, I've got to go.' Without making eye contact or waiting for a response Emily folded the pages into her hand and left the office, the door slamming shut behind her.

CHAPTER 13

The Outskirts of Cairo, Egypt

The parcel was wrapped, as always, in plain paper with no markings.

The Librarian held it under his robe as he descended the steps. The corridor below was dark, but he knew the way well. For years this exchange had been carried out in the same way. Always in silence, always in darkness.

He stepped softly over the old stone flooring, covered in a scattered layer of desert sand and dust. The corridor angled sharply left, descending. He braced himself against the wall, reinforcing his footing. His legs were no longer strengthened by the nimbleness of youth, as they had been when he had first made this descent. He took practised care, now, coming to the end of the corridor, walled off unknown centuries before.

Feeling his way along the rough facade in the blackness, his fingers caressed the familiar spot. Two limestone blocks met at an awkward angle, creating a small fissure of empty space. Taking the parcel from the folds of his robe, he slid it carefully into the nook, pushing it as far back as the space would allow.

The scraping of paper against stone echoed through the silence of the space.

The deposit completed, he turned and retraced his steps upward. The month's collection and compilation had gone well, and the next month's had already begun, all in the same, ancient cycle by which it had been run for thousands of years, though with history's most consistent mark – change – firmly imprinted upon it.

It was a never-ceasing source of amazement, this routine – even all these years on. Such a simple, quiet act, and yet behind it, upholding it, was an unseen structure he could not comprehend and would never fully know.

Turning the final corner and crouching through the low stone entrance, the old questions still burning just as brightly in his mind, the Librarian emerged into the bright light of the Egyptian sun.

CHAPTER 14

Washington DC – 11.30 a.m. EST (10.30 a.m. CST).

Jason watched as the man exited the Eisenhower Executive Office Building, carrying an expensive briefcase and walking with confident strides. He matched perfectly the photo Jason held in his hand, down to the ridiculously pinstriped suit and overly coiffed hairdo. *A man*, Jason thought, *who thinks far too much and far too highly of himself.* That fact alone meant Jason would enjoy what was to come, quite apart from the righteousness of the cause and the need for the act. He'd only flown in from the Midwest a half hour earlier, en route to New York, but Jason didn't mind the scheduled detour. Arrogant upstarts like this deserved what came to them.

As the man rounded a corner on to West Executive Avenue, Jason got up from his park bench, pocketed the photograph and folded his newspaper beneath his left arm. Sauntering nonchalantly, he followed two blocks behind his target as the young man passed down H Street and turned left onto I Street. Exactly as Jason knew he would.

The surveillance of Mitch Forrester had been ongoing for

months. Another Friend, Cole, was assigned to the vice president and had planted himself in the heart of both men's professional environment with ease. His intelligence was thorough. Forrester's habits at the end of the workday repeated like clockwork: he didn't own a car and, rather than take the metro or bus, preferred to walk the 14 blocks from his office to his apartment. Jason imagined that this, too, was a vanity, aimed to keep himself fit and allow himself to be seen by as many people as possible.

Today, like every day, he walked an identical course through Washington, gradually winding his way from the Capitol Hill political district to a posh neighbourhood north of Washington Circle Park, where he rented an apartment in a swanky building on Newport Place that clearly cost far more than a political aide earned. So he had family money, too.

Jason gradually closed the gap between himself and Forrester as they progressed further from the heart of DC, with its routine patrols of covert agents and host of surveillance cameras. The chances of being caught pursuing his target in the residential districts were far smaller, and as they approached the apartment building, he allowed himself to get only a few dozen yards from the political upstart. Then, as Forrester stopped at the door and swiped his keycard for entry, Jason closed the gap entirely.

'I'm sorry,' he blurted, switching into the role of locked-out resident with ease. 'I can't believe it. I've left my key inside. Any chance you could let me in? My wife's at work and my phone is in the apartment – I'm a bit stuck!' Jason did a perfect rendition of the exasperated-yet-effusively-friendly neighbour.

Mitch peered back at the stranger. Jason caught his brief hesitation – a predictable response to his not having seen him around the complex before – yet he trusted that he could rely on Forrester not having met a fair number of the residents in the building. Jason also felt confidence in his ability to sell his role of the flustered tenant.

'No problem,' Forrester finally replied.

'Thanks so much,' Jason glowed with appreciation. He allowed Mitch to hold open the glass doors, and then walked to the elevator. Forrester lived on the fourth floor, so Jason knew he would be headed the same way. 'I'm up on six,' he offered, as he pressed the call button and the doors immediately parted. 'After you.'

Mitch stepped into the elevator, pressing 4 on the panel on his right, then 6 as another kindness to his newfound neighbour.

As the doors slid closed, Mitch felt the knife enter his back. The sensation of the four-inch blade piercing his skin and sliding between his ribs was so strange that at first he didn't know what was happening, and he attempted to turn towards the other man. Jason took his free hand and grabbed Forrester by the shoulder to keep him from moving.

'Listen very closely,' he said, his voice soft but chillingly firm and controlled. 'This knife is currently in your kidney. As long as the blade stays in, you stay alive. The moment I pull it out, you've got about thirty seconds until you bleed to death.'

Mitch's horror was instantaneous, and came mixed with confusion.

'What? I don't und—'

'Don't ask questions,' Jason cut him off. 'Just do what I tell you, and I might walk away and leave the knife right here in your back, ready for some hospital to stitch you up. Understand?'

Mitch had never known terror like he felt now, and as the pain from the blade in his organs shot through his body, he could only grunt in affirmation.

'Good,' Jason said calmly, flipping a switch on the elevator's call panel, halting the car in its ascent. 'Now I want you to tell me everything you know about the vice president's little plot.'

CHAPTER 15

Minnesota – 10.40 a.m. CST

Emily entered her office, closed the door and let down the blinds to the window that opened into the common room beyond. Though she wasn't entirely sure why, she felt she needed privacy, and to be removed from the gaze of colleagues and students.

The second page of Michael's fax continued to confound her. It looked like a collection of clues – but clues to what? And at what point in her morning had she become part of a mystery novel in which receiving a letter filled with clues was something to be expected?

She had to speak with Michael again, now that the contents of the envelope he'd received were in her hands. Anxiously, Emily took up her BlackBerry and dialled his number from her contacts.

'You're back,' Michael said as he picked up on his end. Then he added, with a certain smirkiness, 'I told you that you wouldn't believe it.'

'That's one point I'm more than willing to concede to you,

love.' Emily tried to keep her mood as light as Michael's tone as she unfolded the two faxed sheets of paper, adding them to the original page she had received from Arno.

Though normally keen to engage in some teasing, on this occasion Michael was willing to defer to the serious nature of the moment.

'Emily,' he asked, 'what's all this about?'

'That, I whole-heartedly confess, is entirely beyond me.' She could think of few reasons why Holmstrand would have chosen to involve her in his affairs. Only the broad arenas of their academic work were related: antiquities, history and religion. Was that enough? Did that common realm of interest bind them together in a way that Emily could not yet see?

Her thoughts brought silence to the conversation. Michael's reaction suggested he still felt a lighter tone might be required.

'Well, thank you very much for that insightful contribution, Professor.'

Emily chuckled at his candour. From their first conversation four years ago at a college dinner in Oxford, she and Michael had bantered in this way. He, a former history undergraduate turned proud architecture postgraduate, had tried to sum up his admiration of modern design by giving favourable mention to the 'Gherkin', London's landmark skyscraper that looked like a glass cucumber preparing to take flight. 'It's an eyesore – inexcusable!' had been Emily's understated and objective opinion, freely and energetically offered in response. 'And I'll never believe, not for a minute, that you actually like it. To say you do is just an architect's obligation, like a music student feeling he has to admit to admiring

Bach on principle, even if he would rather hear fingernails scrape across a blackboard than listen to five minutes of the Brandenburg concertos.'

Whether it was due to an admiration of her dark-blue eyes and seemingly effortless beauty, or her forthright tone and strength of will, Michael had taken to Emily immediately, and a casual interest fast became a genuine romance, blossoming into heartfelt love. He had proposed to her only last year, just before their third Thanksgiving dinner together, and though Emily was often the more assertive of the two in their relationship, she had relished the traditional proposal, complete with diamond ring and bended knee.

'Maybe you can start with what you do know,' he urged. 'Both letters mention the Library of Alexandria – that Holmstrand has found it.'

'Not precisely,' Emily interjected. Arno's precise language had struck her. 'He doesn't actually say he's found it. He says that it exists. That I must find it.' Something about the phrasing felt awkward enough to be significant.

'Okay,' Michael agreed, 'but the point is that there's still some finding to be done. I hate to ask this, but . . . were the library and this "society" lost?'

'It's a good thing you're handsome,' she mocked, 'because your knowledge of history is appalling, and makes me wonder if you were ever really paying attention back in your BA days.' Ever since he'd given up historical studies in favour of a better-paying career path in architectural design, she'd craved opportunities to taunt him about it. Emily waited for his laugh in response, and it came as expected. 'But yes,' she continued, 'it's lost. Or rather, the library was destroyed – I'm not sure what "the society" refers to. Perhaps simply the library's organization.'

'When was it destroyed?'

'I'm not sure,' Emily answered.

'And you want to accuse *me* of not knowing history? At least my ignorance isn't prefixed by a PhD in the subject!'

Emily smiled.

'I don't know the answer, Mike, because nobody does. It's a mystery. One of the great mysteries of the ancient world. The Library of Alexandria was built sometime in the reign of Ptolemy the Second, King of Egypt, in the early third century BC, and became the largest library in human history. And then, a few centuries later, it disappeared.'

'Disappeared?'

'There's not really a better word for it,' Emily replied. 'Most people presume it was destroyed, though we don't have any concrete evidence for that. It simply disappears. A genuine mystery.'

'Well, if it's really a mystery,' Michael answered, 'you do have a page full of clues.' This quip, however, caused neither of them to laugh.

Emily looked down at Arno's third page.

'Could it be true that he actually found this library?' Michael finally asked.

Again Holmstrand's strange language lingered in Emily's mind. *'The Library exists . . . as does the Society . . . neither is lost.'* She mulled over Michael's question before answering.

'If it was anyone else claiming they knew where such a library was, I'd dismiss it in an instant. Too sensational, too implausible. But this is Arno Holmstrand. His reputation is hard to match.'

'Yes, I remember your amazement at him,' Michael offered. He knew Emily respected the man's intellectual prowess, and he even had a certain fondness for Holmstrand himself. He'd met him once, at one of Emily's faculty receptions. Michael had confessed to her after the dinner that the professor reminded him immensely of his grandfather – a man with gentle eyes and a respectable brow, who had seen the world yet hadn't been hardened by it. But Michael's tone now was a reminder that Holmstrand's death was involving Emily in something neither of them could yet explain. 'Can't famous men also lie?' he finally asked.

'He wasn't just famous, Mikey,' Emily answered, 'he was a world authority.' Arno Holmstrand had begun to shine out on the academic scene even in his undergraduate days. He had followed a Yale education with a Master's degree at Harvard, and Emily had heard the rumour that he'd completed the degree in under a year. In the same timeframe Arno had managed to publish his first book, *Cross-Cultural Dynamics: The Flow of Knowledge Between Africa and the Near East in the Late Classical Period*. The title might not have rolled off the tongue, but the book had immediately become a classic in the field. Though now decades old, Emily still taught from it in her courses.

None of which, she knew, would impress Michael. Given the circumstances, and Michael's generally bold character, he would be more readily swayed by the adventurous side to Arno's work. And there was plenty of it to go around.

'This is a man who earned his fame on his first archaeological expedition with the University of Cambridge,' she said with great enthusiasm. 'He was only a doctoral student at the time, and his group scouted on maps he had drawn up himself from research in the British Library. They discovered not one but two military fortifications in North Africa, both dating from the reign of Ptolemy the Second of Egypt, long since buried by the sands.' Emily couldn't help but find it exciting.

'The same Ptolemy that's connected with the library?'

'Exactly. And if that wasn't enough, the find was followed by a whole set of Hollywood-style adventures. As I heard the story told, resident militias in the villages surrounding the digs viewed Arno's work with suspicion, and twice raided the sites – on the second occasion binding him, beating him unconscious and depositing his body twenty miles into the open desert.'

Michael allowed a lull to form in the conversation.

'So,' he finally said, 'Professor Arno Holmstrand the Great is the kind of man who just may have found your long lost library.'

Emily leaned into the phone. The discomfort of the morning was edging away, little by little, revealing a rising level of anticipation. 'Yes, he easily could have been. But remember, that's not what his letter says. What he says is even more incredible: that it was never lost at all. That he knows of its existence. I don't know how that can be, but it's what he claims.'

'And now, in death, he wants you to find it?'

'He seems to. Yes.'

'And that doesn't . . . bother you?'

Emily hesitated. Michael's voice had now entirely lost its sense of light-hearted banter.

'No,' she admitted, curious. 'Why should it bother me?'

'Because Holmstrand's history isn't exactly danger-free, the way you've just described it.'

Emily made to respond, but before she could, Michael continued.

'To put it more bluntly, Em, the man is dead. And these letters, these clues – they seem to point you along the very path that earned him three bullets in his chest.'

CHAPTER 16

Mitch gasped for breath, every movement of his chest accentuating the pain caused by the blade piercing his abdominal cavity.

'What do you mean! What plot?' He was genuinely confused, as well as terror-stricken.

'We know about the vice president's plot,' Jason answered, his voice remaining as calm and steady as the fist that held the knife in Forrester's back. 'And his ambitions.' Mitch couldn't turn to see him, so he stared at Jason's half-reflection in the metal panelling of the elevator's control box.

'I don't know anything about a plot!'

'Don't lie to me,' Jason answered, gently nudging the knife. 'It's unbecoming.'

Mitch's eyes watered with the new pain. His breaths were growing more troubled.

'I'm . . . not lying.'

'We also know that a list of the people involved in the VP's plot has been leaked,' Jason continued, unfazed by the

65

agonized man's protestations. 'And it's been leaked to the one group that might actually have the power to stop it.'

'Why . . . why would I want to act against the vice president?' Mitch wheezed. 'He's my boss!'

'Ah, but he isn't, is he? Not really. We know where your true political affiliations lie, Mr Forrester.' Mitch's eyes widened at the allegation. Jason leaned forward, speaking into his ear. 'We know you're not really working for the VP's office, whatever your ID badge might say. Your ambitions are to work your way into another office entirely. One with round walls.'

Mitch couldn't answer. He'd been found out. Perhaps his disdain for the vice president had become too transparent, and people had started to suspect the truth: that he'd been working for three months to secure an appointment on the president's staff.

'So somehow you realized the VP's intentions,' Jason continued, 'and leaked details to his opponents.'

Mitch's mind raced as his body seared with pain. He had practised denials and fabrications in case he was ever found out, but this man seemed to know the truth already. And he had a knife in his back.

'I only found out names,' he finally spurted out. 'I don't know concrete details of his plans, only the people involved.'

Jason raised an eyebrow.

'What names?'

'Gifford, Dales, Marlake . . .' he took another pained breath. 'A few others. But I never told them to anyone. I was compiling a list on my computer. Thought it might make a good motivational document some day. No one's seen it.'

Jason knew the latter statement to be false, though Forrester might be honest in not having shown it to anyone else. Not willingly, or knowingly. Unfortunately, as Jason knew only too well, their opponents had ways of getting to information.

He turned his attention back to the man before him.

'What else was in that document? How much of the plan do you know?'

'What plan?!' Mitch cried, as much from genuine confusion as from the pain. 'I only started to see a pattern – of the president's supporters dying, and the VP's supporters becoming more prominent. But no . . . no plan.'

Jason gazed at the dim reflection of Mitch's eyes on the elevator wall. He paused a long moment in thought before he spoke.

'Do you know, Mr Forrester, I believe you are telling me the truth. I genuinely believe you don't know anything else.'

Mitch managed a relieved sigh through the pain.

'Thank God. I've – ' he winced, but carried on ' – I've never done anything but serve my country.'

Jason gave a half smile.

'Not anymore.' With a smooth motion, he pulled the knife from Mitch Forrester's back, and at once a thick stream of almost black blood began to pour from the wound. He turned the man around to face him as he wiped the blood from the blade on his victim's jacket and flipped the switch for the elevator to resume its ascent.

Horrified, Forrester groped his hands to his back, his face going white as he brought them back before him, covered in his own blood. 'I thought you said you'd let me live if . . . I . . . cooperated.' He leaned back against the elevator wall, growing faint and sliding towards the floor as the rapid blood loss pulled at his consciousness.

Re-sheathing his knife at his side as the elevator chimed and its doors opened onto the empty fourth-floor landing, Jason looked down on the pitiful wretch before him.

'You of all people should know,' he said, a satisfied grin on his face. 'Never trust a man in Washington.' He stepped out of the lift, its doors gently gliding closed around a man who had already taken his last breath.

CHAPTER 17

His brief interrogation of Mitch Forrester confirmed what Jason needed to know. The list had been obtained by the Society through Forrester's computer, which must have been under surveillance by Marlake. That leak had meant the Keeper and his Assistant had both had to be dealt with – tasks he'd already seen to personally. Now, with Forrester out of the way, the leak was well and truly sealed. The Society's obsession with secrecy and closed networks of accountability would ensure that no one else knew. The mission could proceed unabated.

What remained now was the unexpected material from Minnesota. On his way out of this life, the Keeper had proven himself more than just a potential, if capped, leak. The book, the pages . . . something else was afoot. Something even bigger than the mission itself.

Jason's skin tingled as he made his way out of the apartment building. Things were changing. The horizon was starting to look different.

CHAPTER 18

Their conversation had gone on another few minutes before the back and forth of banter and discernment came to a crux.

'Listen,' Emily at last said, 'it's a little past eleven. My flight to Chicago is due to depart at two-ten. With Thanksgiving weekend traffic, that means I'm going to need to leave soon. If I'm going to get there.'

Both she and Michael knew that the last remark was more of a question than a statement.

'If,' he repeated. Michael turned over the printed e-ticket Holmstrand had booked his fiancée. The choice was Chicago or England. Somehow, he knew, it wasn't really a choice. Emily had always been addicted to adventure – the one 'missing ingredient', as she often called it, in her otherwise fulfilling scholarly life. Still, what was presenting itself was more than just an adventurous curiosity.

'Emily, you should come home. You don't need to fly to England just because a colleague asks you to, however tempting the draw. Especially given the fact that he was killed shortly after issuing the invitation.'

Emily thought about the possibilities thrust before her, thought about the mysterious correspondence Arno had left – it was all so much more than she was used to. She'd been in her academic post at Carleton College since completing her doctorate a little over a year and a half ago, returning to the source of her scholarly inspiration. Though she'd left Carleton after completing her BA, going on to study at some of the biggest and best institutions in the academic world, she had eagerly returned to her first stomping grounds. The post she now held was tenure-track, and all else being equal she would hold it until retirement. As a thirty-two year old academic, the approach offered Emily remarkable job security, although it didn't necessarily offer the kind of excitement she'd once hoped would mark out her future. She tried to keep her adventurous streak tamed by remaining an avid runner, and more recently by taking lessons in Krav Maga, the high-impact Israeli martial art. She'd even taken the occasional skydiving lesson at a nearby airfield, but she'd had to come to grips with the fact that the academic world simply didn't pose the thrills she naturally craved.

The present moment, however, did: a mystery, however vaguely defined. Strange letters, even stranger clues. A ticket across the Atlantic. But there was also her fiancé, Thanksgiving, and the rare, precious opportunity for them to be together. Chicago had seemed a great deal closer to Minneapolis when they'd decided Michael's architectural apprenticeship there would be a workable commute.

'We have to decide on this together,' Emily finally said. 'It seems I have two plane reservations today. Which am I going to take?' She found herself holding her breath as she awaited Michael's response.

'England,' Michael said at last, realizing his earlier protestation was going unheeded. 'That's a lot further than Minnesota.'

Emily tensed in eagerness.

'Not just to England,' she added. 'Back to Oxford. Our old stomping grounds.'

'So it would seem,' Michael answered, looking back over Arno's letter. 'But to do what precisely, Emily?' He spoke with an energy that confounded his usual English composure. 'You're simply going to land in England with a sheet of clues and somehow discover something lost to history for centuries?'

Emily wished she were closer, wished she could reach out to take his hand. She sensed his apprehension, and there was a fear present in her own excitement as well. But even as Michael painted the strange picture, it appeared more inviting.

'Think about it, Mike. Arno managed to know my plans, my life – you – well enough to get this information to me, today, despite his own *death*. Come on.' She drew in an eager breath. 'That's *got* to pique your interest.'

No words of argument came down the line.

'And now he's left me a ticket for the UK,' Emily continued. 'Somehow, I think he's thought ahead. I'm sure

I wouldn't be wandering around England aimlessly for long. Besides, if it all falls to pot, it wouldn't be the end of the world. Just a free trip back to your homeland.'

The gentler expression of the doting fiancé at last began to return to Michael's voice.

'But without me.'

Emily's own tone became softer. 'You could always come with, you know. A little adventure, together? Back where we first met?'

Though Emily could not see it, there was a glimmer at the corners of Michael's eyes. But he knew the invitation couldn't be accepted. 'You university types may have an extended holiday, but I have a presentation on Saturday, Thanksgiving weekend or not. It's my first major pitch to a commercial client, remember?'

'Of course. I know.' Michael had been preparing for the moment for months, as one of the last major hurdles in moving from apprentice to fully qualified architect.

'Besides, he says you're supposed to go alone. Heavens only knows what you will be doing over there.'

Emily's ears perked up at his phrasing. Her mind was already made up, and it sounded as if she'd just received the agreement she'd been hoping for.

'Will be?'

'Come on,' Michael answered. 'Let's not pretend for a minute you're not going to go, with or without me.'

And there it was: the longed-for acknowledgement that the adventure was simply too great to pass up. Michael knew her well and wasn't about to hold her back from such an opportunity. A smile covered Emily's face as she leaned into the phone.

'Don't fret, Mikey. I'll bring you back something nice.'

CHAPTER 19

When she hung up the phone a moment later, Emily's pulse was racing. As unsure as she was of what would follow, her immediate plans were set. She would aim her sights at the Minneapolis International Airport, and from there to England. There was just enough time before the flight for her to call her old Master's degree supervisor in Oxford, Professor Peter Wexler, to see about being picked up from the airport and taken to the city. And from there, the adventure would begin.

For better or for worse, the last will and testament of Arno Holmstrand was about to be executed.

CHAPTER 20

New York – 2.30 p.m. EST (1.30 p.m. CST)

The video connection hesitated a moment, and then flickered to life. The Secretary's image connected to those of six other members of the Council. The executive body had been called together for a special session. Circumstances more than demanded it.

He leaned into the small camera perched atop his flatscreen monitor.

'Gentlemen, events have taken a certain turn.'

There was a low rumble of muttering from the six small windows that sat perched next to his on the screen.

'Were your associates not able to complete the task?' asked one member, the words rough, marked by a thick Arabic accent.

'The task was carried out as planned,' the Secretary reassured.

'Then the Keeper, too, is dead?' The question came from another window, with another accent.

'He has been dealt with in the same manner as his Assistant, last week. And only a few hours ago, the source of the leak was capped.'

The six senior members of the Council received the announcement with wordless nods of affirmation. A long silence followed, the Secretary's hands clasped calmly on his desk, before one of the committee again spoke.

'It seems, then, that our work is completed. We know how their structure functions. These were the only men who would have had access to the data. The leak is effectively plugged.' The man's tone was satisfied, but his claims of success were marred by a distinct air of disappointment. The mission could now continue and the short-term aims could be met. But with both the Keeper and his Assistant gone, the longer quest, the quest that had gone on for centuries, was now out of reach. Something had been gained, but much, almost unimaginably much, had been lost.

'Yes,' the Secretary answered, 'the leak has been plugged. Our mission will continue. But – ' he paused to point his next words ' – something new has arisen.'

At the unforeseen remark, eyebrows in every window lifted and the Secretary felt a small surge of power. The ability to hold his colleagues in suspense with the news appealed to his inbuilt sense of dominance. He knew what they did not. They would know only because he chose to share.

'I do not understand,' another member said. 'If they're both dead, our task is accomplished. The threat of exposure is eliminated, even if that means our door to . . . other things . . . has been closed.' The Council member's halting call on 'other things' softened the reference to what everyone on the monitor knew had long been the only thing, the sole aim, for which their ancient institution existed.

The Secretary heard the man out before continuing.

'Gentlemen, the highest aim may still be attainable.' He paused again, revelling in the mystified silence of his colleagues. He had never felt a greater sense of his own authority. 'The Keeper spent his last moments attempting to keep something from me. From us. Something more than just the ability to expose the players in our current drama. His final moments were one last act of deception, one final attempt to keep us from our goal.' His fingers moved to the large, hardcover book the Friend had delivered to him. A meaningless bit of coffee-table dross that had suddenly become a highly valued possession: a pristine copy of Prest's *Illustrated History of Oxford University.*

One with all its pages intact.

'Gentlemen, in death even our worthiest adversaries slip. The Keeper's last deception has failed him.' He stared intensely into the digitized faces of the Council.

'This country is not enough. The Library itself will yet be ours. The race, gentlemen, is not finished.'

He closed the video connection with a keystroke, and turned to the grey-suited man in the shadows to his left.

'It's time you got yourself to Oxford.'

CHAPTER 21

Minnesota – 3 p.m. CST

'I can't tell you how grateful I am for this,' Emily said, looking across to the driver's seat of the roomy Mazda. A few hours earlier she had sheepishly approached Aileen Merrin at her office, asking whether Aileen might be able to drive her to the airport. Emily's original intention had been to park at the airport for the duration of her short visit to Michael's in Chicago, but with the recent change of plans she'd had to modify her arrangements. She had no idea how long her journey to England might last.

'Don't worry about it,' Aileen answered. 'I'm finished teaching for the day, and to be quite honest, with all that's gone on I'm happy to get away from campus for a little while.' She smiled, but her hazel eyes, bordered by graceful lines, were tight with emotion.

'Did you know him well?' Emily asked, knowing Aileen had taken the news of Holmstrand's murder harder than most others.

'No more than you would expect, really,' Aileen answered.

'I'd known his reputation for years, of course. But I only started to get to know him after his arrival here. He was a – ' she searched her vocabulary for the right word ' – spectacular man.' She became pensive, but when she glanced in Emily's direction, her expression was soft and caring. 'You know, you and he are not so different.'

Emily couldn't have thought of a less likely comparison.

'In what conceivable way? He and I are worlds apart. The great and the small.' Though more than able to hold her own in scholarly circles, Emily knew her place when called on it.

'Well, you're young,' Aileen replied, 'and Arno isn't. Wasn't. The best of his career was behind him. At least we can be thankful for that.'

Emily remained silent, allowing Aileen a moment of emotion.

'But the two of you share so many common interests and approaches,' the older woman continued, sitting straighter in her seat and attempting to regain her composure. 'I remember reading your application materials. You were bit by the teaching bug early, just like Arno. How old were you when you first thought of teaching? Ten? Fifteen?'

'Yes,' Emily confirmed. 'I've been on this path for a very long time.' She hadn't known that Holmstrand had a similar background. For her part, Emily had wanted to teach for as long as she could remember. As a schoolgirl in rural Ohio, it had been her elementary school teachers that had sparked the idea in her adolescent mind. She had loved science because her third-grade teacher loved science, and art because her fifth-grade teacher had shown her that she could revel in the subject. She was never quite sure, looking back, whether she had loved these subjects in themselves, or because the enthusiasm of her teachers had been so infectious – but it was precisely that which had implanted in her a love for teaching.

'Arno's interests went back to his own childhood, too,' Aileen noted. 'And just like you, he went after them with a flare. Of course, it was a different world back then. But you each went for what interested you, in your own ways. And you both liked the fights.'

'The fights?'

Aileen grinned.

'The battles, the conflicts. The big moments. History in action.'

It was a good characterization of Emily's interests. When she had gone to university, she had been exposed to the ancient Greeks and Romans, Egyptians and Arabs, Assyrians and Hittites. As these strangers became her friends, she found what would become her real love: their collisions; their conflicts; the earth-shattering moments when cultures collided. Greeks *battling* Romans, Arabs *conquering* Egyptians, Assyrians *oppressing* Israelites. Friends becoming foes, foes waging battle and then becoming friends once again. There was something in the action of struggle and defiance against the odds that sat well with her character. She'd excelled at sports as a teenager and climbed up the male-dominated academic ladder as an adult through something of that same fighting spirit.

'And don't pretend your career hasn't had a certain thrust

to it, either,' Aileen continued, 'despite your youth. A Rhodes Scholar at Oxford, a Ph.D. at Princeton.'

'You remember all this?' Emily asked, 'from my application interview almost two years ago?'

'Some people make an impression,' Aileen said with a smile. Her thoughts returned to Holmstrand. 'Arno is the only faculty member we've ever had who regularly had as many colleagues attending his lectures as students.'

Emily nodded, knowingly. During Arno's first year on the faculty, she had religiously attended at every opportunity. Arno was of the type that couldn't help but reminisce, and each of his lectures inevitably became a romp through memory lane – a journey that few could match.

But Emily had never known him well on a personal level, and she found herself envious of the degree of familiarity Aileen demonstrated for the man. Emily knew him chiefly by reputation and by an awareness of his eccentric quirks, which one forgave – and, Emily secretly confessed, admired – in an old professor of his stature. Famously, Arno was enamoured of aphorisms. Little nuggets of wisdom were inserted into his lectures as well as ordinary speech, at times relaying profound points or otherwise simply expressing an older man's peeves and preferences. 'Knowledge is not circular. Ignorance is circular. Knowledge stands in what is old, yet points to what is ever new.' That had been the opening line of his inaugural lecture, and his pithy retorts against circularity had proven a consistent refrain in all the lectures Emily had attended.

Arno also maintained the habit, which had become something of a trademark, of threefold repetition of key points in his seminars. 'There was no Golden Age in Rome. No Golden Age. *No Golden Age*.' Such triplets punctuated every discourse. Queried on the habit during a seminar on the Oxyrhynchus papyri that Emily had particularly enjoyed, Holmstrand had replied emphatically, 'Say a thing three times and people know you mean it. Once, it might have been an accident. Twice, it could be a coincidence. But when a man says something thrice, he says it for certain.'

Thrice. Emily had smiled at the archaism when it was delivered, and she smiled again at the memory.

'The past is always alive,' went another of Holmstrand's gems, 'if it is remembered. Knowledge has life, and power, as long as it is saved from human forgetfulness.' That pearl had so impacted Emily's neophyte academic idealism that she'd written it into the syllabus for her courses the following year. A great mind was not simply to be treasured, it was to be used.

Emily's memories of Holmstrand culminated with an encounter on the topic of technology – a distinct memory that stuck in her mind. It was a few months earlier, and she was sat at a kiosk in Carleton College's Gould Library as she and Arno both searched the collection's electronic catalogue. A bespectacled, white-haired, tweed-clad professor sitting before a computer screen was an out of place image in any circumstance, but Arno at a computer was something else. The older man had seemed entirely out of sorts with technology, as if each push of a key utterly confounded him, and yet he knew his way around the system with surprising alacrity.

There was, even here, something of a curious paradox to the man.

He had turned to Emily – one of their few personal encounters – and exclaimed with intensity, 'You know, it's amazing, these catalogues!'

Emily, too startled by the spontaneous conversation to respond properly, had merely nodded in reply.

'Have you ever observed,' Arno carried on, 'how so many universities, all over the world, use this same archaic software? One version here, one version there, but at its core it's all the same. I've used this contraption in Oxford, in Egypt, in Minnesota. Not once has it cooperated nicely. This very system, Emily. Everywhere.'

Emily remembered grinning sheepishly, permitting herself the one coy gesture. The miniature diatribe against technology notwithstanding, somehow the old professor had known her name. A touch of fame, however minuscule.

That had been one of their only private conversations, which made the receipt of Holmstrand's letters all the more mysterious. Why, anticipating his death, had he contacted Emily of all people? Why, if he had discovered the location of the Library of Alexandria, one of the greatest lost treasures of antiquity, had Arno chosen to share this with a junior colleague? And why mention it in such guarded tones?

Her reverie faded as the car passed over a bridge with a series of thumps at its connecting rivets. She couldn't tell Aileen about the letters, she decided. If Arno had been so close to Aileen and had wanted her to know, he would have told her himself. Emily did not feel comfortable breaking that unspoken trust.

At length, Aileen too came out of her reverie and glanced across at Emily. 'Are you going home?'

'Pardon?'

'Your flight tonight. Are you going home? To spend the holiday with your family?'

'Not precisely,' Emily answered. She wasn't sure what else to say.

'Spending some quiet time alone, then?'

Emily felt her stomach tighten as her hand glanced across her jacket pocket, where Arno's letters were folded. She might be travelling alone, but somehow Emily doubted very much that what lay ahead was going to be quiet.

CHAPTER 22

Shipu Harbour, outside Ningbo, China

Plain, brown paper surrounded the parcel, secured with thin, black string. The common method of wrapping packages in the region made this look like any other, save for the fact that it bore no markings. No address, no name, no sender.

The Librarian took the parcel from his woven bag and placed it in the rusted metal locker. The hinged door closed with a pronounced creak and he tapped it severely to secure it in place. He slipped the unassuming, equally rusted padlock he had removed a few moments before back into position, squeezing it closed with a clenched fist.

This was his twelfth deposit since his appointment, and the new Librarian made it with great devotion. The pattern he had been given by his mentor, a year earlier, was followed exactly. He ensured he was alone, that he was not followed, that he traced an intricate, winding route from his home to the drop location. The parcel was produced exactly according to the specifications, its format precise. He spoke to no one of his task, and maintained his usual employment and work.

Following the guidance to the letter, he never lingered in the deposit location. The old fisheries warehouse was remote, tucked into the trees at the side of the harbour, and after ensuring the locker was secure, he took to the trees and the familiar path, making his way back to the town.

His noble goal was met for another month. The Librarian's heart swelled with pride as he contributed his hand to an ancient project, the full details of which he would never know.

CHAPTER 23

9.46 p.m. CST – In flight over the
St. Paul-Minneapolis International Airport

'*Use that historical mind of yours, Emily.*' The advice that closed off Holmstrand's final correspondence forced the project of sorting out his mysterious instructions squarely into Emily's court. Even in death, the professor remained a teacher, demanding that answers rise out of his pupils' efforts, rather than doling them out as unearned, unclaimed deposits of intellectual welfare.

Which is bloody annoying, Emily thought to herself. Despite her admiration for the best in teachers' instincts, she would have been glad to be spoon-fed the information she required. Her excitement was mounting, and the lack of concrete details was hard to bear.

The flight from Minneapolis to Heathrow would take a spritely seven hours and forty minutes, assuming smooth flying. Nearly eight hours stuck only in her own head, left to anticipate what lay ahead and what had happened to bring her to this point. As the aircraft's landing gears tucked themselves neatly into the fuselage, locking in place with a motorized whine, Emily clutched Arno's letters to her chest. Their presence was what transformed her current journey into something unique. Something filled with excitement. Their implication was epic. Yet with the excitement came trepidation; she held a dead man's words, letters from the victim of a murder less than 24 hours old. The fear she had felt earlier in the day began to return.

Calm down, professor. She had been scolding herself since check-in but her heart continued to race. She had never been connected to a murder, even at second-hand. Nor had she ever been involved in anything as mysterious as her current journey. Unfolding the letters, she read through them for at least the twentieth time. Their contents burnt into her near-photographic memory, she refolded the pages and watched their edges flutter as her fingers shook.

'. . . we'll be climbing to thirty-five thousand feet – ' a soft male voice droned over the cabin speakers. Emily had been too distracted to notice until then that the captain's remarks had begun '– at which point our cabin crew will come through the aisles with snacks and refreshments.'

Not soon enough. Emily was ready for a drink to calm her nerves. She phased out the remainder of the captain's announcement, succumbing again to her own thoughts on the strange course her day had taken.

Arno's claim – and Emily had to remind herself, despite the concrete reality of the aircraft around her, that a claim was all it could yet be called – was that the Library of Alexandria was not lost. With a disquieting intensity, Emily realized that the professor had provided almost no additional information. All further details, assuming that Arno's subsequent contributions would be as enigmatic as those he had provided in his letters, rested with Emily herself.

Emily's awareness of the Library of Alexandria rested in the sidelines of her past research. The little historical data that could be known with any certainty fell within the scope of her interest in Graeco-Egyptian history, and she had years ago become familiar with its basic contours. But to even the most interested scholar, those contours were vague and mysterious. With almost every detail, the line between legend and reality was blurred, impossible to determine with any finality. Few academics dwelt on it more than in passing, because so much of the topic rested on hypothesis and speculation, realms in which scholars toyed only with hesitation. Historical research was meant to be a thing of facts, and of hard facts on the Alexandrian library there were precious few.

The library, properly called the Royal Library of Alexandria, was thought to have been founded under Ptolemy Philadelphus of Egypt, also called Ptolemy the Second, whose father's service to Alexander the Great had earned him honours and, from 305 BC, the title of king. As part of the glorification of his new empire, Ptolemy had dedicated a famous temple to the Muses, a *Musaion*, from which the Latin-speaking Romans, and all subsequent history, had claimed the word 'museum'. The *Musaion* had not been a library in the modern sense, but a religious temple dedicated to the gods of poetry, the arts, inspiration and learning, containing items worthy of their veneration. Carefully organized shelving contained texts dedicated to every related subject.

It was the king's son, Ptolemy the Second, who had expanded the *Musaion* into a collection, not just of sacred knowledge, but all knowledge. The empire was changing and growing, and it seemed right to its king that it should rule by power, including the power of knowledge. So he founded, funded and fostered what became the world's first great library: a sacred home to all written knowledge and recorded fact.

The project was the largest and most expansive in history. Ptolemy set an initial goal of obtaining 500,000 scrolls for his shelves and established extraordinary practices to accomplish this. Volumes were sought out and bought wherever they could be found, and it even became an imperial requirement that all visitors to Alexandria surrender their books, scrolls and any other written materials on arrival, so that these could be copied by librarian scribes and committed to the collection. Alexandrian librarians were then sent out to other, older centres of learning to obtain copies of important volumes at cost, or borrow them for copy at the expansive *scriptorium* that grew up at the library itself. Texts in languages inaccessible to the scholars and thinkers of the Empire, who by and large thought and read in Greek, were translated by committees organized through the library's expanding infrastructure. The most famous among these translation projects was the translation of the Hebrew Bible into Greek, which had involved the commissioning of no less than seventy Jewish scribes – a number, *Septuaginta* in Greek, by which the translation was known even today.

'Peanuts, pretzels or cookies?' The chirping voice that suddenly broke through Emily's reverie clashed dramatically with the subject of her thoughts.

'Excuse me?'

'What would you like,' the stewardess asked, 'peanuts, pretzels or cookies?' She wore a smile that looked as if it had been plastered on before the flight took off, immovable and fixed across her face.

'Er, peanuts, I suppose,' Emily responded. 'And a whisky. And the peanuts are optional.'

The stewardess reacted to Emily's attempted wit with the same plastic smile. 'Do you have a preference for your whisky? We have Bushmills, Famous Grou—'

'Whichever is largest,' Emily interrupted, waving off the rest of the list with a small gesture of her hand. The stewardess lifted an eyebrow, casting Emily a glance that questioned the ladylikeness of such a comment, but Emily responded with an expression that made it equally clear that the stewardess's opinion was not required. Handing Emily a bottle of Famous Grouse and a plastic cup filled with ice, the woman moved on to the next row of cramped passengers. 'Peanuts, pretzels or cookies?' she chirped, as if powered by a CD on repeat.

Emily twisted the plastic cap off the small bottle and poured its contents over the ice. A long draw of the fiery liquid calmed her frayed nerves, and she closed her eyes, leaning her head against her seat and slipping back into her thoughts.

The Alexandrian librarians became famous throughout the

ancient world for their scholarship and knowledge. With the world's largest collection of documentary resources at their fingertips – a collection that included knowledge of every sort, from the arts, the sciences, history, biology, geography, poetry, politics – these librarians attracted other scholars, and the library became a centre for research and learning. Its head librarians, the keepers of the vast collection, included names familiar to any historian of the period: Apollonius of Rhodes, Eratosthenes, Aristophanes of Byzantium, and a litany of others.

No one knew just how large the library eventually became. The initial objective of 500,000 scrolls was surely surpassed quickly, and the library grew so vast, its influence so great, that other political centres began to found rival institutions across the empire. The library at Pergamum was the strongest, and would have threatened its dominance had it not been ransacked in the mid-first century BC by Mark Antony, who plundered more than 200,000 scrolls from its vaults as a wedding present to Cleopatra, a descendent of the first Ptolemy. Hollywood, Emily remembered, had been more infatuated with their somewhat seedy love affair than with the library that had been his romantic gift.

Alexandria's collection now required multiple buildings, special storage structures and vaults. Its research ethos prompted the construction of dozens of reading halls, lecture rooms, *scriptoria* and administrative offices. Rumours, which could easily have been true, claimed a collection of over a million scrolls and codices. As a storehouse of knowledge and culture, the world had never known anything like it.

And then, somewhere around the sixth century AD, it had all vanished.

In a mystery no historian or scholar had ever been able to solve, the greatest library in human history had simply disappeared. There were many theories, Emily knew, as to what had happened to it. But they were all simply theories. Speculations. The only thing known for certain was that the largest repository of human wisdom the world had ever known had ceased to be. All the knowledge and power it had provided were lost. The library had vanished.

Or had it? The question, which Emily had never given much serious consideration before this morning, was suddenly the only question that mattered, and one that caused her heart to race with excitement. If Holmstrand's message spoke the truth, the possibilities for what lay in store to be discovered in its vaults were almost beyond imagining. What was known of history would change for ever.

Thursday

CHAPTER 24

Fifteen minutes before American Airlines flight 98 touched down for its taxi into Heathrow's Terminal 3, the wheels of a much smaller aircraft gripped the tarmac. The custom-designed Gulfstream 550 was painted a uniform white, with no markings apart from the aircraft number stencilled in black lettering across the tailfin.

Jason peered dispassionately out of one of the aircraft's small windows. The setting inside was a stark contrast to the jet's plain exterior. Plush carpeting and leather seats coloured the cabin a professional beige, augmented by burled walnut highlights. A small table, topped in a matching, perfectly polished walnut, supported a crystal tumbler containing the remnants of his drink, as well as the folder containing his notes and instructions.

And high-quality photocopies of the three pages of the book that had sent him here. He had first encountered the pages as flakes of ash and charred remains in the Keeper's office. He'd later found them in their glossy, full form in a new copy of the book from which they'd been torn. Now their contents were burnt into his mind, the long flight having been spent committing their every detail to memory.

It was not unusual for his work to take him across the Atlantic, nor for it to be done privately, cloaked in stealth and secrecy. Jason had been given the title of Friend seven years ago, and every day since had been a day of intrigue. He had risen through the ranks in the intervening years due to his efficiency and dispassion. There were jobs to be done, and no one could better accomplish them than he. He had never been a man who sought to make the great decisions, to have power and authority in that traditional sense. His power existed at the ground level, in the severity with which he took his orders unquestioningly and enforced them ruthlessly.

He watched as the glitter of the airport passed by his window, the jet taxiing towards a small lot reserved for private arrivals. He was here because he had earned the trust of the Council's most senior member and garnered the post of his chief assistant. The responsibility the Secretary had laid on his shoulders today was vast. Their ultimate aim, the very reason for their being, was not in fact gone from their sight – and might be closer than it had been in centuries.

He had no intention of letting that aim be lost.

CHAPTER 25

Heathrow Airport, London – 11.34 a.m. GMT

Moments later, the thud of 150 tons of Boeing 777 meeting the runway roused Emily Wess from a sleep that had been long in coming. The local time, according to the well-rehearsed voice tinning throughout the cabin, was 11.34 a.m., the weather partly cloudy and 13 degrees centigrade.

Emily rubbed the sleep from her eyes as the announcement concluded with a chirp. 'To all our American passengers on board, may we wish you a very happy Thanksgiving in Britain.'

CHAPTER 26

London – 12.25 p.m. GMT

Professor Peter Wexler had selected the Jaguar S-type for a specific set of reasons. A fan of classic British design, despite the unfortunate history of Jaguar's purchase in 1989 by Ford, and then more recently by the Indian firm Tata Motors, it had seemed the right car to echo his status: a clean finish, a smooth interior and just the right balance of luxury and practicality. It showed class, but not pomp. It was a car in which he was as comfortable driving as being driven, and its classic looks mirrored the classical stature of his institution.

The car's maroon colour, however, had been the working of his wife. No university professor, not even an Oxford don, had the authority required to have the last word against Elizabeth Wexler, and her agreement to the purchase of a car tailored to her husband's tastes had been contingent on her choice of trim. The exterior shone a metallic maroon, the shade of fine velvet, and the interior a cream leather finished in polished Ash.

Peter Wexler sat, emasculated, in what he now called 'my wife's car', as Emily entered through a rear door to his right. With its newest passenger collected from the airport car park, the sedan was filled to comfortable capacity: a driver at the wheel, Wexler to his left and Emily in the back, sitting next to a young man unfamiliar to her.

'Welcome back to England, Miss Wess,' her former supervisor emoted. He was genuinely pleased to see his student of not so many years ago. Emily Wess had been one of his brightest pupils with a quick mind and fighting spirit. He admired her tenacity as much as her intellect.

Signalling the figure next to Emily, he continued. 'Meet Kyle Emory, a new student of mine. Trying to fill your shoes, I should imagine.'

The young man smiled, holding out his hand to Emily.

'Pleased to meet you.' His handshake was firm and energetic. Clean-cut, young, polite – the man made a good first impression. The prime cut of graduate student material, from Emily's quick judgement.

'He's another Colonist,' the professor continued, oblivious to the exchange of pleasantries taking place behind him, 'but one who at least has the good decency to keep the Crown on his currency.'

'A Canadian,' Kyle offered, clarifying. 'I've come here from Vancouver.'

'None of your nonsensical rebelliousness up there,' Wexler strained on, pushing the point for his American protégée. Emily had always been receptive to his penchant for British cultural superiority, and Wexler had consequently always piled it on thick when she was around. 'The Canadians, now there's a people that knows what's good for them!'

'You'd say that of any nation that had the queen on its banknotes and still considered horses the latest in police transportation,' Emily tossed back.

'Quite right, quite right. Horse guards, mounted police – these are venerable, ancient traditions, my dear madam. None of the nonsense you and your fifty tribes get themselves into. Note how the Canadians *aren't* being eaten alive in today's news – ' he motioned vaguely toward the car's radio, through which the BBC's midday news summary could still be heard ' – for the scandalous way *their* president has manhandled the Middle East.'

Kyle bit his tongue, feeling that pointing out that Canada had a prime minister, not a president, was probably tangential to the professor's taunting point.

'Well, you and your Canadian friends can come by any time,' Emily responded. 'Our rebellious colonies will be happy to introduce you to the twenty-first century. Or should we start with the twentieth, or nineteenth? I can never remember which one you're stuck in.'

An enormous grin now covered both of their faces.

Kyle observed the exchange, feeling a bit like a teenager caught in the good-natured teasing of older friends, yet somehow bearing the brunt of all their jokes.

Wexler propped himself against a leather armrest and turned to face his guest. 'Well, now that we've caught up, allow me to cut to the point. I've brought Kyle along because the good

Canadian has something of a passion for your subject, Miss Wess.'

Emily prepped her tongue. *That's* Doctor *Wess, Professor.* She wasn't entirely sure whether the slip was an intentional continuation of Wexler's good-natured jibes, or if the older don had actually forgotten that Emily had gone on to get her doctorate after their work together.

'The Library of Alexandria has been a hobby of mine for years,' Kyle interjected.

Emily checked her amazement, as well as the slight tinge of an instinctive worry. Should this stranger know her business here? She'd been on solid ground in England less than 45 minutes and already she had a professor's assistant sitting beside her, getting down to the matter at hand. Her eyes turned back to Wexler.

'Such efficiency,' she said.

'I rang him up immediately after you and I spoke on the telephone,' Wexler replied. 'Once you'd told me about this letter of yours, I knew I had to bring him along. I hope you don't mind. I know you wanted to keep things rather hush-hush.' He tapped a finger against the side of his nose, the universal sign of comic sleuths badly concealing state secrets.

'No, of course not.' In truth, Emily wasn't entirely sure whether she minded or not. Her instinct was to keep her new information to herself, but someone with more current knowledge on the library would be helpful.

'Can I . . . can I see the letters?' Kyle held out a hand, open-palmed and expectant. Emily considered his request at length, not quite able to overcome her reserve. Turning her eyes to Wexler, she looked for guidance. The don gave her his first serious look of their meeting.

'Emily, he's one of my best pupils. No one will be able to help you more than he.'

Hesitating a moment longer, Emily at last reached into her pocket and extracted the bundle of letters. Kyle received them energetically, disappearing into his own world as he read. Emily turned again to Wexler, who continued to survey the scene with interest.

'As I told you on the phone, Holmstrand was killed yesterday – or I guess it's two days ago now, with the flight. Tuesday night.'

'Poor Professor Holmstrand,' Wexler responded. 'A good man. He reviewed one of my books a few years back.' The review had been a scathing dissection of one of Wexler's studies, and he had loved every word of it. In higher academia, being criticized compellingly was as sought after as being praised.

'Then you know his reputation.'

'He's a man one takes seriously.' *Was.* Wexler immediately noticed his failure to adapt to the circumstances at hand. It was not easy to move from the present tense to the past when human lives were involved.

'That's exactly why I'm here, rather than at home with my fiancé, enjoying a Thanksgiving turkey and laughing off Arno's note as an old man's game.' Emily adjusted her seatbelt, which seemed to bind her uncomfortably into the leather seat.

'Ah, yes, your good sir Michael,' said Wexler. 'How is our ex-patriot?'

'As wonderful as ever. He sends his greetings. Wants you to know how loathsome he finds his English past after spending a few years on holy ground in the States.'

'The boy never did know what was good for him,' Wexler threw back with a devious nod.

Emily smiled, but her mind was too drawn into Arno's notes to stay engaged in friendly banter.

'Holmstrand's letters claim that he knew where the library was located,' she said, nodding at the papers in Kyle's hands, 'as well as some "Society", and that he was being killed for that information.'

'Miss Wess,' Wexler slipped into his familiar master-to-student tone, 'historians have sought the library for centuries—'

'I know,' Emily cut the lecture short with a raised palm. 'Believe me, I know. But his claim cost him his life. I'm inclined to think it's worth following up.' She took a few deep breaths, trying to piece together the portions of the puzzle she knew thus far. 'What's most confusing for me, Professor, is the way he died. It wasn't simply a run-of-the-mill murder. It was apparently carried out by a professional. And he knew it was coming. These letters were sent the day *before* he died. Why kill the old man?'

Arno's assassination, which had motivated the letters and clues he had given his life to protect, was the central event that had brought Emily to this place, and yet she couldn't make sense of it. 'It just doesn't figure. Admittedly, the library's resources were once vast. But to kill a man? What resources could the library possibly hold now that would be worth such a death?'

'It's more than that.'

Emily had grown oblivious to Kyle's presence, so the graduate student's interjection came as a surprise.

'Excuse me?'

Kyle looked up from the pages, now strewn across his lap.

'Sorry, doctors, but the library alone is not the whole of it.'

Given the solemn air of the moment, Emily felt a slight twinge of embarrassment that she still swelled at the recognition – at last – of her proper title.

'Look at this,' Kyle continued, handing one of the sheets to Wexler. 'Read down about two-thirds of the page. The single sentence there on its own.'

Wexler scanned the line.

'*It exists, as does the Society that accompanies it. Neither is lost.*'

'I'm not sure I follow, young man.' Wexler handed the page over to Emily.

'He doesn't just say he knows about the library,' Kyle explained. 'He wrote, "It exists, *as does the Society* that accompanies it."' He paused while Emily looked again at what was now Arno's familiar scrawl.

'And that . . . well, that makes a world of difference.'

CHAPTER 27

'How much do you know about the various theories on what happened when the library was destroyed?' Kyle Emory was now the focal point of both Emily's and Wexler's attention. 'I mean, in particular, the theories about its ongoing existence?'

Emily was already hesitant.

'Speculating about its disappearance is one thing. Theorizing about its continued existence is quite another.'

Kyle gave her a probing look. 'Given. But you're here on speculation that it might still exist, so let's at least remain open to the possibilities.' He paused, waiting for Emily's nod of acknowledgement, and continued when it came. 'Let's take a step back and start with the theories on how it disappeared.'

'Scholars basically agree that it was destroyed,' Emily complied, 'but as to when, and why, and by whom, there is no consensus.'

'Right. The most common claim, which has been the favourite of armchair academics for years, is that it was burnt to ashes, intentionally or accidentally, during Julius Caesar's conquest of the city in 48 BC.'

'Just a few years after Mark Antony had made his great deposit to impress Cleopatra,' Wexler interjected. 'Bloody good wedding gift, if I do say so myself. My wife only gave me a first edition of Tolkien and an engraved humidor. Cheap wench.'

Emily and Kyle both chuckled at Wexler's unique approach to romance.

'Okay,' Kyle added, refocusing. 'But as romantic as the image may be, with Caesar burning the city and library to cinders out of his rage over Cleopatra's affair, the theory has been largely discredited.'

'We have journals and travelogues from ancient writers,' Emily affirmed, 'recording their use of the library decades and even centuries later.'

'Exactly. It's a nice story, but the evidence doesn't add up. But there are two theories where the facts and dates work a little better.'

'The Muslims and the Christians,' Emily offered.

'Precisely!' Kyle sat upright in the car's leather seat, excited that Emily was current on the basic theories. 'Even if it wasn't done by Caesar, most people still agree that the library probably fell when Alexandria was sacked. And that's happened a few times. In AD 642, as the new Muslim armies of the east moved westward, the troops of Amr ibn al'Aas overcame Alexandria's defences and took the city, razing vast portions of it as they advanced. He was a ruthless general. Seeking to root out older religions in favour of the new faith of Islam, he tore down heathen temples, and monuments to heathen wisdom went with them.'

'Is there any direct evidence that the Library of Alexandria still existed at the time of his conquest?' Wexler asked. 'Or that his troops destroyed it?'

'Nothing direct. We only know that he sacked the city, and that such an action would fit his general profile.'

'The hypothesis about it being destroyed by the Christians is about the same,' Emily offered, 'though the dates are a little earlier.'

'Right. That theory puts things around the time of Theophilus.' Kyle nodded to Emily, and she carried on with the description.

'Theophilus the First reigned about midway between Caesar and al'Aas, toward the end of the fourth century. He was a Christian emperor, and one of the first to enforce Christianity not simply as a permissible religion, but as the only acceptable religion. He issued a decree ordering the destruction of all Pagan temples in the realm, and the bishop of Alexandria, also called Theophilus, readily complied.'

'The library might have been spared,' Kyle interjected, 'but its historical connections with Pagan worship remained potent. It had begun life as a temple to the Muses, and not long into its existence had been expanded to include a *Serapaeum*, or temple to the god Serapis.'

'As far as this theory goes,' Emily concluded, 'the inseparable connection of Pagan learning and Pagan religion sealed the library's fate, and it fell to the mobs of Theophilus sometime around AD 391.'

'So we've signs of love and tolerance all around,' Wexler added, sarcastically.

'A dimension to history we all know far too well.' Emily felt she could speak for all three of them. No historian could be surprised by such stories.

'But what's really interesting,' Kyle continued, 'are the legends built on the possibility that the library's destruction was only partial, and that some remnant carried on.'

Emily's innate suspicion began to return.

'Some people love nothing more than a good conspiracy theory.'

'Fair enough,' Kyle offered. 'But you can't simply dismiss the possibility outright. To many people, and I would include myself, it seems all but inconceivable that so vast a library would simply vanish. No emperor would let such a treasure burn. No ruler, however strongly motivated by religious zeal, whether Muslim or Christian, would simply cast away so irreplaceable a resource.'

'There are some fairly dramatic moments of world history that might disagree with you,' Wexler noted.

'And more than that,' Emily pushed, 'such theories exist on pure speculation. Perhaps the library was burned in subterfuge, a ploy against the city's conquerors, its collection having first been rescued to safety. Perhaps the collection had been moved, established in another, carefully guarded location, leaving only a complex of buildings and temples to suffer the violence of the Alexandrian mobs. And on, and on. It's all guesswork.'

'And so without end.' Wexler added. 'Conspiracy theories, by nature, fuel themselves with endless suspicion.'

'That may well be,' Kyle answered, 'but of all the theories running around out there, one that's never faded out fully is about a group that continued to operate the library in an unbroken link from its foundation, through its destruction, throughout history. And remember, Professor Holmstrand's letters both mention a group that accompanies the library. He says that it exists, too.'

Emily tried to envisage Arno buying into such theories – a hard sell for a committed academic. Still, his letters made the existence of some sort of group, which he referred to in each simply as 'the Society', a pronounced point.

'So, what would we be talking about?' she questioned, probing the concept. 'Some huddled group, hidden away in the darkness, holding down the fort over a million scrolls?'

'Not quite.' Kyle was speaking to his passion, his whole body emoting energy. 'The legend goes that the group was made up of the library's staff itself, whose task had always been to collect new information, consolidating it into the collection. Seek, collect, store. Seek, collect, store. When the library was threatened, moving it was only a small part of the project. What they were really interested in was carrying on the library's mission: gathering information and collecting knowledge.

'With Alexandria sacked and the whole world believing the library lost, it became clear that the best way to ensure the library's existence was to keep it a secret. You know history better than I do, Dr Wess – ' Kyle looked intently at

Emily ' – so you know that burning books is pretty well a recurring theme. It was too great a risk. So the biggest library in the world went underground.'

Emily saw a problem in Kyle's logic.

'What is the point of an underground library? If the world's greatest store of knowledge can't be accessed, what good is it?'

'That's where this legend takes a somewhat unexpected turn,' Kyle answered. 'Knowledge that can't be accessed is, as you say, meaningless. But too much knowledge, made too open, becomes a risk. There's the practical risk of someone not liking what they read and destroying it, but there's also the intellectual risk of people wanting to know too much, for the wrong reasons. You have to remember, the Library of Alexandria wasn't just filled with poetry and the arts; it was the repository for the cumulative knowledge of an empire. Historical documents, geographical and cartographic resources, records of scientific discoveries, military annals, architectural plans. When some new technology was discovered in a foreign land, its details were recorded and eventually made their way into the library. When new battle techniques were perfected that gave one army advantage over another, generals kept journals that eventually were copied into the library. When scouts were sent into enemy territories, they drew up maps of fortifications and defences, which were eventually copied and—'

'And made their way into the library.' Emily finished the sentence for him, seeing Kyle's point.

'That's right. The potential for constructive learning that

the library offered had to be tempered with the potential for misuse. No one wanted to see what the wrong hands could do with that kind of information.

'So, the legend says, to protect the library from the wrong people, from evil intentions, an absolute decision was taken for all. The task of seeking out new information continued, but now would be carried out covertly. The Librarians scattered themselves all across the empire, so they could be positioned to collect new information as it became available, depositing it into the collection once it was gathered. And so the collection grew, and continued to grow throughout history.'

Emily held her silence, allowing Kyle's story to roll around in her spinning mind. It was not impossible. Not every secret society was a myth. What Kyle was describing was essentially an ancient form of covert data collection – something governments still did today, and still did in secret. But one detail still tugged the wrong way.

'With these Librarians scattered everywhere, taking in new material, did nothing ever go out? Did the library just become a vast sinkhole of knowledge?'

'Who knows?' Kyle responded with a shrug of the shoulders. 'I've picked up on various strands of the tradition that say the Librarians occasionally disseminated portions of the library's information when they felt it was beneficial to the greater good. But this is where the common thread of the tradition breaks into many different strands, and it's hard to get a concrete feel for what might be fact and what's pure fiction. Some of the theories really start to spin wild, with covert planting of old manuscripts so archaeologists could "discover" them, the leaking of military data against oppressive nations, and so on. You dream up a way it could have worked, you can bet somebody's guessed at it.'

Emily lifted an eyebrow.

'You're saying some materials did go out from the library, despite its being hidden. We just don't know how?'

'Right. The group of Librarians and their successors determined, one way or another, what information to release to the public, whenever they deemed it appropriate. Assuming the legends have some truth to them, that's a lot of power and influence in a small number of hands.'

Emily looked down at Arno's first letter. As passionately as Kyle had spoken, as much as a part of her wanted to believe that so strange a legend made a kind of sense, it seemed too surreal to be possible. So much speculation linked to her current journey only by vague comments written in Holmstrand's hand.

'*It exists, as does the Society that accompanies it. Neither is lost.*' Emily turned to the second letter. '*The Library exists, together with the Society that guards and keeps it.*'

What Kyle said next would erase her every doubt.

'There's one other thing, the reason I brought any of this up at all.' Kyle leaned forward as he spoke, his eyes focusing on the page with Emily. 'This group, this collection of Librarians who kept up the library through history, became known simply as the Society.'

CHAPTER 28

Jefferson Hines approached the familiar bench in Folger Park with an equally familiar sense of insecurity. He knew that everywhere in Washington at least half a dozen cameras recorded his every move, but he also knew that hiding in plain sight was often the best way to avoid overly scrupulous surveillance. Any meeting he set up, particularly 'behind closed doors', would be meticulously scrutinized. A casual meeting in the park, however, could still be considered just that. It would be watched, of course, and undoubtedly listened to by a Secret Service that had the ability to pluck words out of thin air through a technical wizardry that went beyond his understanding. There was no way that could be avoided, but here he could at least sit and talk, so long as he and Cole kept their comments veiled and stuck to the code phrases they had long ago agreed upon. Besides, sometimes being overheard was the whole point.

Cole approached a few moments later and sat down next to him. Both men wore the long winter overcoats of the

115

political upper classes, leather gloves and woollen scarves helping to keep out the wintery chill. The first times they had met together in a public space had made the vice president nervous, but Cole's assurances since had proven themselves. Having integrated himself into the VP's office environment through regular visits as an apparent lobbyist and ideological political supporter, it was no longer a curiosity-rousing sight to see him and Hines together. There was always the cover of perfectly legitimate matters to be discussed, and as a political manoeuverer Cole worked magic. His promises never went unfulfilled, and he brought in both support and funds as any good activist and supporter should. Far from being a man who aroused suspicion, he had become one that Hines's inner circle looked forward to seeing with a certain, drooling eagerness.

He sat now, next to the vice president of the United States, with political activism and professional cover the furthest things from his mind. The VP's Secret Service detail maintained a prescribed distance, intently surveying the surroundings.

'The way things are unfolding is not entirely unexpected,' Cole noted, feeling no need for pleasantries or delays in getting to the matter at hand. He kept his words general. 'Things are going just as we'd planned,' would have put them both at risk. But given the news reports unfolding minute by minute around the world, the agents surely listening to every word would hear only a concerned supporter discussing the latest political scandal of the day. 'There are no known leaks, yet the truth has started to come out.'

'The truth' was the ironic code that Cole had chosen to represent the lie around which their whole mission centred. Their lie was to become the nation's truth. And with that truth, the Council would step up to a new altar of power, to augment the resources already in its vast and ancient arsenal.

'Yes, my staff reported it to me this morning,' Hines replied. 'All the major networks are already beginning to report on new revelations surfacing in the president's handling of Afghanistan. His connection to the Saudis was mentioned explicitly by both CNN and ABC. Something about illicit dealings in the reconstruction effort, drawing out resentment among the insurgents. There are even reports of a video clip of some cell in the desert, threatening jihad and retaliation for his treachery.'

'Give it a few hours,' Cole answered, 'and that connection will be on every set of lips in the country.' It was the kind of speculative comment any interpreter might make, but both men knew that Cole's words were not speculation.

A moment of silence passed between them. Finally, Hines gave voice to the thought at the front of his mind.

'My aide, Forrester, didn't come into the office today.' He allowed the statement to linger in the cold air.

'Not everyone stands by your side through thick and thin,' Cole finally replied. 'It's best to forget about those whose support is not . . . freely offered.' He offered nothing more, and Hines understood the matter to be closed. They had not discussed the execution of Mitch Forrester, which the vice president was fairly certain was the reason for his absence, but then the men Cole represented had made it clear that Hines would not be informed of many of the mission's working dimensions. Nor would his thoughts on them be especially welcomed or required. He sat quietly on his park bench.

'It seems that President Tratham's advisors have been having a bad week,' Cole continued, changing the subject. 'Did your staff show you the Reuters report on Burton Gifford that posted a few hours ago?'

'Not yet.' Hines, however, knew precisely what the report would contain. That assassination had been a part of the plan from the beginning.

'You might want to take a look,' Cole continued. 'Damned shame, a man shot down in the prime of his life like that – with Dales just five days before. Looks like the president's top advisors are being popped off one by one.' He took in a long breath of the crisp November air, his eyebrows raised in feigned exasperation at the sorry state of the world. 'I wonder if any of it's connected to all this news about his shady dealings in the Middle East.'

And with that comment, the mission moved into its next phase. It would take only a matter of minutes for his words, intercepted by the vice president's Secret Service detail, to be passed along to the FBI, and from there to the whole network of Homeland Security's vast, disorganized infrastructure. From there the dots would start to be connected in earnest – dots that Cole and the Council had already lined up in their proper arrangement. The picture they would create would change the course of the nation.

The two men sat a moment longer, Hines appearing to

mull over his political supporter's suggestive interpretation of the day's news.

'I wouldn't know,' he finally said, standing up and extending a hand towards him, 'but I'm sure every possibility will be explored.' *You can damned well bank on it*, he didn't add. He took Cole's hand and shook it. 'Just don't let this little bump in the road sway your support, or the support of any of your colleagues at the Westerberg Foundation, from our Administration. You're a valuable supporter of our party.'

'Of course not, Mr Vice President. You have now, and you will always have, my full support.'

CHAPTER 29

1.50 p.m. GMT

An hour after they had left Heathrow, Peter Wexler's Jaguar rolled over a cobblestone square and into a reserved parking bay at Oriel College, near the centre of Oxford. The remainder of their journey had been quieter than its first half, as Wexler and Emily digested the information Kyle had offered with such enthusiasm. At its base, the legend of the 'Society' was of about the same stock as any other conspiracy theory, but there was something chilling in the connection of names and titles with the mysterious references in Holmstrand's letters – something that gave Kyle's speculations a substance that neither scholar could entirely ignore. It was enough to pique an already heightened curiosity.

The heavy air of Oxford, weighted down by the humidity of the Isis and Cherwell, two rivers that met in the city, lingered in Emily's nose and brought a coolness to her skin as she stepped from the car. Even given all that had happened to bring her here, and despite the strange shape of the conversation over the past sixty minutes, it was good to be back. Oxford was a place like no other on earth.

She turned to Wexler as they both stretched their cramped muscles.

'I need to call Michael. It's only early morning back home, but he'll want to know I got here okay.'

'You can use the box upstairs,' Wexler answered, waving towards his office window. Emily, however, extracted her BlackBerry from her bag, giving it a tap in reply.

'Actually, I think this ought to work over here. I have it on good authority that this new fangled invention called the mobile telephone has finally made its way to Britain.' She held her thumb on the small key to power it up, savouring the opportunity to have got her own back, however slightly, for Wexler's earlier jibes. The older professor simply grumbled in response, a contented grin covering his face as he made his way through the building's ancient door.

'When you're finished, come and join us,' Kyle offered, as Emily waited for the phone to find a network and connect. 'I want to have a word with you about this third page.' He held up the faxed copy of Arno's list, the page that appeared to be a collection of clues.

'Fine. See you in a minute.'

Kyle Emory pocketed the pages, then grabbed Emily's bag and followed Peter Wexler into the ornate building as Emily's phone came online. She pressed the first speed dial option after it found a network, and a few moments later was met by a familiar voice. Michael greeted her exuberantly, and they exchanged customary comments about Emily's flight and arrival.

'Michael,' she finally said. 'If this whole situation wasn't strange before, you're not going to believe what it's become now.'

CHAPTER 30

1.55 p.m. GMT

Three streets away, two men donned slick suits and fastened forged identity cards to their lapels. The fake shields on their belts were exact replicas, and if anyone suspiciously ran the numbers on either, they would find them properly recorded in all the required national and Interpol databases. Their technical team, working from an almost futuristic bank of computer terminals in an unmarked warehouse building in London, were on standby, monitoring telephone and radio communications. Were the two men's cover challenged and if anyone should try to phone up the ranks to enquire after their legitimacy, their call would be seamlessly intercepted, re-routed to a voice that would confirm their status, their place and their right to be there.

But it almost certainly would not come to that. Jason and his partner were experts in their roles, and the crime scene they wished to investigate was crawling with officials. Given their appearance of officialdom, it was likely they wouldn't even be noticed.

Straightening their coats and mentally reminding themselves that from this point on it was British accents only, the two men rounded the corner. The rubble before them was impressive, the destruction vast. But their aim was focused, and they would not be swayed by a challenge.

The Keeper's secret was here. They would not leave before they held it in their hands.

CHAPTER 31

The Secretary brought the Scotch to his lips calmly, savouring the fruits of twenty years in port-barrel oak – the best the Highlands had to offer. While he wasn't a connoisseur in any formal sense, he knew what men of power ought to drink, and this was a drink that only powerful men could afford. Each bottle cost him over four hundred dollars, chiefly because he had them flown over directly from the distillery in Scotland, hand bottled for him by a man who, he was assured, did this for no one else. His was a drink that, quite literally, no one else on earth could enjoy.

Before him, the book lay open to the critical pages. He flicked through them for the hundredth time. It was so clear, so obvious. There was no question to what they pointed.

Absolutely no question. It was almost as if the Keeper had wanted them to discover their contents.

Jason had flown out nearly nine hours ago. By now the Council's most trusted Friend would be in Oxford. The church, described in the book and accompanied by a clear black and white photo, was a focal point of the city – or at least, it had been. The BBC, received across a satellite connection linked to his office, was reporting that over half the structure had been reduced to rubble in an explosion that had rocked the ancient building almost two days earlier. The Secretary took careful note of the details. The explosion had occurred at 5.30 a.m. Wednesday morning, English time. That time matched, almost to the minute, their termination of the Keeper, 4,000 miles to the west. Telephone records, easily obtained, had confirmed that the old man had placed a call to Oxford earlier in the day.

The Secretary could see through the Keeper's infantile, retributive scheme. The old man had clearly known they were coming for him. He had been given the list inadvertently leaked by Hines's incompetent aide, and he knew they would not let him live, knowing what they were plotting. He also knew that his own execution would bring to an end over thirteen centuries of the Council's seeking, and the little bastard had chosen to go out rubbing their noses in that lamentable fact. He had wanted them to find his little pages, to locate the site, and then watch as he denied them what was in it – the last hope of obtaining their Highest Aim, ripped from their grasp. He was teasing them, even in death, making sure they would see just what lengths he had gone to, in his final hours, to keep them at bay.

Foolish man.

The Secretary's only regret was that the adversary he had faced for so many years never had the opportunity to see the full power they had pitted against him. Now that they had discovered his ruse, the Council would act with all the force of its accumulated centuries to bring their quest to its necessary end. They would take their target in America, nothing could stop that now; but the far greater aim, the library itself, would also be theirs. The Secretary could feel it in his blood.

CHAPTER 32

Oxford – 2 p.m. GMT

Emily Wess ascended the wooden stairs towards Professor Wexler's rooms. The staircase had been built centuries after the building proper, yet was itself also an antique. Emily remembered fruitless attempts, in her postgraduate days, at making the ascent without being noticed by her supervisor. The creaking of old wood had foiled her every time.

The professor's office, coupled with a lavatory, kitchenette, sitting area and small bedroom – collectively termed his 'rooms', in old Oxbridge fashion – were located on the second floor of one of Oriel College's buildings off of Magpie Lane. It was here, amidst sagging bookshelves and decrepit lounge furniture, that Emily had sat for her Master's tutorials, studying under one of the field's greats. Their discussions would stay with Emily for ever. Wexler had a way of cutting through the dross and forcing his students to defend their position with an intensity they didn't know they possessed. Eminently a teacher, he had gradually become a close friend.

The door into his rooms had been left ajar, and Emily entered with a light knock.

'Come in, come in,' Wexler said. 'I've taken the liberty . . .' He did not finish the sentence, but simply handed Emily a familiar glass, filled with a familiar liquid. 'To your very good health, and your perplexing return to our halls.'

Emily took the sherry and raised her glass, and Kyle joined them in the toast.

'Michael is well, I presume?' The professor indicated an empty space on the sofa, next to Kyle, and Emily took her seat.

'Very. He sends his greetings.'

Her phone call to Michael had been brief, but long enough for her to assure him of her safe arrival. He had been filled with joy at hearing from her on their special day, even though they'd spoken only hours before, but his tone had become more serious when Emily had shared what she'd learned since arriving in Oxford. News of a legend that, if it were true, fit her current activities into a story larger than either of them had imagined.

Kyle fidgeted from his corner of the sofa, his sherry glass already emptied and set aside.

'Listen, about this third paper,' he said, taking up the final page of Arno's second letter.

'Now, now,' Wexler cut him off. 'You're too quick to business. I may not be one for small talk, Mr Emory, but I am altogether one for enjoying a civilized drink.' He motioned Kyle to set the papers aside.

Kyle did as he'd been bid with visible hesitation. His was

a mind accustomed to running with ideas with all his energy. He knew that this fit the stereotype for doctoral students who were famous the world over for developing one-track minds that could contemplate little else than their subject – even if that 'else' was eating, or bathing, or engaging in normal human conversations. But it was who he was. *And this, this* . . . he glanced at the papers. *This is interesting.*

The three academics sat in silence for a few long moments. Kyle continued to fidget in his seat.

'Well, I see that we've exhausted our casual conversation,' Wexler finally offered, breaking the silence and setting down his glass. 'Very well, Mr Emory, you may continue.'

The look of relief on Kyle's face was unmistakable.

'This third page,' he said, 'it's entirely different from the other two. Since Professor Holmstrand says in his second letter that he can't be sure you'll see his notes before "they" do – whoever "they" are – it seems clear that this third page contains guidance, designed to conceal itself under the guise of an enigma.'

'Guidance concealed under the guise of an enigma?' Emily raised a brow. 'You really are a graduate student! Listen, you don't need to pad the word count for your thesis here. If you mean "clue", you can say it.' She offered a small grin, but from the look on Kyle's face it was apparent that he didn't know whether he was being teased or scolded. Emily cast a bemused glance at Wexler and then reassured Kyle, 'Yes. I do agree that the third page looks like a set of clues. To something.'

'Right.' Kyle absorbed Emily's sarcasm, but his enthusiasm

remained undimmed. 'Clues, precisely. And as to their context, the note at the top of the page gives us some hint. "Two for Oxford, and one thereafter." There are three statements later on the page. It seems a safe guess that two of them apply to places here in the University, and one to somewhere else.'

Emily glanced over at the page. Kyle's reading was logical, and it had the advantage of creating an order to the otherwise random phrases. Rather than four 'clues', there were three, prefaced by a note that gave them their bearings. Two for Oxford, the third . . . elsewhere. For the first time it occurred to Emily that what lay ahead might take her yet further afield than her present surroundings.

'So,' Kyle continued, 'that leaves us the job of figuring out what the three clues mean.'

'As well as the crest,' Wexler interjected, 'the lettering at the top of the page, the symbol in the frame. Surely it also has some significance.'

Having focused so intently on the handwritten phrases surrounding it, Emily had all but neglected to consider the simple crest, drawn near the top of the page. A frame surrounding two Greek letters. This was going to be harder to decipher than the enigmatic phrases, whatever they were supposed to mean.

It was not Emily's only assumption of the day that would prove to be incorrect.

'Ah, that,' Kyle replied. 'I think I've figured that one out.'

Emily's eyebrows lifted involuntarily, and Wexler's followed suit.

'Already?' She took up the paper and peered at the lettering. 'How? There are no indications on the page as to what it might mean, or how to interpret it.'

'Not on that page, no,' Kyle agreed. 'The key is on the page before.' He picked up Arno's second letter and presented it to Emily. 'Look there, at the end. The two underlined words.'

'"Our library",' Emily read aloud. She glanced in Wexler's direction, but the older professor had his gaze set on Kyle, awaiting an explanation. His stare was intent, his mind running over possibilities, trying to trace out his student's discovery for himself.

'Obviously,' Kyle continued, 'Professor Holmstrand wanted to draw attention to those words – it's the only phrase he underlines anywhere in the three notes.'

Suddenly Wexler came alive.

'You clever boy!' He nearly leapt out of his chair, recognizing what Kyle had seen. 'It's a tag, an indicator! Hansel and Gretel's breadcrumbs in the forest.' His face was abeam with recognition, and Kyle nodded fervently.

'I'm sorry,' Emily interrupted their exchange. 'I have to admit, I don't follow.'

Kyle took up the third page again.

'Here at the top of the page the crest is made up of two Greek letters, *beta* and *eta*. The small stroke above them looks like an accent mark, but it isn't.'

'No,' Emily agreed. 'That's a *titlo*, the old indicator of an abbreviation.' The Greek penchant for abbreviations had been forged back when words were not written with pen and ink but carved in stone. Two letters rather than ten required less muscle power and expense to produce.

'Exactly. Normally this kind of flourish indicates an abbreviated term, placed above the first and last letters of the full word it's meant to shorten. But here, here I believe it's meant to abbreviate two words. A phrase.'

Recognition dawned in Emily's eyes. She looked back to the underlined words in Arno's second letter. *Our library*.

'That's right!' exclaimed the professor, seeing the recognition in her expression. 'In the language of the Alexandrian library itself, *beta-eta* is an abbreviation for *bibliotheche emon*, "our library".'

'The same words Holmstrand underlined in his second letter,' Emily muttered. The pieces fit. Arno was urging them to understand.

'My guess is that Holmstrand has drawn you a symbol representing the library itself,' Kyle pressed on, 'and given you clues on how to find it. I'm willing to put a fiver and a round of drinks on this crest, this symbol, being found at whatever spot these clues point to.' He held the paper up before the gaze of Emily and Wexler.

'If this little symbol is, as you say, out there somewhere to be found,' Emily said, finding Kyle's explanation compelling, 'we need to sort out these three comments.'

This time, it was Wexler who took the lead in the conversation.

'Assuming the first two refer to Oxford, then their meaning seems clear.' He drew in a deep breath, preparing for his explanation. 'The first clue, "University's Church, oldest of them all", is hardly encoded at all. Just round the corner, in the heart of the city, is the University Church of St Mary the Virgin, which, apart from being the central hub of Oxford's official religious life, is also the oldest building of the University proper.'

The University Church was not the oldest building in Oxford, nor the first to be used for collegiate life. It was, however, the first building to be used collectively by the various halls and colleges that had arisen in the twelfth and thirteenth centuries, which would eventually produce the university in its lasting form. In that sense, it certainly had a claim on being 'oldest of them all'.

As she looked up, Emily noticed that both Kyle and Wexler now wore puzzled expressions. They glanced at each other, halting, before Kyle turned to face Emily.

'I take it you've not been watching the news?'

'Not recently,' Emily answered. 'I've been rather . . . busy with other things.' Her day thus far had been spent almost entirely in transit.

'Well,' said Kyle, nodding, 'the news you've not heard is significant, especially now and especially to you. Apart from coverage of the scandals afoot in Washington, the main story here today has focused a little closer to home.' He accentuated his next words. 'The University Church has been destroyed.'

'What?' Emily couldn't contain her shock. 'How?'

'A bomb blast, yesterday.' Kyle kept his gaze connected to Emily's.

'But we mustn't let that deter us,' Wexler interjected. 'If

this line does refer to the church, then it helps make sense of the second clue. The church that's just been destroyed is dedicated to the Virgin Mary, a woman of many titles. Mother of Jesus Christ, Sovereign Lady, Ever-Virgin—'

'And Queen of Heaven.' Emily was pacing her mentor.

'Precisely,' Wexler affirmed. 'I've not examined the church for some time, but I can remember that it has just what you'd expect. more than one image of St Mary adorning its walls. Holmstrand's "To pray, between two Queens", the second of his clues . . . I'm willing to bet that symbol – ' he pointed at the crest at the top of the page ' – is found at some point midway between two Marian statues in the University Church.' He paused. 'Or, rather, was, before the explosion.'

The small group was silent for a few lingering moments, pondering over Wexler's apparent solution to Arno's puzzle.

'What about the final phrase, "Fifteen, if by morning"?' Emily asked.

'On that one, I'm afraid I've no idea.' Wexler held up his hands, signalling at least a partial defeat. 'Even the English can't solve everything over a single stiff drink.'

'But give them a second . . .' Emily smiled as she completed Wexler's quip.

'Remember, though,' Kyle noted, 'it does say that only the first two clues point to Oxford, the third to somewhere else. Finding this first location may shed some light on it.'

Emily leaned back, sinking into the wilted curves of the old sofa. Her mind was a blur of emotions. She felt a tension at the news of the University Church's destruction, but she also felt a sense of disappointment that took her by surprise.

She had expected the secrecy of Arno's guidance to be more difficult to unlock. As it was, the great mystery she half-thought was to form some kind of glamorous quest, appeared to have been largely solved over a single sherry and her first half-hour in the city.

A half-hour.

It was that thought, that passing reference to time, that sprung her mind into action. *Time*, she thought. *The time matters. The time changes everything.*

Emily bolted forward in her seat and stared directly into Wexler's eyes.

'Professor, I have a question to which I'm going to need a very precise answer.'

Wexler looked back at Emily, puzzled by her sudden burst of energy.

'As you wish. I'll do what I can.'

When Emily continued, her focus was singular and her heart was racing.

'At what time, exactly, did the University Church explode?'

CHAPTER 33

Oxford – 2.10 p.m. GMT

The rubble around the Friends was impressive in its anarchic disarray. The scene was made yet more chaotic by the crawling sprawl of officials seeking to examine it; forensic examiners, crime scene photographers, even structural engineers were already on site. Uniformed officials roped off areas deemed unsafe with bright tape, while others took down details on notepads, and an almost endless flow of investigators spoke into radios and mobile phones, reporting their findings up the ladder.

It was precisely the traditional jumble of large-scale crime scene investigations that Jason and his partner had counted on. Amidst the sea of different agencies, all with their own dress codes and uniforms, areas of interest and methods of examination, the two men were essentially invisible, allowing them to carry out their work without interference.

And that is what the Friends were here to accomplish: a study, more than an investigation. They knew the cause of the explosion; they knew its motivation and intention. The specific details the police would query – type of explosive, method of trigger – were of little interest. Their focus was on studying what remained, and through it determining precisely what had been destroyed. What had been hidden through the destruction. For this was a game, the Friends knew. A game of hide-and-seek, though the Keeper had intended that they should not be able to seek, that they should only be able to lament the loss of what he had destroyed. The dead man, though, would not have his way.

'Keep it as steady as you can,' Jason ordered his partner. The small device in the latter's palm, barely larger than a personal camcorder, was slowly sweeping across one of the long walls of the church. The images it took in were routed to a computer on Jason's knee.

'Don't let it wobble,' he added. 'We need the contours to line up.'

The other man held his arm as steady as he could, coming to the end of the smooth motion.

'That's the fourth complete,' he said, switching off the device's input.

Jason looked down at the computer as the fourth latitudinal scan of the building's interior uploaded to his screen. The software receiving it was already at work, digitally stitching it to the previous three. Gradually, a three-dimensional map of the structure was being assembled.

'Start on the roof,' Jason ordered. The second man pressed down on a small red button on the camera, and began a fifth scan, this time aiming it skyward, slowly arcing from one end of the church's ceiling to the next.

Jason snapped open his phone. A few button presses later, he was connected to the London team.

'You're seeing this?'

'Yes,' came a dispassionate voice. 'Connect the two-way link and we'll show you ours.' Jason worked his way through a small series of menus on his computer, and the one-way connection to the London servers was made bidirectional. Immediately, the imagery from the lab began to stream to his display.

'I'm getting it,' he affirmed. On his monitor, a similar three-dimensional model of the church's interior began to appear. In most of its features it was identical to the imagery he and his partner were now creating, with one notable, crucial difference. The model from London was of the church without the disfigurement of its recent destruction. It was the church in pristine condition.

'We've assembled the images from various sources,' the London team captain said. 'What you're seeing is the interior as it looked no more than seventy-eight hours ago, though most segments are even newer.' The Council's electronic resources were vast, and their operators' skills adept. Though he had long grown accustomed to it in practical terms, Jason remained amazed at just how much of the earth was photographed in detail and available online, through a combination of official photographs, satellite data, even tourists' blogs and personal albums. With enough focused effort, the exterior and interior of almost every notable building on the planet could be retrieved.

Such extensive efforts had not been required here, however,

he knew. The Council had been keeping its eye on Oxford for decades. The library's resources were mobile, and the city's connections historic. Though no primary connection had ever been established to it, Oxford was a site known to the Council, and for that reason featured prominently in its databases. Scout teams of Friends routinely updated their records with new surveillance, photography and recordings. More recently, over the past six months, the Keeper's interactions with the English city had raised red flags and drawn their attention even further. Though he had always encrypted his emails and telephone calls so that they could not know their contents, the Council had at least been able to see that he had been corresponding with groups in Oxford routinely since May. Accordingly, their men on the ground had stepped up their surveillance.

'We've almost got enough to start the comparative scan,' the man on the phone continued. His terminal in London, like Jason's in Oxford, showed both models side by side: the first, the church in its pristine state; the second, in its current state of manipulated ruin. Ready to be compared. Ready to be examined.

'Use the pre-explosion model to catalogue every item that was present in the segments now destroyed,' Jason commanded. 'Every painting, engraving, statue, window. Anything that's a possibility. Send it up to the Secretary.'

Everyone assigned to the project knew that the Society had destroyed the church, presumably to hide something from view. But unlike the police all around them, the Friends would require no digging, no guesswork. By reconstructing what had stood in the areas now destroyed, they could cross-reference everything they saw, using it as a starting point for further investigation.

'Got it,' the second Friend interjected, lowering the camera to his side. 'That's everything.' Jason nodded in affirmation. Within moments, the second 3D model on his screen was complete. The digital cross-referencing would be done on the higher-powered computers in the London office. Jason had only to wait for the results to be itemized, which would take a few minutes.

He looked up, gazing again at the scene around him. A day earlier, he had stood in the Keeper's office. He had felt the great surge of power as the trigger of his gun came back to its casing and the shots had fired. He had watched the glow depart from the old man's eyes. Minutes later, he now knew, this building had been destroyed. The Keeper, hearing him coming, had orchestrated this last-minute ploy, a desperate attempt to keep something from him.

Jason held back a contented grin. The man should have known better than to think he could hide anything from the Council.

'We're coming for your secrets, old man,' he whispered to himself. He took great pleasure in knowing the Keeper could no longer answer his threat.

CHAPTER 34

2.30 p.m. GMT

Emily could barely contain her impatience as Wexler scanned through the morning's paper for details on the precise time the University Church of St Mary had been destroyed. She had a hunch that the detail was significant, a hunch that instinctively she felt was correct, but one which was just far-fetched enough that she wouldn't quite believe it until the time could be confirmed.

'The explosion was yesterday, early in the morning,' Wexler spoke as he scanned the paper. 'A bomb at the base of the church's tower, according to first reports. Thank God it was early . . .' his voice trailed off as he continued to read. Then, his back straightened as he found the detail he wanted. 'There we are. The explosion happened at precisely five-thirty in the morning. No one was inside, and no one was hurt. But the tower is gone, and so is most of the rest of the building. They were able to pinpoint the time because the hands on the tower's clock stopped as it was destroyed.'

'The local and national media have been all over the story since it happened,' Kyle added. 'According to the BBC this morning, the falling tower took the central part of the church with it, including its old library. The two ends of the main body are still standing, but I haven't heard yet whether they're structurally sound enough to avoid having to be torn down.'

'Immense tragedy,' Wexler added. 'She was a beauty of a church.'

'The whole area's roped off,' Kyle continued. 'They spent most of yesterday scouting the rubble for stability, making sure it was safe for investigators. The Thames Valley Police moved in this morning.'

'And not just the police. With the terrorism watch what it is, you can be sure it will be investigated by the government as well.' Wexler spoke of the government with no little hint of superior distaste. It was, he firmly believed, the divine right of educated intellectuals to know far more about governance than any government ever would. Of course, such men would never deign to actually govern – that was far beneath the dignity of any good scholar. But it was satisfying to know that one *could*, and undoubtedly to far greater success than anyone else.

Emily dismissed the show of traditional snobbery, her mind absorbed in the shocking information.

5.30 a.m. She counted back on her fingers, her heart racing. Even before she started, she knew where the facts were leading, but she had to be sure.

'Five-thirty on Wednesday morning, less six for the time difference . . .' Emily spoke at half volume, entirely to herself.

143

'That means the church was destroyed at eleven-thirty on Tuesday night, Minnesota time at Carleton College.'

Kyle and Wexler kept their eyes on Emily, not seeing whatever connection had come into her mind.

'That is the very moment Arno Holmstrand was killed, according to the rumours circulating in my office. Sometime between eleven and midnight on Tuesday.' Emily spoke the observation into her hand, her fingers still poised from their counting. Then she said the words she would never have expected her sceptical mouth to utter. 'These two events have to be connected.' The church had stood for centuries, only to be destroyed at just the moment she was sent to find it? A lifetime of loathing conspiracy theories aside, it could not be coincidence.

Kyle and Wexler kept their eyes trained on Emily, waiting for more.

'Holmstrand and that church are already connected,' she continued, fleshing out her own thoughts. 'The clues point directly to it. What he's written here clearly directs me there.' She waved a hand from the letters to a photograph of the church on the front page of the Oxford paper, still straddled over Wexler's lap.

'And then, at the same moment he directs me to find something concealed in the church, it's destroyed by a bomb blast.' Emily halted. 'The implication of this seems clear.'

'Do share,' Wexler urged.

'Whether or not they know he passed on these clues to a third party like me, somebody clearly did not want anyone to find the very thing Arno Holmstrand has said I must. And my God, they were willing to go to dramatic lengths to ensure no one does.' Emily allowed herself a moment to reflect. The fact that someone didn't want information relating to the library to be found confirmed for her the validity of Arno's revelations, and even of Kyle's theories on what the 'Society' might be. Some group obviously wanted the library's secrets to remain secrets.

And that fact alone made her want to find them all the more.

Emily raised her gaze to Wexler.

'Professor, destroyed or not, we have to get a look at that church.'

CHAPTER 35

2.45 p.m. GMT

Getting that look was going to prove more easily said than done.

'It's taped off,' Kyle had protested after Emily had made her pronouncement, 'and the church grounds are crawling with police. I don't see how we'll get in.'

In the midst of the confusion and hesitation, Wexler made the move to rise. 'My boy, where there's a will, there's a way.' With Peter Wexler, such a statement was definitive. No more discussion needed to take place. He knew what he wished to do, and he intended to do it, whatever the obstacles might be. His face beamed a confidence that suggested the younger scholars could learn a thing or two from the example.

They followed his lead and stood up as Wexler grabbed an umbrella and a flat cap. The bright blue sky, devoid of even a single cloud, was an irrelevance to his customary attire for walking the streets.

Emily smiled, the professor's enthusiasm infectious. Placing Arno's notes into her bag, she followed Kyle through the door, down the stairs and into the heart of the City of Dreaming Spires.

CHAPTER 36

Washington DC – 9.30 a.m. EST (2.30 p.m. GMT)

'This doesn't look good, no matter how you slice it.' General Huskins flung one of the photographs back onto the long table, tracing its path back to the others with evident disgust. 'All his closest aides, his most influential advisors!'

The other men around the table were silent, each a mixture of anger and alert mental activity. The meeting had been called by Ashton Davis, the secretary of defence, in response to the escalating crisis that was flooding every news outlet from the *New York Times* to the inchoate ramblings of the blogosphere in every language the CIA tracked, which was most of them. Normally, tactical meetings of the nation's defence, intelligence and homeland security heads would be held in the White House situation room, but, given the circumstances, that was not an option. Davis had instructed the small gathering of men to assemble in a soundproof 'quiet room' in the third ring of the Pentagon, where they could speak openly without being seen or heard. By anyone.

'You're overstating the matter,' the secretary of defence

responded. 'Only three of the president's advisors have been killed. That's a far cry from "all".'

'Four,' the general snapped back, 'if you count the VP's man, Forrester. The little upstart spent as much time with the president's staff as his own. And besides, these are just the four we know. Who knows who else has been offed?'

Huskins glared across the table at his counterpart from the Secret Service, Director Brad Whitley, whose head was nodding in agreement. 'In any case, four is no small number,' Whitley added. 'Especially in a single week.'

'How the hell did you let this happen, Whitley?!' The secretary of defence fired his accusation at the last man to speak, thundering a fist down on the table. The Secret Service director, who'd held his position through three administrations, responded calmly, focusing solely on the facts before them.

'Our job is to protect the president, the vice president, their families and visiting heads of state,' he spoke steadily. 'The Secret Service is not tasked to protect the president's aides or advisors.'

Davis breathed firmly, letting his anger reside. Whitley was right, of course. This wasn't an institutional failure. It was, according to everything that they – and every media source in the world – had at their disposal, the fault of the man in charge. The president, it appeared, had brought this upon himself, and upon the nation he was supposed to lead.

'Let's get back to the data on the assassinations,' the secretary of defence replied, dropping the previous point. 'That's the bit that determines whether this is just one holy great breakdown in the war on terror, or a culpable treachery by the commander in chief.' Davis's words were the first occasion that any of them had voiced the real extent of the events unfolding around them. A poignant silence followed.

'Dammit, talk!' the secretary of defence demanded, slamming down his fist again. Snapped back to the gravity of the moment, General Mark Huskins leaned forward and rattled off what his military investigators had discovered from the crime scenes.

'In each case, except the VP's aide, the men were killed by multiple handgun shots at centre-mass. These were formal executions. Professional hits.'

'So it could be anyone, or any number of groups,' Davis thought aloud, his voice hopeful.

'No,' the general countered. 'Ballistics show that the bullets in each case were from the same calibre handgun, and three of the casings still had ample markings for a source trace.'

'What sort of trace?'

'Assuming the rounds aren't too deformed on impact, we can trace manufacture through form, chemical constituents, alloys and other key markers. Helps us keep track of munitions suppliers and traffickers around the world. We do this routinely on all terrorist sites, tactical combat areas – anywhere we have an opportunity to gain munitions from forces other than our own.' He stopped, and sat back, summarizing for the secretary of defence. 'Bullets link bad men, Mr Secretary.'

It was that link that they were all here to determine.

'And?' Davis probed. 'What did the trace show?'

The general realized the gravity of what his answer would mean, but his job was not to mute the terrible facts for these men. When he spoke, he spoke with certainty. 'All the rounds fired in the assassinations of the president's advisors came from a batch of ammunition with identical physical and chemical characteristics to munitions we've tracked solely to one other locale. That locale is north-eastern Afghanistan.'

So, there it is. Every man's mental reaction formed in silent unison. The suspicions that had brought the group together were now substantiated by solid, forensic fact.

'Holy hell,' Whitley answered. Given this data, his job description as head of the Secret Service was suddenly starting to look rather different.

Davis tried to bring the news into the broader context of the day.

'The reports we've all seen flooding the media demonstrate a clear pattern of corrupt dealings by President Tratham. Whoever leaked that cache of documents may have to rot in the deepest belly of one of our finest prisons for the breach of secrecy, but the fact of the matter is they leave little room for doubt. The president's been double-dealing for the reconstruction with his Saudi friends.'

'And that's obviously pissed off the Afghans,' Whitley responded.

'The connection to the dead advisors?' Secretary Davis wanted clarity. Certainty. This time it was the director of the Secret Service who could provide it.

'Each of them – Gifford, Dales, Marlake – they have all advised him on his foreign policy determinations. They've all been part of his inner cadre for the post-war reconstruction negotiations.'

'What about Forrester?'

'He was with the vice president, even if he was aiming higher up. But he was on foreign policy, too.'

'The VP as well! Has the whole damned administration completely lost its mind?!' The secretary of defence's face was red, and he was visibly livid.

'Hold on,' General Huskins interjected, 'we don't know for sure that the vice president is involved. The documents we have only show ties to the president's office, and your taps on Hines – ' he glanced in Whitley's direction ' – seem to indicate he's as surprised by all this as anyone else.'

Davis spun towards Brad Whitley.

'I want you and your men at the Secret Service to find out, and find out for sure. The president has clearly engaged in illegal dealings in Saudi Arabia that have provoked insurgents to kill government advisors, on American soil, right here in the capital. If the vice president has had a part in this despicable treachery, I want to know. If it's the last thing I do, I'll crucify them both.'

CHAPTER 37

Oxford – 3.10 p.m. GMT

The scene at the edge of Radcliffe Square was just as Peter Wexler had described it. Opposite James Gibbs's monumental Radcliffe Camera, Britain's first round library – which now served as a detached collection of reading rooms for the central Bodleian Library – the University Church of St Mary sat in dejected ruins. The great twelfth-century tower and spire, long the focal centre of the city and one of Oxford's major tourist attractions, had been completely destroyed in the blast and existed now only as an unrecognizable pile of collapsed, blackened stone. The church itself had buckled at its middle, its east and west ends standing obstinately in the face of the destruction but the centre half-fallen, crushed as beams connected to the tower had collapsed. The famous round-stone cobbling of the square, as impractical as it was beautiful, was covered in a layer of pebbles and dust emanating out from the epicentre of the church.

As Kyle had anticipated, the whole area was roped off with yellow police taping, and uniformed local patrols stood guard at various points along the line. Behind it, the scene crawled with investigators. The Thames Valley Police were easily distinguishable by their reflective yellow jackets, each emblazoned with the Oxford Ox and force crest. They were joined by members of the fire brigade and a number of inspectors that had come up from London to survey the damage. Men in black suits represented offices and government departments Emily presumed wished to be kept anonymous, though it was obvious to everyone, particularly the local media, huddled in pockets around the site, that MI6 – the street name by which the British Secret Intelligence Service was universally known – would be involved in the investigations. A bomb meant terrorists, and terrorists meant terror and, as English politicians, like their American counterparts, were always ready to remind, there was an ongoing war on terror.

Kyle had been right, too, in his warnings about access. There was no obvious way that the public could get any further than the police tape surrounding the ruins of the church. Emily glanced in the postgraduate student's direction for any sign of guidance, but Kyle had taken himself away from the scene to the stone wall surrounding All Soul's College, bordering one side of the square. He sat there now, and Emily noted the way he looked not at the scene but away from it, lost in his thoughts.

Peter Wexler, on the other hand, took his umbrella in tow and made straight for the line. The old professor clearly intended to go where he wished, all warnings against it be damned. Emily followed at his side.

They were stopped by an officer standing post outside the

stretched yellow tape. 'I'm afraid I can't let you past. This area is closed to the public.'

And with that, their little game began.

'This we can see,' Wexler answered, removing his cap with a deliberate show of pomp. 'I, however, am not a member of the public. I am a member of the University Council, and long-time governor of these grounds.'

The officer looked only half-convinced, and didn't make to move.

'This young woman – ' Wexler raised a dismissive hand towards Emily ' – is my assistant, which means she is a crony who does what I say.' Emily bit her tongue, and forced herself to nod submissively in agreement. She would share one or two choice thoughts on the details of this description with Wexler later.

'And those men – ' Wexler motioned to a group of three men in grey, conversing amidst the rubble inside the line ' – are my colleagues, already looking mildly annoyed that I am here, and not over there.' He paused to let the officer soak in his meaning. 'Now, I should be grateful if you would let us in, as this little mess has put rather a lot on my agenda for the day.'

The officer hesitated, but Peter Wexler was an imposing, elder scholar in a city run by scholars, and at this moment his commanding gaze rested firmly on the officer's face as if chastising a small child.

'Very well, sir,' the officer finally conceded, buckling under the pressure. Oxford was full of pompous dons who held immense clout. He could let the old man have his way now, or let him have it later, after receiving a thorough chastising by his superiors for putting his foot in the mouth of fragile town-and-gown relations. 'But do be careful. The building's stable enough now, but the footing is not.'

'Our thanks,' Wexler answered efficiently, grabbing Emily's shoulder and pulling her along. The two ducked under the yellow tape and began a deliberate walk towards the other men.

'Your assistant?' Emily muttered from the side of her mouth, incredulous.

'Don't be sensitive, I also called you a crony,' Wexler added. 'I gave you the full treatment. Double-barrel degradation. It seemed appropriate in the circumstances.'

'And I'm sure it just crushed you to play the role of the refined old stooge.' Emily rolled her eyes as they walked. 'I don't imagine any of what you said was actually true?'

'That depends very much on how precise you want your truth to be.' Wexler did not turn to her as he spoke, but Emily could sense a look of content self-satisfaction beaming from his face. She switched her focus to her feet, navigating around stones and bricks that had only too recently been features of the Oxford skyline. With all the rubble, her penchant for practical, flat footwear was an asset.

'I'll go give my colleagues there a quick hello,' Wexler said. 'A little reunion and group lamentation – you know, the gentlemanly way to approach destruction. You have a look round. But don't dally. I imagine they'll kick us both out of here eventually.'

He veered right, directly to the group, as Emily carried on

to the edge of the church. The damage, which was impressive from a distance, was all the more so at first hand. Stones that reached shoulder height sat at awkward angles, gargoyles and carved figures broken and crushed beneath them. Emily paused at a statue, apparently an angel, that for centuries had looked down from its lofty height on town and gown below, now split in two and gazing at her ankles. The sight was overwhelming. She stood in the midst of history, as if her textbooks and old documents had suddenly come to life. The construction of this university church had marked a change in western learning, a turning point in intellectual history. Lectures on the great advances in science had been delivered here. The Reformation had taken its toll here, as had the Inquisition.

And here she stood, one of the first to survey its destruction.

Emily fought back the temptation to entertain nostalgia. She was here for a reason, and that reason required her complete focus. Attempting to look as if she had a purpose and right to be there, Emily edged around the west end of the building to the long wall facing the High Street. This side had suffered the least damage, and Emily made her way to the door, walking through without glancing at the uniformed guard who stood patrol against tourists and passersby. Eye contact would only provoke questions, and she was not certain she could improvise as convincingly as Wexler.

Inside, there were almost as many investigators as Emily had seen outside the church. She tried to mimic their observant behaviour as she surveyed the scene. The west end of the church, which housed Charles Kempe's famous stained glass representation of the Tree of Jesse, had miraculously survived unscathed, and, in fact, the whole far area stood in relatively good condition. Glancing through the nave to the opposite end, the same appeared to be true there. The chancel, re-built in the mid-fifteenth century and adorned with intricately carved, wooden choir stalls from the same period, stood as she remembered them from her visits as a student.

The long space of the church between, however, had taken the brunt of the blow. The ceiling was shattered over the central altar and pulpit, and the wall that connected north and supported the tower now lay collapsed in an enormous pile of rubble. The side chapel, named after Adam de Brome, the church's fourteenth-century rector and founder of Oriel College, had been completely crushed. Light shone through the space at awkward angles, entering for the first time in centuries not through the church's stained glass – the work of masters such as Pugin and Kempe – but through gaping holes in the ceiling and walls.

Despite her efforts at restraint, the historian in Emily brought the emotion of the scene flooding forward. This had been the church in which Cardinal Newman had preached before leaving the Anglican Church for the Roman Catholic; in which John Wesley, the founding father of Methodism, had delivered his sermons before being banned for his provocative comments on the sloth and religious indifference of the University faculty; in which the Protestant Reformation had faced some of its first English tests, when the church was used as a courtroom for the trials of Latimer, Ridley, and

Cranmer – two reforming bishops and an archbishop eventually executed on a pyre not far from the church for their refusal to bow to the pro-Roman movements of a new queen. Emily counted herself neither a Catholic, nor a Methodist, nor even a Protestant, but this building, which now stood in broken disarray, had been the site of events and moments that had shaped modern history.

And perhaps it would be again, if indeed it bore some connection to the long-lost Library of Alexandria. That thought, which less than an hour ago would have struck her as utterly fantastic, seemed less ridiculous in her present circumstances. This was deliberate destruction, clearly linked to the murder of Arno Holmstrand.

Emily moved along the church's south aisle towards the rubble at its centre, muttering Arno's enigmatic guidance under her breath: *to pray, between two Queens*. In a church dedicated to the Virgin Mary, Queen of Heaven, there had to be statues, paintings, something depicting the building's heavenly patron.

She looked across at the rubble consuming the middle of the church. *If it's in there, it's gone*. Any statue that might have survived the crushing weight of the tower would be buried for weeks before recovery. The circumstances of the past two days, however, were enough to convince Emily that weeks were not at her disposal.

She looked back, surveying her route. There was no statuary of any note along her path, and nothing leapt out at her from the side windows. She craned her head up further, and, not for the first time in her life, stopped to marvel at the splendour of the great west window. Even the destruction now lying all around it could not detract from its beauty. It depicted that great vision of the prophet Isaiah, in which Christ was prophesied to come forth from the 'tree of Jesse', part of the ancient lineage of King David. The window interpreted the vision literally and was a stunning portrait of a great tree with branches weaving across its space, each supporting images of kings, prophets, patriarchs and ancestors. At their centre, as the fulfilment of the vision, was an image of Christ himself.

Held in the arms of his mother.

Emily focused on the window's central panel. The Christchild was held in his mother's arms, borne up on her knee like a throne. She wore regal attire, every bit the image of the Heavenly Queen.

To pray, between two Queens.

Emily's breath shortened. Glancing around the nearby frames of the vast window, she scanned for another image of the Virgin. Had the symbol been crafted into the window by Kempe himself, balanced by two portraits of Mary? Was the path on which Arno was directing her that old?

Emily's gaze covered the intricate stained glass several times, but she could find no second appearance of the Virgin. *The second must be somewhere else in the church*, she thought. The idea, as she pondered it, made more sense than it being in the window itself.

Find another image of Mary, and then the space between.
Emily expanded the field of her search. The surrounding walls yielded nothing, and her heart sank as she once more looked

to the rubble-filled, middle section of the church. Beyond, her gaze passed through the chancel arch to the stalls behind. Francesco Bassano's painting of the adoration of the shepherds still stood above the altar on the far east wall, holding defiantly fast against the shock of the explosion.

Above it, in what Michael had several times insisted Emily call the *reredos*, but which she always thought of simply as the 'altarpiece', stood seven statues. One in particular fast became the singular object of her attention.

Directly above the altar itself stood a statue of the infant Christ, held in the arms of his regal mother.

To pray, between two Queens. Each end of the long church had at its centre the same image of the Virgin Mary, the one in glass, the other in stone. The focus of Arno's clue suddenly crystallized in Emily's mind. The library's small symbol, and whatever other information or insight might accompany it, had to lie midway between these two images. *Between two Queens*. A spot precisely at the centre of the church.

And directly beneath a thousand tonnes of fallen stone.

CHAPTER 38

Oxford – 3.50 p.m. GMT

When Emily exited the Church a few moments later, her expression was dour. As she stepped through the small alley known as Catte Street at the building's east end, she felt little concern over whether she was stopped now by the police and removed from the scene. Her discoveries inside had removed any hope that the information Arno Holmstrand wanted her to find, which Emily was now certain had actually been there, could be accessed. Arno had written that others were after the knowledge. It seemed clear that they had got here first, and covered their tracks in a dramatic way. Whatever was there to be seen was now entirely inaccessible. Emily had no idea whether it would take weeks or months for the heap of stones to be cleared out of the church's midsection and, even once they were, whether the clue she sought would still remain.

Looking across the grounds, she met eyes with Wexler who was visibly relieved to see her outside the building. Muttering a few quick farewells to the group around him, he nodded to Emily and they both made their way to the edge of the site, crossing beneath the tape to the unrestricted area beyond. They walked over to Kyle, still perched in thought on his stone bench, before they spoke.

'I was beginning to wonder how much longer I could maintain that little ruse,' said Wexler. He looked hopefully towards Emily. 'I trust it was time well spent?'

'In a way,' Emily answered. 'I found the two queens: an image of Mary in the western window, and another as a statue over the far altar. But to pray between them isn't possible just at the moment.'

The professor raised an eyebrow, questioning.

'The midpoint between the two images,' Emily said, 'is currently a massive pile of rock and rubble.'

Wexler cast his gaze back to the church, and as his eyes took in the ruins of the tower, he comprehended Emily's point. The professor appeared physically pained at the news.

'I'm not sure I see a way to continue,' Emily admitted, trying to keep the hint of defeat from her voice. 'Whatever's lying beneath that rubble, there's no way I'm getting to it. At least, not now.'

Suddenly, Kyle stood. Silent to that point, he was now the only one of the three with a look of hope on his face.

'Actually, Dr Wess, I don't believe it's as big a problem as you think.'

Emily, in her frustration, was taken by the positive note.

'Not as big a problem as I think? Professor – ' she turned to Wexler ' – you know how to pick the optimists!' She returned her gaze to Kyle. 'Listen, I know hope springs eternal, but a dose of realism is good for the soul.' Yet as Emily spoke, the young man's face continued to light up, and his look of hope became one of resolute satisfaction. Rather than becoming downcast at the rebuff, his face settled into a wry smile.

Emily didn't understand.

'You don't think the entire crushed frame of a stone church constitutes a problem?'

'No,' Kyle answered, resolute. 'Not for you. Because I'm absolutely certain that under that rubble there is nothing at all.'

CHAPTER 39

New York – 10.30 a.m. EST (3.30 p.m. GMT)

A growing unease churned in the Secretary's stomach.

Jason and his men were in place in Oxford, coordinating with a local street team and their London branch. All his men in England had proven themselves skilled agents; the crew Jason had taken as his support for this task were City businessmen as covers, adept at knowing their territory and unfailing in their delivery of results. Like Jason, they were perfect images of loyalty, secrecy and efficiency: the Secretary's ideal companions. Just as he was a man who wanted only the finest drinks, the finest food, the finest suits, so he wanted only the finest men in his employ. Men who knew his power and their place, who feared the former and embraced the latter. Not yes-men, but men who said nothing. Men who simply *did*, and fulfilled his will to the letter.

The small team was now entrenched in the process of comparing the two digital mock-ups of the church, copies of which sat on the Secretary's computer monitor before him. A small window to the left of the models updated continually with the list of items the team's cross-referencing was verifying had been destroyed in the blast, including full details on their provenance, design, heritage and background. The summaries were intricately detailed. Any minute point could be important, and the team therefore produced extensive listings. The mission was going well.

And still, his stomach turned.

The Secretary received telephone reports at ten-minute intervals, but the time between calls was growing intolerable. Each second seemed to bring new doubts, new concerns. His mind continually rolled over the unsettling collection of details that had accompanied Holmstrand's termination.

The Keeper's last act. A phone call earlier in the day. The book, with its missing pages. The church. The explosion.

He twirled a paperclip through the fingers of his left hand, a nervous twitch he'd carried from childhood. *Something is not right.* He looked down again at the book, at the pages Arno Holmstrand had tried to prevent him from seeing, yet seemingly, at the same time, had also wanted him to seek out and find.

The church. The explosion. The open book. The plainly visible, open book.

His stomach tightened further. The Keeper, he knew, was a man of deception. Of ruses and ploys. He was not a wise man, the Secretary believed, at least not in any noble and true sense. But he was smart, and a master of deception. He had known what they were planning in Washington, but even the sight of the power they were going to wield from the inner sanctum of the American political machine had not stopped him from investing his final energies in this, this . . . other task. This scornful, shaming mockery of the Council's whole *raison d'être*.

It was at that moment that the Secretary's epiphany came. With a clarity that emerged only when circumstances provoked his truest, deepest wisdom, the Secretary suddenly knew the Keeper's final act was not merely a mission of revenge and scorn. No, it was more. Much more. And in the same moment, the Secretary knew that, up to that minute, he had been approaching it wrong. *Liars always lie*, he scolded himself. He was allowing too much credence to the outer appearance of Holmstrand's final work.

The Secretary reached across his desk to the phone, selected a speed-dial option from the large digital panel and pressed the receiver to his ear.

'It's me,' he announced, certain that the man on the other end of the line would need no further qualification. 'I want you at the Keeper's college. Now. Get me information on every person Arno Holmstrand worked with, and everyone he talked to in the past five days.'

He set the receiver back in the cradle, his hand leaving an outline of sweat and vapour.

The old bastard didn't aim his last volley at me at all, he mused, energized by his new perception. *His breadcrumbs were left for someone else. And I'm damned sure going to find out who it was.*

CHAPTER 40

'What are you talking about?' The question came from Peter Wexler, whose confused expression spoke for Emily and himself.

Kyle ran a hand through his short hair as if brushing away any remaining flakes of doubt.

'While the two of you went inside to explore, I've been trying to wrap my head around this whole situation,' he answered, 'and the thought I've been unable to get out of my mind is how glaringly obvious all this is.' He waved an arm at the scene around them.

'Obvious?' The word conflicted with the overwhelming sense of intrigue Emily took from the scene. The only thing obvious to her at the moment was her confusion. And her frustration. And perhaps her increasing annoyance at the younger man's optimism.

'Think about it,' Kyle continued. 'Arno is murdered, and the church blows up at the same moment. Pretty obvious connection, given that he pointed you directly to Oxford and bought you a ticket here before he died. It's not going to take a master sleuth to connect the dots.'

Emily waited for more. She wasn't yet sure where he was leading, but his words resonated with her earlier discomfort at the apparent simplicity of Arno's messages.

'Then there's the clue that pointed us here,' Kyle continued. '"University's Church, oldest of them all." I mean, come on.' He tossed his glance back and forth between Emily and Wexler, exasperated that they didn't seem to see his point. Another man might have taken glee in having beaten two scholars to the solution of a riddle, but Kyle Emory was too consumed by the intrigue of the affair. He wanted them to see what was now so clear to him.

'I think the reason we were able to crack this clue so easily,' he finally said, 'is because it was simple. *Too* simple. What we Canadians call a no-brainer. Anybody who's ever been on a two-penny walking tour of Oxford knows this church is the oldest university building – and if that weren't enough, its name is in the clue itself. If your professor had managed to discover a library that no one else has been able to find for one and a half thousand years, you're telling me it was hidden behind clues a five-pound-an-hour tour guide could crack?'

Emily remained silent. The kid was good, in that annoy-ingly industrious, accurate sort of way. He had chosen to focus on what had seemed only an aside to both Wexler and herself, each of whom had been swept up in the thrill of a little amateur detective work. His focus had paid off.

'You're right. His messages are too . . . too—'

'Obvious.' Kyle allowed the smallest look of satisfaction to linger on his features as he repeated his earlier pronouncement.

Emily nodded in grudging, though admiring, acknowledgement.

'And then there's this business of the two queens,' Kyle continued. 'Dr Wess, you were in there all of ten minutes, and despite half the church being blown to ash, you still found two queens. Found a point in the middle. Found it covered with rock, yes; but you still found it. As clues go, these have all been glaringly straightforward. Right?' Kyle's intensity was heated, his drive curiously energetic. 'If this is all really about the Library of Alexandria,' he continued, drawing his observations together, 'and the clues Arno Holmstrand has left are meant to keep its discovery out of the wrong hands, then they suffer from one key problem.'

'And that is?'

'They won't. They're ridiculously plain, totally unsuited to the goal. Give them a few days and school children could decipher these.'

'Arno Holmstrand was nobody's fool, Kyle.' Wexler leaned into the conversation. 'I find it hard to believe that he couldn't come up with effective means of concealing his real intent.'

'Professor, you're absolutely right,' Kyle answered, now totally taken up in the moment. His excitement caused his shoulders to rise and his open hands to move in front of him, accentuating his points as if the real solution to the afternoon's riddles was suspended somewhere in the air between them.

'The fact that these clues are so plain, so simple, doesn't make me think they're bad. It makes me think they're . . . brilliant.' He looked squarely at Emily, whose curiosity was now fully piqued. 'I think that your professor has crafted these little bits of guidance specifically to be misleading. Twice. Once, just mysteriously enough to draw you in, make you realize there really is a puzzle, get you enthusiastic as the pieces start to fit together and you think you've sorted it. In other words, if someone else finds these, half-suspecting that they conceal some secret, he wants them to feel like they do. To reinforce the expectation, and then lead them astray. But they must have a double function. They conceal something the second time round. Their first read is a deception, hiding their true meaning. If they fall into the wrong hands, their new owners get led on a goose chase toward nothing.'

A double ruse. As Emily listened she turned over the possibilities in her mind, and found herself more and more convinced. Yet one key fact set Kyle's theory on edge. A fact that, quite literally, lay all around them. 'But what of all this?' Emily waved at the scene of destruction filling the square. 'Destroying the church seems to confirm the simpler reading. If the clue doesn't point here, why would someone bomb the tower? Obviously someone else either knew, or strongly believed, that an important piece of information was contained here.'

Kyle paused, but only for a moment. As unlikely as it would sound, he was certain he was right.

'A ruse,' he answered. 'Intended to give credibility to the false reading.' Emily gaped at the suggestion as Kyle confirmed his meaning. 'I don't think someone else blew up this church. I think Holmstrand did it himself.'

'Good Lord.' Wexler gasped aloud, his wide eyes again surveying the scene. The immensity of Kyle's suggestion was baffling. All this destruction as a ploy. If he was right, if Holmstrand or whoever else was involved was willing to cause such devastation – physical as well as historical – just to throw would-be pursuers off the track, then whatever it was that Emily Wess had become involved in was bigger than Wexler had expected. Bigger than anything he had seen in his long academic career. Big enough to do what to any historian would seem unconscionable: destroy a piece of history itself to protect a secret.

The three academics stared long at the fallen rubble of the ancient church.

When Kyle spoke again, his voice was calmer, resolute. He kept his gaze on the ruined landmark as he spoke.

'Whether it's the old Library of Alexandria or not, whatever you're meant to find must be worth a damned fortune.'

Emily finally pulled her eyes away from the scene, turning back to the others and snapping out of the intensity of the moment.

'So, Canada wins the culture wars for the morning, seeing what Peter and I couldn't.' Wexler, in agreement, touched the brim of his cap in acknowledgment of Kyle's work. 'Let's assume, then, that you're right, Kyle,' Emily continued. 'If you're wrong, there's not much we can do anyway. But if you're right and the clues are meant to mislead, how do we find their real meaning?'

Kyle's answer thrust the puzzle's veil back over them all.

'It seems, Dr Wess, that you've still got to figure out how to pray between two queens.'

CHAPTER 41

'You're not going to like this,' the man said solemnly into his small cell phone. Trent was a long-serving Friend, and the Secretary allowed him a degree of informality that he would never permit in his other men.

'Get to it,' the Secretary replied. Though his voice betrayed nothing, the comment drew his attention and he sat forward in his chair.

'We've done a full check on everyone in the Keeper's department at Carleton College. Every member of his department is accounted for – either at home for the holiday or resident on campus. Every member, that is, except one.'

The Secretary's clutch around the phone drew tighter.

'Who is it?'

'A young professor, Dr Emily Wess, is not where she should be.'

The Secretary mouthed the name silently to himself. It was familiar only inasmuch as he had seen a listing of the Keeper's fellow colleagues at the college once they had learned of his identity. But the name did not stand out. They had checked out every person on the list, but none had raised any flags – including Emily Wess.

'We checked out the department months ago,' he reflected. 'Wess didn't stand out.'

'No,' the Friend answered. 'She's an upstart, from the look of her file. Young, new, junior. But – ' he leaned into the phone '– the subject of her doctoral research is . . . of interest.'

The Secretary was already calling up Emily Wess's information on his computer. Every background check the Council ever performed was stored in perpetuity, precisely for moments such as this. As the material appeared on his screen, the knot in his stomach became a rock.

'As a postgraduate,' Trent continued over the line, 'Dr Wess wrote on Ptolemy. On Egypt.' His words confirmed what the Secretary now read.

'That's in her file,' the Secretary said again, though his tone was now unusually terse. 'We checked her out. The woman has an interest in Egypt and history, but there was no connection we could establish, either to the Society or the Keeper specifically. We had her on watch, given the fact that she worked at the same institution, but nothing we observed gave any reason to suspect a connection.'

'I know,' the Friend replied. 'A lot of people study history, even ancient Egyptian history. But Dr Wess's file becomes a lot more interesting once you know where she's decided to spend her Thanksgiving holiday weekend.'

'Where?' the Secretary demanded.

'England. Emily Wess flew into Heathrow this morning.'

CHAPTER 42

Oxford – 4.35 p.m. GMT

Emily parted company with Kyle and Wexler a few minutes after their discussion outside the University Church. It was mid-afternoon, and the two Oxford locals had obligations. For her part, Emily felt she could use some time to herself to think over the confusing revelations the day had brought. Whether it was jet lag, shell shock at the magnitude of events or simply the vast amount of information she'd had to absorb in the few hours she'd been on UK soil, her head throbbed and she desired some time alone. The group agreed to meet up that evening for supper at Wexler's home, which the professor had also graciously offered to serve as her base for as long as she was in the city. He'd given her the address and assured her that he'd see her small bag made it to his guest room, relieving her of the need to carry it around the city.

Leaving the square and the church, Emily turned left onto the gently curving pavement of the High Street. Traditionally, the High Street was the street in most English cities marked out by national retail chains and high-end shops, but Oxford's was different. Rather than the glamour of overpriced clothing outlets and electronics stores, it was home to a row of colleges, coffee houses and a few local storefronts. The retail quarter had moved, Emily had no idea how long ago, to the nearby Cornmarket, leaving the High Street relatively uncommercial, though entirely overrun by bus and taxi traffic.

Emily made her way down the street to a familiar haunt from her postgraduate days. A small coffee house sat on the corner of a side street and the High Street, just opposite the Examination Schools building, where the majority of the University's lectures were held. The shop was an unassuming establishment that met with Emily's approval in every way: the coffee was strong, the location convenient, the ambiance satisfying. She took a seat, ordered a double espresso, and cast her gaze out the window over the constant stream of passers-by.

After Kyle had stated his case, Emily's conviction that he was right had set in quickly. The clues, as they had been reading them, were too obvious. Arno's fear that someone else would find the letters before Emily had evidently been strong enough to warrant encoding even the codes. Oxford's landmark church, the very heart of the historical university, had been destroyed as part of a ploy to keep would-be pursuers off the proper track. Emily tried to comprehend the urgency that Holmstrand must have felt, making the decision to destroy such a piece of history.

Just who was this man? Emily asked herself. *What sort of connections, what sort of power, did a man need to be able to*

177

concoct the destruction of such a building from his office in rural Minnesota?

And what on earth does any of this have to do with me? It was a question Emily could not get out of her mind. And it was one to which she didn't yet have even the beginnings of an answer.

The real question, though, was how she was to decipher the meaning of the clues Holmstrand had gone to such exceptional lengths to conceal. Emily knew she was going to have to think differently if she was going to get into Arno's head. She turned Holmstrand's words over and over in her mind. *University's Church, oldest of them all.* If the name of the church was obvious, it was also definitive. There was no other church in Oxford that bore the institution's title. If Arno had meant it to point to something else instead, did Emily then need to look further back into Oxford's history? Was there another church named for the University after this one, perhaps only for a time? History ebbed and flowed; maybe there was a period in which this wasn't the religious centre. Was 'oldest of them all' the ploy?

A group of tourists passed before the shop windows, holding up cameras to record the vision of the college that sat beside it. Emily looked on vacantly as poses were struck and the moment committed to the memory-card film of the digital age. She took a long sip of her thick, black coffee.

Or maybe 'University's church' is the ploy? If the first part of the clue was meant to mislead, then Emily needed to be looking instead for the oldest church in Oxford, irrespective of University affiliation. That would be a project and a half.

Would it be the oldest complete church, still standing? The oldest foundation? Oldest tower? Emily could think of at least half a dozen structures within a one-mile radius that claimed to be remnants of the 'oldest' building in Oxford – oldest towers, oldest walls, oldest foundations, oldest floors. In a city that seethed with antiquity, everyone tried to up the ante by proclaiming themselves more antiquated than anyone else.

She tried to re-focus. *To pray, between two Queens*. Outside the context of the University Church, Emily didn't know where to begin decoding Arno's second clue. Setting aside all the 'Queens of Heaven' that existed in a city filled with churches and depictions of the Virgin Mary, Oxford was also a royal city with a long history of interaction with the monarchy. Buildings, streets, signs, squares, statues, churches – there was at least one of just about everything dedicated to one queen or another. It was an impossible array.

Emily took another draw from her cup, finishing off its contents. As much as she enjoyed the drink, she suspected a walk might better relieve the frustration that grew with every new reflection. Laying down a few coins to cover the bill, she exited the shop and crossed to the other side of the street. Finding herself behind one of the city's famed 'walking tour' groups, she fell into slow step and listened to the monotone voice of the bored guide describe the sights around him. Emily had signed up for such a tour many years ago on her first visit to Oxford as an undergraduate on a year abroad. For a moment, her mind lightened as she thought back to the sheer awe with which she'd taken in the fairy-tale like surroundings, the great stone facades, the covered markets, the fortified college enclaves and chapel spires. Even as a student, she'd suspected that the poorly paid guides on these tours made up half the 'facts' with which they enthralled their packs of tourists, but she strangely hadn't minded. Oxford was as much myth as fact, equal parts romantic dream and concrete reality.

'. . . in direct challenge to the claims of Merton College, which sits behind it.' Emily drifted back into the present as a lull in traffic made the voice of the guide more audible. 'But despite this, University College, here on our left, still claims to be the oldest College in the University, dating back to the middle of the thirteenth century.' A dozen cameras swung left and began photographing the stonework being described.

What? Emily felt her heart jump. Before she realized she was speaking, her mouth had opened and the question was pouring out.

'Excuse me, would you repeat that?'

The guide turned to her and with a practised politeness, he assented. 'Of course. University College is one of three colleges claiming to be the oldest in the University. The others are Merton and Balliol, which we'll see in just a moment.' The guide gave a broad smile, but his eyes glistened with a certain suspicion, as if to suggest that if this questioner, with her unusually vivid, deep-blue eyes and attractive looks had paid the £10 for the tour, he hadn't seen it.

Emily, however, had stopped in her tracks, leaving the group to move on as she fished into her bag for Arno's letters.

Retrieving the third page, she read aloud words that suddenly had new meaning.

'*University's Church, oldest of them all.*' The simple brilliance of the guise now leapt out at her, as if the words had been re-written with new clarity.

Emily, like Wexler and Emory, had from the first been reading 'The University Church' – a familiar name of a familiar landmark, and one which Arno had obviously wanted to jump to mind. But his wording was precise. Not *the* University's church, but *University's* church: the chapel of University College. *The oldest of them all.*

Emily stared at the sturdy wall of University College, imposing itself on the street below. With a new conviction, she was certain this was the object of Arno's instruction.

She had come to a stop in front of the easternmost gate of the college wall, which was no longer used for access. To enter the complex, she would need to walk a little further up the street to the main gate, but for the moment she wanted to collect her thoughts. She ascended the few steps that drew up to the walled-in archway, turning to take a seat on the topmost step. Emily closed her eyes for a moment, savouring the lack of visual distraction, enthused by the speed with which Arno's little mystery was beginning to make sense. *This might not be a wild goose chase after all.*

She opened her eyes and again looked over the handwritten words. '*To pray, between two Queens.*' Emily felt a new determination welling within herself. She would find the object of this riddle, too.

A. M. DEAN

Its solution came sooner than she anticipated. Raising her head from the page, she found herself gazing into an immense stone visage. On the opposite side of the street, surrounded by eight white stone pillars that supported a canopy over her head, stood the noble form of a queen. The statue stood in a private cupola, perched above a decorated wall at an angle along the road. Emily now faced it at eye level only because she had ascended the steps outside University College's unused gate.

Queen's College. Her pulse raced as she quickly searched her mind for the few facts she knew of the place. Founded in 1341, named for Queen Philippa the wife of King Edward the Third, famous for producing good organ scholars and historians. Emily had attended a seminar there in her second year as a Master's student and, even then, she'd remarked at the statue over the front gate. Few queens merited such a scholarly monument.

She's the first. I need a second.

With a knowing certainty, Emily turned her gaze from the right to the left and, even before the motion had begun, knew what she would see. There, at almost the same distance away in the other direction, stood the buckled shell of the University Church of St Mary the Virgin.

Emily stood, she now realized, between two queens. To her left, the Queen of Heaven, in the form of a church dedicated to the Virgin. To her right, a Queen of the Realm, in the form of a college dedicated to a fourteenth-century monarch.

182

And behind her, concealed from view by the College's thick wall, was *University's Church, the oldest of them all.*

Emily shoved Arno's letter into her bag and flew to the door.

CHAPTER 43

4.55 p.m. GMT

The sequence of events that followed Emily's epiphany came quickly. Arriving at University College, she paid a small fee for the honour of touring the grounds and entered the college's ancient enclosure. Inside its limestone walls, she crossed through the manicured gardens and headed straight for the college chapel. The great building stood next to the college hall, the two impressive structures concealed from regular public view by the walled-in design of the college itself.

Emily entered the chapel with a singularity of purpose. Every feature of the beautiful interior – the statues of former Masters in the antechapel, the ornately carved wooden screen, the Van Linge stained glass dating from before the Civil War – attracted her attention only as a potential location of the library's symbol as it was drawn on Arno's letter. On any other day, she would have lingered at each detail of the sacred space, glorying in the historical and religious significance of those she recognized, seeking to learn about those she did not. She had spent hours doing just that in chapels and churches throughout her life, infused with the in-built belief that there was something almost sacrilegious in standing near something ancient and not revelling in its meaning. But not today.

Emily had no idea what form the crest would take: whether it would be shining in stained glass, chiselled in stone, carved in wood or woven into fabric. She only sensed, with everything in her being, that it would be here somewhere. Every feature, every surface, was a possibility. She glanced again at the third sheet Arno had sent her, with the small crest drawn near its top, the Greek letters *beta* and *eta* surrounded by a small decorative frame.

She walked past the wooden screen into the main chapel. A few other visitors dotted the space, some standing to gape at the surroundings, others seated in the old pews in various poses of devotion. Emily walked past them to the altar, scanning her eyes over every surface. Nothing bearing any resemblance to Arno's symbol appeared. She turned to the right-hand side of the church and passed her gaze over walls, pews, windows and floors as she walked down the aisle. *Nothing.* She returned to the altar end and examined it again, then repeated the process with the opposite side wall and pews. *Again nothing.*

Frustrated, she craned her neck to the quasi-Gothic styling of the chapel roof, with its great swoops, pointed arches and imposing curves. The ceiling glared back down at her silently, revealing nothing.

Emily lowered her eyes from the roof, scanning back again

towards the altar end of the nave, the chapel's clear focal point. It was separated from the main space of the church by a traditional rood screen, carved elaborately in darkly stained wood. Master carvers of some previous generation had created lattice-work and foliage of the solid wood that seemed almost as light as air, marred only by a layer of grey dust in its harder-to-reach areas and a few scratch and scuff marks from centuries of use as an active worshipping space.

As she scanned the screen, Emily's attention was caught by one of the small, scratched sections in its corner. Visible only from the altar end, where she was now standing, the somewhat rougher section was shielded from the normal view of visitors and worshippers. And from where she stood she could see it was not only more defaced than other areas, but also that the disruptions to the dark wood were bright, as if they had been made recently. She took a few steps and moved closer, and the scratch marks began to take a coherent shape. What had appeared a small patch became more clearly a roughly etched square, and jagged lines revealed themselves.

Letters, words, surrounded by roughly etched lines, and a small sign. *The* sign.

Emily had found it.

Scratched crudely into the wooden frame was a symbol identical to that at the top of Arno's letter: the Greek letters *beta* and *eta* beneath their abbreviation mark, surrounded by a decorative border. The unassuming, simple crest depicting 'our library'. Beneath it, etched into the wood within the small square, was a series of disconnected words.

CHAPTER 44

Emily stared long at the mystifying text, the sense of history, of adventure, suddenly tangible and real. Despite her best intentions, her mind slipped back to Hollywood blockbusters with their papier mâché temples and fake-gold statues. A rural Ohio upbringing not being inherently packed with excitement, Emily had since childhood fostered an almost tomboyish love of adventure films. The release of *Indiana Jones* had been a favourite.

This is the real thing, Indiana. Her satisfaction was immense.

This was Emily Wess's first genuine discovery. On its own it might be worth nothing: a few scratch marks on the back of a church wall. But its significance was far greater. Emily was now completely convinced that Arno's talk of the Library of Alexandria was true, and that this was a piece in a puzzle that would yield a discovery like no other she could imagine.

And if she could come this far, she could go further.

She looked again at the makeshift etching in the

woodwork before her. There was Arno's crest, clear as day. And beneath it, in rough lettering, a series of words:

Ptolemy's Legacy.
GLASS
SAND
LIGHT

Despite the familiar name of the Egyptian king, the remaining words meant nothing in particular to Emily. Her delight in having made the find not withstanding, the contents of the message were even more baffling than those that had come before it.

But there was a clear way forward. She had come this far through the insight of others, and Emily realized she would need to use them again to discover the steps ahead. She needed help.

Taking her BlackBerry from the pocket of her favourite Salvatore Ferragamo jacket, she pressed a silver button to activate its camera. Accompanied by the digital clicks that confirmed the action, she took three shots of the etched scrawl, wanting to be sure it was clearly visible in at least one. Her mind was determined. Though she and Wexler hadn't arranged to meet again until dinner later that evening, Emily knew her discovery was far too important to wait. Pocketing her phone, she departed the chapel and made for the professor's home.

CHAPTER 45

New York – 12.30 p.m. EST (5.30 p.m. GMT)

The sense of clarity, of revelation, the Secretary had felt two hours before had settled since into a controlled, focused determination. He forced his shoulders to relax as the phone line clicked through its various international connections, waiting for it to culminate in the distinctive double-ring of the British network.

Just over an hour ago, his men in Minnesota had confirmed his new interpretation of the Keeper's mysterious end. The Council had been set up, providing cover for the Society to draw in another. The Secretary's own men sent scrabbling through rubble while the Keeper drew a new helper into his cause. The errand on which his most trusted men in England had been sent was, the Secretary was more and more certain, a goose chase. A deception. Arno Holmstrand was teasing him, even in death.

But now he knew who the new player was. That Dr Emily Wess had travelled to England, that she was there at the same time as his own men, confirmed the Secretary's vision.

The situation at hand was now different. The facts were different, at least in their meaning. He could no longer believe that the explosion in Oxford had been a ploy to conceal something from his Council. At least, nothing that was in the church.

The Keeper's plot had been deceptive but flawed. Tearing a few pages out of an easily accessible book, he had clearly known that the Council could recreate his missing pages without batting an eye. As it was, they hadn't even had to go through the expensive, slow but generally reliable process of chemically treating the charred remains, knitting them back together and seeing what the man had wanted hidden. Jason had simply gone to a local bookstore and bought another copy of the book. Holmstrand had been deliberate enough to ensure it was not a rare edition that he used in his plot, helping ensure they could track down a clean copy easily. The pages he had torn from his volume were found in theirs in all their glory – and their reference was clear. The University Church of St Mary in Oxford. A landmark.

Then, even as the Secretary had discovered the object his foe had known they would discern, he had learnt of its destruction. An explosion, only minutes after the Keeper had been terminated. The connection was clear, and though the extent of the ploy surprised him, the desire of the Keeper to spite them, by leading them to a treasure only to rip it from their grasp and make them watch it be denied them, did not. Holmstrand had engaged in such vindictive taunting before.

The next steps had been automatic, and the Secretary realized now that this had been his error. An obvious target, an obvious concealment – he had sent the Friends on their obvious errand without hesitation: deny the Keeper the benefits of the destruction. Find what lay beneath the rubble.

At some level deep within, beyond the realm that he would ever admit, even to himself, he knew he should have known better. He should have stopped. Should have looked beyond what seemed apparent and seen that he was being toyed with. Manipulated. After all these years, he should have known the Keeper's game.

Still, hindsight was twenty-twenty. It might be a cliché, but it was true nonetheless. He sat now at his desk, certain beyond any doubt that he had found his way through his adversary's ruse. He had been led off the path, but he had found his way back. The men in Minnesota had done their jobs well.

The line connected, and the double-ring sounded in his receiver. A moment later, a voice answered.

'I'm here.'

'Where, precisely?' the Secretary asked.

'Just outside the scene,' Jason replied. 'It's gone dark, so the local police have asked us all to stand aside while they install boom lighting over the rubble. The delay won't be much longer. We'll be back in the church in a few minutes. The listing from London is complete, and they've instructed us to seek out a few dark zones on the scans – a few areas for which they don't have complete coverage. There might be something there.'

'No,' the Secretary said, flatly. His statement, as he

expected, provoked no questioning, no argument from the other end of the line. Just silence, awaiting explanation and instruction. His closest aid, the one among the Friends to have his complete confidence and trust despite his young years, was well trained, reliable.

'Circumstances have changed,' he continued. 'There is nothing in the church. It's a diversion.'

On the other side of the Atlantic, Jason's frame tightened. Though he said nothing, he felt the signs of anger in himself. He did not relish being deceived.

The Secretary suspected his mounting anger.

'Do not worry, my friend. We have seen through it, in the end. As we always do.'

'What is our next step?' Jason asked. The only effective way to combat frustration was to set another aim, another target, and to conquer.

'To play the hunter, rather than the miner.' The Secretary drew himself upright at his desk. 'I'm sending a file to your phone with a photograph. This woman, Dr Emily Wess, is there in Oxford. She is now your priority. She's got a BlackBerry with a registered number. Your team should be able to use it to track her location.'

Jason felt his phone vibrate at his ear even as the Secretary spoke, indicating a new message had come through.

'Hold on,' he said, lowering the phone to eye level. A message was on the small display with Wess's information. He scanned it quickly and put the phone back to his ear. 'Got it.'

'This woman is now your number one priority.'

'How is she involved?' Jason asked. 'How much does she know?'

'I don't know yet – I only know she is, and right at the heart of things.' The Secretary paused. To any other man, he would not admit such apparent weakness, but Jason was trusted with his every thought. 'Her name was in our files already but had never thrown up a flag. She was, as far as we knew, a non-critical associate of the Keeper. But she flew to England immediately after the termination, on a ticket booked by him.' The background work the Secretary's men in New York had undertaken was already revealing connections to the past day's events. 'She's involved. I'm certain of it.' He paused. 'We're at her house now, seeing what she might have hidden away. Find her and keep her in your sights. I don't want her terminated until we know exactly how she's involved. Report whatever you see.'

The Secretary ended the call, and Jason turned to his partner.

'We've got new instructions. Take this.' He handed his cell phone to the man, Emily Wess's data still displayed on its small screen. 'Get her phone tracked, and get us to her.'

'Give me a zone,' the other Friend answered. 'Where do we start the tracking?'

'She's here. Emily Wess is in Oxford.'

CHAPTER 46

Oxford – 6 p.m. GMT

Emily had phoned Professor Wexler on her way out of the University College grounds and proceeded to travel across the city as quickly as she could. Once she had told him of her discovery, his voice on the line had sounded as excited as hers. At her arrival, Wexler opened the door with gusto.

'Come in, come in.'

Emily stepped into the Victorian house and hugged her host. Decorum took second-stage to her new energy.

'Off with the shoes,' Wexler instructed. 'The Madame won't stand for you mucking up her floors.' Even given the immensity of the day's discoveries, certain protocols were expected to be followed.

Emily obeyed, kicking off her loafers, and followed Wexler in sock-clad feet to the elegantly decorated living room.

Wexler had an air of childlike excitement about him as he gave a half-bow to the woman sat regally at the sofa.

'Emily Wess, my lovely wife, Mrs Professor Wexler.' Wexler's wife rose from her seat and embraced Emily warmly.

'Ignore him,' she smiled. 'It's Elizabeth, and it's a joy to meet you after all these years.'

Emily smiled back as Elizabeth Wexler continued.

'Peter's spoken of you often. Never more so than today.' Elizabeth Wexler spoke with the air of a woman who knew her husband's energy well. 'Please, Emily, make yourself at home. I'll go and tend to the oven while the two of you get settled in.' She moved to the door as Wexler stepped in to take her place, drinks already in hand.

'A drink, Miss Wess. And take a seat.'

Emily took the glass and did as instructed. She noticed as she sat that the furniture in the professor's home was of a vastly more refined style and condition than in his office. Wexler's sense of the showmanship of academia meant a studied appearance of the dishevelled and absent-minded. But at home, all showmanship could be set aside.

'I've been able to do nothing since you rang,' Wexler said, still standing, pacing the room. He moved to a coffee table and lifted a worn book. 'I've been trying to occupy myself, waiting, with some refresher material on Alexandria and her library, but the old mind's been hard to keep focused.' He set the book down and took a seat across from Emily. He stared at her, expectantly.

Emily extracted her phone from her jacket wordlessly, switched on the screen and handed it to the professor. Wexler gazed at the image intently.

'Amazing. Wonderful!'

Emily tightened her grip around her glass.

'Listen, if you tell me you understand it already . . .' Her tone was half jest, half challenge. She had been thinking about the contents of the etched message since she'd discovered it. Wexler had seen it for less than twenty seconds.

'No, heavens no,' the professor quickly reassured her. 'I don't have a clue what it means. Not yet. But it's simply wonderful that it was there, don't you think? That you found it! That there's genuinely something to all this curious subterfuge.' He looked at Emily, raised his glass dramatically and took a long, celebratory swill. Following it with a sharp breath as the whisky singed his throat, he settled back into his chair and let the moment's excitement shift into a spirit of focus.

'Do you – do you have you any thoughts on its meaning?' he asked.

'Just a few observations at this point.' Emily straightened in her seat, her posture analytical. 'The first thing that strikes me is that the message is in wood, not stone or paint. And it's etched, not carved. Recently.'

The last word resonated with them both. A symbol fashioned recently was an interesting juxtaposition on the idea of concealing something very old.

'So it's a new message, not some historical piece of the woodwork,' Wexler commented, his eyes remaining on the BlackBerry's small display.

'It would seem so. The wood looks freshly disturbed. The message isn't faded into the polished surface like other carvings. And it looks like the words were scratched into the wood with – I don't know – a pick, some rough metal edge. Like it was scratched out quickly, with whatever tool someone happened to have handy.' Emily paused, allowing time for her observations to settle in. The curiosities didn't end there.

'The second thing that stands out,' she continued, 'is the language. The message is in English, whereas almost every other inscription in the chapel is in Latin.'

'That caught my eye also,' Wexler agreed, continuing to stare at the photograph.

'Both of these facts suggest the message is recent, and I'd say very recent. This etching could have been made yesterday, or last week. It's definitely not part of some ancient trail of clues.'

'Which means it couldn't have been placed here by Holmstrand himself,' Wexler noted, 'at least, not physically – unless he was able to disappear from your campus and gallivant around the globe in such a short span of time, which doesn't seem likely. He must have had help.'

Emily considered the implication of Wexler's point. Clues were being left for Emily to discover, and Arno was behind them. But he was not acting alone.

'So Holmstrand, before he died, had somebody help him plant this message. Something new, planted for a reason.'

Wexler considered Emily's comments for a long moment. When he spoke, his words were a continuation of her thoughts.

'Planted for a reason, and planted *for a person*.'

Emily didn't immediately follow. Wexler looked up from the phone and set his gaze on his former student's face.

'Planted for you, Miss Wess.' He passed the phone back to Emily. 'This little clue was hidden away, its location spelled out in a series of letters delivered to you. It's written in

English, which, despite your proficiency in others, is your language – or at least the American bastardization of it.' Passing up the opportunity for a bit of friendly slander was simply out of the question. But Wexler's point was serious and he continued. 'And it begins with a comment on Ptolemy, who, I'm sure I needn't remind you, was the subject of *your* past research.' Wexler assumed a more emphatic tone. 'I don't know how many letters one has to line up before an alphabet starts to make sense, but we've got a, b and c here, all pointing in the same direction. This is not a generic sign. This is a message put in place for one purpose and one alone: to be discovered by Dr Emily Wess.'

It was now Emily's turn to stare at the phone's small screen, scrutinizing the display in silence as the professor spoke. Her finger clicked a slider on the side of the keypad, cycling through the three photos.

'This puts a whole new twist on things,' Wexler continued. 'Kyle was right before: these clues are designed to have one meaning, hidden away beneath something more obvious. But that meaning is aimed at you, Emily. They must be meant to make sense *to you* in a way that might not be obvious to others.'

Emily emerged from her quiet introspection, looking up to Wexler.

'If you're right, then this new clue, too, is supposed to speak to me. So, what do we make of it?'

Wexler appeared pleased that Emily was in agreement with his assessment of the situation, and that she kept to 'we', despite the sudden personalization of the day's events.

A long silence followed, as the two scholars tried for answers.

'Ptolemy's legacy,' Emily said, finally breaking the silence, 'is exactly what we're searching for. The Library of Alexandria itself. It was founded by the first Ptolemy to come to power and expanded by his sons.'

'Precisely,' the professor answered. He took a long drink, his eyes still on his books. 'But, of course, that can't possibly be what the clue means.'

Emily lifted her eyes to probe Wexler's, realizing the elder professor had an idea.

He turned to face her, suddenly every ounce a teacher before his pupil.

'There are two good reasons why "Ptolemy's Legacy" cannot refer to the ancient library of Alexandria. First, we already know we're looking for the lost library, so a clue whose coded message is "Go, look for the ancient library" is hardly helpful. Even if Arno had thought you were so thick as still to be confused about the matter, simply telling you to go and find it does little to tell you how."

Emily allowed herself a laugh at the professor's point, as well as at the mockingly condescending tone in which it was delivered. The ability to be chided like a little schoolgirl apparently didn't fade, no matter how many degrees one held.

'Secondly,' Wexler continued, 'is the word "legacy". A legacy isn't something that has been lost; it's something left behind, passed on. Something accessible.'

Emily picked up on her mentor's thought.

'Of course. When we talk about a politician's legacy, we're

talking about what he's left after him. What we have now that we owe to his work. To his life.'

'Exactly. As clues go, "Ptolemy's Legacy" wouldn't be pointing you to something lost, but to something we possess. Something that exists today that we can trace back to the ancient king.' Wexler rose from his chair and walked over to a bookshelf on the opposite side of the room, continuing his thought uninterrupted. 'Which leads me to an interesting idea, my dear.' He scanned over the row of books deliberately, seeking out a specific volume. Finding it with the tap of a finger, he removed it from the shelf and began flicking through its pages as he continued to speak. 'The work of Ptolemy *was* his library, and the legacy of Ptolemy *is* his library. After a fashion.'

Emily listened intently, trying to work ahead and see where Wexler's conclusions were taking him.

'You may be after something old, something hidden, but to get you there Professor Holmstrand is pointing you towards something new. Something obvious.' Wexler walked back to Emily, turned the open book towards her and extended his arm.

Emily took the book. It was spread open to a colour photograph of an immense modern building, circular in structure with a dramatically sloping roof, angling down to meet the sea at the edge of a bustling Egyptian metropolis.

'May I present you, Dr Wess,' Wexler announced, 'with Ptolemy's legacy: the Library of Alexandria. The *new* Library of Alexandria, opened by the Egyptian government in 2002. Five to one on this as the object of your most recent message.'

The magnificent structure stared up at Emily from the page, its modern lines and imposing contours reflecting in her eyes. The new library held no direct connection to its ancient forebear, but it stood in the tradition of that original project. It was a grandiose monument to its royal Egyptian past, marking out the coastline of Alexandria with a building unlike any other on earth.

As Emily took in the image, she sensed it was a building she would have to see for herself.

CHAPTER 47

Chicago – 2 p.m. CST (8 p.m. GMT)

Michael Torrance sat on a bench in the green quadrangle outside his apartment, a thick leather jacket keeping out the cool air of a blue autumn day, when the phone in his pocket sounded. Emily's name flashed across the screen, next to a small photo he had snapped two years before, moments after she'd woken up on a camping trip sporting hair only a fiancé could love. His current apprenticeship in Chicago meant they spent considerable time apart and the small flash of her face on the screen made the distance a touch more tolerable.

Though the distance had grown exponentially in the past 24 hours.

'Emily,' he announced happily, drawing the phone to his ear, 'I wasn't expecting your call until later.'

'Hi, love. Am I interrupting your afternoon?'

'Not at all. I'm just enjoying a lunchtime moment to myself.' Michael paused, knowing his next words would strike up Emily's sentimentality. 'Happy Thanksgiving, dear.'

'Still is,' she teased back, 'just like when I phoned you a few hours ago.' Her voice was all warmth.

'A man can't greet his lady twice? Being back in the old country is making you a minimalist, Em. Soon you'll be telling me that the "I love you" I expect to hear loud and clear on our wedding day will be sufficient for the whole marriage.'

'I thought that was understood,' Emily replied. 'I mean, we're both busy people. No time for unnecessary repetition.' She laughed into the phone, and was suddenly aware of the distance between them, of the day and its meaning, and with a renewed vigour she wished they had not agreed for him to stay behind in America. 'Happy Thanksgiving to you too, Mikey. I'm sorry I'm not there. But I'll make it up to you.'

'You bet you will.' A tease echoed in Michael's voice.

'But at the moment,' Emily continued, 'there is something you can do for me.'

'You expect me to let you boss me around from the other side of the globe?'

'I don't boss,' Emily protested, feigning innocence. 'I just strongly suggest.'

He laughed. 'What do you need?'

Emily spent the next minutes updating him on the events since her arrival in Oxford. Michael listened in amazement to descriptions of shattered buildings, ancient churches, wooden etchings, and, at last, of the Egyptian government's new masterpiece of historical and scholarly appreciation.

'The New Library of Alexandria? Emily, it's one of the most amazing buildings constructed in the past thirty years. It's an architect's dream.'

'You architects do have a one-track mind!' Emily accosted playfully. Amongst the explosions, the wreckage, the breaking into a crime scene and the other dramatic details that so enthused her, it was the architecture that captured Michael's interest.

'Don't worry, Em,' Michael answered. 'I'm still suitably impressed by your sleuthing and witty brilliance. But this building . . . we're talking architectural perfection.'

'Wouldn't you like it if I could give you a first-hand account?' she asked.

'You're going?' Michael suddenly realized that Emily wasn't simply mentioning the structure, but planning a second stage to her impromptu trip. 'You're going to Egypt?'

'If you can help me out, I am. I can't find a pointer like this and not follow it up, right?' It was a rhetorical question, yet there was more to Emily's proposal than simply chasing an interesting academic lead. There was a danger she already knew was involved. If she drew closer to the library, given what she had seen this morning, that danger would likely increase.

Michael let out a long sigh, expressing a nervousness that Emily knew he must be feeling in the face of the news. But her fiancé knew that she was driven, and Emily felt his concern all the more potently for the silence with which he restrained it.

'As long as you promise me you'll be careful,' Michael finally said, 'I'll help you in whatever way I can from here.'

'I promise. I have every intention of coming back home to you. Now, do you think you can book me a ticket?' It would be easier, and faster, than trying to do it via her BlackBerry.

'Sure,' Michael answered. 'It'll actually be a good distraction for me. The online booking sites are probably the only places on the Internet that won't be covering the scandals. I haven't been able to stop hitting the refresh button on CNN's homepage since all the proverbial faeces started to hit the fan this afternoon.'

'I don't follow.'

'Well, well, dear,' Michael teased, 'you really have been tied up in your adventures if you haven't heard what's been going on over here. Do yourself a favour: take a look at the news before you get on your plane. The whole country's imploding back on this side of the pond. Presidential scandal, terrorists assassinating Washington insiders. It's like the political apocalypse.' He followed his characterization with a potted summary of the situation consuming Washington.

'At least I'm not the only one surrounded by intrigue,' Emily said when he had finished. 'You see, we're sharing a common experience today, after all.'

CHAPTER 48

Oxford – 8.25 p.m. GMT

The timing of their conversation had, by chance, served Emily well. A Turkish Airlines flight to Alexandria left that evening at 10.55 p.m., and so long as Wexler's wife would allow them to live down their walking out on her home-cooked dinner just as it was about to begin, they could make it to Heathrow with just enough time for Emily to grab a quick shower and change her clothes on her way out the door. The thought of another stint in a cabin filled with recy-cled air seemed impossible without first freshening up.

The professor had agreed to drive Emily to the airport himself as soon as Michael confirmed the ticket had been booked. At the thought of the exploits that lay ahead of his former student, the old don was childlike with anticipation.

'You'll want this,' he said, thrusting a book from his shelf into Emily's hands after she'd emerged from the guest room, showered and changed. It was the third book he had offered her since she'd appeared. 'And this.' A glossy travel guide was added to the stack. 'I picked that up when I was there for the library's opening in 2002. Splendid structure. It will tell you all about it.'

Emily smiled gratefully. The volumes in her hands covered everything from the history of the ancient library to the politics of modern Egypt that had produced its new masterpiece. Even with an eight-hour flight ahead, it would try her concentration to make it through them all. 'Thank you, Professor,' she said, sincerely. 'But these will have to do. If we don't leave now . . .'

'Yes, yes. Quite right.' Wexler pulled himself away from the bookshelf. The two caught eyes for a brief moment. He could not restrain a smile. 'Heavens, if this isn't exciting! If I'd only known your visits would prove so interesting, I'd have invited you back more often.'

They shared a laugh, and Wexler pocketed the keys to the car.

'My love, we're off,' he announced in the general direction of the kitchen, already on the move to the front door.

'Before we go,' Emily interrupted, 'tell me, is your phone able to receive picture messages?'

'I think so,' Wexler answered. 'I've never tried, but it's one of these newfangled things. I'm sure it must. Why do you ask?'

'I'd like to photograph these letters from Arno and send them to you. For safekeeping.' Emily hesitated, but something made her feel that having an electronic backup of the materials was in order. The day had already provided so many uncertainties and mysteries. She did not know what lay ahead.

'Very well,' Wexler replied. 'Good thinking. You can do it in the car. Now, let's make a move.'

Emily picked up her small travelling bag, and with her books in hand stepped towards the door, the car, the airport, and beyond them – Alexandria.

CHAPTER 49

Oxford – 9.35 p.m. GMT

Unlike most men, whose views were formed by Hollywood blockbusters and cheap crime dramas, Jason knew that tracking a target in the modern world was less about running after people on footpaths or tailing them in cars and more about sitting astutely in front of a well-equipped computer terminal. Not that tailing and chasing didn't figure occasionally, but it tended only to come at the final phase of an operation, when a tail was ready to be captured – or eliminated. The actual tracking was much more effectively done with technology and modern resourcefulness.

The tracking of Emily Wess was a case in point. The telephone number for her BlackBerry had been easily traced to a SIM card, which had since allowed them to keep a digital lock on Wess's location, accurate to within a third of a city block. It also allowed them to listen in on her telephone calls, which had revealed both a local interaction with an Oxford academic named Peter Wexler as well as a fiancé in Chicago called Michael Torrance. Background on Wexler confirmed a longstanding relationship with Wess, as well as a specialist standing in ancient Egyptian history. If there was any question over a connection to the library's interests, it was now well and truly removed.

The trace on Wess's call to her fiancé had revealed her intention to travel, and from a search of airline databases Jason now knew full details of Emily's flight booked to Alexandria, down to her seat assignment and meal preference. He had since put a continual trace on all of Wess's credit cards and wiretaps on the ten most frequently called numbers from her cell phone. Wherever Emily Wess went, whatever she did, whomever she spoke to, the Friends would now know.

The thrust of Jason's work for the past twenty minutes had then been to focus on Alexandria. Before he phoned the Secretary, he wanted all the information at his fingertips. Just as it now was.

He picked up his phone and dialled.

'Update,' the Secretary demanded, seconds later.

'Emily Wess has booked a seat to Alexandria on Turkish Airlines flight TA1986 out of Heathrow at 10.55 this evening, local time. The ticket was booked online, from a computer in an apartment building in Chicago belonging to her fiancé. We'll have men there shortly.'

'Alexandria,' the Secretary replied, repeating the significant location.

'I've already prepped our main team there,' Jason continued, 'and I'll be flying over as soon as we're done here.'

'Go as soon as you can. Leave the follow-up in Oxford to the others.'

'Of course.' Jason paused, and looked up to the notes on his screen. 'We have four targets in Alexandria that we've been monitoring for months. We know there has to be a Librarian in the city, given its significance, and our best intelligence says it's one of these four, all of whom work in the Bibliotheca Alexandrina, which is Wess's destination.' He knew the Secretary had the details already – the Alexandrian surveillance was a longstanding operation – but he sent the condensed details across the connection anyway. 'I've ordered our men there to stay with each of these four constantly over the next forty-eight hours. Chances are good Wess is going to meet with one of them. And if she's been guided there by the Keeper, it's likely she'll make contact with the one that matters.'

'And you?'

'We'll stay on Wess herself,' Jason answered, glancing across to his partner. 'We'll be there when she lands, and we'll stay with her, just in case she doesn't head towards one of our known candidates.'

The Secretary allowed himself to sit back into his chair on his end of the line. The Friends were on top of their game.

'One more thing,' Jason added. 'Wess is en route to the airport and busy browsing through various news websites via her BlackBerry's 3G connection. All of them about the situation in Washington.'

Damn, the Secretary thought, almost speaking the word aloud. While it was clear that this Emily Wess was somehow connected to the library, it now also seemed that she was informed on their mission in DC. The Council's leak wasn't as capped as they'd thought.

'So, she's been given information on the current mission. Holmstrand got it out before we got to him.'

'So it seems,' Jason replied.

The Secretary pondered his next words long before speaking them into the phone.

'You're going to have to stay on Wess tightly, now. She may be our only living link to the library's location, so we need her alive and unaware of our presence for as long as possible. If she does anything that puts the Washington mission at risk, you'll have to step in. But consider it a last resort.'

'Understood.'

Another silence passed before the Secretary closed the conversation.

'Now get yourself to Egypt, and find out what Emily Wess really knows.'

CHAPTER 50

London – 10.55 p.m. GMT

The only seat Michael had been able to find for Emily on the night flight to Alexandria at such late notice had been in first class, which was a category of luxury she had never before experienced. As she was led to a plush and roomy seat, already covered in a woollen blanket and adorned with a welcome bag of small gifts, she was suddenly grateful that Wexler had offered to foot the bill. After a day spent rummaging through ground zero of a foreign explosion and decoding clues left by a dead man, she was grateful for the small signs of civility. Bottled hand lotion and a refreshing towelette had never looked so comforting.

The flight from London to Alexandria, including the short clearance stop on the tarmac in Cairo, was a tidy and precise eight hours in length, departing from one of the western world's oldest airports and arriving in one of Egypt's newest. Borg El Arab was a shining new wonder of glass and metal, shaped – inexplicably, Emily felt – like a boat. Michael, not surprisingly, had exuded an endearing passion when he had described it on the phone, though Emily had wondered even then whether the details of an airport, however new, constituted something only an architectural student could love. Even if the nautical design was meant to convey the connection between modern air travel and Alexandria's ancient fame as a shipping port, connecting every corner of the old Mediterranean world, it was still an airport, with all the annoyances of airports everywhere.

Emily relaxed into her seat. That experience was still eight hours away, and she might as well enjoy the peace and quiet while she had it, and read through some of the material Wexler had given her. That, and eat the largest meal the airline would serve her. The ravenous churning in her stomach was an increasingly uncomfortable reminder that she hadn't had more than a cup of coffee since she'd arrived from America.

Waiting for the meal service to begin, she took advantage of the in-seat power point and clicked in her mobile phone charger, then turned her attention towards her books. Borg El Arab, she quickly learned, wasn't the only new piece of modern architecture to spring up in Alexandria over the past years. The travel guide Wexler had given her in Oxford, which she now opened across her lap, was filled with example after example. Since the mid 1990s, the local government in Alexandria had made it an aim to revitalize the city, to reclaim it from the general picture most foreigners had of Egypt: that of a poverty-stricken, uneducated, just-this-side-of-uncivilized stereotype of the Third World. Alexandria, which in ancient times had been one of the great capitals of world trade and learning, was becoming a new metropolis of culture and civic showmanship. The same expensive shops that lined Fifth Avenue in New York and Oxford Street in London now lined Alexandria's Corniche, and every new building that went up in the city was an example of thoroughly modern architecture – as far from baked brick and pyramids as the imagination could travel.

The new library was a case in point. Desiring to reclaim something of its ancient reputation as a world centre for learning, the city had decided decades ago to build a new library as close as possible to the site of the old. But the location could be all that the new Bibliotheca Alexandrina had in common with its forebear. The structure itself looked, as far as Emily could ascertain from the photos, as futuristic as any she had ever seen. The main building was an enormous granite disk, sloping down at an angle towards the sea, becoming an image – the literature was quick to point out – of the sun of knowledge rising out of the water. Around its sides were inscriptions in over 120 of the world's known languages and scripts, symbolizing the collection of all the world's wisdom for which the original library had been known.

It was little wonder that Michael loved it.

Every figure Emily read about the structure was overwhelming. The central disc of its design was 160 metres in diameter. The main reading room alone covered over 70,000 square meters. It had cost $220 million dollars to build. It had shelf space for over 8 million books.

When modern Alexandria built, it built big. Not so different, Emily thought, from ancient Alexandria.

The big difference between the old and the new came in the societies surrounding the two libraries. In the ancient city, the library had been the favourite of the king, and society did what societies were wont to do in the ancient world: they followed their king. Ptolemy used the library to make his empire great, and his people followed eagerly. Whether they followed because they loved their king and cherished his library, or because they had little choice save follow or die, made little difference in the end. The library received the support of the nation.

Modern Egypt, though, looked little like the kingdom of Ptolemy Soter, and the stunning price tag for the new Bibliotheca Alexandrina was not the only detail that had made its construction a matter of intense debate at street and governmental levels. Equally as significant was the question of just exactly what it was supposed to be for, given that the majority of the Egyptian populace remained illiterate, and Alexandria had not been a capital of learning for centuries. The long-governing president at the time might have supported it entirely, viewing its existence as a means to recreate that older reputation, but a president is not a king – a fact that had been emphasized by the uprising that had since ejected the ruling government from power. Where the Ptolemies had commanded and the people followed, the modern regime had to face democratic elections and international media caricatures. It was a different world: a world that was volatile, manipulative and insecure.

Emily's thoughts trailed back to the news reports she'd read on the drive to Heathrow. It was hard to believe what she'd read on the BlackBerry's tiny screen: she'd been out of the country less than 48 hours, yet already the capital had been riddled by assassinations, apparently by Middle Eastern activists, and seemingly because the president had provoked their wrath through his own illegal wheelings-and-dealings. *I wonder if I'm going to have a country to go back to*, she mused to herself. It wasn't every day the terms 'political coup' and 'presidential treachery' were applied to reports on the United States, but these had been two of the tamer headlines she'd read from the car.

But she wouldn't allow herself to be distracted. The scandal in Washington served for the moment as a good example of the fickle nature of world politics – the very kind of political fickleness that had made the new Alexandrian library such a challenge to complete. Nevertheless, it had been built, and in 2002 the world once again was home to the Library of Alexandria, with her new face and image.

Outside the window, the Channel gave way to coastline. During her reading, they had already made it already as far as France. Not for the first time that day, Emily wondered at just how she had found herself in the middle of so much . . . enormity. It was hard to believe that only two evenings ago she had been straining her muscles and focus in her usual Krav Maga lesson, and yesterday morning she had been teaching her usual class on a manicured rural campus in Minnesota. Now, here she sat, tucked into a first class seat on a Turkish flight to Egypt, following the advice of a scratching she'd discovered on a church wall in England, while the political world back home appeared to be imploding.

The churning discomfort in the pit of her stomach grew, and not solely from her hunger. If this was all a wild goose chase and led her nowhere, so be it. At least she would have seen Alexandria. But if it was more, and she was sure it was more, then she might actually succeed in this little quest. And if she did, then she would possess the same information that had earned Arno Holmstrand three bullets in his chest.

Emily closed her eyes. Seven hours still separated her from the Egyptian coast. In that moment, Emily wished it were far, far more.

CHAPTER 51

The group called together by the secretary of defence to address the mounting crisis in the administration was gathered again in the quiet room within the Pentagon. Ashton Davis had reassembled the small team that he knew would soon be undertaking one of the most monumental tasks in American history: the forcible removal from office of the president of the United States.

'Impeachment is not an option,' he stated flatly. 'Impeachment is a formal process that takes time, and only once it is completed can a sitting president then be removed from office. We don't have such time at our disposal. This man's actions have provoked a clear and present threat to the security of our nation. Political advisors, even staff who work in the West Wing itself, are being assassinated. The man who is provoking such activities must be removed from a position where he has the power to do so, whether or not he is the president of the United States.'

Though the reasoning was clear, the thought made the director of the Secret Service nervous.

'Never in American history has a president been forcibly removed from office by anyone other than the voters.'

'But never in American history has a president brought assassins into Washington on a vendetta against his illegal activities abroad, Director Whitley,' General Mark Huskins answered.

'Which is precisely why our response is being staged as a military reaction,' the secretary of defence added. 'We're not just talking about illegal business dealings or bad political moves. We're talking about a man endangering our national security. A man who's all but brought the Middle Eastern conflict into the innermost courts of our democratic capital.'

Whitley squirmed slightly in his seat. Everything the other two men said was accurate – but even so. It was an unprecedented step.

'Is there any formal provision in the Constitution for a military removal of power of a sitting president?'

'Not explicitly,' Davis answered. 'Despite the fact that the president is the commander-in-chief of the armed forces, he can't be brought before a normal military court martial. The title of commander-in-chief is not actually a military rank.'

'But if there is no military provision, how do we proceed? The US Army can't arrest a private citizen on home soil outside the instigation of martial law.'

General Huskins leaned in to the table.

'We can, if that citizen is supporting or encouraging the combat operations of combatant enemy forces in wartime.'

Whitley's eyes widened.

'You're suggesting we arrest the president of the United States as an enemy combatant in the war on terror?'

'We've arrested other American citizens on the same grounds for less. Good God, President Tratham's illegal activities have brought assassins into Washington itself! They may be here in retaliation, rather than his invitation, but the fact of the matter is that they are here, and if he had been obeying the laws he's supposed to uphold, they wouldn't be. The man must be stopped!' The general spoke forcefully, with conviction.

Director Whitley knew there was little point to protest. Huskins was right. The president had to be stopped before the situation got completely out of hand.

'What about the vice president?' asked the secretary of defence. 'Has any connection come up on him?'

Whitley turned toward Davis with a hopeful look.

'My agents have been working with the FBI, checking out every possibility since our last meeting. The good news is that Hines looks clean. His main support base, when it comes to his foreign affairs dealings, has been from Alhauser, Krefft and the Westerberg Foundation – all of whom have strong track records in promoting above-board business dealings in the Middle East. The last two of those groups have actually lobbied in Congress for transparent accountability on reconstruction work in Iraq and Afghanistan. The VP seems to be in with the right kind of groups, not the kind that are going to provoke militant responses for illicit behaviour.'

'Keep checking,' Davis ordered. 'The man better be spotless, or he and the president will go down together.' He stood up, drawing the meeting to a close with a final note on the gravity of their responsibility. 'Men, this country's government will not be brought down by the criminal acts of its leader. We owe it to every American citizen to see to that. Now go, make sure the VP is ready for what's coming. Before this week is out, his role in the administration is going to look a hell of a lot different than it does today.'

Friday

CHAPTER 52

The wheels of the Turkish Airlines jet touched the tarmac only a minute later than their scheduled arrival time. The sun was beginning to rise on the horizon, and the night-time cold had not yet shifted to the steady heat that even a November day would bring.

Within an hour, Emily was in a taxi, headed north and east to the city centre. She craned her neck to the window as they drove, hoping to gain a clear view of the city in the distance. She had seen precious little during landing, and as she now realized she was mere miles away from a city she had studied since her childhood, the fear that had poisoned her stomach over the past hours began to soften with a familiar sense of adventure and discovery.

In the distance sat Alexandria, the city of Alexander the Great himself. It had been one of the most famous cities in the world since Alexander founded it in his own honour in the early 330s BC through to its gradual shrinking from international view in the seventh century AD. Its lighthouse, the *Pharos*, had shone out over the bay as one of the seven wonders of the world, while its reputation as a centre for trade, industry and intellect had been almost as famous. Sitting along the coast at the far western edge of the Nile delta, the 'Pearl of the Mediterranean' – as Alexandria had for millennia been known – had always held a central place in shipping and military power. Today it might be more notable as a centre for tourism, serving as a popular resort destination and cultural hot spot, but as Egypt's main port, it retained something of its old importance as a shipping centre.

Alexandria had sat at the heart of three empires, and as a key hub in at least five distinct cultures. The ancient Pharaonic dynasty, which had transformed in its final centuries in to the reign of the Ptolemies, stretched its significance back through the millennia. In the final few centuries BC, it had become the centre of the Jewish diaspora and the single largest body of Israelites in the world. Then, in the years following the conversion of the Empire to Christianity, it had become a capital of Christian learning and influence, producing some of the Church's greatest bishops and thinkers, as well as some of its most insipid heresies. The Council of Nicaea, the first Ecumenical Council and the assembly that had produced the first form of the creed Christians still recited today, had taken place in response to a heresy that had originated in this city and quickly spread across the Christian world.

Alexandria's Christian fame was destined to last for centuries, but not to be indefinite. Following a series of conquests in the 640s, it had finally been conquered by Muslim armies and had become the heart of a new Islamic North Africa, though its conquerors had quickly founded their own city to rival it. That metropolis had later become Cairo, today the more famous, if younger, cousin of ancient Alexandria.

Emily was impressed with the city that came into view. Many ancient capitals of culture and knowledge had come and gone over the course of history, but usually, when they went, they remained gone. Alexandria was fighting back, reclaiming its heritage. It saw greatness on its horizon, and was intent on claiming it.

That spirit had, literally, changed the landscape of the city around her. It had created a modern metropolis, a gleaming contribution to the culture of the continent. And it had created the new library. Before Emily had a chance to ponder that feat further, she felt the taxi slow and swing around a tight corner into a small city plaza. Before her stood the unmistakable form of the building she had come to see.

Within its depths, a man sat patiently, awaiting her arrival.

CHAPTER 53

10.25 a.m.

Emily exited the taxi with determination, the usual spring in her step muted only slightly by the fatigue of travel, yet strengthened by a belief that she was on the right track. The granite facade of the library stood before her, seeming to shine white in the morning sun, and the modern structure fused with a front portico covered in statues of ancient Egyptian gods and kings, blurring the line between the futuristic present and the antiquated past. She had to admit that the design worked. She felt overwhelmed, even awe-struck, at the sight before her.

A wide collection of glass doors marked the entry, and Emily pressed her way through them eagerly. She had used the brief journey from the airport to work out the basics of a plan. She would sign up for one of the guided tours of the library that were offered every fifteen minutes, and use that to orient herself to the building and its contents. She had no idea where to begin looking for whatever it was she was supposed to find here, but a basic orientation seemed a necessary first step. Once she had her bearings, she would settle into the task of seeking out the next piece of Arno's puzzle.

Desks surrounded the library's central foyer, helpfully marked in a variety of languages for the benefit of visitors like Emily. She scanned the signs for one marked 'Tours', and having found it, made her way directly.

'Entry and tours are ten pounds,' a clerk notified Emily, before she'd even asked the question. As she opened her wallet and extracted the required local currency, which she'd bought at a ridiculous commission at an airport exchange counter, the clerk continued a well-rehearsed spiel. 'Our guides will lead you through the library on half-hour visit, in which all of history will become clear to you.' Emily held back a laugh. Occasionally, broken English made for more grandiose promises than intended. But on the up side, 'all of history' seemed a pretty good deal for 10 Egyptian pounds.

The clerk handed Emily a small, colour map.

'Tour just left five minutes ago. Next one at eleven. Wait by the statue and your guide will come.' She motioned towards a white stone statue that stood in the middle of the foyer, dominating the lobby. Emily recognized the figure as Demetrius of Phaleron, the famed Athenian orator who had spent his golden years in Alexandria under the patronage of the first Ptolemy.

But Emily was too anxious to wait. She looked at her watch, and then back to the clerk.

'I'll just join the one that's started. Which way did they go?'

Emily followed the clerk's hand gesture, and stepped quickly across the foyer to a set of stairs leading towards the main reading room where a small group of mostly American tourists was huddled around a young and serious-looking guide. Emily could spot a student a mile away, and immediately felt certain that the guide was a university student herself – by her age, probably a postgraduate. Working off tuition was apparently a tradition that knew no international borders.

Emily stepped closer to the group, smiled courteously as the guide noticed her arrival, and held up her ticket to ensure the guide knew she was meant to be there.

'Sorry I'm late,' Emily mouthed, mostly to herself. The guide smiled in return, and carried on with her words. She spoke in an educated and clear English, her accent softened by careful practise.

'The Bibliotheca Alexandrina, or *Aktabat al-Iskandar yah*, is a gem in our modern Alexandrian cultural heritage. Officially opened in 2002, it is the intellectual centre not just of Egypt, but of the whole Mediterranean.' She led them further up the steps. 'Our city once had the greatest library in the world. Today our collection may not be the biggest, but it's growing fast, and we hope one day it will be.'

'How big is it?' A predictably dressed tourist asked the predictable question.

'The library has space for 8 million books, as well as several hundred thousand maps and special volumes. However – ' the guide added with a slight hush, as if revealing a state secret, ' – our current collection is only about 600,000 volumes. Which is why, as you're about to see, most of the shelves are half empty. The collection we do have was donated when the building was completed from countries all over the world. Many of our largest donations came from Spain, France and Mexico. Now we gather books from all across the Middle East, Asia, Europe and the West, and the collection grows every day. One day, all these half-empty shelves will be full.'

With a carefully rehearsed deliberateness, these final words were uttered precisely as the group reached the top of the staircase and set eyes upon the focal heart of the library: the main reading room. Audible gasps came from every side, and Emily was not ashamed to let one escape her own lips.

Before them was a truly spectacular sight. A huge, sloping ceiling of glass and stone beamed light on to a library that looked like a cross between the archives of a spacecraft and a postmodern, upper-class executive lounge. Lacquered wood floors cascaded down the immense angular space, storey after storey, connected by sculpted stairways and gently arching ramps. Row after row of shelves were constructed of a light ash, bordered in brushed aluminium and tastefully illuminated with in-shelf bulbs. Glass partitions accentuated smaller reading and work areas, while artistic balconies overlooked lower levels. Around the forest of immense silver pillars that supported the striking roof, desks sat in rows and clusters, some bare surfaced and waiting to be covered in books and papers, others – hundreds of others – furnished with computer terminals, scanners and printers. Recessed lighting cast a calm and professional glow into those corners where the sunlight, beaming through the skylights above, did not reach.

The guide allowed her audience a moment to take in the scene.

'The sight before you was the creation of a Norwegian architectural firm chosen by UNESCO to create our landmark library.'

'The firm was Snøhetta, wasn't it?' Emily recollected the detail from Wexler's guidebook.

The guide appeared suitably impressed.

'Yes, madam.' She cast Emily a provocative glance. 'Snøhetta won the contract based on their vision of the old and new meeting in a single structure, symbolizing the rebirth of our city in the twenty-first century. But also because their design, in addition to being visually stunning, is also practical.

'Our library can seat thousands of readers at any given moment. Books are easily accessible through an entirely electronic catalogue, and we maintain active collections of periodicals and news from all over the world. The main reading room, where we are now standing, spans seven sloping stories. All around the edges of each floor are computers, providing free Internet access to anyone who wishes to use them.' She paused, apparently particularly proud of this last point. 'The Internet may not yet reach to every corner of Africa, but here in these walls it is free and fast to whoever wants it.'

She began to lead them through the stacks, weaving through clusters of desks and impressively lined shelves.

'There are also many other resources here, beyond the books we all expect from a library. Within the main space are separate collections for maps, a whole wing solely for multimedia resources, and a scientific laboratory dedicated to restoring old books and manuscripts. We are also the only library in Egypt to have our own collection of materials for the blind, with thousands of books in braille. On the upper floor we extend our reach from earth to the heavens with a fully digital planetarium. And if you have time after that experience, we also house eight complete museums displaying over thirty special collections, all within these walls.'

More gasps. Emily gaped with the rest as they moved down a flight of steps towards a sub-level of volumes that appeared to be dedicated to Eastern European history.

'You may also be interested to learn,' the guide continued, 'that the Bibliotheca Alexandrina is home to the world's only complete copy of the Internet Archive, housed on a bank of over two hundred computers donated by the archive at a value of over five million US dollars – though today its value is estimated at over ten times that amount. Every page on the internet between 1996 and 2001 was contained in the initial donation, and is archived here on over one hundred terabytes of storage space – and it has been expanded ever since with a complete snapshot of the whole Internet, taken every two months. This incredible resource is employed by hundreds of thousands all over the globe.'

They moved along, taking in row after row of glistening shelves, shining facades, relaxing lounge areas and conference spaces. The guide continued to provide detailed commentary on the sights surrounding them, but after a few minutes Emily had reached a threshold of amazement. The place was clearly stunning. Impressive. Unparalleled. But she wasn't here merely for the show-and-tell, and the more facts the guide relayed, the more daunting the project before her seemed. Even if she had known precisely what she was looking for, finding it in a structure of these dimensions would be an immense errand. But Emily wasn't sure she had the faintest clue just what she was here to discover.

I need to get off on my own. The thought hit her strongly, and she acted on it swiftly. A moment later, as the guide and her group rounded a corner, Emily did not. The guide's voice trailed into the distance, and Emily found herself standing before 600,000 books, alone.

CHAPTER 54

10.35 a.m.

'. . . the main reading room, where we are now, spans seven sloping stories . . .'

The two men paid only enough attention to the young guide's words to keep her relative volume consistent, using the simple technique to maintain a stable distance between the group and themselves whilst remaining out of sight. They had not had time to change clothes since their arrival, and their black and grey business suits, which had helped them blend in in Oxford, made them look conspicuous in the ranks of Egyptian academia. Better to maintain a distance and keep out of unnecessary public scrutiny.

They kept their position behind the rows of shelves, trailing and to the side of the tour. Each Friend engaged in a practised and convincing show of scanning the shelves, picking up and leafing through the odd book here and there, to any outside observer appearing only as keen readers exploring the library's collection. But their attention was trained on one thing only: the young woman they had tracked from Oxford.

Dr Emily Wess, whose precise connection to the Keeper remained a mystery, but whose involvement with the library was now beyond question. Emily Wess, whose commercial flight from England had taken an hour longer than their private jet, making preceding her to Egypt a simple task. Emily Wess, whose every movement was now tracked, whose whole life was becoming the complete focus of the Council. Even as they tracked her here, a team was at her home in Minnesota, seeking further information.

Emily Wess, who now stood alone, separate from her group.

The second man looked over an open book to the first. He, too, had seen that their target had removed herself from the tour and was now alone. Accessible.

Wait, Jason thought firmly to himself, knowing that the look in his eyes would convey the message to his partner without the need for words. *Wait, and follow. Don't engage*.

Their men were in place throughout the library, staying close to each of the four employees the Council had been tracking for the past months. Each of these men was considered a potential candidate to be identified as the Librarian working covertly in Alexandria. They knew that their foes, the Society of Librarians, had an operative in the city – that much had been clear for years – and they had gradually narrowed down their pool of potential subjects to these four. As yet, however, the Council had been unable to find anything conclusive that would reveal which of the four men it was. But that task was about to be accomplished for them. Emily Wess simply needed to make her way to whichever one the Keeper had guided her towards, and they would know their man. A Librarian working in this location would have to be high-ranking in the Society's hierarchy, someone the Council could tap for new details and information. Emily Wess would lead them right to him. And then, if that was the extent of her knowledge, they could strip her of both it, and her life.

CHAPTER 55

10.40 a.m.

The hardest part was determining where to begin. The sheer size of the library made any decision Emily might make arbitrary, but she knew she had to start somewhere. She walked back up the small flight of stairs her tour had descended a few minutes before she left its ranks, to a plexiglass display panel outlining the floor plan of the main reading room. Pulling her BlackBerry out of her pocket, she flicked on the display and called up the etching she'd photographed in Oxford.

I've found Ptolemy's legacy, she thought to herself, re-reading the hand-carved first line. Beneath it were the three words she felt must guide her to something here in the Bibliotheca Alexandrina: glass, sand, light.

Let's start at the very beginning. Glass. Emily had little idea what glass could have to do with her quest for the lost Library of Alexandria, but whatever section of the building's collection dealt with the historical city couldn't be a bad place to begin.

Recalling the tour guide's pride in the public-access computer terminals scattered throughout the Bibliotheca Alexandrina, Emily made her way to a nearby computer and called up the English language version of the catalogue system from a menu before her. A familiar search interface appeared, so much like those of academic library catalogues she'd encountered at other institutions in her work, and she quickly clicked her way through to the appropriate screen and entered her search criteria. Scanning over the rows of resulting matches, she located 'History: Alexandria (Ancient)', with a series of digits beside the entry directing her towards level 4, stack rows 25-63. Returning to the plexiglass display, she found a route to the location on the library's floor plan, and turned to follow her path.

Making her way across two levels of galleries and down to the fourth cascading floor of the reading room, Emily arrived at row 25, where the larger collection on ancient Mediterranean history began to hone in on Alexandria proper. The books were arranged in clusters on their shelves, slightly larger in their bunches here than in the other areas she had passed by. Indeed, the shelves looked more like what one would expect of a library, and the contrast stood out. Emily realized that the rest of the place, for all its splendour, had a certain sad, haunted air about it. One of the world's most spectacular facilities, mostly empty – as if it were showing off to the world the sheer might and power of its potential for learning, but hadn't yet quite figured out what it wanted to say.

She worked her way down the long rows, scanning spines with titles printed in French, English, Spanish, Russian, German, Arabic. *God help me if it's in Arabic*, she thought. Most Romance languages she could manage, along with the traditional scholastic Greek, Latin, and enough Slavic type-face to get by. But Arabic was branched further out on the family tree of world languages than she had ever dared to climb.

By the time she made her approach to the fifth and final shelf of row 63, the last of the section, she already sensed she would find nothing. The last cluster of books addressed the city's declining years, but there was nothing in any of their titles, or any of those that had come before, that bore any association with glass. *As if there would be*, she mused.

Emily straightened herself up and walked across to the polished balcony handrail, artfully separating her floor from the one beneath it. Maybe she was thinking in the wrong direction. Glass, however far back in history it may stretch, always had a modern feel about it. Maybe she shouldn't be looking at history at all. Modern glass? Glass-making? Glass technologies? Emily directed herself once more to one of the library's ever-present computer terminals, entered a new set of search criteria into the standard interface, and within a few minutes determined directions to the collection on 'Materials, Modern: Glass', and began her walk to another stylized quarter of the complex.

A scan down its shelves resulted in the flip side of the

problem she had faced in her survey of the historical stacks: here every book she touched was on glass, but none bore any connection to Alexandria, or the library. Different conditions of disappointment, but the same end result.

Think, professor! The thought almost came out aloud, as if by sheer, aggressive insistence she could force herself to figure out the path she was meant to follow. *Glass, sand, light – what on earth is that supposed to mean?*

Think creatively. Perhaps the answer lay not in finding one term or the next, but in their combination. Glass, everyone knew, was made of sand. Or at least, that was as far as Emily knew the science of glass-making herself. Light . . . light was also among the terms. Light clearly passed through glass.

She closed her eyes, trying to achieve some epiphany by combining the words creatively.

Was Ptolemy's legacy some kind of process? Converting the Egyptian sands to glass? Letting in the light? It was a stretch, but it was better than nothing. She headed back towards the history collection, this time intent on locating every volume she could on Ptolemy. *But which Ptolemy?* Even as she walked, Emily knew the possibilities were too numerous to be useful. There had been fifteen kings in succession, all called Ptolemy, and at least twice that number of generals, princes, rulers and commanders that had borne the imperial name throughout the late Egyptian dynasty. Each of them had a history. And Emily was sure that each had at least a small collection of books written on him.

This is getting me nowhere.

She stopped before she had climbed back to the fourth floor, and sidestepped across the landing to one of the small huddles of chairs that dotted the library. Running around the stacks at every whim was counterproductive. She needed to sit, to think and to sort out exactly what she was meant to be seeking.

She sank as far as she could into a stiff, bluish-grey chair and let the sunlight from above distract her from the sights all around. Again she closed her eyes, seeking focus.

The clues in Oxford were deceptive, she reminded herself. *Their language was precise, designed to mislead at first reading.* She took out her phone, stared a hundredth time at the photograph from the chapel.

Ptolemy's legacy. Emily thought back to Wexler's words on 'legacy': something possessed now, today, rather than something lost. That guidance had brought her here. Perhaps she needed to heed it again, to re-adjust her approach. Rather than probe the library looking for something that contains a key element of the king's legacy, Emily told herself, *let's start from the premise that this is his legacy. I'm sitting in it.* She opened her eyes and took in the scene anew. *What is it here, in this place, that links these three terms together?*

A woman at a nearby computer terminal pounded away on her keyboard, music emanating from small white head-phones firmly planted in her ears. Emily couldn't be certain, but it sounded as if the woman was humming along. Music, humming, typing, computer blips – it was as if she had sat at that desk, at that computer, at that moment, specifically to distract Emily.

Emily closed her eyes and leaned her head back on the stiff chair, allowing the sunlight to cover her face and calm her blood.

And then it hit her.

Sunlight. Light, pouring down from above. There was only one way that could happen. Emily's eyes snapped open.

Glass. The massive, sloping ceiling was a spectacular network of glass panels streaming in the Egyptian sun. Each was framed in its granite alcove, forming a criss-crossed network of panes that transformed the golden-yellow light into a soft grey that filled the library below.

Emily sat upright. *Glass, sand, light.* She looked again to her BlackBerry and all at once the picture on the screen appeared different. New. There was something she had not seen before: shape. Whoever had scratched the message into the wooden altar screen in Oxford had not written these words side by side. They were scratched into the wood vertically. 'Glass' did not stand beside the others; it stood over them.

> *GLASS*
> *SAND*
> *LIGHT*

Emily looked up once more at the ceiling slanted high above. Here, in the midst of Ptolemy's legacy, glass stood over everything.

Could these words be a map? A basic plan she was meant to follow?

The top of the library was glass. It was built on the Egyptian sand. Emily looked back to the photograph. *Beneath the sand, light.*

I have to get to the basement.

CHAPTER 56

11 a.m.

Even as Emily descended staircase after staircase, occasionally sidestepping into the shelving stacks to avoid her determined gait attracting the attention of the few curators and attendants on duty, and worked her way down to the bottommost floor of the library, she felt her certainty rising. The three words in her photographs were a plan, telling her to move down to whatever part of the structure lay beneath the sand, beneath ground level. There, she was certain, she would find the 'light' that sat beneath the other two words of the clue. Light, as any historian knew, was a symbol for truth in almost every culture.

The truth is beneath these walls.

Her pace quickened as she approached the bottom floor. It looked much like every other: collections of desks, computers and tables in the sunlit front landing, with row upon row of illuminated shelving recessing into the stacks that ran back beneath the floor above.

Emily moved from the staircase to the rows of shelves, and

made straight for the wall at their rear. The surroundings were darker here with only the artistic in-shelf lighting on the stacks illuminating against the darkness that came from standing beneath eleven stories of modern design.

She reached the far wall, whitewashed and clean. Occasional portraits and posters broke up the long, flat facade, which, Emily noticed, was otherwise punctuated only by three sets of wooden doors: one at each end, and one in the middle. She made her way impulsively to the door on the left. She tried the handle. *Locked.*

A moment later she was at the central doors. They appeared identical to the first set, and were also tightly locked. Her certainty, however, did not wane. Despite two misses, she was convinced she was on the right track.

As she approached the third set of doors, Emily's heart raced.

The sign she sought was there, waiting.

In the upper corner of the door, scratched in rudimentary strokes through the lacquer and wood, was a symbol she had come to know all too well, with its two Greek letters surrounded by their embellished frame. The library's crest. She allowed herself only the briefest moment to glint a confident smile, and then put her hand to the third set of closed doors.

And this time, they opened.

CHAPTER 57

The three men had overturned every surface in the small residential house, just off the Carleton College campus, rented by Dr Emily Wess. Sofa cushions had been knifed open, the mattress deconstructed to its springs. Carpeting had been torn up from the floors, and even wallpapered walls had had their paper torn off in the search for any covered holes or concealed hiding spaces. All the searches undertaken by the Friends were thorough, so when the Secretary ordered one to be 'full', he meant that a location was to be disassembled, torn down to its bare skeleton if needed.

The Friends had done this, yet the search had been fruitless. There was nothing, not a single item, anywhere in Emily Wess's residence that bore any obvious connection to the library, to the Society, or to the Keeper. Only a personal library that contained a stereotypical collection for a college professor, intriguing solely in the clear love that Emily Wess bore for her post-graduate alma mater of Oxford University.

Books on its history, architecture and culture took up almost three full shelves of her living room bookcase.

As they had been instructed, the men had removed the hard drive from Wess's computer and bagged all the books from her shelves. If anything was concealed in either, it would be discovered back beneath the blue lighting of their Minneapolis satellite station.

Collectively, all three men hoped the scrutiny there would turn up something. No news was not good news in the Secretary's eyes.

One of the men snapped open his phone and dialled. A moment later, the line connected. Neither party identified themselves.

'Are you finished?' came the query from the far end of the line.

'Yes. We've found nothing. The house looks clean. Her books and computer will be at the lab within an hour.' He glanced over the ransacked remains that had once been Emily Wess's home, convinced that they had not missed anything.

He turned his attention back to the phone.

'And you – are you on site?' he asked.

'We've just arrived at his place,' came the reply.

'Good,' he answered. 'When you've extracted what you need from the fiancé, report immediately.'

'Of course.' With that, both men ended the call.

In Chicago, the two Friends adopted a professional demeanour as the brass elevator doors parted on the fourth floor of a mid-level apartment block in the centre of the city.

A few steps later, they stood before the door marked 401. The lead Friend knocked.

'His last name?' his partner asked beneath his breath. In the 'interview' to follow, he would need to maintain a professional protocol. 'Remind me of his last name.'

'Torrance,' the other man answered. 'The target's name is Michael Torrance.'

CHAPTER 58

11.05 a.m.

Emily pushed open the wooden door, which gave way on well-oiled hinges. Beyond the white wall at the back of the library's lowest floor of stacks a different scene appeared before her. A long ramp descended further into the belly of the structure, the walls here a dark, stone grey, the lighting suddenly the flickering, stale blue of fluorescent strip bulbs rather than the warm glow of recessed fixtures that marked out the public spaces behind him. There were no signs beyond the door of the cream and pale-grey commercial carpeting that ended on a metal seam just before it: the floor was bare concrete, already marked with long and wavering lines from the wheels of transfer carts repeatedly pushed along it.

This was clearly an entrance into the working underbelly of the gleaming Bibliotheca Alexandrina. As Emily skirted her way down the corridor into the complex of hallways and rooms to which it led, she couldn't help but feel that this was where the real work of the Middle East's foremost centre of learning took place.

As she made her way into the main corridor, the entrance to the first in an interconnected series of rooms and offices appeared at her right. She glanced cautiously into the small room, wanting to ensure it was empty before she passed by the open door and exposed herself to being seen. Fortunately, the room was unoccupied, as was the next one after it, and she was able to continue her descent along the downward-sloping hallway. The studio-designed shelving of the reading rooms above gave way here to old metal racks, painted an industrial green found the world over, bending under the weight of books and papers that were more piled than stacked upon them.

Occasional sounds of activity reminded her, however, that this was a working area, and that she was not alone, however barren many of the offices and workrooms looked. Emily heard muffled voices from the next room down the corridor and stepped lightly as she approached. Edging her left eye to the small window in the door, she gazed in on what looked like an ordinary office meeting – colleagues looking over papers, typing at glowing computer terminals.

Before she could be noticed, Emily ducked her head and moved past. Though in another context she might have enjoyed nothing more than a professional meeting with the people she saw, she could not risk an encounter now. This was obviously not a public area, and she was here without invitation. An employee zealous for protocol would see her to the door as swiftly as she had entered it, and she could not afford to be ejected from these halls.

These halls hold an answer, Emily told herself. *Light. Truth. Whatever it is I'm supposed to find.*

She moved further down the corridor until she came to its end, scanning surfaces, doorways, shelves and anything else she could spot for some sign of her aim.

Doors here were mostly marked only with numbers or left plain. A few, though, bore engraved nameplates that began 'Doctor' or 'Professor'. It came as a certain comfort to Emily to see that English had been chosen as the international language of scholarship in Egypt. Her memory glanced back to an anonymous afternoon in her childhood, seated in the French classroom of her middle school in Logan, Ohio, as the teacher had proudly insisted to her students that French was the universal language, the true and literal 'lingua franca' the world over. The teacher had managed to convince them at the time, and Emily had carried on with the language for years. But the world had clearly changed.

The corridor terminated in a sharp right turn, marking the beginning of another. Emily descended into the increasingly poorly lit substructure of the library. More offices lined this corridor, which branched off into three other, shorter hallways to the left, causing the whole ensemble to form a network of forked hallways connected like an immense backward letter 'E'. Tucking herself behind the corner of a shelf or into an empty room whenever she heard a sound, Emily moved along slowly, scanning the complex with strained eyes and avoiding the sweep of the surprisingly few security cameras present in the basement.

Beneath the sand, light. Clearly, any light she was going to find down here wasn't going to be coming from the sun, nor did she believe that the septic blue fluorescent bulbs flickering above her were substantial enough to produce anything like the illuminating revelation she was seeking. *It must be a symbol, or a representation. A figure, instead of the reality.*

What symbolizes light?

The further Emily progressed, the older the walls around her appeared to look. They had begun concrete, but now – were they stone? If not, the brick used was a good approximation. The edges of each long rectangular slab looked weathered, slightly decayed.

Could they have built all this on the remains of some older structure?

Emily remembered that the Egyptian government had wanted to build the library as close as they could to the site of the old library. Egypt was also a land in which every shovel cast into the earth came up with at least one ancient artefact. It was entirely possible that not every wall down here in the belly of the new complex was as modern as those above.

She turned into the middle of the three side-corridors. The rack shelving here was mostly empty, revealing more of the walls behind it as Emily made her way down the short length. The lights in this area were out completely, but as her eyes continued to adjust, the graffitied state of the stone brickwork was unmissable. The stonework was covered in scrawls and designs. The markings, however, were not painted. They were scratched.

Scratched.

Emily's pulse quickened. Both signs she'd been given so far had been scratched – into the woodwork of the University College Chapel in Oxford and on the door of the reading room above. For the first time since entering the basement complex, she felt as if she might be making progress.

Her eyes surveyed the etchings on the walls. Most were in Arabic, though some in a Latin-based script she didn't entirely recognize. But she could tell that most were names. People's names.

As quickly as they had come, thoughts of great antiquity vanished, and Emily smiled at what she realized she was seeing. Her thoughts returned to Willis Hall at Carleton College, where years ago as an undergraduate in her senior year, she and a group of friends had kept an old and venerable school tradition. Late into a May night, working in the dark to avoid the surveillance of campus security's ever-present patrols, they had secretly climbed up the yellow-brick building's tower, taking pens and inscribing their names on the old and generally unseen walls. They added their scrawls to hundreds of others already there, stretching back untold years into the college's history. It was something of a rite of passage: leaving your mark on the stone of the campus before departing for whatever came next. As Emily now scanned the dozens of names scratched into the stone of this basement corridor, she realized it must be the Egyptian construction workers' equivalent of the tradition at Willis Hall: etching their names into history, into a structure their hands had fashioned, but which most would likely never enter again.

She stepped further into the short corridor and came to a doorway. No nameplate marked its surface and the door was locked. She tried the handle twice, jiggling it with increasing force, but it did not budge. Emily felt a surprising desperation. *What if it's in there, whatever it is I'm looking for, and I can't reach it?* The host of names carved into the wall, however unrelated they might be, had increased her adrenaline levels and sense of expectation. But the door would not give.

She moved forward, reached the end of the small alcove and turned to scan her way back along the other side. A second door stood opposite the first. Again it bore neither number, nor nameplate.

And then she saw it. Freshly scratched into the stone, in small and rough English script, was a single word.

LIGHT

So, I won't need to decipher a sign, after all, Emily thought. The light she was looking for was a little more – obvious. She trained her eyes on the word, as if it might reveal some secret if she gazed at it intensely enough.

This is the spot, she knew, *and this is the door.* She lowered her gaze to the wooden door before her, and as she did, she felt her skin go cold.

The door now stood open. Within it loomed a man, dark skin concealed behind a black beard, with black eyes trained directly on Emily.

CHAPTER 59

11.35 a.m.

The man's gaze bored into Emily's now ashen face. He was dressed in a traditional suit and tie, each a different shade of light brown. His olive complexion was accentuated by a short, attentively trimmed jet-black beard. The thinning hair atop his head was the same formidable colour, but softened around the temples and ears by touches of grey. His eyes drilled into Emily with a singular focus.

'What do you want?' The man spoke abruptly, the sternness of his tone made blunter by a guttural Arabic accent.

Emily had no idea how to respond. How she should answer depended entirely on who the man was, and whether or not he was connected to Emily's investigation and the word scratched above his office door. Was he attached, somehow, to the messages and signs Arno had left in the library? Or was he simply a library worker who happened to be in the room? Emily was at a loss even for a beginning of an approach.

'I, I'm . . .' Emily faltered.

The man looked her over slowly as Emily fumbled and went silent. At length he brought his gaze directly back to eye level. He said nothing, only waited. Whether by deliberate ploy or simply bluntness of character, he wasn't going to make this easy for Emily.

I have to get past this man. I can't let him stop me. Emily's mind raced for the right words, but all she could conjure up was the obvious excuse. She struggled for a relaxed tone.

'I'm very sorry, I think I've lost my tour group and I'm lo—'

'I'm sorry,' the man cut her off. 'I am very busy.' Yet he remained squarely planted in the doorway, his eyes not moving an inch from Emily's. Nor did he raise an arm, or glance in the direction of his desk, or make any other gesture that would normally accompany the attempt to shy away from an unwanted conversation. He stood absolutely stoic, hands unmoving at his sides.

The silent, awkward moment grew, as if the man expected something more. Then, after what seemed an unyielding moment, he moved his hand to the doorknob.

'I'm afraid I will have to ask you to leave, if you don't have anything to say.' His eyes bored once again into Emily's, strangely, almost imploringly. Then he took the door in hand without ceremony, stepped back fully into his office and closed it between them.

For the second time, Emily stood staring at the surface of the unmarked door, now shut inches from her face. Her heart raced, but no longer solely from fear. She felt a panicked excitement. *Clearly, this man knows something.* She knocked on the door, even as she realized that she didn't know what she would say when it was opened.

The opportunity didn't come. The door remained firm before her.

Think! Emily commanded her mind to attention. Something was strange about the man's final remark. 'I'll have to ask you to leave, if you don't have anything to say.' It was a peculiar comment, and in the confusion of the current moment it tugged at Emily's mind. *'Anything to say'? What is he expecting me to say?*

Emily looked around herself for some sort of guidance, and her eyes ascended back to the word etched above the door. 'Light.' *Is it a passphrase? Am I supposed to use it as an entry word, like Ali Baba at his cave, after the thieves had gone?*

Worried that whatever opportunity an encounter with the man might present was slipping away, she acted on impulse. 'Light!' she announced, the word echoing in the small corridor.

Nothing. The door remained firmly closed, and the only sounds Emily heard were the reverberations of her own voice. The simple answer, it seemed, had been too simple. The pattern of looking for the obvious solutions to Arno's clues was apparently at its end. She should have guessed as much.

So what the hell am I supposed to say?

Beyond the writing on the wall, the sole resource she had at her disposal was her bag full of papers from Oxford. She pulled out Arno's two letters and page of clues. Shuffling through them, Emily quickly scanned over the hand-written text, forcing herself to slow down and see whatever might be there to help her. The letters, though, revealed nothing that seemed relevant. The texts had got her as far as Oxford, and from there to the small chapel inscription, but they said nothing of what she was supposed to do here.

At least, they didn't appear to. But that, Emily realized, had to be intentional.

The connection to Oxford sparked a memory, and Emily flipped the pages until she came to the sheet that had first made her journey feel like a quest – the page containing the small crest that had been her guidepost in both cities, with the three clues she had been forced to decipher. And at the top of the page, a short inscription: 'Two for Oxford, and one thereafter.'

What was it Kyle said? Emily asked herself, thinking back to Wexler's assistant's comments as they had sat together in the professor's college rooms. *'There are three statements later on the page. It seems a safe guess that two of them apply to places here in the university, and one to somewhere else.'* As the memory came, Emily was overwhelmed with an admiration for the young man she'd met in the city. If her hunch was correct, this was going to be the third time that Kyle had steered her aright in a moment of frustration.

Emily scanned down the page, beneath the crest, to the three statements Holmstrand had penned for his attention. The first two were familiar, and had already proven their worth. Beneath them ran Arno's third and final clue.

Fifteen, if by morning.

The phrase meant nothing to Emily, but at that precise moment she wasn't looking for meaning. She was only looking for something to say.

She brought her eyes back up to the door, and with as firm a voice as she could manage, spoke the meaningless phrase past it, into the office beyond. 'Fifteen, if by morning.'

An interminable moment passed, in which Emily's every hope seemed to vanish and every doubt emerge out of the darkness. *What if this isn't it at all?* It was the last clue she possessed.

Then, a click.

Emily's gaze snapped down to the doorknob, and she watched as it slowly creaked to the left, stopped and went still. The door silently swung open. Behind it, the man stood firm as before, his eyes once again drilling into hers. Without shifting his gaze, he spoke.

'Come in.'

CHAPTER 60

11.40 a.m.

Jason and his partner had stalked their target from a comfortable distance, following her down corridor after corridor, pausing as she darted into empty rooms and offices. The woman's dedication to her mission was intense, surprising only in that she hadn't seemed to know what it was she was looking for. The Friends knew far more about her goal than she, even if the identity of her target had remained unclear until just minutes ago.

The identity of the Librarian Emily Wess was groping to find had become clear to them the moment she had entered the underground complex. Of the four candidates the Council had determined as potential Librarians in the city, three worked in the upper offices of the Bibliotheca Alexandrina. Only one worked in its depths. As the clues the Keeper had left for Emily Wess drew her down deeper and deeper into the structure's belly, Jason had narrowed his choices and found his target.

'It's Antoun,' he'd relayed to the whole team through a group broadcast SMS. In the basement corridors, with their stone walls and hard floors, he couldn't risk being overheard by Wess, even at a whisper. The Friends throughout the building understood immediately what the two-word text meant and began to reconfigure themselves accordingly. The man who had been tracking Antoun withdrew from his position: once they knew he was the target, they didn't want to be too close. A spooked Librarian, much less a spooked Emily Wess, were not useful. Jason and his partner had continued to follow from behind.

Their only concern had then been to avoid being seen by either Wess or the man she was to meet. The Friends did not share her obvious worry over being spotted by others down in the halls. Fabricated access cards and badges had been waiting for them on their landing in Egypt, and each wore them pinned to their lapels. If their grey suits had looked out of place among the tourists and students above, they suited them well in the working basement. Any inquisitive mind would discover two technology specialists, surveying the library for the content and condition of its scanners and optical devices, of which there was no shortage. They looked the part, and the Friends had extensive experience in playing their roles convincingly.

After several minutes of searching and scanning, the target had stopped before a certain door. Something had caught her attention there. Jason signalled to his partner, and each took up a position at the corner where the shorter corridor met the longer hallway. In the darkness they had the perfect vantage point to see and not to be seen.

When the door had opened and the man appeared, Jason had acted quickly. Taking out his phone, he snapped a silent portrait of the man, and with a few button presses sent it to the Secretary.

Antoun, he thought, confirming the identity. They had their Librarian.

Emily Wess, however, clearly didn't know the man. A strange scene of doors being closed, Dr Wess shuffling papers and talking to herself, was followed by the door reopening. The dark-skinned Antoun, outwardly a respectable employee of the library, stared at Wess coldly. 'Come in.'

Jason knew it was time to act. As Wess entered the office and Antoun closed the door behind her, Jason moved forward and extracted a small digital device from his pocket. Soundlessly, he fastened the specialized microphone to the doorframe and plugged an earpiece into his left ear. Touching his finger to a series of buttons on the display, he adjusted the microphone to its optimal settings. It performed its function perfectly, and he could hear through the door as if it were not there.

A few additional button presses and the device began to beam the digitized conversation over a short-range WiFi broadcast. The second Friend, his palmtop computer already out and opened, picked up the signal and routed it through a live connection to the Secretary's office.

As the two people within the office spoke, their words

flew seamlessly across the vast network of digital space, being broadcast with crystal clarity from two small speakers in a New York office only milliseconds after they were spoken.

The Secretary sat at an oak desk, listening to every word.

CHAPTER 61

11.45 a.m.

'Come in.' The man spoke the words slowly, a mixture of command and hesitation. The plan that the Keeper had set in motion was at a critical stage, and the work that had already been done to prepare Emily Wess for her role – wholly without Wess's knowledge – was growing closer to its culmination.

He stepped aside and Emily entered the concrete and brick, windowless office. The man shut the door behind her, sliding a small bolt lock into place.

'Please, sit down.' He motioned Emily towards a wooden chair in the corner – the only surface in the office that wasn't covered in piles of papers, books, folders and computer equipment. This was an office that was heavily used.

Emily took her seat. The man moved to his place at his desk, sat on a creaking swivel chair and turned to face her. He kept his hands flat on his knees, staring at his visitor without saying a word.

Finally, Emily broke the silence.

'My name is—'

'I know who you are, Dr Wess.'

Emily started at the sound of her own name. This man had known her all along.

'I don't understand,' she replied. 'If you already know who I am, why didn't you let me in when I first knocked? Why the bizarre interrogation at your door?'

The man's gaze remained constant.

'That is not the way we work. We are based on . . . trust. I had to be absolutely certain that I could trust you.' Behind his words there was a mixture of conviction and relief.

'I don't understand,' Emily repeated. 'What made you decide you could trust me?'

'Because,' the man answered, 'you knew my name.'

'Your name?'

'"Fifteen, if by morning".' The man motioned towards himself. 'In the flesh.' There was a slight lift at the edge of his mouth, almost a smile.

Emily remained suspicious, and sat motionless at the revelation.

'I'm sorry, Dr Wess,' the man said, sensing her reserve. It was important, critical, that Emily Wess understand what was at stake. He would need to help her along.

'It is not actually my name, of course,' he explained. 'My name is Athanasius, though here my colleagues know me as Dr Antoun.'

The man spoke sincerely, and the more obvious forthrightness calmed Emily's nerves slightly.

'And the phrase, "Fifteen, if by morning"?' she asked.

'It's what we call our persona. Think of it as an identifier. A simple way to speak of one another without our real identities being employed.' He waited, looking for a sign of understanding to appear on Emily's face. Emily, however, retained her confusion and suspicion.

This time Athanasius rose, realizing he was going to have to do more to earn Emily's confidence. He took a single step across the small office to a filing cabinet and retrieved an unpretentious sheet of paper stacked there amid countless others.

'I received this last week,' he announced, handing the paper to Emily. On it was a brief, handwritten note: *Dr Emily Wess should arrive imminently. If she knows what to say, tell her what she needs to know.*

Emily felt her throat constrict. The handwriting was Arno Holmstrand's, identical to the script on the letters in her bag. Even the rusty brown ink was the same.

Athanasius Antoun returned to his seat.

'So, what is it, Dr Wess?'

Emily looked up.

'What is what?'

'What is it that you need to know?'

The sudden jolt into question-and-answer took her by surprise.

'What do I need to know? Anything. Everything. I have – literally – crossed the world in the past 24 hours, knowing only that I'm looking for the lost Library of Alexandria and – ' she fumbled through her bag, extracted Arno's papers and shifted her gaze to the first letter '– and this "Society that accompanies it."' She looked up to the man opposite her. 'Can I assume you are a member of this "Society"?' She figured she might as well lay her cards on the table and probe the man for what few specifics she had at her disposal.

Athanasius paused. Under normal circumstances, no Librarian would ever speak of his role, or of the Society, or of the library. Many throughout history had chosen imprisonment, even death, rather than reveal their part in its noble course. But the Keeper's instructions had been clear. Emily Wess had been chosen for a role, and she needed to know the truth, even if giving it to her meant breaking centuries of protocol.

'Yes,' he finally answered, honestly. 'But I must correct you, Dr Wess. The library you are looking for, it is not lost.' He paused, allowing Emily a moment to take in his words. 'It is hidden.'

Emily immediately chased up the point.

'So Arno discovered it,' she said, 'and you're working together to keep it secret?'

'Not exactly.' Athanasius fidgeted in his chair. Wess's understanding of the situation was poor. 'It did not need to be discovered, because it has never been lost. It has always been hidden, cared for. Intentionally.'

Emily absorbed the revelation. Kyle, it seemed, had been right again. 'Since when?'

'*Always*,' Athanasius emphasized. 'The myth of the library being destroyed, or lost, has always served us well. But it is not dead, and never has been. It is very much a living, active entity. Just like the library upstairs, our collection is always growing.'

Emily kept her eyes on Athanasius, but her vision moved elsewhere – tracking back through history, to legends and myths, documents and discoveries. The theories she had discussed with Kyle and Wexler now had chilling, substantial merit. In the world as she had known it until today, no one knew what happened to the Library of Alexandria, but everyone agreed it had disappeared. Everyone knew that it was gone and had been for centuries.

Everyone . . . except this man sat before her and the group to which he belonged.

'Our role,' Athanasius continued, 'is to make certain it is kept alive. The Society exists to ensure that the library remains what it has always been: the most extensive collection of knowledge in history, with a purpose to fulfil in the course of human events.'

Emily's vision snapped back to the present, and to the question that burned in her most strongly.

'So, you know where it is?' She leaned forward, anxious for the answer. When it came, it was not what she expected.

'No.' Athanasius anticipated the look of disappointment that crossed Emily's face. 'None of us know where the library is located. That has always been our Society's most closely guarded secret, kept even from us who work in its ranks. Only two men know its location.' He caught himself. 'Or did. Both of these men have been killed in the past week.'

Emily felt something tighten in her chest. Her memory flashed back to Arno Holmstrand, murdered in his office.

Had there been another killing, more death? The scope of what she was finding herself a part of was expanding dramatically.

Yet, despite the immensity of that story, and even the fact that two recent deaths were involved in the details, Emily's curiosity got the better of her fear. One point, a key point, wound its way out of Athanasius's words and onto Emily's tongue.

'Tell me how it works,' she said, ensuring Antoun saw the earnestness of her demand. 'How do you maintain a hidden library?'

CHAPTER 62

Athanasius settled back into his office chair. If the story was to be told, it needed to be told well and thoroughly. He had been a Librarian, a member of the Society, for well over twenty-five years, dedicating the most productive part of his life to its service and work. Emily Wess had been exposed to its existence for only minutes, and yet its very future depended on her. How Athanasius went about informing her of its work, and drawing her into its fold, was critical.

'The how of our work,' he began, 'can come after the who and the why. Our full name is the Society of the Librarians of Alexandria. For fifteen centuries our role has been the same: to maintain the library's archive of past knowledge, and continually update it with new material. Upstairs – ' he waved a hand towards the immense institution above '– they are proud to have an archive that goes back to 1996. Ours goes back . . . well, let us say, somewhat further.'

'To the time of Ptolemy the Second,' Emily offered, thinking back to the famed founder of the original library.

'No, Dr Wess. Much, much further. That may be when the library was founded, but it sought out information, documents and records from centuries before. We have archives in our collection that go back thousands of years. In reference to some cultures, to the very beginnings of their written history. King Ptolemy had a vision, that man must live by truth, and have access to all truth, of every age. We have always tried to maintain that vision.'

As Athanasius spoke, Emily felt an air of nobility about the man and his words, which was a strange complement to the atmosphere of death, which, as those same words reminded, had brought her here. The original project of the Library of Alexandria had been a principled one. Working for its continuation seemed equally elevated.

'The Dark Ages may be behind us,' Athanasius continued, 'but the darkest are yet to come, and will arrive the moment we are blinded to the past. In Ptolemy's day, people called his project the "New Dawn", the rising of wisdom out of chaos, the ordering and accessibility of knowledge. But new dawns are not always welcomed. You are a historian, yes, Dr Wess?' Emily nodded. 'Then you are well aware of the vicissitudes of history. Tribe fights tribe, nation battles nation. Ideology struggles to conquer ideology.'

Emily knew the trends of human history only too well. It was what fascinated her about the field, even if the constant conflicts spoke to something rather depressing about the condition of mankind. Name two cultures at peace, she had often quipped, then give a historian a few centuries and they could show you two cultures at war. And those would be the

optimistic statistics. In too many cases to count, the time-
line was marked in decades, not centuries.

'Between the rise of Christian anti-Paganism in the fourth
and fifth centuries,' Athanasius continued, 'and the advent
of Islam and its approaching armies in the sixth, the climate
in which our library existed was becoming unstable. The
knowledge we possessed, the materials we had collected, were
becoming either the envy or bane of too many cultures and
powers. We knew that, left on open shelves in a known location, the library would never be safe – and the world could
hardly be safe from the kind of knowledge it possessed. You
must remember, Dr Wess, that the library is not simply filled
with literature. It possesses—'

'Military information,' Emily interjected. 'Political materials, information on states and governments.' She flashed
through the types of materials a king would want at his
disposal. It seemed impossible that what they were discussing
was actually real.

'Scientific advances, technological research,' said
Athanasius, continuing the list. 'The kinds of information
that are . . . dangerous.'

Emily leaned forward at the word. She hardly felt in a
position to correct Antoun, but his final comment touched
a topic that was important to her.

'I trust you mean threatening,' she said. 'Information isn't
dangerous, only what we do with it.' She'd been accused of
a juvenile naiveté in the past for maintaining this distinction, but it was one she happened to believe.

'I mean dangerous, Dr Wess,' said Athanasius, his features

tightening. 'A threat is one thing. Real danger is another. Information is not simply a romantic idea. Raw information can be deadly.'

Emily felt, and looked, uncomfortable. This was a point intellectuals had debated for centuries, and which would never leave the table. Is it what we know that is dangerous, or what we do with it? She and Michael had debated the question more times than she could remember. He approached it in what he called a 'more protective, guard-like' way than she, convinced that information itself held power, that what men did, they did *because* of the knowledge they possessed. It was not an either-or proposition. 'Evil men can't do great evil without the tools,' he had told her more than once. Emily held a different view. She was less convinced of the usefulness of holding back information than she was of the dangers of oppression, cruelty and domination to which censorship traditionally led.

She was about to interject, to raise her ideological point on the distinction between knowledge and action, when Athanasius pre-empted her.

'Think of modern history. Imagine that full details for the construction, delivery and detonation of a nuclear device were publicly available in 1944, with three world powers all out to destroy one another at any cost. Would you consider such information merely a threat, or a genuine danger?'

Emily said nothing. Visions of mushroom clouds over Nagasaki and Hiroshima flashed through her mind.

'Empires were overtaking empires,' Athanasius continued, returning to antiquity, 'new cultures were progressing, conquering and defeating ancient civilizations. What would have happened if one army was given full details of the military might of every other? If the secrets of a government were known to their enemies, down to the most minute of operational details? That is the kind of depth the library had attained, after centuries of blurring the lines between collecting information and proactively seeking it out. The Librarians were not just processors and cataloguers; they had extended their role to reconnaissance and action, the world over. The materials they had assembled were unparalleled. No, it had become clear that this knowledge was too much for a warring world to bear. We had to protect the world from what we knew.'

Emily listened, though her attention wavered between awe and trepidation. Inside, deep in her gut, a new knot was forming. Attaining knowledge was close to her heart, but hiding it from the world – it was censorship by another name. Despite the kinds of dangers Athanasius had mentioned, the world had too often seen what censorship fostered in the end.

'The decision was made,' Athanasius continued, 'by the chief Librarian, the Keeper of the Library, to take it underground. And so our Society was formed. The transfer itself happened in the early seventh century, and we have looked after it ever since, ever since it was "lost" to the world. In fact it was moved to Constantinople. The imperial city was by then already several centuries old, but compared to Alexandria it was new, and it was taking over as the intellectual heart of the Empire.

'The transfer must have been an incredible task.' Athanasius's eyes wandered, his mind attempting to recreate such a scene. 'Millions of scrolls, manuscripts, books – all loaded secretly on to ships to sail covertly across the Mediterranean to the Bosporus, to a new underground complex that had been constructed there to house them.'

Emily's imagination followed Athanasius's. With the size the library had attained after so many centuries, the flotilla involved in its transfer would have had to be enormous. Pulling it off secretly, under the cover of darkness, would have been almost impossible. Still, in all the centuries of recorded history since, Emily had never encountered a single mention of the project. Either Athanasius's story of the library's move was simply a lie, or it was the revelation of a monumental ancient cover up.

'The collection remained in Constantinople until sometime in the middle of the sixteenth century. In the decades and centuries that followed, there were continual attempts to discover it, but its cover remained – though only just. The Society was becoming increasingly worried about the risk of leaks. Our staff is human, as susceptible to bribes, to threats, to manipulation as anyone else. Should any one of them succumb, centuries of attention to secrecy would be compromised.'

Emily felt she knew where Athanasius was leading.

'So, you had to hide it, even from your own people.'

'It was decided to take the library's concealment to the next level: to move it again, this time leaving its location unknown to all but the smallest handful of privileged individuals – only two, who would live far apart, in remote regions of the Empire. Should one die, the knowledge of the library's location would rest with the other, and he would choose a new "second". In this way, the location of the collection would never rest only with one individual, in whom it could be lost, but it would also not be known to many, in whom it could be compromised.'

At least, Athanasius thought to himself, *that's how the system normally works.* '*When the Keeper sees his own death coming, without a Second yet in place, some plans have to be improvised.* But he bit his lip on this detail. Wess was not yet ready for that dimension of the story.

'By the end of the sixteenth century, the labyrinth of tunnels beneath the former Byzantine imperial palace, home to the library for centuries, was empty.'

CHAPTER 63

The director of the Secret Service, Brad Whitley, stood in the vice president's office, the door locked and the curtains drawn. He'd already instructed his men to switch off the wiretaps on the office, and to ensure their meeting wasn't interrupted. Some discussions required focus with no distractions or prying ears.

'This is all very hard to believe, Director Whitley,' Vice President Hines said. 'This is really going to happen in two days?'

'Yes, Mr Vice President,' Whitley answered. 'The secretary of defence and his top military commanders agree that this is a matter of national defence that must be handled immediately. The president is going to be removed from office under the provisions of military law, despite the protestations of innocence he's been making to the press since this broke. He is a man that has brought the foreign enemy into the homeland. Were it not for his illegal activities we would not

281

have terrorists and assassins taking out political figures in the capital.'

'You're sure of the connection?'

'Yes, sir. The evidence is irrefutable. The military has been able to tie the assassinations directly to Afghan enclaves through traceable munitions, and the materials that have come out on President Tratham's activities in Saudi Arabia leave no room for doubt. Surely you've seen them.'

'Of course I have,' Hines confirmed. His staff had been keeping him up to date with a nearly continual flow of documents since the story had first begun to break. He cast a perplexed look at the secret service director. 'What is the procedure for something like this?' he asked. 'Are there provisions for a military arrest of the president?'

'Not as such,' Whitley answered, 'but the generals are convinced that standard military law and the provisions of the Patriot Act are more than adequate for the arrest, detention and charging of any individual, including a sitting president. Once he's arrested on such grounds, his executive privilege ends immediately.'

'And then?'

'And then the constitutional chain of succession plays out as it is designed to.'

Hines appreciated the gravity of this innocuous phrase. The chain of succession transferred executive control to the vice president on the president's incapacitation or inability to carry out the duties of his office; and if that incapacitation were long-term, would transfer the presidency itself to him.

'You should know, Mr Vice President,' Whitley continued, 'that Secretary of Defence Davis and his team have been investigating you thoroughly. There is treachery and treason in the air, and he – we – are determined not to let it infect our system of government any more than the president has already caused to happen. You need to know that every dimension of your political life is being scrutinized.'

Hines straightened slightly at the words.

'I'm glad to hear that,' he answered, his tone that of the serious, accountable politician. 'I have nothing to hide.'

'Yes, sir. That's what our investigations have confirmed so far.'

'And my main advisors and contributors on international matters are Westerberg, Alhauser and Krefft. If you've looked into them, you know that they're famous for being completely transparent in their foreign dealings. The Westerberg Foundation has even—'

'Right,' Whitley interrupted, 'it's lobbied for accountability on reconstruction dealings. We've done the background. They've publicly stood out against the very kinds of wheelings-and-dealings that have got President Tratham into trouble.'

Vice President Hines nodded, sure of the stature of his supporters. He had no question that they would turn up clean at any level of scrutiny.

'So,' Whitley continued, 'unless there are secrets in your chest that are yet to come to light . . .' He let the thought linger.

'There aren't,' Hines answered firmly. *At least, none that you will ever know.*

'Then you'd better start preparing yourself, Mr Vice President,' the director of the Secret Service added, rising. 'Before the weekend is over, I doubt very much that "Vice" is going to still be part of your title.'

CHAPTER 64

Alexandria – 12.02 p.m.

Emily attempted to digest a story that at the very least challenged a vast segment of history as she had learnt it. History, and present reality. Mixed together with Athanasius's flood of details were the concrete facts of a murder, perhaps two, and a bombing – more than she could contemplate. Emily had never known her excitement to be so intermingled with fear that the two became almost indistinguishable.

'Your Society,' she blurted, 'it's the continuation of the old Librarians' work: seeking out materials and adding them to this hidden collection?'

'In part,' the Egyptian man answered. 'Our role as individual Librarians is to seek out and collect information – something librarians had done in Alexandria since the library's earliest days – and over the years we have spread out over the globe to accomplish our task. But the Society as a whole also has a tactical mission.'

'Tactical?' The comment took Emily off guard. The word seemed out of place in a discussion of books, knowledge and documents, and served to heighten the rising apprehension that kept her on the edge of her seat.

'You must understand,' Athanasius continued, 'that the library long ago moved from simply being a repository to being an active force in the world. Already by the first century, it was playing a part in world events. If some knowledge needed to be hidden, other knowledge had to be shared. The good of mankind is facilitated by the right information influencing the right people at the right times. Our Society's aim has been to keep the library, but also to use it.'

Emily sat back, struck into silence. This added an entirely different dimension to the history of the Library of Alexandria. It hadn't just collected information on world events: it had helped orchestrate them.

'To what degree?' she asked. 'How involved has the Society been in influencing the world from the wealth of its resources?'

'Our degree of involvement has varied throughout history. In ideal situations, we do not have to play too direct a role. But history is often far from ideal.'

'Give me specifics,' Emily said, surprised by her own self-confidence. She felt her pulse increasing, unsure how to feel about this newest revelation.

Athanasius lifted his brow, but complied.

'Nero.'

'Nero?'

'One of the worst emperors in history. You and most of the world know him as a deranged madman who played his fiddle while Rome burned, but in his day his exploits were well concealed by his inner court. The Empire suffered, not knowing that it was at the hands of its leader. We, however, knew the details. It was through the library's release of key information to the right people that Nero's role in the decline of Rome was made known, ultimately leading to the change of public opinion that drove him to take his own life.'

Emily listened in complete awe.

'Or, if modern history is more compelling, I could mention Napoleon,' Athanasius said. 'After his coup in 1799, his power spread across Europe with almost unstoppable force. He was an Empire builder of the most egotistical fashion, and states were falling left and right at the power of his "Grande Armée".'

'But somehow you got involved?' Emily probed.

'The Society provided the core reconnaissance and intelligence that allowed the Sixth Coalition to defeat him at Leipzig in 1813. It was the battle that turned the tide on the Napoleonic dynasty.'

'The Society stopped Napoleon?' The idea beggared belief.

'The Society influenced the events of that age,' Athanasius corrected, 'as it has influenced the events of every age at times when the tactical sharing of information has allowed the common good to prevail.'

Emily sat back, overwhelmed.

'You're saying that you use the information at your disposal to manipulate the events of the world around you.' Once again, the majesty of the revelation was tempered by her innate moral objections to what she was hearing, which grew ever stronger.

'Not events, just knowledge. And I wouldn't use the term

"manipulate".' Athanasius searched for a word that would better suit Emily's temperament. 'Better to think of it as . . . sharing. The careful and deliberate sharing of knowledge, when it will help, rather than hurt. The library has always been an institution of good. We strive to make moral decisions that will benefit humankind.'

The knot in Emily's stomach returned, tighter than before. There was nobility and moral conviction in the Society's cause, yes; but censorship had long since been surpassed. The library was a force for active involvement and change, with resources beyond imagining. Who could handle such power?

She tried to combat her growing unease by returning to practical questions.

'How did the Librarians do their job, once the library was hidden even from them? Influencing the world seems impossible if you don't have access to your own resources.'

'Knowing the physical location of the library has never been at the heart of the Librarians' work,' Athanasius answered. 'A physical connection to the collection became less important over time, and today it is not necessary at all. Individual Librarians collect and feed information in, and only those in charge require access to the collection itself. Our whole structure is compartmentalized. We remain headed by the Keeper of the library and his Assistant. Only these two people ever know the location of the collection, and only they have access to it. It is the Keeper who oversees its organization and the distribution of information into the public domain as appropriate. There is a large support crew, spread throughout the world, who assist in the management and the processing of new materials. The remainder of the work is done by us: the Librarians. There are one hundred of us at any given time, located all over the world and given a simple charge: to gather information in the realm of our remit. That information might be raw materials or intelligence that leads towards the Society's further involvement in local or international events. Some Librarians, such as myself, actually work in libraries.' Athanasius indicated his surroundings. 'I have worked in library sciences all my life, and my role is, let us say, traditional. I ensure that a copy of all printed books, newspapers, journals, magazines, even pamphlets and posters that come through the major Egyptian publishing houses and presses, find their way into our collection. Those that are not produced through mainstream means, I seek out and acquire. There are ten or so of us with roles like this, at the British Library, the American Library of Congress, and similar institutions across the world. The majority of our Librarians, however, are more specialized. Their work involves collecting information on political and social activities in their regions, but chiefly to seek out the "great and the good" of their societies. The movers and shakers of the world. Anyone of any significance is sought out, followed, explored, with background information collected and assembled, narrative histories composed, interpersonal networks scrutinized, and so on.'

Emily took in the enormity of the organization Athanasius described. If it truly was what he said it was, the Society of the Librarians of Alexandria constituted not simply a network of individuals sitting on an unparalleled vault of information and knowledge, but also one of the largest, and oldest, espionage operations in history.

The scope of the project seemed impossibly vast. Emily's blood pressure continued to rise, her pulse to soar, but she couldn't resist knowing every detail.

'How are you chosen? How are you trained for your roles?'

'There is a very old process we faithfully follow,' Athanasius answered, 'allowing us the ability to recruit new Librarians and train them fully in their roles, without their ever knowing the identity of the Keeper and others in charge. Potential candidates are shadowed and researched for at least five years, to determine their character, suitability and trustworthiness. The Keeper assigns one Librarian to this role who is charged to get to know the candidate personally, though obviously without revealing his reasons or connections. Ideally the two become colleagues, even friends, and we are able to get to know the candidate through their mentor. When the time comes for the candidate to be made aware of the Society, and the role to which they are being invited, the approach is always made by another Librarian, one from a different country. In this way, the Librarian nearby, the one who has come to know the candidate and screened them, is never known by the new recruit to be involved. If they reveal their invitation, or any aspect of their role to their mentor, we know that candidate is not capable of being trusted with the kind of information we have at our disposal. Ultimately, if everything goes well, the new candidate is formally appointed from afar by the Keeper, and sworn into the Society. They are given their instructions, their oath, their duties, and then the Librarian departs. The two will never meet again.'

'So the new Librarian joins a Society, of which they have only knowingly ever met one member? And of which they're given no names of any other members?'

'Precisely,' Athanasius affirmed. 'The Keeper's identity is never revealed. No one should be able to identify what you Americans call "the man at the top".'

The complexity of the system reinforced the general sense of mystery Emily felt before the Society, but also added to its foreboding character. Emily felt wonder, coupled with intrigue and anticipation.

'I can't imagine,' she finally said, 'what that must be like. To be courted by a group of such history, of such resources. For such a task.'

'In point of fact,' Athanasius answered, 'I think you can.' Emily's eyebrows lifted at the remark. 'And more directly than you think.'

'What do you mean?'

'You know at least one person who has gone through just the sort of covert preparation I have described.'

Emily hesitated.

'Who?'

Athanasius's eyes again drilled into hers.

'You.'

CHAPTER 65

12.20 p.m.

'Me?' Emily's heart, formerly racing, all but stopped at Athanasius's latest revelation. 'What are you talking about? I wasn't being prepared by anyone!'

'How would you have known?' Athanasius questioned back. 'The whole point of the preparation is for the candidate *not* to know. Not until the end, until they've proven they are trustworthy. In the normal five-year progression, the candidate is only made aware of the library and the Society in the final six months.'

'But, I—'

'You were not yet at that stage,' Athanasius interrupted. 'Your candidacy had only been ongoing for a little over a year.'

'A year!' Emily couldn't believe she'd been watched by the group at all, much less for so long a period of time. 'But who was "mentoring" me, as you put it?'

Athanasius's expression tightened.

'Under normal circumstances, you would never have

292

known. But, Dr Wess, our circumstances today are not normal. I think you know full well who was watching you, preparing you. He was the man at the top. The Keeper himself.' He let the silence draw out between them.

Emily knew there was only one person it could possibly be.

'Arno Holmstrand.' Her eyes were wide but convinced. Early on in Athanasius's description of the Society, Emily had guessed at the identity of its Keeper. Now she was certain. 'The Keeper was Professor Arno Holmstrand.'

Athanasius's expression softened at the name.

'Yes, Dr Wess. Arno was the Keeper, and your mentor. And a good man.' Evident emotion seeped into these last words.

Emily would have joined Athanasius more obviously in expressing their common sense of loss – for she, too, felt a sorrow at Arno's death that resurged at every mention of his name. That sorrow now took on a new dimension in the knowledge that Holmstrand had been personally involved in her life for so long without her knowing. But Emily's chief emotion at the moment was a confused, fearful yet anticipated excitement. Her involvement in the events of the past two days was not accidental or circumstantial. She had been under the eyes of the Society for over a year. Holmstrand, its Keeper, had been watching her for over a year. Preparing her.

For what? What was Emily meant to do? Part of her felt a fear that told her to tuck tail and run as far as possible from all this novelty; but a stronger part felt emboldened by the new knowledge, and infused with a power to look further into its depths. If she genuinely was to become a Librarian, she had to know what that role would entail.

She turned back to Athanasius.

'So what normally comes next? After this elaborate recruitment programme, how do the Librarians actually go about their work? Nothing you've said accounts for the fact that collecting and depositing information remain impossible if you don't know where the library is.'

'The fruits of our collections are submitted to the Keeper each month by parcel.'

'Parcel?'

'You know: small packages, tied with string.'

Emily balked, but Athanasius carried on before she could offer the incredulous remark moving towards her lips.

'They are not mailed to him, of course. There would be far too much risk of exposure. Instead, they are collected. Each month we assemble our new information into a parcel, and leave it for collection.'

'Where?'

'The drop point is different for each Librarian. We are told where, and how, and when we are to deposit our contributions as part of our recruitment. Then, month after month, we make our drop as prescribed. The Keeper assigns a team of three assistants to each Librarian – people the Librarian does not know, or ever see, but whose responsibility is to see to the Librarian's work, and to collect the parcels from the drop point each month. The arrangements are personal, developed for each recruit. Just like they were being developed for you.'

Emily didn't meet his eyes at the last remark, trying to bypass the discomfort that came, along with a new gleam of sweat on her skin and goosebumps on her arms, as she learned of details related specifically to her. The broader details were overwhelming enough, and the library's redundancies for secrecy and accountability bespoke a regimented structure. Not only were the Librarians kept in the dark as to the library's location and the identities of their fellow workers, but none of them would be able to know the larger meta-narrative into which their specific information was being fed. Each member of the Society simply collected specific data, and passed it along. What it meant, how it fit together with other material, was kept out of their grasp.

The very thing that impressed her, however, also begged the question that was behind her racing heart and tingling skin. At length, Emily could not continue without asking it.

'Why all this secrecy surrounding a force for good?' She edged forward on her chair, sincere in her question. 'All this control, this subterfuge, these trails that can't be followed. It seems, well, excessive.'

Athanasius met Emily's expression with kindness, but his brow drooped wearily.

'Because, Dr Wess, every search for truth has its opponents, and the possession of great truth earns one even greater enemies.' He watched Emily for a sign of recognition.

'We are secretive, because we have a foe.'

No sooner had the words departed his lips, than the eerie silence of the subterranean surroundings was shattered by a loud thump outside the door. Emily's heart seemed to shoot into her throat, and she leapt out of her chair in surprise. Before she could speak, Athanasius's hand was cupped around her mouth.

'Don't make a sound.'

CHAPTER 66

12.29 p.m.

'Down!' Jason whispered the command to his partner with all the intensity he had at his disposal. It took the two men less than a second to retreat around the bend into the main corridor, taking refuge behind two bookshelves, well out of the sight of Dr Athanasius Antoun's office.

Every urge in his body was to turn to his partner, to shout out his displeasure. *What the hell happened?! What did you do?!* But circumstances would allow none of it. Jason took a deep breath, controlling his anger. Gently edging one eye beyond the corner, he glanced back towards the office door. On the floor, across the small hall, a book had toppled from an imbalanced pile on a metal shelf. The unexpected noise had not been the fault of his partner, simply a fluke. An 'accident', to use a term the Secretary insisted was never to be spoken.

Jason drew back his head with a snap as the wooden office door began to creep open. Glancing across to his partner, he held a finger to his lips. Both men stopped their breathing, afraid that even the sound of their breath in the echo-prone corridors might give away their presence.

The large Egyptian scholar glanced warily out from his cracked door, letting his gaze linger long to his right, then to his left. The dark passageway showed no signs of intruders, no presence of unexpected visitors.

Athanasius lowered his gaze, looking down. On the floor, a book lay upside down, its cover open. Raising his eyes upward, he noticed the lop-sided pile of books and papers on which it had sat, midway up the stack of storage shelves. At the sight, the beat of his heart slowed, and his sigh of relief was audible throughout the halls. Still, Athanasius gave the corridor another long looking over before drawing his head back into his office and again closing the door.

As the latch clicked into place, Jason and the other Friend slowly, silently, released their constrained breaths.

That was too close.

Jason pulled himself up to full height, and gazed again around the corner. In the darkness, the small microphone and transmitter they had affixed to the door was almost invisible. He could only hope Antoun had not seen it.

CHAPTER 67

12.32 p.m.

'Dr Wess, please sit back down.' Athanasius locked the door behind him, and returned to his position opposite her.

Emily's eyes were wide, her breath short and racing. The adrenaline rush was clearly affecting her, as her body struggled to adapt to a level of stress to which she was not accustomed.

'Please, sit,' Athanasius repeated. He put a hand to her shoulder and nudged her back into the chair.

'It was a false alarm,' he added. 'Forgive me.'

'What the hell was that?'

'Just a book, falling off too crowded a shelf. Nothing more. I'm sorry if I frightened you with my response. I'm a little on edge these days.'

'I should say so!' Emily took a series of long, deep breaths, forcing away the dizziness and slightly sick feeling that came with her shock. 'Just who did you think was out there?'

Athanasius sat again in his own seat.

'I was just mentioning the reason for all our secrecy. Our work does not go unopposed.'

Emily forced her fingers into tight balls, squeezing away her stress.

'You thought they were outside, these foes of yours?' She forced her eyes at his. 'Just what sort of people are these?'

'We do not know precisely how, or exactly when, the Council came into being.' Athanasius's shoulders slumped slightly as he spoke. 'That is what they call themselves, Dr Wess. We know that its formation happened some time in the century following our taking the library underground. The first reference we have of it in the collection is from AD 722. According to a brief document submitted by a Librarian in Damascus, it was already an organized group with designated leaders and an efficient structure. And it was already known simply as the "Council".'

Emily lifted an eyebrow at the title, wringing the adrenaline stiffness from her wrists. Despite her fear, she couldn't help but think it seemed fitting that an opposing organization with a 1,300-year history should have so innocuous a name.

'The power the library's collection held for international dominance,' Athanasius continued, 'for power plays between kings and factions had been our reason for hiding it in the first place. But then division sprouted in our own ranks. The Council's origin was in a coup. Certain men within the Society felt that its power was not being adequately used. There was a desire to be more . . . forceful with our resources and influence.'

'Power corrupts, as they say,' Emily offered. It was a challenge to return to constructive conversation after their scare, but she reminded herself it had only been a falling book. There was no one outside.

'When the Society wouldn't allow its resources to be used for monetary gain, for the support of immoral armies and similar aims,' Athanasius continued, 'the coup attempted to place its leadership in new hands. It failed, but the men who had fostered it came together in a new organization. The Council had been born.

'The expulsion of these men unfortunately created a new unity amongst the Society's opponents. The leaders of factions who had been warring for generations came together. Militants, dissidents, even generals and the leaders of whole states were suddenly allies – but not for the greater good. Their coalition had one distinct aim: to rediscover what we had hidden. To lay claim to a knowledge that every one of them knew they would use unhesitatingly against one another. To discover real and undefeatable power.

'Their aims grew and expanded with their numbers. At their centre was a desire to find the library and gain its resources, but such intentions led to new ambitions. Hidden out of the public eye, the Council extended its reach into any group or organization from which it might claim more power, more influence. It began to have members in armies, in governments, in trade and business – and it used all of these to exercise influence across the world.'

'You're saying there's another organization out there trying to manipulate world events. Not just your Society.' Emily saw Athanasius recoil at her comparison of the two groups, but the man quickly regained his composure.

'The Council's desire is only power. Domination. Its "Highest Aim", the discovery of the library with all its potential for truly unparalleled dominance, has never faded. They work tirelessly to locate the one thing we want hidden and they want to find.'

'So they are just as active as you?'

Athanasius gave a weary frown.

'Yes, Dr Wess. They are active, and extremely powerful. That bump outside may have only been a book, but my caution was not misplaced.'

Emily stared on at the almost physical discomfort that seemed to come over Athanasius as he continued to speak.

'We know that the Council is headed by a committee that includes officials in state courts, governments, and the administrations of a dozen nations. Some of these individuals we know, many we do not. They have learned to be as secretive as we are.

'We do, however, know the identity of one key figure.' Athanasius instinctively lowered his voice. 'The Council is headed by a secretary who wields tremendous power over its operations. The organization may technically run by committee, but it is a committee in which the head outranks every other member, and has his own ranks of "Friends", his assistants who carry out his orders with chilling efficiency. We have been attempting to discover his identity for decades – and then, six months ago, we were finally successful. The Council's Secretary is an American entrepreneur and businessman in New York by the name of Ewan Westerberg, the head of a large foundation that invests in businesses and political causes all over the world.' Athanasius removed a photograph from a thick manila folder on his desk and passed it to Emily. His voice hesitated. 'He is a very dangerous individual.'

The name meant nothing to Emily, nor the face in the photograph. The worlds of business and entrepreneurship were well outside her realm of experience.

'Once we discovered his identity,' Athanasius continued, 'our aim was to use this knowledge to our advantage. We knew who was at their helm, but they still knew nothing of our Keeper or his Assistant. Or so we thought.' He stopped, allowing his mind to contemplate the reality as his hand tugged at his beard. Finally, he returned his gaze to Emily. 'We were wrong. Somehow, the Council had discovered their identities, just as we had discovered Westerberg's. Our Assistant Keeper was Collin Marlake, a high-ranking patents clerk in Washington DC. He had been with the Society for thirty-seven years and was nearing retirement, both from his office job and his role with us. A week ago, two men appeared in his office shortly after opening, and efficiently – ' he spat out the word as if it were poison ' – shot him twice in the heart.'

Emily sat silently and took in the report.

'At first, we didn't know why he was suddenly killed, but the reason became clear to the Keeper soon enough. One of Marlake's final submissions to the library contained a listing of names he'd hacked off an aide's computer in the office of the American vice president.'

'The vice president's office?' Emily started. The chill in her spine suddenly returned. 'What sort of names?'

'They were divided into two unlabelled categories, though we determined quickly enough that one group was of individuals close to President Samuel Tratham, and the other contained the names of men supporting the Council, together with men close to the vice president. Beyond this, the meaning of the list wasn't immediately clear. It didn't become so until we discovered that the individuals from the first list were starting to show up dead.'

'It was some sort of hit list,' Emily speculated.

'In part. But one with more manipulative ends than just revenge. The end-game here is . . . more dramatic.'

Suddenly the news reports on the scandals in Washington flashed into Emily's mind. The president's advisors being killed off, presumably by terrorist insurgents. The president's actions bringing this on himself, his treachery putting American security at risk. Talk of the imminent collapse of the administration.

'Wait, you're talking about a coup. A conspiracy?'

Athanasius's head gave a slow, knowing nod as his eyes remained fixed on Emily's.

'It doesn't look like President Tratham is going to survive this scandal.'

'But you're saying the scandal's based on a lie,' Emily interjected. 'The online reports I read were saying that the president's aides were being killed off by foreign insurgents – that he's put the nation at risk by behaving in a way that's causing insurgents to attack us on our own soil. You're

suggesting this isn't true – that they weren't killed by terrorists at all.'

'Well, not the kind of terrorists that people suspect. It's
not hit men from the Middle East that are attacking your
compatriots, Dr Wess. Welcome to your first display of the
Council's handiwork.'

CHAPTER 68

12.38 p.m.

Emily's mind stumbled before the magnitude of the revelation. The story that had begun with a colleague's murder and a lost library now encompassed two secret societies, the ancient and ongoing manipulation of world events, and apparently an active coup in Washington. And somehow, ominously, in the mix of it all, there was apparently a role for her. Her earlier mix of fear and anticipation was now at a height.

'But why?' she demanded, breathless. 'Why would this Council go to such lengths to smear the president? What does it have to gain from the act?'

'You've heard that nature abhors a vacuum, yes?' Athanasius questioned in response. 'Well, given what's happened over the past week, it looks as if there will soon be a vacuum at the top of the Executive Branch of the American government. If you want to bring yourself into a position of power, what better way than to create a situation of political suction that will draw your man to the top?'

'But that won't work,' Emily said, her mind racing. 'The

US has a clearly defined chain of command. If the president leaves office, the post doesn't go to some outsider. The vice president will automatically take the office.'

Athanasius's eyes were wide as he connected the final dots for Emily, his voice again almost a whisper. 'Whose name do you think was at the top of the second group on the list?' He gave Emily a long moment to digest the true degree of the conspiracy. He knew that for the young professor, the ancient world and the modern were colliding in almost incomprehensible terms. 'We're not the only ones who know how to use the information at our disposal,' he finally added.

'This is . . . unbelievable,' Emily whispered back. The weight of the information seemed to suppress any more daring speech.

'Our Keeper,' Athanasius continued quietly with his narrative, 'received the list and pieced together its meaning. But by then the Council knew it was in his hands. Two days ago, he met a similar end to his Assistant's.' There was a long, emotive pause before he continued. When he did, his eyes were glistening but firm. 'The only difference was that this time, he knew they were coming. Arno was a practical man, and he knew that if they had found the Assistant Keeper, they would also find him, and that this would certainly mean his death. They couldn't let him live with both the knowledge of their plot and the power of the library at his command. So even though they were killing off the only remaining man who could lead them to the library's location, they took that drastic step. And Arno, rather than strive to protect himself, spent his last days putting a new plan into action.'

Emily's foreboding sense that the story was coming back to herself was confirmed by Athanasius's next words.

'He decided to speed along your recruitment, Dr Wess. He no longer had an additional four years to recruit you, to follow our normal pattern. He had a mere matter of days – days in which to set in motion your entry into the Society.'

'Why didn't he just come and tell me?' Emily queried. 'In those last days, he could have talked to me. Shared this himself. Helped me along.' Emily's sense of loss returned, knowing now that Holmstrand had spent the last days of his life focused on her. But that loss was not just emotional. She suddenly realized she had lost a man who, in the face of what seemed real danger, could have helped her.

Athanasius gave an appreciative smile.

'It is not the way we work,' he reminded her. 'Some things cannot just be given. They have to be discovered. What Arno spent his final days doing was concocting a plan that would both throw the Council off our trail while at the same time helping you to discover the library, our Society, and your role.'

The strange split in Emily's racing mind returned. On the one hand she did not want to hear of 'her role' – of any part she was meant to play in a centuries-old drama steeped in deception, death and destruction. But even through the fear, that other part of her screamed out: the part that relished the need to take a stand, to be strong for a cause that went beyond herself. The tension tore at her. What had before seemed an inspiring quest, a thrill ride that might yield a reputation-building academic discovery, now weighed upon her shoulders like an impossible yoke. She was not sure she wanted such a burden, much less whether she had it in her power to accomplish it.

Athanasius seemed to sense the line of her thought, and leaned forward towards Emily, full of seriousness.

'It isn't an option, this task,' he said. 'Given the magnitude of what is at stake, you have an obligation. You must continue, carry it through to the end.' He watched her expression closely. 'Besides, there is really no choice. You can be absolutely certain that the Council knows who you are by now. Once they know you are connected to the library, they will stop at nothing to find you, to get what you know.'

The words congealed all her amorphous fears.

'But I don't know anything!'

'You do. You are here, with me,' Antoun answered. 'And the Keeper has entrusted you with a charge, one which only you can accomplish. You will need to be on your guard until you complete it.'

Emily's spirit chilled, yet a curiosity swept over her, strong enough to distract her momentarily from the thought of pursuit.

'If everything in the Society is so secret,' she asked, leaning in towards Athanasius, 'if everything is hidden from view, even to you as Librarians, how is it that you personally know so much? How is it that you possess all the details you've just passed on to me?'

Athanasius looked weary, even sad.

'Because, Dr Wess, I was being trained up to be the new Assistant Keeper. Marlake was to retire in two months and

I was being readied to take over his role. That timetable had been moved up after his death, but now, given our current circumstances, things have changed again.' His voice was lower now, barely more than a suggestive whisper. 'A second in command cannot be second without a first.' He kept his gaze steady as Emily leaned towards him.

'Finding the new Keeper has something to do with my recruitment as a Librarian?' Emily asked. 'Am I meant to help you find him?'

'It has everything to do with your recruitment,' Athanasius affirmed, 'but there is no "him".' When he spoke his next words, his eyes were as wide as Emily's. 'Come now, Dr Wess. Surely you understand. I never said you were being recruited to be a Librarian.'

CHAPTER 69

12.45 p.m.

A situation whose dimensions were so vast, so far reaching, that it couldn't possibly get any bigger, just had.

'The Keeper? Holmstrand was training me up to *replace* him?'

'You were the one he had selected,' Athanasius affirmed. 'Of course, your entry into the role wasn't meant to be so . . . dramatic. Or speedy. But when the Council began their attack, the Keeper's intentions had to be stepped up.'

Emily continued to struggle with Athanasius's pronouncements.

'But, why not you?' she asked, sincere in the question. 'You were already in line to become the Assistant Keeper, and you clearly know far more than I do. Why not make you the Keeper and have you train up a new second?'

'It is hard to understand, I know,' Athanasius answered, almost consoling, 'but there is an order and reason to the way we operate. My experiences, my skills, these have been trained and conditioned for a specific role. It is one of importance,

311

one of action, but also one of support. The Keeper saw in you something different – something he felt was important, critical to the role not of supporting, but leading. Something that outweighed your inexperience. Experience can always be gained, and you can learn what you do not know. But the Keeper trusted you, and found in you the degree and scope of character he felt was crucial to the role.'

For most of her academic life, Emily had craved recognition – recognition as intelligent, creative, authoritative. But to hear her character being lauded in such a way now filled her with terror. She was uncertain whether she could ever live up to the expectations set before her, and she saw that the stakes for failure were far higher than a bad journal review or a poor class rating.

At the same time, her intellectual streak remained uneasy with the details Athanasius had related about the library's history and the Society's operations. Clearly they had a powerful foe, but Emily could not shirk the feeling that the library's caretakers had edged around censorship, had blurred the line between 'sharing information' and the outright manipulation of world events in a manner not entirely dissimilar to that of the Council's current presidential plottings. She felt herself positioned between a moral black cloud, and one that was lighter, but still grey.

Is such action right? Precisely what kind of group am I being asked to join? To lead?

She knew, however, that she could not walk away from the task Arno Holmstrand had set before her. What risked being lost for ever was simply of too much value. The object of the Society's care was unparalleled in human history. If its dimensions were as vast and detailed as Athanasius had indicated, then it was, even today, a resource that had no match or equal. It could not be lost. The chilling prospect of being pursued by the Council would have to be met.

With customary speed, Emily's acceptance of a situation congealed into a firm resolve. Whether she had asked for it or not, there was work to be done. She decided to take her courage into her two hands.

'How am I supposed to find it?' she blurted out, breaking the stagnant silence that had settled over them.

Athanasius looked up. His own heart, saddened by the recounting he'd given Emily of the library's recent history, was encouraged by the woman's resolve.

'By carrying on in the same manner you have thus far. By following the guidance the Keeper has left for you.'

Emily hesitated.

'I managed to find my way here because Arno left me two letters and a series of clues in America, which led me to etchings he had somehow managed to have engraved in England and here in Alexandria. But the clue that that pointed me to you was the last one he left. From here, I have nothing to go on.'

Athanasius stood upright. 'That is not precisely the case.' He returned to the filing cabinet from which he had retrieved Arno's letter instructing him to await Emily's arrival. He now picked up an envelope and passed it to Emily.

'I would advise you to keep following the Keeper's lead.'

Emily looked down at the envelope in her hands.

'It came with the letter to me,' Athanasius clarified. The Keeper had always thought two steps ahead.

On the envelope Emily found the same brown ink and handwriting that had characterized Arno's earlier correspondence. Tidily written was a plain phrase: *For Dr Emily Wess – To be collected on arrival.* Evidently, Holmstrand had been more confident than she of her making it this far.

She turned the envelope over and tore it open. A single sheet of paper was folded inside, on which was written a solitary line that she read aloud.

> *Between two continents: the house of the king,*
> *touching the water.*

'Our Keeper was always one for making you think,' said Athanasius, bringing the edges of his lips into a wry smile.

For the first time in the conversation, Emily smiled back with a sense of knowing certainty.

'That may be,' she said, 'but this time, I don't have to. Arno would have known that this would be obvious to me, and it's all the more clear after our conversation.' Athanasius waited. Emily rose to her feet and started to pace the small office in excitement as she drew out the meaning of Holmstrand's cryptic message.

'There is only one city in which a royal palace lies straddled between two continents, and it's a city that you've just finished telling me was part of the library's past. Constantinople, modern day Istanbul. The city sits on a small protrusion of land in the Bosporus, immediately between the land masses of Europe and Asia. It's been riddled with earth-quakes throughout its history for that very reason.' Emily had visited Istanbul twice as a student, and remembered it well.

She suddenly stopped her pacing, and spun around to stand face to face with Athanasius.

'And I know exactly what he means by "the house of the king".'

CHAPTER 70

One hour later – 1.45 p.m. Local time, Alexandria

Jason sat, nonchalantly, at a small round table at the airport coffee kiosk. It was a typical day, and travellers busied themselves in all directions. The other Friend sat inconspicuously on the far side of the courtyard, detached from his colleague.

Beneath the veneer of calm and casual, however, Jason's mind teemed with conflicting emotions. On the one hand, there was the excitement that came from knowing that Emily Wess was staged to be the Society's new Keeper, and that she might be able to lead them to the library itself. On the other hand, that possibility was theoretical – and in the meantime there were new, very real and very immediate threats to the success of the mission in Washington DC. Too many people knew too much and the Society was too far in to back away now. Everything was at risk if Wess or Antoun talked.

He opened his phone and called the first contact in his phonebook, which was simply marked 'Secretary'. A few seconds later, the line connected to Ewan Westerberg's office in New York.

'You heard the conversation?' As ever, Jason began without wasting time on introductions. Only a handful of people in the world had the Secretary's private number, and both men already knew the subject matter of the call.

'Every word,' Westerberg answered. His tone was terse but professional. His ability to retain a commanding composure whatever the circumstances – whether greeting a colleague or ordering an execution – was what gave the man his reputation. 'We were right. Holmstrand has led Emily Wess directly to the Alexandrian Librarian.'

'He's not just a Librarian,' Jason affirmed. 'He's the future Assistant Keeper. We couldn't have hoped for a better find.'

'We knew Alexandria was going to be important,' the Secretary replied, though even he had been surprised at just how high-ranking in the Society Athanasius Antoun had turned out to be. 'Now we have a critical link.'

That was the good news. But both men were more than aware that the tapped conversation had revealed other, more troubling facts, and not solely with respect to the Washington mission.

'Their information on us is – thorough.' Jason's voice was slightly tense.

'They know more about our structure than we thought,' the Secretary acknowledged. Neither had anticipated that the Society knew the Council's workings to the degree Antoun's description revealed. 'Still, what they know pales in comparison to what they do not.'

Jason remained anxious.

'But they know who *you* are, Father.' Even as the last word slipped off his tongue, Jason froze. The slip was unconscionable. The rules he was meant to follow when speaking to the Secretary were firm and unbending. And he had never before faltered.

Ewan Westerberg's response was icy. In its sudden coldness, it was even more terrifying than in its usual restraint.

'What have I told you about referring to me that way?' The statement was not so much a question as a reminder. A threatening reminder.

Jason Westerberg had worked his way to the top of the Council's active arm, even securing a place among the select group of the Secretary's 'Friends', his closest aides, precisely because he had never allowed himself to think of the Secretary as his father, but only as his employer. His connection by birth was irrelevant; only his performance mattered. The two men had a relationship that was entirely professional, and both – especially Jason's father – preferred it that way. It had been the nature of their relationship since his youth, and he knew it would be until death.

'I'm sorry. Sir.' Jason tried to recover his composure over the phone. 'But the point remains true. The Society does know who you are, and now, so does Emily Wess, the woman who was being trained up as their new Keeper.'

'Don't let such matters trouble you, Jason,' the Secretary replied. His rare use of a personal name surprised his son. It was a turn from his icy tone a moment ago. This was as close as Ewan Westerberg came to showing affection, offered now to calm the younger man's agitated state. 'They may have learned something of us, but we have learned something far more critical of them. Even now, we are tracing out every detail on Antoun's life. The overview information we had on him as a candidate Librarian was inconclusive, but with the new materials we've gained from his conversation, I am confident we will be able to break through his guise and find out far more.' He paused. 'Did this man see you?'

'No.'

'Keep it that way. It is better that he not be aware we know anything about him until we've had time to flesh out a deeper background profile. Then you can – ' he paused, giving emphasis to the double-meaning of the words to follow '– *invite him* to share with you whatever else he knows. His tone with Wess was too guarded. He knows more, and he can lead us to his colleagues in the Society. Let the other teams in Cairo keep him in their sights while we gather our intelligence on the man. We'll bring you back in when it's time to convince Antoun to cooperate.'

'And in the meantime?' Jason looked across the small plaza at the other Friend. He knew they would not simply be sitting idly while that research was done.

'You two stay with our principal target. Dr Wess has already determined her next stop on the Keeper's little initiation quest. Don't let her out of your sights.'

'Her flight to Istanbul leaves in under an hour,' Jason noted. 'Our jet will precede her by twenty minutes. I've already arranged for us to be met on arrival. I'll have four men at my disposal there, if they become necessary.'

'Take what you need,' the Secretary replied. 'There cannot be many more steps in this little game the Keeper has arranged for his would-be disciple.'

Jason embraced the thought. The sooner his game was at its end, the sooner Emily Wess could be taken out of the picture all together. Rather than a new threat, the woman might prove herself a double gift to the Council. She would lead them to the library, and by her death would ensure that their work in Washington was not revealed. They would end up with control of the collection as well as the last world superpower.

Jason's adrenaline spiked at the mere thought of the power that lay ahead of them.

From across the Atlantic, the Secretary sensed his son's drive.

'Don't lose your focus, Jason – a little more patience. Emily Wess will show us the door to the object of our attention for thirteen centuries. And when she does, then, my son, you can do what you need to do in order to ensure it is we – and not she – who walk through it.'

CHAPTER 71

Istanbul – 4.55 p.m. Local time (GMT+2)

The wheels of Emily's flight touched down at Istanbul's Ataturk airport at 4.55 p.m. The short flight had been uneventful, but Emily's mind had been too full to allow for the kind of wandering reverie she had experienced on her flight from England. Her thoughts swarmed with the information she had learned from Athanasius in the basement of the Bibliotheca Alexandrina.

A rush of adrenaline had hit her as she learned that Arno Holmstrand had left her another letter, another clue, and one that she could decipher. Istanbul, the modern Islamic and secular face of ancient Christian Constantinople, made sense on every level. It had a royal palace that sat on a point of land jutted between two continents. It had a long intellectual past, which Antoun had confirmed played its part in the library's ancient history. It even followed Alexandria itself in being a royal city named after its founder – the Egyptian metropolis named after Alexander the Great; Constantinople named after Constantine, also called 'the Great'. The parallels were everywhere. Emily knew that this was where she needed to be.

Athanasius had helped to organize the last-minute flight to Istanbul. Twice in the past twenty-four hours Emily had been able to go from the first thought of travel, through booking tickets, boarding and flying, all in a mere matter of hours. The Internet did at times show its helpful face.

Athanasius had also arranged for a local driver to collect Emily at the airport, rather than leave her to struggle with Istanbul's notorious taxi drivers, known to every local for their penchant for overcharging tourists by taking them on the longest possible route between any two points. In a city whose streets wound around hills and coves in an intricate maze, it was easy to fool a passenger. Both Athanasius and Emily had agreed that time was of the essence, and not to be wasted on such unnecessary meanderings.

'The driver is a friend,' Athanasius had told her. 'He'll meet you at the limo ranks. Look for my name.'

Their conversation had ended, and the two of them had parted ways without further discussion. Emily felt that a certain bond had formed between them, but it had arisen out of the dire circumstances at hand. They had left on business-like terms.

Now, 700 miles away, Emily walked off the sky ramp and into the terminal of Ataturk International airport. Her flight had arrived at the tail end of the business day, and the airport bustled with activity.

Slinging her small bag over her shoulder, she scanned the signage for English, marked out in yellow, and began to make her way toward passport control and the exit. The former went more smoothly than she had anticipated, and within minutes she walked out of the far side of the glass corridors at customs, her passport newly stamped with her Turkish entry details, including a visa sticker designed to look like an ornate Turkish rug. Her next stop was a nearby exchange counter, to withdraw an ample supply of Turkish Lira for the day ahead. Athanasius had warned her that few small businesses in Turkey accepted anything but cash.

A satisfying clutch of wrinkled banknotes was soon in hand, and Emily switched on her BlackBerry to phone Michael. She hadn't been able to speak to him since she had left England, and from her perspective, the world itself had changed since then. Michael was more than due for an update, and she could do with the consoling sound of his familiar voice.

The phone rang a few times without connecting, and Emily instinctively felt something was awry. Not answering on the first few rings was unusual. Michael's caller ID always let him know who was calling, and though he screened his calls surreptitiously, hers was a number that always prompted a response. Michael had rarely answered later than the second ring since the first phone call she'd made to him, requesting their first date. She had broken with custom and taken that initial step herself, but on that occasion Michael had taken to the third ring to answer, and Emily had confessed later that she had almost lost her nerve and hung up. That third ring had nearly cost them their relationship, and Michael had never forgotten the symbolism of it.

Emily now glanced at her watch as the phone rang a fourth

time, and a fifth. *5 p.m here* . . . she counted back eight hours on her fingers. *That's nine in the morning in Chicago. He should be up.* She tried to run through Michael's Friday morning routine in her mind. He wouldn't normally go to the office for another hour. Had she forgotten some activity that would be keeping him away from the phone?

Before she could wonder any further, the line connected.

'Hello?' Michael answered. His voice sounded faint over the distant connection.

'It's me,' Emily said, her own voice filled with a relieved happiness.

'Em!' His full voice came across the line. Emily's worries faded.

'I'm so glad you're there,' she said. 'You won't believe what's happened since I talked to you from Oxford.'

There was a slight delay. 'Where are you now?' Michael asked.

'Istanbul.'

'Turkey? I thought you were going to Egypt!'

'I was. I did. I was there. Believe me, Mike, I was there. But it led me here.' She recounted the story of the past day – of her searching the structure in Alexandria, her finding the crest, her discussion with Athanasius. She told him of the library, the Society, the Council, the changes to history as she had known it that these facts suggested. She told him of Arno's latest clue, of her latest ticket and her recent flight. And she told him of the role she was apparently meant to fill. The fear tingled at her spine as she spoke, but she stated the facts clearly and boldly.

As she did, she realized just how fast-paced her life had been over the past forty-eight hours. Somehow, she'd managed to set foot on three different continents in the past day alone.

She continued to fill him in quickly in broad details as she walked the long hallways of the airport towards the taxi and limousine ranks. Then, at the end of her enthusiastic report, she finally paused for breath.

Michael remained silent – for too long. He was not one to keep quiet. Emily's earlier sense of worry swiftly returned, and she realized that Michael had not commented on the news of her strange recruitment, nor even when she spoke of the Council, or the strange role she was apparently meant to fill in the Society. He was simply quiet.

'Mike, what's wrong?' she finally asked.

There was another delay before he answered.

'Emily, your office at Carleton. It was burgled. Your house, too. The police called me about five or six hours ago, in the middle of the night, trying to find you. Somebody broke into both, and made a mess of everything. Shelves emptied, drawers overturned. It sounds like they were completely ransacked.'

Emily's pace slowed. Michael's revelation was immediately deflating, and her temporary rush was all at once at an end, with Michael's news changing the look and feel of everything she had learned.

Conscious of her silence, she asked the first question that came to mind.

'Do they know who did it?' Thoughts of the Council, of its ruthless leader, of the men at his disposal, swirled through her mind.

'No. But . . .' His voice trailed off.

'Mike, what is it? Tell me.' Something more was clearly upsetting him. Emily was now almost at a standstill.

The words he spoke next froze Emily in her tracks.

'Em. These men. They've come for me.'

CHAPTER 72

5.15 p.m.

Emily's tongue seemed locked in her throat. She had never before had the occasion to experience emotional panic, and as she took in Michael's announcement it hit her all the harder for its unfamiliarity. Her skin seemed to go cold, sounds seemed to evaporate from the air around her, her mind became a disorganized fog. And she felt, for the first time in her life, a sense of complete helplessness. Helplessness and a desperate confusion.

'What do you mean, they've come for you? Who? When? Are you okay?' Her words clipped together as she tripped over one on the way to the next. She stood fast in the middle of the airport corridor, fellow passengers shuffling past her, butting arms and jostling as they moved by. But Emily Wess was oblivious to anything other than her fiancé's reply.

'A few hours ago, two men came to interview me,' Michael answered. 'They showed up here at the flat – the apartment – first thing in the morning. At first, I thought they were here about the burglaries at your place, though it seemed strange to me that they would come all the way to Chicago.

'But all they wanted to know about was you. How long you'd worked at the college. Where you had studied before. What your interests were. Whether you spend time away with people that I don't know about, or travel without explanation.' He hesitated, wondering whether to share a final assessment with her, but opted for full honestly. 'These men were sinister. There's no other word for it.'

Emily took in his words as best as she could, her heart now beating at the same frantic pace she had last experienced in Athanasius's office. Michael's quiet tone throughout the conversation now made sense.

'They asked about your travel plans,' he continued, 'what flight you had taken. They even wanted to know how you had booked your ticket – whether it was online, in person, through a friend. Things that couldn't possibly be important in figuring out why your place was robbed.'

'Mike, I'm so sorry. I'm so sorry.'

'And then there were a whole series of questions about political dimensions to your work.'

'Political?'

'Whether you had business partners in Washington, how much you knew about members of the administration, whether you received funding from political parties or lobby groups. The line of questioning was absurd, but aggressive.'

'My God, this is unbelievable.' As her fiancé spoke, Emily felt a rising hatred for the men whom, she now realized, were taking the business of the Library of Alexandria and making it personal. Athanasius had warned her in Alexandria that its opponents would know who she was and would set their sights on her. His warning was proving its worth.

'These men,' Michael continued, 'there was something about them. They were . . . intense. They wore the same grey suits, had the same haircuts, the same behaviours. It was like they were clones of each other. And I'll be damned if either of the bastards work for the local police, or the government. There wasn't a legitimate bone in their bodies.'

At the tones of Michael's defiance, Emily breathed a small sigh of relief. Michael Torrance was nobody's cowering victim. Though Emily's self-assured demeanour and tenacity often caused others to characterize her as the dominant partner, the truth was they were equally matched. He had a strength and resilience about him that inspired her own.

'But,' Michael added, 'I wouldn't want to cross those men again. They seemed to know the answers to their questions before they asked them. I had the distinct sense I was being tested, not questioned.' This time the pause in his voice was noticeably longer. 'I don't want to know what they would have done if I gave them an answer they weren't expecting.'

Emily tried to temper the swirling mix of emotions surging through her: anger, hatred, fear, confusion. She needed to follow Michael's example and think calmly about what this meant. The Council – that was what Athanasius had called the group that worked against the library – had to be the group behind this. Behind the ransacking of her office and house, behind the 'interview' with Michael. They were obviously looking for her.

They were looking for her, and were willing to get to her

by whatever means were required. Even her fiancé. The hatred in her gut rose again, overpowering the hard ball of fear. She was no longer safe, but she was also no longer an objective observer. Up until this moment, the quest on which Arno Holmstrand had set her had been precisely the sort of mystery that Emily had always secretly hoped one day to be involved in: the kind that takes a small, insignificant person and thrusts them into the full dimensions of history. And here she was, a novice professor, cast into a full-feature role in a drama that stretched from Pharaohs to modern governments, across centuries and continents. It was, to that point, utterly perfect. But with the attack on Michael – and she considered it an attack, an invasion, even if they had only questioned him – that scope was inverted. Emily was no longer simply being thrust into history; history was being thrust at Emily Wess. What had formerly been impersonal events were now entirely, unacceptably personal.

'Michael,' Emily interjected, returning to the moment, 'these men, these people, they're dangerous. I had no idea they would come after you.'

'You know who they are?' Michael wasn't sure whether the thought comforted him, or only made him fear more for her safety.

'I have an idea,' she answered. 'The man I spoke to told me that this other group, this Council, has what I suppose amounts to operatives. He called them their "friends".'

'But why were they asking about Washington?' Michael persisted. 'What does the library have to do with what's going on there? Is it somehow connected to the scandals?'

Emily almost replied, wanting to draw her fiancé into the secret of the century, but she bit her lip. Instinctively, she felt that filling Michael in on the details of the Council's plot with the vice president would only put him in more danger, and in this moment she acknowledged her own protective instincts. That information had been behind the death of Arno Holmstrand, but also, she now knew, at least four other men.

Instead, she made an emphatic pronouncement.

'I have to come home.' The idea was not one she had thought through; it was not a plan. It was simply the obvious action that had to be taken. She couldn't continue on her little quest when her life and his were clearly at risk. She might love adventure, but she was not that selfish. 'I'm still in the airport. I'm sure I can get a flight back later this evening.'

There was another lull in their conversation, but when Michael answered, it wasn't with the response Emily had expected.

'No. Absolutely not.'

'Mike, I'm not about to keep playing detective without you when the stakes are this high. This was meant to just be a quick trip away to find a library for a colleague.'

Michael's sudden firmness of tone, however, suggested he had come to see the situation as a challenge and wasn't about to let Emily abandon it simply for his sake.

'Em, use some sense here. They've had their little interview with me. Unpleasant yes, but done. And they've gone. They've no reason to come back for me. But you, you – ' he looked for the right words '– you can't possibly still think this is all some little game of pretend detectives. Even I can see real history here, and more than just ancient, if it's connected in any way to what's going on in DC.' His tone was forceful, resilient, and Emily heard the resolve in it.

'I still think I should fly back,' she said. 'I can investigate what I've learned from there. Do some research. Get things in order. Be with you.'

'No way,' Michael answered. 'You're not using me as an excuse. Fly here if you like. My door will be locked.'

Emily finally smiled properly, with a laugh to match. She was marrying the right man. Adventurous, strong, belligerent. Wonderful. Yet even as the laughter subsided, Michael seemed to sense that Emily's suggestion of flying back might not only be out of concern for him. Even a strong woman could feel fear.

'I could fly to you,' he suggested spontaneously. 'Join you for whatever's ahead.'

Emily's emotions urged a 'yes' to fall from her lips, but she held back the word. She did not want them both in danger, if danger was to come.

'No, you hold down the fort,' she finally answered. 'But I'm giving this one more day. That's all. And only if they leave you alone. If you so much as get a phone call you weren't expecting, I'm out of here. I want a husband to come back to.'

'Sounds fair,' he said. He, too, knew when to give in.

What Emily wanted to say next seemed trite, but she had to say it.

'Be careful, Michael. I love you.'

'Me? I plan on being in my office twenty-four hours a day for the next three,' he answered, 'getting my project ready, and hopefully running with the plans once I make the sale. Try not to worry. Just make sure you take your own advice. If these men came here, Emily, it means they are willing to go anywhere.' He let his words sink in. 'Watch your back.'

CHAPTER 73

5.25 p.m.

The aftermath of Emily's conversation with Michael was a tension that settled in her chest.

It was enough to make any sane person paranoid, and Emily noticed a new nervousness in her step. The crowded airport felt less secure than it had before the call and she glanced suspiciously at every passerby.

Don't panic, she told herself. *It's irrational to overreact*. It was one of those commands that was easy to issue, but tended not to work in practice. Her nerves were in no way calmed.

Emily rounded a corner and came to a long set of glass doors leading to the exterior of the airport and the kerbside limo ranks. Men with small placards lined the ranks, each standing next to polished black sedans, looking the picture of expensive perfection and professionalism.

Each, save for one. At the right of the row of cars, a small man leaned against a diminutive, grey Audi with a sign marked 'Dr Antoun'. His suit was tattered and crumpled, and his hair looked as if it had never been threatened by a comb, though he wore an enormous smile, so wide and gaping that it almost appeared manufactured. He grinned and nodded at each passerby, waiting for one to nod back and step towards him.

Athanasius may indeed have arranged for Emily to be met by one of his friends, but it was apparently a friend on a budget.

She nodded to the driver and approached the small car.

'I'm Emily Wess, Dr Antoun's – ' she didn't know what word to use ' – colleague.' She stood as the small man opened the Audi's rear passenger door with a smile, saw her in and closed it behind her. Emily took to her seat and fastened her belt.

As she settled into the car and it pulled away from the curb, Emily's whole body suddenly tensed. Just at the edge of her peripheral vision, a patch of colour grabbed her attention. Or rather, a patch devoid of colour: one of muffled, conspicuous grey. As the sight registered, she spun her head back to the curb. She was sure that she'd spotted two men, dressed in grey, standing off to the side, just out of plain view, but when she looked closely, there was no one there but the other drivers, waiting for their charges.

I'm being paranoid, she chided herself, straightening in her seat and counting her heartbeat back to something approaching normal.

CHAPTER 74

5.29 p.m.

Three streets behind her, Jason Westerberg edged up the speed of a black sedan, keeping a steady distance from Emily Wess's car. In the back seat, his partner sat calmly, playing the part of his passenger. The silencer affixed to the gun in his lap was the only thing that set him apart from a routine airport pick-up.

Without speaking, the Friends followed their target.

CHAPTER 75

General Brad Huskins looked across the limousine's interior at the vice president. Given the circumstances, the man looked composed, confident and prepared – all qualities that were desirable in a nation's chief political leader.

'The arrest of the president is planned for Sunday morning at ten a.m.,' the secretary of defence stated. Seated next to the vice president, Ashton Davis had spent most of the journey's first five minutes running through the procedures ahead of them. Ahead of the nation. 'As the arrest will take place under the regulations of military law, it will be performed by military hands.'

'I will arrest him myself,' General Huskins noted.

The vice president nodded and turned to Brad Whitley.

'I trust you can ensure that there is not going to be any protest or interruption from your agents in the White House?'

'None,' the director of the Secret Service answered. 'Both

337

the presidential and vice presidential details are being briefed this afternoon, and our entire Washington staff will have their new marching orders within seconds of the operation taking place.'

'I don't want some service agent botching a smooth and controlled arrest by attempting to throw himself in front of the president,' the general stated.

'It's not going to be an issue,' Whitley insisted. 'My men are tasked to protect the president of the United States. The *legitimate* president. They are not going to resist the legal removal of a traitor.'

Both General Huskins and the secretary of defence nodded, understanding. Davis looked out the tinted window of the limousine and saw the marble of the Capitol building shimmer in the sunlight. Behind it stood the smaller, but for today's business more powerful, complex that housed the United States Supreme Court.

'We'll arrive at Chief Justice Angela Robbins's office in a few moments,' he said, turning his attention back to the other men in the car. 'She'll clarify the constitutional details on the transfer of executive power and run through the process. Whether or not you immediately take up Tratham's office of president, or whether you simply take up executive control as vice president until such time as Tratham is convicted of treason and thus ineligible to hold office, will be her call. But in either case, the practical result is the same.'

'You'll be running the show.' The comment came from General Huskins, who uttered it with full seriousness.

A silence lingered for a few moments. It was broken only

as the car approached the back entrance to the Supreme Court building.

'This is going to be the biggest trial our country has faced since its founding,' Brad Whitley said.

'Thank God we've got clear and reasoned men like you to see us through it.'

CHAPTER 76

Istanbul – 5.35 p.m.

The small car Athanasius had arranged to collect Emily now sped her along the main coastal road between the airport and the heart of Istanbul: a smart, modern highway with the unlikely name of Kennedy Caddesi. The old Audi, which looked to be about twenty years shy of the newest model in their fleet, creaked and groaned with the effort of the drive. Her driver, whose smile seemed immovable but who clearly spoke no English, obviously intended to get to their destination as fast as possible.

Emily strove to piece together the evidence of the day. Focusing on the actual data at hand helped keep her mind from dwelling on the worry she felt for Michael and the nervousness she felt for herself. If she didn't feed her attention with the facts of the puzzle before her, she felt she would go mad – either from anxiety for Michael's safety; or the ongoing sense of guilt she felt at continuing here, away from him; or the threat to her own safety that she knew was real, even if unseen. So it was to the materials she had learned over the past day that she forced her mind to turn.

Whatever had been the cause of its departure, the original Library of Alexandria had obviously left the city. Scholarship had thought it lost, or destroyed. She now knew it had been hidden, and covertly moved. Relocating it to Constantinople made sense. The new imperial capital of the Empire was secure and safe. The city had become a dominant world centre after the decline of Rome, and would remain so until it fell to the Ottoman Turks almost 1,000 years later, in 1453. Even then, it had remained a city of imperial significance, becoming the heart of the great Islamic Empire, with its powerful Sultanate and unstoppable armies, until that, too, disappeared. The advent of modern Turkey in 1923 had changed the landscape. For the first time since Constantine had consecrated it for himself in AD 330, the city was not a royal stronghold.

If the library had indeed been here, then it made a certain kind of sense that Holmstrand would lead her to the spot as part of its discovery. Emily couldn't help but feel that Arno was deliberately causing her to trace out the history of the library in her own journey, as if this would somehow bring her closer to it . . . personally? Emotionally?

Whatever the drive, one fact was of particular interest. If Athanasius was right, and the library hadn't left Constantinople until the middle of the sixteenth century, then it had remained here through the great transfer of powers the century before. It had arrived in the Imperial City under the banner of a Byzantine king. It left under the flag of the Ottomans.

Which meant that 'the palace of the king' that Arno's latest clue described couldn't be the residence of the Byzantine Emperor who had been enthroned in the immense Hagia Sophia Church, now a museum. As Emily's car drove past it, she felt certain that this was the surface meaning of Arno's words, meant to be easily deciphered but pointing in the wrong direction. Constantinople's kings had been glorious, and their palace, though now largely in ruins and in a state of showy excavation, was a famous tourist attraction in the modern city. Mention 'the king's house' in Istanbul, and it was there that you would be directed.

But if the library truly had existed here past the fall of Byzantium and Constantinople, into the period of Islamic conquest, then the palace of the king must refer to something different. It must refer, Emily felt certain, to the residence of the Ottoman Sultan. The same residence, known as Topkapi Palace, towards which the small Audi was now barrelling with all the speed it could muster.

CHAPTER 77

6.05 p.m.

As the car rounded a sharp bend on to Kabaskal Street, two brief pings emanated from Emily's jacket pocket, followed a moment later by two more. She reached into her jacket and retrieved her BlackBerry, its small screen illuminated and announcing the arrival of two text messages. A moment later Emily examined the messages listing, seeing next to both a country code and number she did not recognize.

Opening the first, its source quickly became clear. A brief personal message began the text: FROM ATHANASIUS: SO THAT YOU HAVE EVERYTHING IN YOUR HANDS WHEN YOU ARRIVE AT YOUR GOAL.

Emily spun her thumb over the trackball to scroll down, the rest of the message containing a listing of names – names she did not recognize. Then, in the second message, another list of names. But on this list, the names stood out.

The first was Jefferson Hines, the vice president of the United States of America.

As the car pulled to a halt outside the Topkapi Palace, Emily realized what she held in her hand. It was the list that had sent Arno Holmstrand to his grave.

CHAPTER 78

The secretary loomed over the men at the black table, peering over their shoulders as their fingers danced atop the keyboards attached to their dedicated computer terminals. They, like all employees of the Council, were among the best in their field, and the materials they had already assembled from Athanasius Antoun's conversation with Emily Wess were formidable. More continued to be compiled as they traced out names and places from the transcript, hacked into personal records and telephone logs, and cross-referenced the backgrounds of persons whose identities they had taken from face recognition scans of people entering and leaving the Bibliotheca Alexandrina. 'Leaving no stone unturned' was a method of investigation that had become vastly more detailed with the advent of computer hacking.

Ewan assessed what he already knew.

'We know Antoun's been trained up to take on the secondary role in the Society,' he said, his words aimed at no one in particular. 'Which by his own admission means he would have become one of the two people who know the location of the library itself.'

'But he hadn't yet taken on the role,' one of the advisors noted. 'We got to Marlake first, before the succession happened.'

'So Antoun said,' Ewan confirmed. He looked down at the transcript on the table. 'It still stands to figure, however, that his work over the last several months would have been centred on assuming the role – learning the information he would be required to know, making contacts, establishing groundworks, and so on.'

'His phone records are extensive,' a computer tech interjected. 'The number of calls made and received began to increase dramatically in February, and has remained high ever since. I've spot checked random recordings from the taps we've had on the Bibliotheca Alexandrina's telecommunications system, but none of his conversations are revealing. It's probably why they never raised any alarms before. If they're discussing anything related to the library, it's done in a coded way. His conversations are all about books, acquisitions and ordinary business.'

'Of course he's not going to speak openly about the library,' the Secretary replied, 'and he's not going to encrypt his calls. He must know we would spot that immediately. It would have given him away.'

Suddenly, an idea began to form in Ewan's mind.

'Richard,' he said, looking to one of the hackers, 'plot his telephone calls on a map. Give me a visual image of where he's been calling.'

'Yes, sir,' the man answered, and his fingers began to race over his keyboard. In a few moments, a standard Mercator projection map of the world appeared on his screen, and small red dots began to plot themselves on top of it, each marking a specific city. When the red dots were finished, an identical routine was carried out in blue.

'The red points are calls made from Antoun to the location, the blue are calls made to him from the location,' Richard said. 'The plot is for the past six months of phone records.'

The men huddled around the computer's display, scrutinizing. After a few moments of studious silence had passed, the Secretary spoke.

'Tell me what stands out to you about this map,' he ordered. An idea was gaining force in his mind, but he wanted it verified by others.

'Well,' one of his advisors replied, keeping his eyes trained on the screen, 'he's clearly made a lot of calls.'

'Yes, yes,' Ewan answered, annoyed by the vacuous and obvious observation. 'But look more closely. On this map, what location is conspicuously absent, given what we've learned from Antoun's conversation with Wess?' All eyes scanned over the display with renewed focus.

At last, the second computer tech spotted it.

'Got it,' he said, excited. 'It's Istanbul. There's not a single call made or received in the past six months from within Istanbul, or any city in proximity to it.'

The observation exactly confirmed what the Secretary had

noticed. Istanbul, where Emily Wess and Jason and his team were, was a gaping blank on the call record. The conclusion seemed clear.

'The library cannot be there,' he said. 'It may be a historical site of the vault, but it's no longer active. The new Assistant Keeper's contacts confirm this.'

'So Emily Wess is wrong in interpreting the Keeper's message as pointing to Istanbul?'

'No,' the Secretary answered. 'I'm sure she's right. But the Keeper is doing what he always did: deceiving, manipulating, drawing out the routine. It's just another step in his game of cat and mouse. Let Wess go, see whatever drivel has been left for her there. We need to skip a step ahead.' He looked back to the map, as did his colleagues.

'One other location stands out,' the hacker Richard said. 'England is spotted with frequent calls, both to and from.' Ewan looked more closely at the region.

'Zoom in on the UK,' he ordered. A few seconds later, the United Kingdom filled the whole of the display, marked with a concentration of red and blue dots in Oxfordshire, a large number in Oxford itself.

Oxford. Another thought triggered in the Secretary's mind. 'Somebody call up the inventory of books retrieved from Wess's house.' The second tech retrieved the surveillance analysis, and Ewan scanned down the book list. A whole column was taken up with books on Oxford. Emily Wess had been there as a post-graduate student.

'Wess was in Oxford,' he said, thinking aloud, the pace of his words increasing. 'The Keeper had been in Oxford on several occasions over his career. Antoun's call sheet is concentrated here . . .'

'But we were in Oxford yesterday,' an advisor noted, 'at the church. The destruction was a ruse.'

'Of course it was,' Ewan answered. 'The church was a deception. But Oxford, it appears, was not.'

As the Secretary spoke, Richard continued to type, manoeuvring his way through the full record of Athanasius Antoun's email correspondence. For a moment there was a lull in his movements, and at last he looked up to the Secretary.

'Sir, there's something here you should see.'

Ewan moved closer to his terminal and looked towards the screen.

'This image was attached to a blank email sent to Antoun a little over three months ago from a Yahoo account pinged to an IP address in Oxford. It didn't set off any alerts at the time, but then we weren't looking in such detail.' He clicked his mouse, and a postcard photograph of Westminster Abbey appeared on the screen. The Secretary lifted an eyebrow.

'Westminster?'

'Right,' Richard answered. 'But that's not the real picture. Turns out it's an encrypted JPEG file.'

'Translate,' the Secretary ordered. He tended to leave the teching to the techs, and was not familiar with the vocabulary.

'It's a photo file designed to show a certain image when opened normally. But when it is decrypted, the true photo becomes visible.'

The Secretary checked a rising anticipation.

'Can you decrypt it?'

'Of course,' Richard answered. 'I already have. It wasn't the world's simplest encryption algorithm, but it certainly wasn't the most complex. JPEG encryption isn't meant as a high-level encoding system. It's generally used for simple deception. You'd have no idea a second photo was hidden in there unless you were specifically looking for it.'

'I don't care,' the Secretary dismissed, anxiously. 'Show me the real photograph.' A few mouse clicks later, and a different photo appeared on the screen.

A new symbol lay before the Secretary's eyes, carved in stone and taken from a position far beneath. It was a glyph, a figurative carving affixed to a decorative stone ceiling. And its form was distinctive.

In that moment, Ewan knew exactly where he needed to go, and what he needed to do. The library's location was as clear to him as the image before his eyes.

In the same moment, one of the techs looked up from his display anxiously.

'We've just picked up activity on Emily Wess's cell phone in Istanbul.'

'Details,' Ewan barked. The man clicked through a few screens on his computer, speaking as he typed.

'She's just received two SMS text messages, both from the same source. The origin number is in Egypt. We'll have a full trace in a moment.'

'Can you get the text of the messages?'

'Absolutely.' A series of keystrokes temporarily broke the flow of the conversation. When the tech looked back up to the Secretary, his face was sober. 'Both messages are lists of names.'

Ewan walked over to the man's display and looked over his shoulder at the messages shown on the screen. The two text messages together contained the list. The leak. The spreading leak.

Without saying another word to the men in the room, he calmly removed a slender cell phone from his breast pocket, dialled and held it to his ear.

'Your objective has changed,' he said when the line connected through to Jason in a car in Istanbul.

'It is time to terminate Emily Wess. See if she knows anything else, then send her out of this life.'

CHAPTER 79

Istanbul, Topkapi Palace – 6.15 p.m. Local time

Emily paused at the entrance gate to the palace to pay the 20 Turkish lira entrance fee, and then made her way across the cultivated courtyard garden to the main complex.

The palace, like so many other sights Emily had seen in the past two days, was designed to make an impression. But it did so in a way unlike either the lofty and learned architecture of Oxford University, or the glass-and-stone modernism of the new Alexandrian Library. The palace that had been home to the Sultans since it was constructed in 1478 by Mehmet 'The Conqueror' – who had taken the city from the Christians and brought to an end the Byzantine and Roman Empires – was a traditional vision of mixed Islamic design. No two buildings looked the same, and bright colouring – almost entirely absent in Oxford and Alexandria – was the *modus operandi* of the Ottoman decorators. Blue, red and gold tiles lined buildings, inside and out; painted colonnades supported gold-leafed, angular canopies; and fountains dotted every corner and square. The complex itself, occupying some

80,000 square metres on the top of Seraglio Point, was more like a small village of royal buildings and halls than it was a single structure.

Emily knew a little about Topkapi, perhaps slightly more than the casual tourist without a historical consciousness, but not a great deal more than was described in the tour pamphlet she had received with her entrance ticket.

Ottoman Sultans had occupied Topkapi Palace from the days of Mehmet the Conqueror until 1856. In that function it had been home to the immense royal family, including the multitude of imperial wives and consorts and their children. A whole section of the grounds, known as the 'Harem', formed a traditional part of all Ottoman royal residences, in which the regent himself lived with the closest members of his family. The palace, however, was also home to the offices of state, including the residences of viziers and advisors, all of whom the Sultan kept close to home, literally. Within its walls also resided the royal treasury, stables, parade and cere- monial grounds, armouries, hospitals, baths, mosques, audi- ence halls – everything a reigning monarch could require, leaving him with little need to engage in the risky business of going out among the crowded and unruly populace any more than absolutely necessary.

The palace had become a museum in the 1840s, after the Sultans had decided to move elsewhere. It was officially made an institution of the new Turkish government's Museums Directorate by Kemal Ataturk in 1924, and so it remained today. In this function, not only did Topkapi provide a remark- able view and experience of Ottoman life at its highest levels to the tourist, but it also housed collections of Islamic and Ottoman interest that went beyond royal history. The traditional art of painted ceramics and tiles was much on display, and a relic room near one of the palace mosques housed a number of important artefacts of Islamic heritage. Among these was the museum's most prized item: a single hair from Mohammed's beard, preserved in a glass case in a dedicated room, alongside which a Muslim cleric perpetually read verses from the Qur'an.

Emily took in the scene as she walked through the complex, which even through the tense events of the day was a thing of beauty that had to be admired. As the cool of the evening started to creep in over the point, she walked along a stone pathway, bordered by well-maintained flowers, towards the Baghdad Pavilion in the palace's north-eastern corner. Fountains flowed on all sides. One piece of history that pushed its way out of her memory and through her scattered thoughts was the purpose these served: the gentle sound they produced was intended to be more than beautiful and relaxing. It was an effective source of 'white noise', helping to muffle the sounds of conversations the Sultan might have with his advisors in the midst of the crowded palace. Fountains were strategically located near the windows and entrances of all the major audience chambers and privy meeting rooms, keeping any would-be spies at bay, at least as far as they could attempt to hear the royal voice.

The beauty and the history, however, were set today in the context of something far greater, with dimensions that were not only awe-inspiring but terrifying. Emily cast every other glance over her shoulder, seeking any suspicious figures. The men she thought she'd seen at the airport might have been the fruit of paranoia, but reality couldn't be ignored. Athanasius's 'Council' was a reality, willing to stop at nothing to attain its aims. They had sought out Michael, and that meant they knew all about her. Perhaps even the fact that she now possessed the lists of names that were seemingly at the heart of their current actions. She knew they were no longer the foe merely of the Society. They were her foes as well, and Emily felt certain they would be hunting their prey.

She stepped into a red and white marble pavilion, built to commemorate a military campaign in Baghdad in the 17th century, now surrounded by carefully groomed trees and flowers. The kiosk was at the far corner of Topkapi, in the innermost sanctum of the royal grounds. Here, from an artfully concealed vantage point, she saw what, in the heyday of the Empire, few save the upper classes and nobility would have seen: an uninterrupted view out over the city and seas beneath from the vantage point of imperial might and strength. The Sultan had literally been able to stand in his garden and look down upon his empire.

And that view troubled Emily.

From the elevated corner of the palace she could look out at the city proper in one direction, and on the conflux of seas in the other. At the tip of Istanbul's central peninsula, the Marmara Sea, the Bosporus and Golden Horn all converged, giving the city its prime location for shipping and trade. Emily looked down on the waters far below the hilltop enclave.

Far below.

The distance, at this moment, proved unsettling. It did not fit. Emily kept her gaze on the waters below, but her certainty that this was the correct palace was quickly disappearing. Had she made a mistake?

Topkapi Palace stood on its hill, overlooking the water, but Arno's letter in Alexandria had spoken of the house of the king 'touching the water'. *Touching.* It was a strange phrase, but that fact gave it added weight in Emily's mind. If she had learned anything about Arno Holmstrand over the past two days, it was that his phrasing was too precise for it not to be meaningful. When he said something, he meant it; and he meant it exactly the way he said it.

As she forced herself to hear the full precision of Arno's words, the plain fact of the matter was suddenly as clear as the sea far below her. The palace and the seas were in proximity – but they did not meet. They did not touch. Which could mean only one thing.

Topkapi was the wrong palace.

CHAPTER 80

6.30 p.m.

Emily turned on her heels and walked back towards the main gate. Each step solidified the realization that the Topkapi Palace could not be the 'house of the king' toward which Arno's clue was meant to direct her. It was the local variation of Holmstrand's subterfuge that had first had Emily searching the ruins of the University Church of St Mary in Oxford: the obvious solution, designed to throw off would-be pursuers who may have found the clue she now clutched to her chest. The concealment here was two layers deep. The clue did not point to the first imperial palace most would associate with Constantinople – that of the Emperors – but to the residence of the Sultans. But there was a second layer of deception.

The house of the king, touching the water. It had to point elsewhere. There had to be another palace. Though Emily now appreciated the need Arno had felt to conceal his clues, it still left her with a new puzzle to solve.

A young man sat behind the plexiglass window of the

ticket booth as Emily approached, attentively waiting for business. He struck Emily as the kind of worker keen to please, which would be helpful in the course of the strange dialogue she knew was about to come.

'Excuse me, I have a question,' she blurted, even before she'd fully reached the window.

'Yes? How can I help?' The young man sat upright, a professional smile immediately covering his face. Emily's assessment had been correct.

'This isn't the palace I want.'

The man, despite his best intention, gave a confused look. English wasn't his first language, but even if it had been, the statement was unexpected.

'Excuse me?'

'Sorry. I think I'm meant to be visiting a different royal palace. This one doesn't match the – ' she hesitated '– the description I was given. Forgive a stupid tourist!' She tried to coax back the worker's friendly smile. Innocent confusion, rather than glaring intensity, was likely to get her further in this conversation, and more quickly. 'Are there other residences of the Sultans here in Istanbul?'

'There are two,' the museum worker offered, hesitantly. 'Yildiz and Dolmabahce. But this one is the most famous.' He was clearly proud of his surroundings, and his chest puffed up slightly.

'Where are the others?' Emily asked. 'Is one near the water?'

'Yildiz is in the city,' came the answer. 'But Dolmabahce is on the sea.' Emily took in the magic words.

'It is also an important place,' the guide continued,

deigning to give it honourable mention, though only after his own Topkapi. 'Ataturk was there. Very important for Turkish history.'

'How do I get there?'

'You can go by bus or car, but it's faster by ferry. Take the boat from Emınönü, down the hill.' He handed Emily a small brochure for Dolmabahce Palace and a ferry schedule from the stand at his side.

'Thanks, that's great.' Emily beamed her appreciation at the young man.

'But,' the worker added, 'you'll have to wait for tomorrow. Here we are open until seven, but Dolmabahce Palace is open only until five, so it is closed for today.'

The speed at which Emily's demeanour went from excited to crestfallen was astonishing. Tomorrow morning seemed impossibly far away. She had meant what she said to Michael on the phone: one more day was all she was willing to stay away from him.

The man seemed to sense her disappointment.

'That is,' he continued, 'unless you're interested in Franco-Turkish relations.'

Emily looked up.

'Pardon me?'

'There is a lecture at Dolmabahce tonight on relationships between France and Turkey over the past century. The speaker is a French politician – ' he picked up a flyer from his desk and looked down at the name ' – Jean-Marc Letrouc.' He passed the flyer to Emily. 'The talk starts at seven. If you get the last ferry over, you might just make it.'

Emily looked at the man with a sense of overwhelming gratitude. Had they not been separated by a plate of plexiglass, she would have reached over and hugged him.

Emily Wess did not harbour the slightest interest whatsoever in Franco-Turkish relations, but this evening she was willing to make an exception. Whatever it took to get her into the palace. The right palace.

She picked up the leaflets, passed the worker a small handful of change to tip him for his services, and made her way towards the sea.

CHAPTER 81

Jason turned to his partner, a solemn look on his face, anticipation already stirring in his chest. His conversation with the Secretary had been short and to the point.

'Our aim has changed,' he reported to the other Friend. 'Wess is to be terminated at the next available opportunity following the extraction of whatever information she possesses.'

His partner raised his brow, though did not reply. They had invested a great deal of time and energy into tracking her, and she still seemed to be following the Keeper's leads. To kill her now was a surprising turn. There was much that hung in the balance in Washington, he knew, but Wess might be leading them to something far greater – to the library itself.

'We'll stop her the next time she's alone,' Jason continued. 'We've been told to interrogate her briefly, see if she knows anything beyond what we've already gained. You'll relieve her of her cell phone and anything else on her person. We're to make damned sure the list hasn't got further than her phone. When we've got everything, we'll finish the job.'

'We can take her out now,' his partner replied. They were tracking Wess down a steep incline that led towards the ports. She had obviously decided that Topkapi was not the palace she was meant to find, and was making her way towards Dolmabahce. The Council had scouted both palaces multiple times over numerous years. Until minutes ago, the Friends' plan had been to follow Emily Wess on the ferry and in her search of Dolmabahce. But if that was no longer the intention, they might as well eliminate their target immediately. 'We can wait until she crosses the next major road, and take her out.'

'No,' Jason answered. 'The Secretary wants it done quietly, with no witnesses. And out of sight, where her body won't be discovered for a while. We don't need a police investigation marring what's coming.'

His partner nodded. So it would be. Emily Wess would die alone, out of sight, stripped of whatever relevant knowledge she might still possess. He looked at Jason and noticed in his eyes a spark – one that was far more intense than would burn simply for the execution of a potential leak. There was more there. It was . . . expectation. The observation brought him a swell of anticipation. In light of their new orders and the Secretary's call a moment ago, he interpreted Jason's look to mean only one thing.

The Secretary had located the library.

CHAPTER 82

6.45 p.m.

Emily left the grounds of Topkapi palace and pointed herself down the hill toward the northern coast of Istanbul's central peninsula. She couldn't shake the feeling that she was being watched, followed, and yet the need to make the final ferry left her with little option but risk the open streets. The schedule she had been given showed the last boat from the Emınönü port to Besiktas, the closest to Dolmabahce Palace, sailing at 7 p.m. exactly. It was marked as a short journey, only fifteen minutes in length. If Emily could get there in time, and if she wasn't interrupted or intercepted, she would arrive at the palace only twenty or so minutes into the evening's lecture. The introductions and pleasantries before the talk itself would surely take at least that long – Emily knew only too well how important a good introduction was to most academics. She just had to hope that the evening wasn't going to be overly formal on protocol, and that they would still be letting people in.

As long as I can get through the door, she thought, *I can try to find a way to disappear into the palace grounds.*

The walk down the steep central hill of the city, however, was longer than it looked, and Emily increased her pace as she saw the hands of her watch edge closer to seven o'clock. She couldn't allow herself to miss this boat.

She rounded a corner and was faced with a main thoroughfare running along the north-facing coast. Across it, jutting out into the water, was Eminönü: a collection of docks, boats and kiosks crowded with people. Darting through the road's busy traffic, Emily crossed to the port and made her way to the stands of small, two-storey ferry boats lining the wooden gangways.

'Besiktas? Dolmabahce?' she asked a man who looked official in a typical dockworker sort of way: a greasy shirt, tired hat and a hand full of tickets and banknotes.

The potbellied man grunted around his half-smoked cigarette and gestured towards a ferry on the far end of the dock. 'Pay on boat.' He resumed counting his bills.

Emily quickly crossed to the craft, which was already throttling its engines and making ready to depart. Jumping on board, she handed over twelve lira for a ticket and ascended the few steps to the upper balcony level. Only when the remaining crowd of last-minute passengers had boarded and the the ferry was fully in motion, the impressive skyline of the peninsula beginning to recede, did she allow herself to catch her breath. She had made the boat, and leaping onto a moving ferry was as good a way as any to reassure herself that she had lost any potential followers. She moved to the white metal railing at the edge of the balcony and looked out over the scene before her.

To the ferry's rear stood the towering mass of the hill she had just descended, topped by the grand domes of Hagia Sophia and the Blue Mosque, with the walls and balustrades of Topkapi at their side. Minarets from countless mosques lined the whole skyline, and Emily couldn't help but think that it was a scene that could have come out of any medieval Eastern storybook.

She turned her body and faced forward with the motion of the boat. On her left side stood Europe. On her right, Asia, with the Bosporus serving as the narrow straight between the two great land masses. Trade had flourished here for millennia. Even though the buildings on both sides now bore the clear imprints of modernity, dotted with radio antennae and television satellite dishes, and even though cars loudly sounded their horns on busy streets all around, Emily felt that there was something timeless about Istanbul. One city encompassing two continents, serving as the centre of two great Empires – and now, the Turkish Republic. Even if the political capital today was Ankara, it was Istanbul that would always be the heart of Turkey.

On the left of her vision, Dolmabahce Palace began to come into view. The sight couldn't be more different from that of the great Topkapi Palace. Emily unfolded the small brochure the ticket agent had given her, intent to take in whatever basic information she could to prepare her for the search that lay ahead.

Dolmabahce had taken over from Topkapi Palace as the

imperial residence in 1856, when Sultan Abdulmecid I desired to have a state manor that looked more like those of his European counterparts. His wishes were met with a huge complex that mixed architectural styles from across Europe's history: Baroque, Neoclassical, Rococo – anything but traditional Ottoman. Its identity as a palace of the Sultans was to come through its decoration, not its design.

As she watched it come more fully into view, Emily realized it had oddly attained the desired effect of a European look. It seemed a strange mixture of Versailles, Buckingham Palace and an Italian stately home. She couldn't help but think that Michael would consider it an architectural nightmare – an inbreeding of influences that left it with no distinguishable style. But it certainly impressed. The word 'breathtaking', Emily thought, would not be too much.

Inside, her pamphlet continued, Dolmabahce was designed around the traditional Ottoman division of public space and harem, or family quarters, that Emily had witnessed at Topkapi. But everything on the interior was done in spades, and done to overwhelm. Two of the most famous features, the Crystal Staircase and the central chandelier, were cases in point. The staircase's name came from the fact that its banisters were made of solid Baccarat crystal, while the chandelier, given to the Sultan by Queen Victoria, was then and remained today the largest in the world, weighing in at four-and-a-half tonnes and branching out into 750 lamps. Every item in the palace was gilded, bejewelled, embossed or emblazoned, making every item priceless, and every vision overwhelming.

Emily was not at all surprised to read that the only access

to Dolmabahce was by guided tour. None of the free roaming of the grounds that she had experienced at Topkapi.

It's good I'm going after closing, she thought. Breaking away from a lecture into an empty palace sounded less problematic than breaking away from a tour group and having to dodge others.

This palace, too, was now a museum, though it had remained a political building even into the regime of the new Turkish state. Its importance to Turkish history was largely to do with the fact that it had been the residence of Mustafa Kemal Ataturk, modern Turkey's founder and first president, at the end of his life. Turkish citizens, and the Turkish state, idolized their founder in a way that went beyond anything Americans might feel for George Washington and the Founding Fathers. The deathbed of Ataturk, within the Dolmabahce grounds, had become a memorial, a kind of shrine, and one of the most visited features of the palace tour.

What was most significant to Emily, however, was the location. The plot of land that Abdulmecid had chosen for his new palace was once a bay on the Bosporus. It had been filled in by Ottoman gardeners over a long series of decades the century before, and transformed into an imperial garden and retreat. The name Dolmabahce, 'filled garden', kept the memory of its old origins alive. Today, the palace sat on this plot of reclaimed land, literally 'touching the water', which came immediately up to the building's foundations.

Emily looked up at the sight, now immediately off the ferry's bow. There was no doubt she was coming to the right place.

As the boat approached the port and began to slow, she started the short walk to the staircase that would lead her down to the lower deck to disembark. As she turned, her eyes fell to the wider balcony of the lower level, and came to rest on two men.

Two men, both smartly dressed and, although one now held his jacket in his hand, these were men in suits.

Grey suits.

Their hair was neatly trimmed, and they looked almost identical. *Like clones*. Michael's voice rang through her head.

Emily's blood went cold. She had not been paranoid at the airport, nor had her subsequent nervousness been misplaced: she was, indeed, being followed. These clearly weren't the same men that had confronted Michael – there was no way they could have made it here in so short an amount of time – but they had to be connected.

The Council was tracking her. Following her. A voice in her head suddenly screamed a firm command: *keep them following.*

Emily took a quick step back as her heart raced, removing herself from view. Did they know she had seen them? If they believed she was unaware of their presence, it might stave off a confrontation.

Emily could no longer hear the roar of the ferry's engines, nor the chatter of the crowded passengers. All she could hear was her own pulse, hammering in her ears.

Down the steps, off the boat and across to the palace. Down the steps, off the boat and across to the palace – she forced herself to recite the steps ahead mentally, trying to bring focus, if not calm.

Emily swallowed hard, took a deep breath, and stepped onto the metal stairwell. Keeping her eyes directly forward and slightly downcast, she walked directly for the ferry's ramp and stepped onto dry land.

Keep them following. She repeated the mental command as she forced herself forward. *If they want to follow, I'll damned well give them something to pursue.*

CHAPTER 83

7.15 p.m.

The moment her feet were on solid ground, Emily turned towards the immense Dolmabahce Palace on her left and attempted to walk toward it nonchalantly as though her heart were not racing. She tried to keep to the centre of the busy sidewalk.

If I can get inside and slip away, it's still possible to lose them.

Emily tried to comfort herself with the fact that these men had been following her at least since her arrival in Turkey, which meant they must have been with her earlier at Topkapi Palace. They had been with her, but they had not hurt her. They had not even confronted her. She prayed they would keep up the trend.

Just don't look suspicious, she instructed herself. *If they think you're onto them, everything could change.*

She forced herself to slow her step to match the rather leisurely, evening gait of others nearby. To blend in.

The walk to the palace took only minutes. Emily craned her neck to take in the full breadth of the place as she now stood before it. Dolmabahce was a sight to catch one's attention. Despite her fear, she asked herself whether its grand facade wasn't the 19th-century Ottoman form of 'shock-and-awe' when it came to imperial show and tell.

She followed signs to the palace's main entrance, its doors propped open and lights on, welcoming latecomers to the evening's special event. As she approached, Emily slowed her pace even more, smoothed down her designer blazer and pulled back her somewhat dishevelled hair into a tight, professional ponytail. She wondered if, in her current rumpled state, she would be able to pass for an interested scholar, keen to know more about Franco-Turkish relations. She would have to hope she could.

A small, antique wooden table inside the doors served as the registration desk, and Emily paid an exorbitant fee for entry to the evening's lecture. Apologizing politely for her lateness to a receptionist who didn't seem to mind one way or the other, she took her ticket and entered the building.

She was, as she had suspected she would be, immediately overwhelmed. The main entrance, entitled the Medal Hall on a small placard still in place from the daytime tour groups, captured every sense. Its size was vast, with sloping staircases, immense chandelier, engraved tables and imposing paintings. Suddenly, the free champagne and toiletries she'd received earlier that day on her first class flight from England didn't seem to define 'luxury' in the way they had before.

Tearing her gaze from the opulent splendour around her, Emily followed a small trickle of fellow participants still making their way around a corner and into what she could see, even from a distance, was an almost equally stunning assembly room. As she approached, she could see it filled with wooden chairs, each covered in red velvet, and almost all already occupied with attentive guests. A man addressed the chamber from an elegant podium at its front, speaking in French. The talk appeared to have already begun.

Just before she entered the room, Emily put her plan into action. Suddenly 'remembering' that she needed the rest-room, she asked the doorman for directions.

'Two doors over, on the right.'

Emily walked the distance. Then, checking to ensure that no eyes were on her, she rounded a corner and disappeared into the dark palace grounds beyond.

CHAPTER 84

Dolmabahce Palace – 7.27 p.m.

Moments later Emily was alone in the vast, dark corridors of Dolmabahce Palace. As the largest in Turkey, it presented her with an even more daunting task than she had faced in the Bibliotheca Alexandrina. Somewhere in the 110,000 square metres of the palace's floorspace, Arno Holmstrand had left her a clue.

She traced her way in and out of rooms and corridors in the palace's main block, her heart beating not only from the threat of the men following her, but also from awe at the overwhelming sights around her. Even in the dimmed lighting of its after-hours state, the place seemed to glow and shimmer. Fourteen tonnes of gold leaf sparked in the gentle light.

As she made her way towards the famed Crystal Staircase and walked quietly up its edge, she knew that she couldn't possibly search every area and surface of such a place. Nor, she thought, would Arno have expected her to. Holmstrand couldn't have known that Emily would have even as much access to the palace as she now did. He would have left his clue somewhere that Emily would be able to find, presumably on or near the normal tour route. Somewhere accessible.

Signs and red roping marked the route the tours took through the grounds, so Emily tried to keep to these, her eyes peeled for any indication of the small symbol that had marked out Arno's clues everywhere else.

There must be something here he knew would draw my attention, she thought. *Something to narrow down the possibilities.*

Where do you hide a clue in a king's house? The royal foyer? That couldn't be it. In the daytime, it would be constantly filled with guests, presenting no opportunity to scan for a sign. The Ambassador's Hall? Emily hoped that wasn't the location, as the small maps posted at intervals along the tour route seemed to indicate that it was the very room in which the lecture was taking place. If Arno's clue was hidden there, it was going to be impossible to find tonight.

Where else? Emily forced herself to think over every word of the message she had received in Alexandria. '*Between two continents: the house of the king, touching the water.*' The two continents were accounted for, the house was royal and it touched the water. What was she missing?

The king. That was the only part of the clue that still sounded odd. Dolmabahce had been the house of the Sultans for decades, but the Ottoman leaders had never used the title 'king'. Nor had the Byzantine rulers before them, who were known almost exclusively as Emperor. Yes, the terms were all more or less equivalent, but Arno Holmstrand had proven his fickleness for language multiple times already. Usage of this word, in this message, must be precise. Intentional.

Who ruled here, but wasn't a Sultan? Even as she asked the question, she rounded a corner and saw the answer appear before her.

Ataturk. The founder of the Turkish Republic and modern state, who had taken up residence in Dolmabahce Palace even as he had signed a 1922 edict removing governance of the Turkish people from the hands of hereditary monarchy. Ataturk, who had ousted the Sultans but went on to lead his republican government from the glory of their palaces. Ataturk, who had taken ill, and finally died, here in the palace walls. More specifically, in the chamber known today as 'Ataturk's Bedroom', towards which a sign standing in the centre of the corridor now pointed.

This man had attained a kind of prominence in the Turkish national memory that went beyond that of almost any king or leader before him. He had become the symbol of national identity, the 'Great Leader' of Turkish patriotic pride. At 9.05 a.m. on November 10th, 1938, he had died. It was a date, and a time, that any student of modern Eastern European history knew well. All the clocks in the palace had been stopped at the moment of Ataturk's death and marked the moment of national mourning for decades to come. More recently, that ban of mourning had been lifted and the palace clocks returned to show the actual time. All but for one: the small clock that sat on the table in the bedroom where Ataturk had died.

Emily knew exactly where she needed to go.

CHAPTER 85

7.45 p.m.

Emily followed the signs towards Ataturk's bedroom, located in what had been the harem section of the palace. She did not have far to go, and though she was constantly glancing over her shoulder, she could not be certain she wasn't being followed. That uncertainty prompted an urgency to her step.

The room was ceremonially marked but, as she entered, Emily realized it was hardly the most glamorous chamber in the palace. That was not to say it was not lavish and over-done, but it wasn't dripping with flagrant, showy wealth in the same way as most of the rooms through which she had just passed.

The focal point of the room was Ataturk's bed itself: a great wood-panelled, king-sized installation, it was covered in a bold, blood-red Turkish flag as a memorial to the spot where its first leader had fallen. The room itself was wood-panelled with elaborate oriental rugs and a series of floral ottomans and chairs filling up the small space.

Emily stepped over the suspended red cords that normally kept the tours a respectable distance from the venerated bed itself. The area she needed to survey for Arno's clue was now dramatically more manageable. *Somewhere in these four walls.*

The bed itself provided few opportunities for concealing an etched symbol, being mostly fabric and coverings. She gave it a quick survey but sensed she would have more luck elsewhere. Forcing herself to go against her nerves and adrenaline and scan slowly over the contents of the room, she scoped out potential locations for a hidden sign. She examined the small wooden nightstands on either side of the bed. Nothing. The inlaid table to its left, with its small, square clock forever frozen at 9.05, was equally barren. She passed her eyes over every inch of the wooden wall panelling – a prime candidate for the kind of etchings Emily had found in England and Egypt – but was similarly disappointed.

She took herself to the ottoman in the room's windowed corner to sit and reflect. *Where am I not looking?*

Then, out of the corner of her eye, something attracted her attention. Behind a heavily embroidered pillow, the wooden frame of the couch itself was visible. Something interrupted the flow of the grain, just where it disappeared behind the fabric.

Emily stiffened, reached across and pulled the pillow away. Behind it, scratched lightly into the wooden arm of the ottoman, was Arno's final clue. The library's crest provided the header, as it had in every other location along her journey. Beneath ran a single line of text, familiar only in its cryptic form:

'A *full circle: Oxford's divine ceiling, and Library's home.'*

Beneath the text, to Emily's surprise, was etched a second symbol.

CHAPTER 86

8.02 p.m.

Emily pulled her BlackBerry from her jacket pocket and photographed the etching on the ottoman's arm. Manoeuvring her fingers deftly over the small keypad, she began to annotate the photograph for reference, but stopped a few keystrokes into the first word. There was no need to make a note. The reference point of Arno's words and the meaning of the new symbol were immediately clear to her.

Any student at Oxford had at some point been introduced to the university's Divinity Schools: a ceremonial debating hall attached to the central Bodleian Library, which had been the institution's first purpose-built lecturing space. The university itself had been in existence for generations by the time the building was constructed in the mid-15th century, but it had carried out its lectures in the halls of its various colleges and other structures – including the University Church of St Mary, the rubble of which Emily had stepped through what now seemed like a lifetime ago. As the students had grown rowdier and more intense, the university had decided that carrying on its debates and lectures in the church was no longer appropriate and had commissioned the Divinity Schools to serve their dedicated function. Two centuries later, an additional room had been added at its far western end, known as Convocation House. This elaborate room, which even today had no artificial lighting, housed the throne of the Chancellor of the University, and for a period of just over 15 years during the reign of Charles II, during the height of the English Civil War, had served as the meeting place of Parliament.

Every student at Oxford knew the building because it was a masterpiece of odd, overwhelming design that was a 'must see' on any induction to the city; but also because it had not been a lecture hall for decades, and was now exclusively used for graduation ceremonies. One moment of glory in the old hall to impress on the way out the door.

The most famous feature of the Divinity Schools was its ceiling. Constructed in what was known as the 'perpendicular style', it was stylized with elaborate lierne vaulting and covered from one end to the other in hundreds of strange, mysterious symbols, some of which protruded down as hanging pendants. It was almost as if the ceiling had fingers, reaching down towards its occupants below. Emily remembered the somewhat eerie feeling she'd had on her first visit, listening to her college's senior tutor mention something about the man who had designed it: a master-mason by the name of William Orchard.

No one knew precisely what the various symbols on the Divinity Schools ceiling were, and that fact alone inspired countless conspiracy theorists. Some carvings were obviously the crests of houses and colleges at the time of the building's fabrication; others were likely the initials of donors who had contributed to its construction. But others – dozens upon dozens – were simply a mystery. They apparently meant nothing and thus were the source of perpetual fascination among visitors and interpreters.

Emily looked back to the second symbol that Holmstrand had left for her here in Ataturk's room. The line of text, 'A full circle: Oxford's divine ceiling, and Library's home', clearly pointed to the Divinity Schools. Arno could hardly have been more explicit. And the new symbol, Emily figured, must almost certainly be one of those sculpted onto that building's ornate ceiling.

All at once, she became aware of voices outside the door, somewhere down the long corridor. The precariousness of her situation suddenly hit home. She was seated on a sofa – a defaced sofa – in one of the most cherished rooms in Turkey. The amount of trouble she would be in if discovered was almost unimaginable. Emily had heard a few things about Turkish prisons, none of them good. And that was the best-case scenario. If the voices were coming from the two grey-suited men she'd spotted on the ferry, things could get far, far worse.

She quickly replaced the pillow over Arno's etching, crossed the room, stepped over the red roping and returned to the hallway outside. She paused long enough to work out the location of the voices, which were now growing stronger, and moved in the opposite direction. Hopefully they were museum workers, making rounds for the evening, or other seminar guests who had chosen to avoid the lecture itself. In either case, Emily didn't wish to be seen. Now that she had found what Arno had left for her, all she wanted was to get out and get to safety.

Winding her way through the elaborate halls, Emily finally found herself back at the central staircase. She descended it quickly and rounded a corner back to the main lobby. Across its long expanse was the gate back onto the streets of Istanbul.

But to her right, behind one of the pillars at the hall's wide edge, stood the two men in grey suits.

As Emily spotted them now, she locked eyes with one of the men. The man's steeled expression did not change, but his body turned to face Emily fully. As if they were attached at the hip, the other man turned with him. There was no longer any attempt at remaining hidden.

Run! The thought erupted in Emily's mind with an almost uncontrollable intensity. Her adrenaline surged. Yet she knew that if she ran, she would attract even more attention to herself. A woman speeding out of a palace was prone to be stopped along the way, and if she was stopped, these two men would have her at their mercy.

Just walk, straight to the door, and out.

Emily ripped her eyes from the man's gaze and pointed herself across the room. She took long steps, covering the space as quickly as she could without breaking into a jog.

Straight to the door. Straight to the door. She attempted to keep her pace steady with the rhythm of her words.

The space of the foyer seemed impossibly large, and Emily

felt with each step that the next would be accompanied by a hand on her shoulder or a tackle from behind. She kept her eyes pinned on the exit until, at last, it was before her. Pushing the door open with a force she didn't know she possessed, she turned herself out onto the street.

Emily walked straight across the road that ran parallel to the palace, to the sidewalk on its far side. People strolled the pavement, providing as much in the way of cover as she was likely to get. She kept her stride constant, just shy of a run, and elbowed her way through the small clusters of people when they stood in her way. It garnered her upset looks and a few shouts of protest, but Emily didn't stop.

Only after five minutes had passed did she allow her step to slow. Maybe, just maybe, the men were not in the hot pursuit she feared. She had not once glanced back to look. One thing she remembered from every action movie she had ever seen: looking back slows you down.

But it was time to find out, one way or the other. She came to a corner and tucked herself around its edge. Mustering her courage, she turned back and stuck her head past the building's edge, looking back in the direction she had come.

Three streets back, the two men were tracking a course directly towards her.

CHAPTER 87

8.20 p.m.

Emily pulled her body back behind the corner as fast as she could move it. The two men would be on her in a matter of moments. She had to think fast.

Returning to the ferry was a non-starter: she had taken the last one to get to Dolmabahce. *Besides*, she thought to herself, her mind racing, *no enclosed spaces. Keep yourself moving, with places to run.* Emily might not be experienced in evading pursuers, but hardly a day had passed since her teens that she had not begun with a run. These men would not take her without an effort.

She forced her legs into action and moved up the slender side street. She was heading south along the coast, back towards the central hub of the city. The neighbourhood ahead, which faced the famous peninsula of Hagia Sophia and the Blue Mosque, was the bustling market quarter called Galata, filled with tiny alleys and winding streets, each replete with carts and tables and tradesmen selling their wares. Emily remembered it from her former visits as a neighbourhood as much alive in the evening as in the day, always crowded, always full.

It will do perfectly, she thought. She would make her way through Galata and lose her pursuers, then cross over to the main city by bridge from the opposite side of the river.

Emily quickened her pace, and then broke into a full run. There was no reason not to move at full speed now, being free of the palace. Both she and the men behind her knew of each other's presence, and the chase was on. For the second time in her journey, her preference for comfortable, flat footwear was suddenly a logistical asset.

She sped her way up a winding, small street, which opened out onto a larger square, its market bustling under electric lights. Carts were covered in everything from baskets of colourful Indian spices to cheap electronics and twice-recycled batteries.

Emily dodged her way through the carts and crowds. As she reached the far side of the square, she glanced behind her. The two men had emerged out of the same small alley she had used to enter the market. Their motions were coordinated and they seemed to move in step, scanning opposing halves of the square as if it were overlaid by a grid marked out in their minds. One of the men spoke into a small cell phone as he scanned the area. It was like watching something out of a CIA movie, only Emily knew full well that these were not the good guys.

As the men continued their efficient survey of the square, she tucked herself behind a tall cart containing clothing and shoes, but the movement came seconds too late. The man with the phone spotted her and pointed a finger across the square. The other man spun to attention and both started to weave their way through the tables in Emily's direction. They navigated the busy marketplace without breaking line of sight: merchants and shoppers were simply shoved out of their way without hesitation or a second glance.

Emily pushed herself away from the cart and turned into another side alley descending away from the market square. She ran at full speed, changing her direction whenever a new side street emerged. Despite her physical aptitude, she was starting to sense that she couldn't outrun these men. She had to lose them.

She darted into a back lane, her side aching from the combination of adrenaline pulsing through her muscles and the sudden need to use them with such ferocity. Morning runs were what they were, but running for her life was a new experience. Leaning against a wall, she struggled to catch her breath. Then, before she could relax her frame and give her muscles the chance to tense up and lock, she pushed herself off, a clear voice in her mind commanding her along: *keep moving!*

The two men closed the space that separated them from Emily with each stride. Though Emily's technique of veering in spontaneous directions, cutting through side streets and lanes, meant that they couldn't get up the speed of a full sprint that would have ended the pursuit in a matter of seconds, they still had the upper hand on her. They were men used to pursuing targets.

Emily turned hard to the right and tucked herself into

another back alley, completing its length in a few strides of her long legs. Like so many she had passed through in the past seconds, this small lane opened into a broader street, filled with more shops, carts and crowds. But this street held one important, terrifying difference. As Emily kept to its edge and moved along it as fast as she could, looking for the next alley into which she could flee, she realized none were coming. Not a single side street presented itself, not one alley – no way out. She was in a long avenue of shopfronts and buildings, hemmed in by solid walls of structures on both sides.

I'm trapped.

She scanned wildly for anything that might serve as an escape route. Then, to her right, a few feet ahead, an opportunity presented itself: an open set of double doors, leading into one of the area's few churches – remnants of an era when Istanbul had been as much Christian as Muslim.

It's no alley, but it's better than nothing.

She turned and darted through the doors.

The church inside was dark, lit almost entirely by the few candle stands onto which clusters of old women had affixed small beeswax tapers. Behind them, the walls were adorned with romantic pictures of the Lord, of the Virgin Mary, of the saints, with an altar at the far end of the long space, walled off by a small, waist-height screen of wood and images. *Armenian*, Emily's historical mind noted, despite the situation, registering the distinctive interior design of Armenian churches the world over.

To her relief, the church was supported by a series of large pillars dotting both sides of the nave. In the stark darkness they provided what she needed most: a place to hide. Taking an unlit candle from a box at the entrance in case she needed to look pious and blend in, she moved along the left wall until she reached a pillar suitably removed from the small groups of worshippers and disappeared behind it.

She leaned her head, her whole body, back against the cold stone pylon, brushing aside loose strands of her long hair that stuck to the perspiration on her face. Her heavy breathing seemed to echo off the image-laden walls.

Calm down. Deep breaths. Slow. Don't let them hear you; don't let them see you.

She pinched her eyes closed and forced herself to be still. She had never in her life experienced terror like that of the past few minutes, and her body was unsure how to respond. She prayed with everything in her that she'd made it into the church before the men had rounded the corner and seen her course.

No doubts remained in Emily's mind: not about the library's existence, not about the history of the Society, not about the Council. Arno had led her to something real – it was almost in her grasp. But the cost of that reality was a knowledge that bound her to events far beyond her control. Were these men out to kill her because she could lead them to the library? Or were they part of the plot on the American government?

Emily forced her breathing to slow, waiting for her pulse to return to something approximating normal. For long minutes the church was silent. No one entered. No one broke the prayerful quiet.

Slowly, silently, she peered around the pillar. The view confirmed the lack of sound: the place was now almost completely empty. The men hadn't followed her. She had entered alone.

She waited a few more minutes, giving her pursuers time to move on and continue chasing their phantom target down whatever streets they believed she had taken. Only when the church's caretaker appeared and began to close the double doors for the night, did Emily finally emerge from her pillar and move to the exit.

She peered warily into the street before stepping fully out of the doors. A quick scan in either direction produced nothing of alarm. She walked out into the street. A few moments later, she found an alley leading down the hill and disappeared into the bustling avenues of Galata.

CHAPTER 88

9.10 p.m.

Back in the midst of the market quarter, Emily continued to weave her way through as many side streets and lanes as she could find, gradually working her way out of the heavily trafficked areas and into the network of less-frequented back streets at the quarter's fringe. Her body was soaked with a layer of perspiration that was as much from terror as physical exertion. Though she'd caught no glimpse of her two pursuers since the church, she was under no illusions. She wasn't safe. She had to get out of Istanbul, and fast.

Her constant changing of course onto ever more vacant and empty side streets – her own form of tactical evasion – meant that her progress down the long hill of Galata, towards the bridge that would lead her back to the main city and the thoroughfares that would take her to the airport and out of the country, was slow. The delay, however, served a useful purpose: the longer she walked, the more minutes that passed, the more her fear subsided. Eventually her feverish pace relaxed, calming to a measured walk as the trough that followed her peak of adrenaline started to catch up with her.

But though her body was tired, her mind was still racing, and not just from the chase. As the terror of the experience ebbed, her attention was captured by a strange unease at Arno's most recent clue.

Something in the message didn't sit well.

She hadn't misread the clue itself. She might have fallen for a trick in misidentifying the correct palace, but Emily was absolutely certain of the message here. The presence of the new symbol, together with the text, removed any doubt: the clue pointed to the Oxford Divinity Schools, and to a specific symbol sculpted into its ceiling.

The problem was that it *did* point to the Schools. That it pointed back to Oxford. *Back.* Back to the place where her quest for the library had begun in earnest. This final clue made the whole journey on which he had been sent the equivalent of running around in circles. Arno's message stressed this, almost seemed to tease it. '*A full circle: Oxford's divine ceiling, and Library's home.*' A full circle, a circuit, ending up nowhere else than where she had begun.

Something about this felt . . . wrong.

Her ability to dwell on that discomfort, however, came to a sudden and terrifying end. Emily was snapped out of her ponderings by a pointed, distinctive click behind her. She froze in her tracks, midway between the tall buildings that lined the narrow service alley. Though she had never heard it before in her own, real experience, she had seen enough movies to know the sound of a gun being cocked. Slowly, she looked up from the alley's cobbled surface.

Standing before her was the smaller and stockier of the grey-suited men, his pistol levelled directly at Emily's head.

CHAPTER 89

9.30 p.m.

Jason kept his Glock 26 trained directly on Emily Wess. The tiny gun was his favourite for travelling: at just under six and a half inches long and weighing in at only 26 ounces with its ten-round clip fully loaded, it was easy to conceal and astoundingly accurate for its size. The model had gained the name 'Baby Glock' among security personnel the world over, but it packed a punch that was anything but infantile.

When she saw the gun levelled at her forehead, Emily instinctively lurched backwards and looked behind her, only to discover that the other man stood at the far end of the alley, firmly blocking any escape.

'Don't try it, Dr Wess.' Jason spoke clearly, firmly, with an efficiency and calm that made his words sound routine, as if he were not in fact levelling a gun at a woman's face, his finger not poised over a trigger that could easily end another person's life. 'There is not going to be any more running today.'

Emily faced her pursuer, though her eyes remained fixed on the square barrel of the small gun.

'What do you want with me?'

Jason's gaze remained direct, unwavering.

'Nothing that you aren't able to give, or that we aren't willing to take.' His eyes tightened. The expression he bore was not quite a smile, but an almost bemused condescension.

'First, give us what you found in the palace,' he commanded. His father had assured him that whatever had been left there was simply part of the Keeper's attempt at subterfuge, and not a key ingredient in their search. The Council had already found what it needed through the graphic decoded from Antoun's email. Still, it would be good for them to know what Holmstrand's final clue had been.

Emily did her best to make bold in the circumstance.

'I don't know what you mean.' These were not the kind of men she wanted finding their way to the library.

Jason straightened his right arm and pushed the gun closer to Emily's face.

'Don't cross me, Dr Wess. Your phone,' he motioned to Emily's jacket with the gun, 'give us your phone.'

At the word 'us', Emily became aware that the second man had silently approached from the rear. His breath was now audible behind her, almost pressing down on Emily's neck. She suddenly felt claustrophobic. Trapped.

The two men were cleverer than she had hoped. They weren't probing her randomly for information: they knew precisely what she had and where she had it.

'I'm not a patient person, Dr Wess,' Jason continued. 'I know the phone contains information on what you found in the palace, as well as a certain list you should never have seen. Now, I won't ask again.' He held out his left hand, open and palm-up. As Emily watched the gesture, she felt a second gun barrel, this one pressed into her back.

'Okay, okay.' Her boldness was suddenly gone, the desire to remain alive strong and powerful. She had promised Michael she would come back to him, and she needed to keep that promise. 'Here.' She reached into her jacket, removed her BlackBerry and handed it to the man in front of her. She was not worried about losing the materials she had on her person: she'd sent copies of Arno's letters to Wexler, and Michael still had two of the originals. The clue she'd just discovered in the palace, with its strange glyph, was burnt permanently into her memory. The list was stored in her mind, too, and she would be able to get another digital copy from Athanasius. She was certain she could proceed without the BlackBerry. The agony she felt was not the frustration of loss but of handing the information over to such men.

Jason passed the small device to his partner.

'Take everything,' he instructed. 'And double-check the list wasn't forwarded. It was sent to her in two text messages – the second is the key. The one that contains the names of our men.'

The words tinged Emily's ears. *Our men?* Despite her racing heart and the two guns trained on her, the language struck her. *Our.*

Jason turned back to her, the BlackBerry now in the hands of his colleague, who had shouldered his own gun and was wholly focused on manipulating the small device.

'While you're being so cooperative, why don't you give me the papers, too?'

Emily tried to stall, but Jason's gun again moved closer to her face. As with her phone, it was clear that her pursuers already knew exactly what she had in her possession. These men were thorough.

Resigned, she grabbed the bundle of Arno's letters and the faxed copy of the clues from her bag and passed them into the man's waiting hand.

Jason allowed himself a half smile.

'Thank you, Dr Wess. You've been exceptionally helpful.' He paused. 'But you did make us run after you, and that is . . . unfortunate.' He stood tall, a new air of professionalism sweeping over him. 'The Council is grateful for your generosity in assisting us with our aims, but I regret to inform you that your services are no longer required. The time has come for your involvement to end.' He glanced over Emily's shoulder to the man behind her. 'Do it.'

CHAPTER 90

9.40 p.m.

Emily heard the scuffle of fabric as the man behind her raised his gun.

'Wait!' she cried, as her mind raced frantically. 'You can't kill me!'

'You're quite mistaken in that belief,' Jason answered, bemused.

'No, I mean you can't.' Emily's words raced off her tongue as fast as her mind could produce them. 'Not if you want your little game in Washington to succeed.'

The words caught Jason's attention and he raised his left hand in a small gesture, instructing his partner to wait with the execution. He knew Emily was only delaying, attempting to forestall the inevitable, but he was willing to hear her out.

'Don't be ridiculous,' he said. 'There's no way you can throw off our project, dead or alive. Our activity in Washington is almost complete. There's nothing you, or anyone else, can do to stop it.'

'We can still expose you,' Emily threw back. 'No matter

how far you've got, the world won't let you get away with it once they see what you've done and who's been involved.'

'Hence our happy moment here together. Your death will ensure that never happens.'

'Not quite,' Emily answered back. Now it was her turn to take a tone of confidence, despite the panic in her chest. 'The man who sent me your little list, the one that could bring you down – he expects to hear from me with my progress on . . . other matters.' Emily took a breath to steady her nerves, gathering as much composure as the moment would allow. 'If he doesn't, you can bet your last breath or mine that those names, and whatever other details he's got, will be known to every media outlet in the world in a matter of hours.'

Jason bored his eyes into Emily's. Could she possibly be telling the truth? Could Antoun and she have concocted such a plan without him being aware? It wasn't impossible: a quick whisper in the ear that their taps had not picked up. A note. But the chances were far greater that this was simply the desperate ruse of a woman too pitifully scared to meet her end. He spat back at Emily, 'Nonsense. We heard every word of your conversation in Alexandria. Antoun, in any case, is being dealt with, which makes you the last leak in the operation, with the exception of your gallant fiancé, Mr Torrance. But don't worry – soon he won't be talking either.' His eyes almost sparkled at the last threat as he took delight in the extra torture this knowledge would add to Wess's final moments.

'Kill me if you want,' Emily answered, forcing herself to

ignore the threat against Michael and pour all her bearing into the defiance of the man before her. Standing straight, and for the first time looking up from Jason's gun into the hunter's eyes, she spoke firmly. 'But know, as you do, that everything you've been working for dies with me.'

The silence that followed seemed to Emily to stretch on into eternity as the diminutive, muscular man before her pondered whether to kill her or let her live. In that moment, unsure whether she clung to life or death, Emily felt a strange quiet. Almost a calm.

'Enough.' Jason's word finally broke through the silence sharply. His decision had been reached. He nodded his head in a strange, commanding gesture to his partner. 'Do it, now.'

Before Emily could register what he meant, the blow came from behind her, shattering against the back of her head as metal met flesh and skull. The last sound she heard was a satisfied laugh, emanating from the swirling forms in her vision that moments ago had been the clear shapes of the two men. Then the sounds swirled and faded like the images, and the world around her went black.

Emily Wess's body hit the ground.

CHAPTER 91

9.45 p.m.

Jason turned to the other Friend, impatiently.

'Do you have it?'

'Almost.' The second man watched the progress indicator on his small device slide to its endpoint, downloading the complete contents of Emily's BlackBerry to its hard drive. Then he deleted all of the data on the BlackBerry itself. He snapped the cable out of Emily's phone and tossed it onto the street next to her limp body. On his own computer, the materials Emily had assembled would be more useful and easier to scan.

A stomp of his foot later, and her phone was destroyed.

'Done,' he confirmed to his partner. 'We have everything. Both SMS messages were there and neither had been forwarded. I'm checking through the stored memory now. Whatever she found in the palace is in here somewhere.'

Jason walked over and took a position immediately beside him.

'Show me.'

The other man, who went simply by the nickname 'Tech', navigated his way through his tiny, customized computer's touch-screen interface with deft speed and skill. Unlike Jason, who had been with the Council his whole life, he had been recruited into the Friends in his mid thirties. Prior to that memorable afternoon, when he had suddenly found himself surrounded by ominous looking men with cold expressions and an incomparable offer, he had earned a certain degree of underground notoriety as a computer hacker. The Council, realizing that such skills were becoming more important in their tasks of search-and-destroy in the twenty-first century, had followed his 'career' with interest. He was the ideal candidate for the manner of work in which the Friends engaged: talented, brilliant, but equally devious and possessing a clear disregard for fickle matters such as which activities happened to be legal and which did not. His was a 'soft conscience', as the Secretary called it. One that could be moulded to the shape required.

That moulding had gone so well that he now accompanied Jason on almost every mission on which the Secretary's principal Friend was sent. Jason may have been the leader's son – a fact every member of the Council knew, but which none dared mention in the Secretary's presence – but Tech liked to feel, in his rare moments of sentimentality, that he had risen almost as high. There were few others trusted with the matters he was given on a day-to-day basis.

Calling up a folder containing the downloaded contents of Wess's BlackBerry, he tilted the small display toward Jason. Together they gave a cursory scan of its contents.

A knowing smile returned to Jason's face as he came to the end of the materials. Wess had nothing there that they did not already know. The etching she had discovered in Dolmabahce Palace, photograph of which resided on her phone, had pointed to Oxford and had provided a new symbol; but the Council had already determined that the final location was Oxford, and they already possessed the new seal, having found it encrypted beneath the false-front image file in Antoun's email. Wess had been behind the game.

Still, it was satisfying to see the clue itself. It confirmed what the Council had discovered itself, and it contained the magic words that every member of the Council had been struggling to hear for centuries. 'The Library's home.'

We're already on our way. We've got it.

As pride swelled in his chest, he handed the small computer back to his partner.

'Send it up,' he commanded. 'Send everything.' Tech started the process of transferring the downloaded contents to the Secretary. Even though there wasn't much, and nothing new, it would still be scrutinized and examined.

At that moment, Jason's phone rang. He looked at the number, and answered.

'Have you done it?' Ewan Westerberg asked. He was anxious to know that Wess had been terminated.

'Not entirely. It is a work in progress. We've sent her to sleep for the time being.' Speaking openly of an execution over mobile telephone lines was not wise, but it didn't take a great deal of creativity to mask the real topic of conversation.

The Secretary was surprised at the report.

'Why? I thought my wishes were clear.'

'There was a complication. An unexpected hiccup.' He relayed to his father Wess's threat of how Antoun would expose their Washington mission and the full listing of names – including theirs – if Wess didn't report in. His decision to incapacitate Wess, rather than kill her, had been a temporary response while he checked on the Secretary's wishes. As he spoke, he looked down at Emily's body. It was pitiful, seeing the foolish woman lying unconscious at his feet. The thought of ending her life once and for all excited him, and the delay was disappointing.

Having listened to his son's report, Ewan Westerberg answered with an air of composed conviction.

'Let her sleep. I don't want her out of the picture until we're certain her threat of exposure has been eradicated. I'll instruct our men to bring our discussions with Mr Antoun to an end earlier than planned, and then our remaining team in Istanbul can extend Wess's nap indefinitely.'

'Understood,' Jason replied. Antoun would be terminated, removing any potential backlash against Emily's execution, and then Wess herself would finally be taken care of. It was likely an unnecessary redundancy, Jason thought silently, but better safe than even mildly sorry.

'As for you,' the Secretary continued, 'get yourself to Oxford as fast as you can. Leave Wess to the local Turkish team. I've already notified them of your position and they should be there within the hour. As long as she's out of sight, immobilize her and leave her for their arrival. The time has come for you to be on your way. We have everything we need to claim the library, and I want you with me when we take possession of what is ours.' Without waiting for a response, Ewan terminated the call.

Jason looked again at Emily's body, the crumpled woman's chest slowly rising and falling. He was disappointed that he would not be able to see the look in her eyes as she died – to behold the recognition that there was nothing to be done, that it was all about to end. Those satisfying moments would be given to another, but Jason knew he could not focus on the small loss. What he was about to witness, to be a part of, was something infinitely greater. The work of the Council for centuries was about to come to fruition. The power they would gain, the might they would wield, once the library was theirs, would be limitless. To have its resources at their command, together with their man in the Oval Office and surrounded by other Council members in his administration – it would be the dawn of the Council's most glorious era.

He grabbed a pair of handcuffs from his back pocket and, dragging Emily's body to the side of the alley, chained her left hand to a drainpipe running down to the ground. The Alexandrian team would finish with Antoun, and then his partners here in Istanbul would come for her.

'It's time to go,' he barked, looking up from the body. The other man nodded and the two Friends left Emily's fate to the local team. Their glory was now only hours away.

CHAPTER 92

Ewan Westerberg sat anxiously in his car. However fast he instructed his driver to go, he would never get to the private airstrip beside New York's John F. Kennedy Airport fast enough to satisfy the anticipation in his chest. For the Council's Secretary, time had seemed to slow to an intolerable pace.

In the forty-five minutes that had elapsed since the Friends had reported in from Istanbul, sending over a crystal-clear image of Emily Wess's final clue and confirming the Council's own information, all the necessary preparations had been made. Each of the Secretary's advisors had counselled what Ewan already knew: that the information pointed towards a ceremonial building in Oxford, England. Full details on the history, architecture, layout and significant features of the Divinity Schools had already been assembled and would be waiting for him at the plane. His men would scrutinize every fact and detail of the building, making ready for his arrival.

A team in London was preparing for that arrival even now,

while another in Oxford was making the arrangements that would be necessary there. His organization ran efficiently and smoothly. They had been meticulously trained, and the events that lay ahead were the very things for which they had worked ever since the Council's formation, so many centuries ago.

All of history pointed towards this moment.

Jason and his partner were already en route to Heathrow, while Ewan's jet was being fuelled and prepped for its unscheduled flight. Missing the FAA's window for departure planning didn't concern him. Enough power and influence could manipulate any agency to bend its rules, and they had got their way with the Aviation Administration before. Besides, being the key financial supporter of the vice president brought perks in its own right. His flight would depart precisely the moment it, and he, were ready.

Then the two greatest triumphs in the Council's history would come within hours of one another. On Saturday morning he would take the library, and on Sunday he would take the American presidency. He would not sit in the famous Gunlocke chair behind the Resolute Desk, of course, but that had never been the plan. The fact was that a member of the Council would, and his own position would be all the stronger for not being in the immediate limelight. He would have the collected knowledge and intelligence of millennia, more current and extensive today than any government's agencies had ever been or ever would be, at his beck and call, together with the most powerful executive authority in the history of the world. Everyone, everything, would be under his control.

CHAPTER 93

Istanbul – 10.05 p.m.

Vision, when it finally returned, was blurry. As Emily came to on the ground of the small Galata service alley in Istanbul, her eyes at first produced only clouded images, fading in and out of focus. Her ears, too, did not function as they ought, producing only muffled drones of fluctuating noise. Then came an acute awareness of the throbbing pain at the base of her skull, pulsing down and out through the whole of her body. She had never known a pain like it in her life.

Emily pushed herself upright, propping herself into a sitting position with one hand. The other was fastened to what felt like a pipe running up the brick wall behind her. Taking her free hand, she felt the back of her head. Her fingers came back coated in a thick, black layer of partially congealed blood. *At least it's congealed*, she thought to herself. It meant the active bleeding had likely stopped. She blinked heavily several times, squinting her vision back into focus, and glanced at her surroundings. It was the same narrow alley as before, but the two men who had pursued and then attacked her were gone.

Attacked, and left for dead, Emily thought, surmising her situation. *Better luck next time.* There might be little she could do to feel better physically, but she could reclaim her dignity and resolve.

Pulling a bobby pin from her hair, she focused her eyes on the handcuff binding her to the drainpipe. Emily was no locksmith, but childhood years spent breaking into her younger cousin Andrew's locked doors and desks during summers spent together meant this wasn't the first time she'd been confronted with a lock she needed to pick. Nor were standard-issue handcuffs the pinnacle of locking sophistication. A few confident gestures of the pin later, she extracted her left hand from the cuff and rubbed feeling back into her fingers.

Near her feet she spotted her BlackBerry, lying face-down on the tiled stones of the street. Suddenly her only thought was of Michael. Though she'd forced herself to ignore her attacker's threat on his life during their encounter, it was now the only thought on her mind. She had to reach him, to warn him, and somehow to get him to safety.

She reached forward and took the phone, pain shooting through every part of her body and her vision blurring again as she moved. Wrapping her fingers around it, she pulled back to her former position and allowed her sight to clear before turning it over and examining its condition. The screen was dark and cracked down its middle, and Emily's heart started at the thought that he might not be able to warn

Michael in time. She pressed the power button, hoping for the best, but the device was dead.

Damn it, she swore to herself, returning a hand to the back of her head. The hair that had remained in her thick ponytail after her run had absorbed some of the blow's force, and though the pain was terrific, she did not feel shattered bone.

The real blow was the men's success in relieving her of her information and her possessions. *Everything is in their hands now*, she thought. *They've got it all.* She was certain her attackers were from the Council that Athanasius had described so vividly, and they had known exactly what they wanted. Their efficiency in stripping her of it was both impressive and terrifying. These were men who had perfected the skills necessary to obtain what they desired.

And Emily had just let the final clue, the key clue, to the library's location fall directly into their hands. The degree of guilt she felt was unexpected.

Soon they'll be in Oxford, and it will be theirs. The circle of their hunt-and-chase routine will be complete. They'll find what they've been seeking for so long—

She paused mid-lament. There was that word again. *Circle.* It had felt wrong to her as she pondered Arno's latest message during her pursuit, and it felt newly troubling to her as she sat there, recovering from her blow. '*A full circle: Oxford's divine ceiling, and Library's home.*' Circles, running in circles, circular reasoning . . . Emily forced herself painfully to her feet as the true question burned its way into her mind. Why was it that this word was raising such a red flag?

Come on Arno, you're trying to tell me something. What is it?

The clues that Holmstrand had left for her all along her journey had convinced Emily not to dismiss any dimension of this latest one. If something didn't sit well, that was a sign. A sign that Arno had hidden something else within the clue. Something Emily hadn't yet recognized.

She propped herself against a wooden shell containing trash cans from a nearby shop and closed her eyes. The urge to remove herself from the remote alley into a busier, public space, was offset by a pain that was all but immobilizing. Slowing her breathing to help control the pain, she allowed her mind to stretch back over all she knew of Arno Holmstrand – all she had ever known of the great professor's work and legacy, all she had ever heard the man say.

Heard him say. It was there that her attention gravitated. The strange clue didn't sit well with something she had heard Arno speak.

What did Arno say?

Finally, the question provoked a memory: a memory of the first words she had ever heard Arno Holmstrand speak. The words that had formed the opening line of his inaugural lecture at Carleton College.

'Knowledge is not circular. Ignorance is circular. Knowledge stands in what is old, yet points to what is ever new.'

The professor's laments had been consistent on the theme: truth didn't work in circles. Circularity was a deception. And now, in pointing back towards the university city of Oxford, his final clue described just such a meaningless, trivial circle – the very sort of thing he had so publicly, vocally despised.

It was a conclusion Arno Holmstrand would never draw.

With absolute clarity, Emily suddenly felt certain of one fact above all else. The Library of Alexandria was not in Oxford.

CHAPTER 94

10.25 p.m.

Twenty minutes later the line to Michael's apartment in Chicago began to ring. A cheap pay-as-you-go mobile purchased from a street vendor had provided Emily with a new phone to replace her destroyed BlackBerry, and she knew by heart the one number she needed at this moment. She had entered the long series of digits, pressed the dial button and held the phone to her ear. Two short rings later, Michael Torrance picked up his telephone on the other side of the globe.

'It's me,' she announced as the line connected.

'Em!' Michael's exuberance as he greeted her was like a tonic for her wounds. They were connected, she was alive, and she had the strength to warn him.

'Michael, you've got to get out of there now.' She skipped over their usual greetings. She didn't have time to fill him in on details.

'What are you talking about, Em? Are you okay?'

'Mike, just trust me, please. You've got to get away. You're

in danger. You remember those men who came to interrogate you?'

Michael's pulse started to accelerate, shocked into action
by Emily's unexpected urgency.

'Of course I remember them.'

'They're going to come back, Mikey, and this time they're
not coming to ask questions. You've got to get away, to someplace safe.'

'Emily, why would they be coming for me?' He had frozen
in place in the middle of his apartment, phone in hand,
desperate to know the reason for his fiancée's pleading.

'They're coming for you because you're connected to me.
And they know I can expose them. You're a . . . a risk.'

Michael tried to make sense of Emily's words.

'Does this have something to do with the president's down-
fall?' Throughout the United States, the media had already
predicted the end of his regime. 'Forthcoming impeachment'
was the key phrase of the day. He remembered his interrogators' chilling interest in Emily's political involvement.

'It has everything to do with it. And with the library. And
with the Society and the Council. They're all connected.'
She gave him a bullet-point report of the events of her past
hours.

Michael took her news with restraint, demanding repeatedly to know if she was all right – 'I mean, *really* all right' –
but otherwise allowing her an uninterrupted narrative.

'You've got to go, Mikey' she pleaded aloud, thinking,
please just understand!

'Go where?' Michael had already accepted Emily's

instruction and his mind sped ahead to possibilities. 'I could go to—'

'No, don't,' Emily interrupted him. 'Don't say it aloud. They're almost certainly listening. Do you remember where we spent our first weekend after you moved to Illinois?' The weekend after he had taken up his internship in Chicago, the two of them had gone camping near the scenic Starved Rock State Park. It had been a profoundly romantic escape and she knew he would remember it well.

'Of course.'

'Go there, and stay there until you hear from me.' She thought ahead to all the potential ways the Council's men might try to track him down. 'Take a work colleague's car. They probably know yours. Leave your cell phone at home – don't take it with you, not even turned off. When it's safe, I'll send someone to get you. Don't use your credit cards. Nothing. Just go, and wait for me.'

Michael hesitated for a moment.

'Okay, Em. I'll go. Where will you be going? Back to Oxford?'

Emily paused. When she spoke, her words were filled with resolve, but she deliberately kept her answer vague.

'I need to see a new friend one more time.'

Two minutes after she terminated her call to Michael with the firmest 'I love you' she had ever spoken, Emily was standing at the edge of the busy Tersane Street, one of the few artery roads out of Istanbul's Galata district, her arm extended to hail a cab.

There's more that Athanasius hasn't told me, she ruminated. *He's shared the old, the past. But there's still something new, something more I need to know.*

She had never expected that the Egyptian man's accounting of the library, the Society and its history had been complete, but now that she had Arno's final puzzle-piece in hand, she felt she had to clarify its contents with the one man who might know the answers.

She hailed the first taxi that approached. Opening the door, Emily fell into the car's tattered rear seat.

'Take me to the airport.' She closed her eyes once again, seeking to contain the throbbing in her head. 'And all the remaining Turkish currency in my wallet is yours if you get me there in a hurry.'

An hour and a half later, she was on the direct 12.30 a.m. night flight to Alexandria. She would be back in Egypt by 2.30 in the morning. But as she flew, Emily remembered that Michael wasn't the only person her attacker had threatened in his final rant. Athanasius had also been promised an exit from this life. Emily could only hope she would not be too late to warn him.

CHAPTER 95

The two friends moved in practised unison through the dark corridors. Though neither had a military background, they worked and walked in step as if they did, but with an emotion that no legitimate soldier would share. Their actions were always personal. They served the Council: the only true body of real power and might in the world. A Council that for centuries had sought to gain influence, gain control, gain not only the library and its vast resources, but a position of influence that would allow them to use it the way real men should. To rule. To conquer.

Tonight that aim was being furthered in the manner the Friends knew well, and towards which their unique expertise was aimed. Many people would consider their work dark, even morbid. But to both men it was sacred and noble.

The Bibliotheca Alexandrina was closed, and apart from security lighting, almost entirely dark. Yet the two men knew precisely where to go, and they had descended into the underground corridors with ease. Athanasius Antoun had stayed to work through the night, which meant he was contained. It would make their task all the easier.

As they reached his office, both men paused. The first reached down to the knob and tested it. The door wasn't even locked. The pitiful fool.

The second Friend drew out his Glock and chambered a round. An instant later, the first threw open the door. The men burst into the small office, blood lust burning red in their eyes.

CHAPTER 96

11.58 p.m.

Racing down a long, unlit corridor, Athanasius prayed his knowledge of the library's floor plan would provide him with an advantage. Despite their efforts at silence, he had heard the two men approaching. In an otherwise vacant midnight basement, even footsteps were audible. He knew they were coming, and he knew they weren't here to talk. Combatting the nervous twitches of his teeming adrenaline levels, Athanasius had removed his shoes and made his way in the darkness in his stocking feet.

'*The bastard's not here!*' Antoun heard the shout from behind him. His pursuers, finding his office empty, abandoned the struggle for a covert arrival. '*Go after him!*' came the next cry.

He turned a sharp corner and descended a short staircase to the second basement level. The emergency exit lighting cast only a faint, green glow, but he ran as fast as his legs would move. Behind him, the footsteps of his pursuers thumped on the concrete floor, echoing more and more loudly through the subterranean complex.

Athanasius came to the end of the B-Level's main corridor and tried one of the office doors, only to find it locked. Feeling his blood pressure rising, he back-stepped towards the staircase and tried the next. This door opened, and closing it silently behind him, Athanasius allowed his eyes a moment to adjust to the near blackness, then made his way around what appeared to be a table at the centre of the room, to its far corner. There he crouched down, drawing deep and slow breaths as quietly as possible. His pulse seemed to beat at full volume.

The thumping footsteps in the corridor continued, changing direction from time to time, one moment louder and closer, one moment softer and further away. And then, at last, they seemed to fade and go silent all together. A long silence followed and Athanasius slowly exhaled a sigh of relief. Whomever the Council had sent to find him hadn't made it as far as his impromptu hiding place.

Waiting a long moment to ensure that they were gone altogether, Athanasius at last felt a push of confidence and rose from his crouched stance. With a forced swallow he drove the coppery taste of fear from his mouth.

An instant later, the door to the small room smashed open and the bright beams of two lights flared in his eyes. Before Athanasius could fully register the sight, the Friend with the gun leapt across the office in a single bound, grabbing him by his hair and yanking back the Egyptian man's head. Thrusting the blunt barrel of his gun into his gaping mouth, he pushed it deep into his throat.

'Please, no noise,' the second man noted calmly, switching on the room's main lights. Athanasius felt his gag reflex start to rise as he choked on the gun.

'Dr Athanasius Antoun. We've been looking for you for quite some time,' the Friend continued. 'And at long last, here we are, together.' He nodded to his partner, who removed the gun barrel from Athanasius's mouth, renewed his grip on the Librarian's hair and threw him forcefully into the corner of the room. His body slammed into a filing cabinet, and he fell helplessly to the floor. The first Friend casually took a seat in a nearby chair and swivelled it to face him.

'Given some conversations you've recently been having with a certain Emily Wess,' he continued, 'we need to have a . . . let us call it a frank discussion, shall we?'

Athanasius stared up at him in terror.

'These surroundings, though,' the Friend continued. 'They're so impersonal, don't you think? In a moment, I shall have my colleague escort you back to your office, and there we will have a constructive conversation, you and I.' There was a sadistic anticipation in the man's expression.

'But first,' he continued, 'I feel it is important to make sure you understand exactly where you stand in our relationship. I suggest we begin by setting out a few terms for our discussion.' He held out his hand and received the Glock from his partner. Calmly and without hesitation, he aimed it at Athanasius and fired a round directly into his torso. Antoun's body slammed back again into the filing cabinet from the bullet's force, his eyes wide in panic.

The Friend calmly handed the gun back to his partner.

'My terms are these,' he said, looking down at Athanasius as the blood began to flow from his new wound. 'Cooperate, and the hell you're about to face can be made a little shorter.'

Saturday

CHAPTER 97

Oxford, England – 7.45 a.m. GMT

The Secretary's car turned off Oxford's Broad Street onto Catte Street, which ran perpendicular to it and alongside the Old Bodleian Library. The huge, square structure was the focal as well as working heart of the university, containing both a series of working reading rooms for under- and postgraduate students, as well as the famous Duke Humphrey's Collection, which housed Oxford's priceless treasure of rare and ancient books, manuscripts and other literary artefacts. The architecturally distinct Divinity Schools hall was connected to it, protruding out from its side like some strange, Gothic appendage.

The morning crowds were already milling in the streets. The city's resident students were in bed for Saturday's traditional lazy morning, but the small city still bustled. Shopkeepers along the Broad Street peddled their wares – mostly trite trinkets emblazoned with the Oxford logo or college crests – to tourists who travelled from all over the world to gaze on the 'dreaming spires' of one of the western world's great palaces of learning. Walking tour groups formed in huddles along the pavements, and delivery vans scuttled over paving stones and red tarmac to feed the shops for the weekend of business ahead.

Ewan's men had arranged to have the entire Bodleian Library complex marked off and closed for their arrival, and he took pleasure in looking out his window to see the red and white barrier fencing that had been erected around the entrance gates to its fenced courtyard. Signs dotted the barriers, boldly announcing that the ancient buildings were 'Closed for emergency repair works'. A fabricated story about a gas leak in one building, and a manufactured electrical problem in another, and Ewan's men had faced few hurdles in getting the complex closed for the day.

He revelled in such power. *A power that will soon grow, exponentially.*

For a moment his thoughts travelled back to his own childhood, when his father, then the Council's aggressive Secretary, had first begun to indoctrinate him in the power of the position he would one day hold. William Westerberg III, whom Ewan had always called simply 'sir', had sat him in the corner of his home office on a small wooden chair with strict instructions to watch and listen, but not to make a sound. He had watched keenly, entranced by the power his father – and his whole family – commanded, as the older man had made a series of phone calls ordering a crew of FBI officers to release a man he did not wish to remain in custody. One of his Friends had been arrested mid-operation and this had displeased Ewan's father. A few moments later, with surprisingly few words uttered into a phone over a tumbler of expensive Scotch, the FBI was bowing to his wishes. Ewan had remained in the room with his father until the released Friend had been brought in to report. His father had chided the man for being caught, and sent him on his way with instructions to terminate every FBI agent involved in his release, so that no leaks exposing his involvement could ever be found.

In that encounter, Ewan had seen what power was, and he had craved it for the remainder of his life. It was both his birthright but also his project: to gain more power with every action. Every time he did, he thought back to that first experience. His father, he knew, would be proud.

As his car came to a halt, Ewan exited and immediately made his way through a gated door into the Old Bodleian complex. The doorway was a large wooden interruption of the flat stone face of the building's eastern wall, itself covered in the brightly painted crests of a handful of the oldest Oxford colleges. The fixture was itself a much-photographed feature of the building, but today it was of little interest to the Secretary. He walked through the doorway without so much as a sideways glance.

Through the archway, he and his men found themselves in the central courtyard of the Bodleian, open-air and cobbled, surrounded on all sides by the wings of the library itself. Directly across from them was the main entrance into the building proper: a glass-faced gateway into the university's hub of learning.

Flanked by his men, Ewan crossed the small space of the

courtyard, passing the prominent statue of Thomas Bodley, the library's founder, on his way to the entrance. Entering through the glass doors, he stared immediately before him, across the small foyer, to their ancient wooden counterparts. To his left was the readers' entrance to the reading rooms in the wings; to his right was a gift shop selling overpriced merchandise stamped with images of the library.

Directly before him, two massive wooden doors marked the entrance into the Divinity Schools.

'Open them,' he commanded his men. With a slow pull to counter the doors' immense weight, a man in a grey suit prised them open. Before they had come fully to a halt, Ewan and his team had entered the hall.

CHAPTER 98

Having arrived in Alexandria in the early hours of the morning, Emily had been forced to spend a few hours asleep in the airport lobby as she'd had no success in reaching Athanasius by phone. He was listed in the public directory only at his office, and this wouldn't open until a reasonable hour of the morning. *As long as he works on Saturday*, Emily thought. Athanasius Antoun struck her as the sort of person who worked every day, weekends providing little change to his routine.

She had returned to the grounds of the Bibliotheca Alexandrina before its opening, only slightly refreshed after making do with a rinsing off of as much of her body as she had been able to manage in the airport's public facilities. She watched as employee after employee entered the library, hoping to spot Antoun's distinctive features. But, after a series of false sightings, Emily began to realize that possessing a black beard and a suit hardly marked a man out as distinctive in northern Egypt. When the front desk clerks finally emerged to unlock the glass doors to the public, Athanasius had still not arrived.

This is not good. Not good at all, Emily's thoughts began to gain pace once again. She might be too late. Her assailant's threat in Istanbul against the Egyptian Librarian may have already been carried out. *Could another Assistant Keeper have been killed in the latest act of this long power play?*

Yet she couldn't leave without knowing for sure, and Athanasius's subterranean office was the only contact point Emily had for him. She owed him at least enough, and she certainly needed him enough, to make her way down into the dark recesses of the library and seek him out there. Perhaps he wasn't dead. Perhaps he'd simply worked through the night and was already inside.

Entering the great library once more, Emily made her way to the main reading room and retraced the steps she had taken two days earlier as she descended to the lowest floor. At the bottommost level she found the third door against the stacks' back wall and entered into the access corridors in the library's basement. Feeling far surer of herself than she had when she first made this journey, she made her way back to the small side-corridor, with the collection of etched builders' names upon its walls and found herself, once more, before Antoun's wooden door. Above it, Emily could still see Arno's etching, 'LIGHT', that had brought her to her first encounter with the Egyptian man.

She knocked on the door, no hesitation in her actions this time around.

'Dr Antoun, it's Emily Wess.' She waited anxiously for the door to open, barely able to contain the anticipation burning within her to find out the final information she knew Athanasius could provide her.

No answer came from within, and Emily repeated her knock, louder than before.

'Athanasius, please, open the door, it's important.' When the silence continued, she cast her mind back to their first encounter, remembering the 'pass phrase' that had gained her entry then.

Do I actually have to go through this routine again? There was an exasperation to the thought, but Emily didn't have time to dwell on it.

'Fifteen, if by morning!' she announced. She stopped her knocking with the words, waiting – but no reply came, and the door remained closed.

'Enough of this!' It had started only as a thought, but in Emily's energized state it came out aloud. She knelt down before the door and gazed at its knob. *This isn't just a set of cheap handcuffs*, she thought to herself, unsure whether her earlier lock-picking skills would be enough for a proper lock. But when she reached her hand to the knob, it turned easily.

Left unlocked. It was a good sign. Antoun was almost certainly inside. But why wasn't he answering? Sensing something was wrong, Emily stood, turned the knob the remainder of the way and flung open the door, pushing her way into the office. The small room was lit only by a small lamp on the cluttered desk.

Athanasius's body was slumped over on the floor. At first Emily thought he might simply be asleep, reclined in a strange pose before his filing cabinet. But then she saw the pool of blood surrounding the man and soaking through his brown suit. Then the lacerations to his face, and the strange, unnatural way his fingers angled away from his hands. The signs of torture revealed themselves one by one.

Emily's horror and anger were simultaneous. More blood, more death – people were being murdered all around her, she was being attacked herself, and she hadn't asked for any of it. Yet the men responsible were after something she knew they could not be allowed to have, with aims they could not be allowed to accomplish.

Emily stooped down next to Athanasius, feeling the impulsive need to check his condition. Realizing she was an intruder at the scene of a violent assault, and apparently a murder, she tried to remain attentive to her surroundings, avoiding stepping in the pool of blood around him. She grabbed his shoulders, keeping her sleeves from brushing against his bloody chest, and pushed them back, lifting the man's head off his chest. The white shirt beneath his jacket was soaked in blood and Emily could see the puncture wound from a bullet hole near the middle of the right side of his chest. The blood that had poured out of the wound was copious, and Emily saw more of it on Antoun's clothes and on the floor than she imagined could possibly be left inside his small frame.

But then Emily became aware of something unexpected. Athanasius's body was still warm beneath Emily's hand.

Removing a hand from his shoulder, she pushed a finger onto the carotid artery at Antoun's neck and felt a pulse pushing through his veins. It was faint, but it was steady.

Athanasius was still alive.

CHAPTER 99

Oxford – 8 a.m. GMT

High above the Secretary and his men, the ornate ceiling of the Divinity Schools looked down, designed to impress and faithfully fulfilling its architect's vision. Arches and points dotted the strange creation, which seemed to reach down from above with long stone fingers, teasing the students and tourists who for centuries had passed beneath it. Morning light from the room's tall windows cast orange rays and grey shadows across the ceiling's sculpted texture, giving its three-dimensional design added depth.

Ewan Westerberg's eyes, like those of his men, immediately went to the hundreds of carved symbols dotting the ceiling. A total of 455 of the bosses punctuated its surface at regular intervals, positioned at odd angles and inclines, giving the whole room a strangely cryptic, confusing feel.

'Find it,' he barked. His crew had used the flight to scrutinize photographs of the Divinity Schools' ceiling, easily obtained off the web in high-resolution format. The sign they were looking for, the sign that had been encrypted beneath a front image on Athanasius Antoun's computer, was located on the central line of the main arch, near the second recess from the hall's far western end. No resource they had found had been able to identify what the sign was meant to stand for, but that mattered little to Ewan. The symbol's importance lay in the fact that it mattered to the Keeper who had pointed Wess towards it. For Ewan Westerberg it was the only symbol in the room that mattered.

The Friends located the glyph quickly, and Jason snapped an order for a tall ladder to be brought in from one of the vans the men had parked outside the complex, filled with tools and materials for whatever it was that might lay ahead. A few moments of assembly later, and the ladder was in place. Jason lost no time in scaling its height, coming face to face with the ceiling above, and the strange carving that was their focus.

'What do you see?' Ewan demanded.

'Nothing, yet.' Jason scrutinized the surface of the round, sculpted symbol that hung inches below the main surface of the ceiling. Its cryptic face looked the same here as it did below. *But it would, of course*, Jason thought. Whatever he was looking for would be hidden. He scanned every surface, every corner.

'Nothing seems to be written on it,' he called down to his father and the other men below. 'At least, nothing I can see.'

'Keep looking,' Ewan snapped. 'It might not be something written. Look for anything. Anything unusual.'

Jason kept up his search, but the surfaces of the sculpture were clean. The only 'text' it contained, or marking of any kind, was the strange lettering of the symbol itself.

It has to be something else. Jason began to probe the carved image with his right hand. Perhaps it was something etched into the shape? Something to be felt, rather than seen? But nothing revealed itself on the smooth stone surface.

He could sense the mounting frustration, coupled with anticipation, from the Secretary and the men below. It has to be here, he reminded himself. He began to push at the surface, looking for something more immediate, more direct than a message. Perhaps this symbol actually was the means to enter the library itself. He poked a sturdy finger at every surface and contour, hoping for something to depress, or fall away, or otherwise do whatever it was this fixture was meant to do.

Nothing happened.

Finally, only one possibility remained. Balancing himself carefully on the ladder and leaning his hips forward against its top tiers for extra stability, Jason wrapped both of his hands around the edges of the sculpted sign, and pulled. The carving held fast. It was only when, as a final effort, he twisted the symbol, applying what torque he could from his perch, that he felt it give way. His adrenaline spiked as he realized that the whole carving rotated clockwise with his hands.

'It's moving!' Far below, Ewan himself grabbed the ladder and offered his own hand at supporting his son above.

Jason continued to rotate the symbol until he had turned it a full 90 degrees. As it passed that mark, he heard a distinct click and the symbol locked into its new position.

At the same moment, things began to move – in the most literal sense possible. From below, a distinctive, low scraping noise suddenly came from the far corner of the hall, filling its enormous space. As Jason descended the ladder, Ewan and the others crossed the room to examine its source. In the corner, one of the great stone floor segments slowly slid away into the stonework of the building's wall. A dark hole appeared where the rectangular block had previously been.

Within its shadows, a stairway led into the darkness below. Ewan could barely contain his exhilaration.

Two of his men made to descend the steps first and clear whatever room lay beneath, but Ewan would have none of it. This was a moment he intended to possess, to own, for himself. He would lead. Others – all others – would follow.

He grabbed a flashlight from the man closest to him and, pushing the others aside, descended the steps. They proceeded downward for what seemed a surprising length, finally terminating at what Ewan thought must be at least two storeys underground. Beyond the final stone step was a small corridor, lit only by his flashlight and covered in dust and cobwebs.

The corridor was not long, and at its end Ewan could see an old, wooden door. How many centuries old he could not tell, but it, like the whole subterranean structure in which he found himself, looked far more ancient than even the old buildings above.

As the Secretary approached the wooden door, his men descending the steps into the hallway behind him, he noticed a metal plaque fixed to its surface. Covered in a thick layer of dust, he could not make out its wording. He held the flashlight at shoulder level, using his free hand to brush away the dirt to the brass sign beneath.

And there, Ewan read the most beautiful words he had ever seen.

REPOSITUM BIBLIOTECAE ALEXANDRIANAE

The vault of the Library of Alexandria. Found, at long last. He had waited his whole life for this moment.

He pushed on the wooden door, and held his breath as it slowly swung open.

CHAPTER 100

Simultaneously, Alexandria, Egypt – 10.00 a.m.
(8.00 a.m. GMT)

'My God, what have they done to you!' Emily cried, easing Athanasius's head back against the filing cabinet behind her as the man gradually regained consciousness. He had started to come to as Emily's finger pressed into his neck to check for a pulse, and when he had managed to force open his eyes, pulling himself out of the deep sleep that threatened to over-take him, Athanasius had seen Emily's face. It was a face that represented such hope, on which he had wagered so much. It was a face he had not thought he would see again.

'The Friends . . . they were . . . here,' Athanasius gasped. The hole in his chest made speaking difficult. 'In the middle of the night. They wanted . . . to talk.' A terrible, raspy gurgling came from the bullet wound as he spoke. Emily recognized the signs of a punctured lung. She rose and began to move towards the phone on Antoun's desk. If she could call for help, it was possible an ambulance could still arrive in time.

'No,' Athanasius commanded from the floor. Emily turned back to him, meeting his gaze, and the wounded man wheezed out firm words. 'It is too late for that now. At this moment, we must think . . . beyond ourselves.'

Emily hesitated, the instinct to call for help hard to suppress. Athanasius, however, gazed up at her with a pleading expression. It was the face of a man who knew his time had come, and who wanted to make the most of his remaining moments. Turning away from the desk, Emily knelt back down at his side.

'My God, they know, don't they,' she said. 'They came to kill you.' Antoun forced a nod.

'They interrogated me for hours . . . but then, the . . . bastards . . . missed my heart,' Athanasius wheezed. Emily was suddenly overcome by the condition of the man she had come to find. Antoun had spent the past hours alone on his floor in the basement of the Bibliotheca Alexandrina, tortured to a grotesque degree, slowly bleeding to death in silence, alone.

'I told them nothing,' Athanasius added. His face, formerly a dark, olive complexion, was pale, its shadows deeper and his features already taking on a ghostly air. Yet he managed to force himself to speak. 'They tried . . . but I kept . . . our secret.'

'I know, I know.' Emily tightened her grip around Athanasius's arm, trying to convey comfort, trust. 'I'm sure you were strong.'

Athanasius smiled, content that he had performed his duty to the fullest. But then the smile passed. His mind was still alert enough to question the fact that Emily was with him at all.

'Why are you . . . here?' he managed to ask.

Emily sensed Antoun did not have much time, so she kept her details to a minimum.

'I found the final clue. It was in Dolmabahce Palace, along the banks of the Bosporus. I found it in Ataturk's bedroom, on a sofa next to the bed where he died.'

Athanasius raised an eyebrow as far as he could manage.

'It was just like the others,' Emily continued. 'The crest for the library was followed by a line of text. But this time there was a second symbol. Both it and the text – "A full circle: Oxford's divine ceiling, and Library's home" – point back to Oxford.'

Athanasius didn't have the strength to ask again, but his expression repeated his question for him: *so why are you here?*

'I'm here,' Emily answered, 'because I don't believe for a minute that Arno Holmstrand would have constructed a series of clues that led me around in circles. He was constantly ranting against circular logic, circuitous reasoning. And now, he's supposed to have created a series of instructions that has me end up back where I started, just yards away from the University Church where this all began? I'm sorry, I don't believe it.'

Athanasius nodded, but his head began to sag, and his breathing became more laboured. Emily sensed she had to get to the point, to ensure that this man's sacrifice was not in vain.

'Everything you've told me about the library, Athanasius,

about your Society, is old. It's all tied up in the past.' Emily
leaned forward until her face was mere inches from his. 'That
can only be half of your story. There is something you're not
telling me. Please, now is the moment. You have to tell me
what I don't know. What is it that makes the library new –
different? That breaks it out of the circle.'

Athanasius looked back into Emily's deep, blue eyes. He
knew, deep inside, that these were his final moments, and
Wess did as well. He blinked as forcibly as he was able,
focusing on keeping conscious as long as he could.

'Do you remember . . . Dr Wess, what I told you about
our . . . our work as Librarians? About how . . . we deliver
our materials to the Keeper each month?'

Emily's mind raced to their former conversation.

'Yes, yes I do. Something about delivering parcels to be
collected.'

'That's right. We collect our information, and deliver it
by parcel. The Keeper . . . he receives our materials and
updates the library from them.' He gasped and began to cough,
blood spraying from his lips and chest wound.

'On my desk,' he finally managed, using his forehead to
motion towards its cluttered surface. 'It's my . . . most recent
contribution. I was meant to drop it off later . . . today.'

Emily peered up at the desktop. There, among the papers,
was a small parcel, wrapped in brown paper and tied, almost
stereotypically, with winding string. She reached up and
grabbed it.

'Go on . . .' Athanasius insisted. 'Open it.'

CHAPTER 101

Oxford – 8.15 a.m. GMT

With the full weight of history upon him, Ewan Westerberg watched as the door slowly swung open. He was about to set eye upon that which his predecessors had sought since the Council's advent. He was the fiftieth Secretary of the Council, and he had always been proud of this numerical distinction. But with what he had done today, he would be remembered always as the first. The greatest. The one who accomplished what others could only consider a hopeless impossibility. The power and influence he had first tasted in his father's study would reach an extent in him that no Secretary before had ever possessed.

He waited for the thud of the door as it swung fully open and met the stone wall to its left, coming to an abrupt halt. The moment had arrived. Taking a deep breath, Ewan lowered his head and stepped into the library's vault and home.

The single beam of his flashlight was quickly joined by those of his men, and as his eyes adjusted to the light, his breath was taken away by what he saw.

Stretched out before him, deep beneath the ancient city and extending as far back into the dark recesses as his eyes would allow him to see, were row upon row of carefully crafted wooden shelves, reaching from floor to ceiling in careful, deliberate array. Long tables were spread among them, and filing units towered between the stacks. The beauty of the place was stunning, and its dimensions vast. There was room here for hundreds of thousands, even millions of books.

But the sight of the ancient shelves was not what took the Secretary's breath away. It was the fact that every single one of them was empty.

CHAPTER 102

Simultaneously, Alexandria, Egypt – 10.15 a.m.
(8.15 a.m. GMT)

The parcel was tiny and thin. As Emily snapped the string ties and tore away at the paper, she wondered how anything worthy of the library's weight could possibly be inside.

What lay beneath the paper, however, stripped the question from her mind. Emily tried to conceal her surprise. In her hands was a small plastic sleeve, containing a single, silver DVD.

She looked up at Athanasius, but the dying man was already speaking.

'The library may be old . . . Dr Wess . . . but it has always pointed towards something new . . . made use of what is new. We submit our information by disk, rather than bundles of books and papers, because the Library of Alexandria . . . is no longer a storeroom of manuscripts, papers and volumes. The library, Dr Wess . . . is a network.'

Once again, the history of the Library of Alexandria, as

Emily understood it, changed. This was a word she had not anticipated hearing.

'A network?' She stared at the Egyptian man, turning the silver DVD over in her hands. 'You mean, it's online? On the Internet? The web?'

'Something like that,' Athanasius answered, his breathing starting to fail. Still, he had a satisfied smile on his face. 'Though obviously the Internet itself would be too risky . . . too public, too vulnerable. Our version is . . . let us say . . . a little more secure. A little more . . . protected.'

He coughed again, and this time the blood flowed from his mouth and Athanasius buckled under the force of the convulsion. Emily cast the DVD aside, leaned forward and took the man in her arms. She had never watched a man die, and she felt an overwhelming urge to comfort this good man in his final moments.

'It's okay, Athanasius,' she whispered to him, the other man's body gradually going limp in her arms. 'You've given me what I need to know. You've done well.'

With his final ounce of strength, Athanasius leaned his head up towards Emily's face, grabbing her shoulder and putting his mouth next to her ear.

'Did you really think, Dr Wess . . . that we would still be using wooden shelves and filing cabinets? This great city couldn't contain the library 2,000 years ago . . . Do you actually believe . . . any physical vault could do so today?' He bored his eyes directly into Emily's as long as he could, willing her to understand. And it was those eyes, the eyes of the library's new Keeper, that Athanasius saw as his life ebbed from him and he slipped into a sleep from which he would not awake.

CHAPTER 103

The Oval Office, Washington DC – 8.30 a.m. EST
(1.30 p.m. GMT)

The president of the United States gazed across his desk at the assembly of men arrayed before him in the Oval Office. The events of the past three days had been so unexpected, they had come upon him with such surprise and such ferocity, and now they had led to this point. Three of the most powerful men in Washington – the secretary of defence, a starred Army general who served on the Joint Chiefs of Staff, and the director of the Secret Service – stood before him, together with his own vice president. They did not come to identify a way through the trauma, or to reveal that the fraud of it all had been exposed. No, they came to tell him that the events of the past days had been the beginning of the end, and that the end itself was to come the next day. Tomorrow: the day that suddenly looked to be the final day of his presidency.

'I am giving command of the operation itself to the Army,' Ashton Davis said. He spoke, as he had from the beginning of his conversation, with a restrained but firm demeanour. 'It is the military that considers you a threat, and it is therefore under the military's auspices that your arrest will come.'

'A threat!' the president almost laughed back. 'This is ridiculous! I'm no threat! This is nonsense!'

'A series of executions of your closest aides, Mr President,' General Huskins interjected, 'is not nonsense. Terrorists are systematically assassinating political figures, not just on American soil, but in the capital itself.'

'But I have nothing to do with that,' Tratham answered, defiant. 'They were good men. I've never done anything to endanger them.'

'That's simply not true,' Davis answered. 'You may not have arranged for their deaths, but your advisors were killed by Afghans declaring jihad on everyone in your inner circle who's had anything to do with your illegal activities in the reconstruction effort.'

The president's face was now a shade of deep, fiery red.

'How dare you, Ashton! You know damned well I've never had any illegal dealings in the Middle East. Hell, I've spent the majority of my administration fighting to re-build Afghanistan after the destruction my predecessor wreaked on it!'

'While on the side you partnered with the Saudis,' Huskins pointed out. 'What the hell did you think the Afghans would do when you sold out business and construction rights in their country to their sworn enemies?'

'Dammit, Huskins, I've never had dealings with the Saudis!'

'That claim stands at stark odds with the abundance of evidence that we, and the rest of the world, have at our disposal to prove otherwise.'

'The crap in the press?' President Tratham was enraged. 'It's all slander. Lies. You should know better! I don't know where it's come from, but someone is setting me up.'

'Bullshit,' General Huskins answered, his own temperature rising. 'There are documents with your signature, financial records, statements from your Saudi partners, emails—'

'It's crap!' the president snapped. 'I have no idea who could pull off all this, but I've never sent an email to any Saudi "partners" in my life.'

The secretary of defence held a hand up before the general could react. Allowing a moment of silence to calm the emotion of the moment, he spoke again with measured, firm tones.

'Enough. Mr President, let us end these desperate protestations. We have not come here to discuss the issue with you, but to describe what is going to happen in response to it. The future path is set. Your arrest will take place tomorrow morning. We're doing you the undeserved courtesy of a final afternoon to get your personal affairs in order, to see to your family's arrangements and any other personal plans you may wish to make – but mark my words, if you attempt to go to the press, to get away from Washington, to avoid responsibility for your actions, we'll act immediately.' He stared firmly into the president's disbelieving eyes. 'Barring such a necessity, however, tomorrow morning at ten a.m. you will be arrested by General Huskins and taken into military custody at Fort Meade.'

President Tratham took long, slow breaths. He stared into the face of this coup, right in the middle of the Oval Office. His heart was filled with hatred for the men before him.

'On a Sunday?' he questioned. 'You're going to falsely arrest the president of the United States on a Sunday morning? The American people aren't going to stand for any of this.'

Ashton Davis stared back at him with resolve.

'The American people are already calling for your head to be stuck atop the Washington Monument, Tratham.' He dropped all pretence of official respect. 'And besides, from this moment on, you are no longer in a position to speak for the American people.'

Sunday

CHAPTER 104

In the hours that passed after Athanasius Antoun's death, Emily had acted quickly. Pocketing the DVD that constituted Antoun's final 'parcel' for the library, she had given the office a brief but thorough search, looking for any documents or other items that might reveal a connection to the library. She found none – Athanasius had been exacting in his attention to secrecy. Then, moving as quickly as she could in the awareness that the longer she lingered at the scene, the greater the likelihood she would be spotted or caught at the scene of a murder, she had wiped down every surface she had touched, attempting to eliminate anything that would point to her. Finally, she had done her best in the circumstances to give a respectful farewell to the man who had given his life for the library's preservation. She laid the man's body out on the floor, folding his arms across his chest. She did not know what religion Antoun subscribed to, but a small Coptic cross on his desk hinted at some degree of devotion. Emily closed her eyes and said a short prayer for the man's

455

soul, and left his office for the final time, leaving the door slightly ajar so that other workers who passed by would see his body sooner rather than later. Not to be left in that condition for long was the final kindness she could offer.

Now she sat on another Turkish Airlines night flight, soaring through the darkness over the Mediterranean on her way back to England. Since leaving the grounds of the Bibliotheca Alexandrina, she had devoted herself to two tasks: remaining out of sight, and preparing herself for what she needed to do after the flight. The former she accomplished by taking a taxi from the Corniche to a market neighbourhood near the Borg El Arab. There she found an ATM and withdrew all the cash her bank would allow. Stepping into the nearby bank itself, she exchanged the cash for British pounds, and then used her credit card again to exchange the equivalent of another 200 pounds and withdraw 600 Turkish lira. That would be the last time she used her cards. She would buy her ticket to the UK at the counter, with cash, and she would wait to do so until as late as possible before the flight closed. The Council would still be able to track her, but she would give them as little time as possible to formulate their plans from her movements.

Her mind had then been on what lay ahead. In England, in Oxford, she would have more resources at her fingertips than she had in Egypt. She knew the library's vault was not there – that had been a ruse left by the Keeper. In fact, what she now knew meant that the library might not have a vault at all. Her understandings of history had shifted once when she had learned that the Library of Alexandria might have been found, then again when she had learned it had never been lost. Now, to discover that it had progressed through history, with history – leading history – and wound up digital, the stuff of metallic disks, networks and the general space age, history had again been transformed into something new.

Before her flight had departed, Emily had found an Internet cafe near the airport and located a terminal with as much privacy as was available. There she had slid Athanasius's DVD into the desktop's drive, hoping to gain some first-hand experience of the library's contents. As it turned out, the main contents of the disk was encrypted, a fact that Emily realized shouldn't surprise her. But beside an inaccessible folder on the finder's display of the DVD's contents was a text file with a simple, two-word title: 'For Emily.txt'. Athanasius had known this particular parcel would be collected by Emily, and had left her more guidance than their time together in life had allowed. Had he added this file only at the end, after his attack, as he sat alone in his basement office, gradually bleeding to death? Emily's throat constricted at the thought.

The file contained a fleshed-out version of the narrative that Athanasius had begun on the floor of his office. Emily read it with a burning intensity.

'The Library first began its transfer to a computerized form in the late 1950s when the Society's expansive knowledge of the advancing field of computer engineering made such a move possible. The original intention was solely to back up the physical repository with a digital copy, but in the early 1960s two of our Librarians

> *in the United States began to gather information on new packet-switching research being carried out at MIT's Lincoln Laboratory, together with groundbreaking networking design being advanced at UCLA and the government's Advanced Researched Projects Agency Network, known as ARPA. Though the fruit of their labours, which came to be called ARPANET – the precursor to the modern Internet – would not manage its first live transmission until the autumn of 1969, we saw the potential of their work far earlier and, combining it with technologies we had absorbed from Soviet researchers, completed construction of our first fully functional network in 1964.'*

As Emily read over the information, Arno Holmstrand's words again came back to mind. 'Knowledge is not circular: ignorance is circular. Knowledge stands in what is old, yet points to what is ever new.' The transformation of the library in the second half of the twentieth century was testimony to the Keeper's vision. The library had stood on over two millennia of constant operation, with countless additional centuries of collected information, but had pointed the way into the new digital age and led the way there to the world around it.

> *'It was clear that this was where the world was going. We knew this long before anyone else – and so we took the first steps. Then, when the time was right, we helped others along the way, making sure there was a certain balance to the development of these new technologies. This was, after all, at the heart of the Cold War. It was not in our interest, or the world's, that any one power*

should possess this technology alone. We helped make sure it
advanced, and spread as it should.'

Again, as before, the Society of the Librarians of Alexandria
had played its tactical role, not simply of gathering information and knowledge, but using it – 'sharing' it, as Athanasius
had described their work – in a way that Emily could not
help but feel was manipulative. This discomfort had arisen
when Athanasius first told her of the Society's active role in
shaping world events, and it returned every time she pondered
the way they wielded their influence. There was a danger in
such control.

'As the Library's digitization continued, our network expanded
across the globe. Just like the network that became the Internet,
ours was designed to be redundant, failsafe. It is everywhere, and
nowhere. It has nodes across the world, though each simply routes
data. Where the data itself is stored, how it is kept, I do not
know. All I possess is the Keeper's absolute conviction that the
system is undiscoverable. Even if you and I were to find one of
the physical machines that makes up our network, and dissect it
to pieces, it would give us nothing. Nothing is kept hard-coded
or on physical drives. All the data simply "floats" in memory
between the parts of our network. If you discover a component,
attempt to hijack it – all you will find is a bare computer. An
empty box.

'What is most important is that the Keeper was able to access
it anywhere. Wherever he happened to be in the world, he was
able to interact with its contents, make his updates, and release

data as he required. There was an interface he could access when-
ever needed, wherever required. But what that was, I never
learned.'

Emily's optimism had begun to fade as she neared the end
of the file. The thought that the library was a networked
collection, accessible in electronic format, had seemed to
imply it was closer to hand than she had believed over the
past days. There was no need to seek out some deftly hidden
vault or repository: Emily simply needed to log in to the
network, and the knowledge of all those centuries would be
at her fingertips. But as Athanasius's file described the scope
of the precautions the Society had taken to make the library
undetectable and, even if parts of its structure were found
physically, she realized that the way ahead would be chal-
lenging. Then, to learn that the interface itself was not known
even to the one individual who had possessed the most information on the library and Society – with that knowledge the
library started to seem farther away than ever before.

'The Library is everywhere,' Athanasius's file concluded. *'I am*
certain that if the Keeper were still alive, he would be able to
access it right here, in this building, even in my office. But how,
I simply do not know. What you have to find, Dr Wess, is the
way in.'

As Emily had closed the file and ejected the DVD from the
terminal, she realized that over the past four days two men,
by all accounts great men, had spent their final hours leaving

their last testaments for her, and that the course of her life was being shaped by their dying wishes. The feeling of being part of something noble, something great, hit home with a new concreteness.

Emily now sat back, compressed into her small airline seat, gazing vacantly out the small window as the shadowy hills and mountains of Western Europe passed slowly beneath her in the black darkness of early morning. The 'way in'. It sounded so simple. In reality, it was a puzzle Emily knew would not be easy to solve. But as she continued to ponder, her surprise at the latest revelations began to fade. Why should she be surprised that the library had been 'upgraded' to meet with the circumstances of the modern world? The original library had been, in its day, a thoroughly modern, thoroughly ground-breaking creation. Never before had a repository for information in such quantity been devised, much less executed. Never before had a centralized staff been networked, deployed all over the Empire and known world, to gather data for such a collective databank of human wisdom and employ it tactically for human advancement. Was it any great surprise that this library, as it grew, should have adopted new means to further its aims – to keep itself at the cutting edge of new and creative industry?

Her thoughts gradually grew more confident. She had escaped death. She now knew what she was really looking for, with no more subterfuge. Arno Holmstrand had set up the elaborate stage of the past four days to bring her to this knowledge, this understanding, and Emily was convinced that she would be provided with the information necessary to find what still needed to be found. The list of ways Arno had already set her up for success was a long one.

List. The word stuck in her mind, calling her back to the one issue that didn't fit nicely into the greater scheme of things: *the list of names – names in two groups, in two text messages*. She remembered Antoun's revelation that these were part of the Council's plot to gain power in the American government, and she had seen enough news throughout the past three days to know that America's current presidential administration was toppling. The plot, whatever it was, was working.

Those two lists. Emily's memory now flashed to a moment, a comment, that had come from her attacker in Istanbul. As the man had stripped Emily of her phone, he had passed it to his partner with an instruction about the texts containing the list's two groups of names. '*It was sent to her in two text messages – the second is the key. The one that contains the names of our men.*'

That was it: *our men*. From Athanasius Emily already knew that the first group were those individuals that had been targeted and executed as part of the plot to force the president from office. She had assumed the second group were men that the Council wanted to promote – men they could manipulate in a new administration. But her attacker's words had been more concrete than this. '*The names of our men.*' The second list of names was not of individuals to influence and manipulate: it was a list of the Council's men, its own members, who, with the fall of the president, were being situated to step into new positions of power.

Emily's skin went an icy cold. If she was right . . . she almost couldn't fathom the extent of the Council's grasp, or its treachery. They names on the list were names she knew well. Names every American knew well. Names known all over the world. The sheer ingenuity of the Council's plot was coupled with the terrible realization of just how far their power really stretched. As Athanasius had predicted, they were creating a vacuum of power at the top of the American political system; but they weren't doing it in the hopes that they could fill the void with men they might influence. Their men were already in place: they would simply step up to new office. And the vice president was only the beginning.

These people had to be stopped. This Council had to be stopped. Emily had to find a way, however daunting the task. She would land in England shortly and return to Oxford. Once there, she would trace out the final steps required to locate her aim. She would discover what it truly meant for the library to be a network. And she would find a way in.

CHAPTER 105

Oxford – 4 a.m. GMT

An hour and a half after her flight landed in Heathrow, Emily stepped out of a taxi in a residential neighbourhood of Oxford, and into a red British Telecom call box. She'd stripped her new Turkish phone of its battery, crushed the device and left it in Egypt. The Council surely had other ways to track her, but Emily would do whatever she could to make that task more difficult for them.

Dropping a fifty-pence piece into the slot on the phone, she dialled from memory the six digits for Peter Wexler's home phone. It was four in the morning, and the old professor would be asleep, but at least this meant Emily could be certain of reaching him. And Wexler would forgive the hour once he heard what Emily had to say.

'What? Good heavens, who's ringing up at this time of morning?' Peter Wexler mumbled his thoughts into the receiver without any semblance of a polite greeting.

'Professor Wexler, it's Emily Wess.'

Wexler was suddenly alert.

'Dr Wess, my dear! Where are you calling from? Have you made any discoveries?'

'More than you can possibly imagine. The kind that keep me from telling you where I'm calling from.'

Wexler was now sitting upright in his bed, fumbling for the cord on the lamp at his bedside.

'This is wonderful, Emily!'

'It's far bigger than just a historical discovery,' Emily went on. As briefly as she could, she gave Wexler an overview of the council's existence, and of their role in the political situation overtaking the US government.

'The people involved . . . I can't even begin to tell you how far they have infiltrated Washington. It's just terrifying.' She rattled off a few of the key names from the second portion of the list.

'Emily, good Lord, this is something that needs to be made public. And immediately. Nothing's been announced, but all the papers are expecting that something big is going to happen in Washington today. No one knows exactly what, or how, but the rumour is that your president will not be in office by bedtime.'

And the race keeps picking up pace, Emily thought to herself. News of the escalations in Washington was confirmation that she had to find some concrete connection, some hard evidence, to take it public. And she knew where she would find them.

A minute later, with arrangements made to speak with Wexler again later in the day, Emily hung up the phone and began to walk cautiously down the street.

Yet Antoun had told her about the conspiracy in detail, and Emily knew he could have learned the details from only one place. The library. It had to contain information on the people involved, on the plot itself, likely with a fair amount of further information.

The information she required was locked in its vault. Emily spoke the revelation to herself: '*It all comes down to the library yet again.*'

I've got to find a way in, and now. In a few hours it may all be too late.

She quickened her pace.

CHAPTER 106

The Secretary sat quietly at an antique desk in a small home office in north Oxford, the base of his Central England team of Friends. Before him was an open laptop computer, a half-emptied glass of whisky and a series of printouts from various of his men. He forced his breath to remain slow, his temper to remain calm.

A day earlier, his rage had been almost uncontainable. The sight of the library's vault, stripped of its precious contents and barren in its vast underground tomb, had nearly slipped him over the edge into a place as dark as the stone chamber in which he had stood. All he had worked for, sought and struggled to obtain had been there, right at his fingertips, only to be snatched from his grasp. It had been staged with almost impossible cruelty, building his approach with intensity and anticipation. Secret passages, dark corridors, archaic wooden doors and Latin inscriptions – everything that had captivated him had, in that moment of vision, suddenly seemed a vicious attack on his worth, his leadership, his whole life.

He took a long, full sip from his glass, returning to grinding his teeth even before the liquid had fully passed his tongue. Normally he was not a man to drink in the morning, but over the past night he had not slept and the distinction between night and day seemed to matter little.

Recalling the moment was enraging. Ewan had struck out at everything, overturning tables, knocking down row after row of old wooden bookshelves. He had even lashed out and struck his own son, as if all the failings of the moment were his doing. Jason had taken his father's blow without flinching or responding. For all that the discovery of the empty vault had enraged the father, it had deadened the son. Jason had stared vacantly into the empty chamber, his disappointment hardening into a stony, bitter resolve deep within.

Now, in the early hours of the morning after, the Secretary's fury was gradually transforming into focus and determination. As much as the sight had seemed to mark the utter failure of a life's work, he realized that what it truly marked was simply the next stage in the puzzle and game that had always been the Council's work. He had hoped that the puzzle might have at last been solved, the game won; but now it was clear that it must go on a little longer. Besides, the mission in Washington was only hours away from its fulfilment. The arrest of the president would take place at 10 a.m. local time in Washington, which was 3 p.m. in England.

Ewan looked at the clock on the desk. Ten hours, and he would control the most powerful government on earth – whether or not the library was in his possession. His task at this moment was to reclaim his focus as the Council's leader as they prepared for this ascension of power, and to take the necessary steps forward in turning the tragedy of the previous day into something gainful and productive.

The Secretary's moment of self-inspiration was interrupted as Jason entered the office.

'Sir, there's news.' Jason stood in the doorway, formally, his left eye swollen from his father's blow the day before.

'What news?'

'Wess has made a call since landing.' He waited for his father's temper to flare. Emily Wess had somehow managed to make it out of Istanbul before their team there had made it to the site intended for her execution. The Council knew she had then made a second trip to Alexandria, where she would undoubtedly have discovered the termination of Antoun. She had since travelled back to England. Airline records showed her on the night flight to Heathrow, but Wess had done a good job in reducing the number of means by which they could pinpoint her location. She'd stopped using her bank cards after withdrawing a large sum of cash in Egypt, and the tracking signal from her replacement mobile phone had never left the African continent.

Not bad for an amateur, Ewan had thought to himself. *She's even managed to keep her fiancé from us.* A certain, mild annoyance accompanied the thought. The Friends had not been able to locate Michael Torrance since Emily had spoken to him from Istanbul. Presumably she had urged him into hiding, and two of the Secretary's men had been kept busy trying to locate him since. He knew they would find Torrance eventually. Still, he regretted that his desire to keep her alive until they'd terminated Antoun had prevented him from offing her before she gained this newfound persistence.

'Who did she call?' the Secretary demanded.

'Peter Wexler, from a pay phone in Oxford.'

'So,' Ewan mused, 'she's here.'

'The call,' Jason continued, 'it was . . . detailed. She's told Wexler about the list, about the Washington mission. She's been told by Antoun that—'

'By Antoun?' the Secretary interrupted. 'I thought we terminated that leak yesterday?'

Jason's face flushed, causing further pain to his swollen eye.

'Our men went through with the termination, as you'd ordered, but clearly something didn't go right. He was still alive when Wess arrived back at his office. He stayed alive long enough to tell her something important – to her and to us.'

Ewan fought to control a new fury. His men had failed, and at such a simple task. They would pay, dearly.

'DAMN IT!' the Secretary thundered. 'This woman just won't get out of my way!' He clapped his large hands down on the desk and stood. His eyes were filled with venom and he pointed a commanding finger at his son as he spoke.

'Find Emily Wess, now. I no longer care whether she might

one day lead us to the library. I want the bitch dead. You find her, and you put two bullets through her brain. And then you watch until her life is gone. She had better not be breathing when you leave.'

CHAPTER 107

7 a.m. GMT

Walking down Alfred Street as the sun began to rise over the Oxford skyline, Emily knew she was at risk if she remained in public view. The Council would find her. She could imagine them pouring their energy into the task even now. She had to get someplace safe, someplace she could sit and think, and figure out how to gain entry to the library's network, which Athanasius had been so certain could be accessed anywhere.

She turned a corner onto Bear Lane, keeping as close as she could to the built-up edge of the pavement. A few yards ahead was the entrance to her old alma mater. Within the walled compound of Oriel College she would be less visible than anywhere else, and the college also had a library with 24-hour access where she could set herself to the task of finding what Athanasius had called her 'way in'.

Minutes later, she was nestled into a side bay of Oriel's library, the same elderly porter working at its entrance as had been on staff during her postgraduate days, who remembered her fondly and allowed her in with a friendly welcome. A small, personal desk between narrow rows of stacks afforded her privacy, and its computer terminal gave her Internet access. She would have to start somewhere in her search.

Emily began by following the few leads she could draw from the details Antoun had left her in the text file on the parcel DVD. He had referred to the development of the Internet, known in its earliest form as ARPANET and designed by the government's Advanced Research Projects Agency. That seemed a reasonable place to look. Unfortunately, that agency, which had a history of changing its name back and forth between ARPA and DARPA – depending on when the government wanted to stress its defence-based potential – seemed to offer little in the way of insight for Emily's quest. Calling up various websites on the history of their networking project in the 1960s, she learned a little more about the packet-switching technology they had developed, which was the backbone of modern data networks, allowing materials to be transferred seamlessly across multiple branches of interconnected circuits, rather than simply over a single circuit between one machine and another. Was that the key ingredient of technological wisdom that the Society had 'shared' all those decades ago that had sped along the creation of the networks that now dominated the information age?

It was impossible to know. But in any case, it didn't help Emily one way or the other. What she needed was not simply more history, but something to guide her towards the 'way in' to whatever alternative network it was that the library now occupied.

But there was something more. Emily squirmed in her wooden seat. *Something about this search itself feels out of place.* She had been brought to this point by the work and cryptic guidance of Arno Holmstrand, a man Emily would always associate with techno-illiteracy, despite her recent enlightenment as to the library's true form. Could the world of techno-wizardry and computerized networking minutiae really be the arena toward which Arno was now drawing her?

It's out of character, Emily mused. *Every clue he's left me so far has been something I could relate to. Something literary or historical – something in my area of knowledge.* The materials now filling her computer screen, however, could hardly be further from her realm of experience. Emily had never heard of packet-switching before yesterday afternoon, nor of networking protocols, routers, nodes or any of the other technological information these systems involved. She was in completely unknown territory. As odd as everything she had experienced since receiving Arno's first note had been, she now realized that this was the first moment in which she had no reference points whatsoever. Nothing she could relate back to past studies, theorized historical wisdom, or anything of which she'd ever heard or pondered in her life.

And that doesn't feel right. All this techno-investigating is leading me away from what I know.

She realized she needed to get back to her centre. Discovering the way in had to be connected, somehow, with her world of books and learning and historical study.

There's got to be some piece I'm not seeing, she thought. *What connection am I not making?*

Rather than seeking out information on networking and technical matters, Emily needed to return to the historical realm that was her home. If Arno was going to give her a final revelation, a final push, it would come from there.

For this task, Oriel College's own library collection would likely prove a more fruitful arena of research than the Internet at large. Emily minimized the search window on the terminal's display. It would be better to work with the library's online catalogue. She'd not used it before, having always worked from the University's central Bodleian system. But in her experience, most online library catalogues were pretty much the same.

And it was that casual, practical thought that led Emily Wess where she needed to go.

Even as the thought formed in her mind, the world around Emily seemed to go silent. In an instant, her mind was transported back to a sunny, spring day on the green campus of Carleton College. She was sat at a computer desk, searching the catalogue of the Gould Library for a volume on second-century Roman political intrigue. Opposite her, at an identical terminal, was Arno Holmstrand. The professor had looked out of sorts at the computer, yet his fingers had navigated the terminal's interface skilfully enough. It was a memory that had flashed through Emily's mind shortly after she'd learned of Holmstrand's death, and now it returned, the context of the moment having changed so much.

'*Have you ever observed,*' Arno had asked, '*how so many*

universities, all over the world, use this same archaic software? One version here, one version there, but at its core, it's all the same.'

Emily's whole body tensed at the vivid memory, so clear that it was almost as if she and the famous professor were back together again as they had been all those months before.

'I've used this contraption in Oxford,' Holmstrand had continued, *'in Egypt, in Minnesota. Not once has it cooperated.'* He had leaned a little forward, his weathered eyes beaming straight into Emily's. *'This very system, Emily. Everywhere.'*

And in that memory, Emily knew.

All the confusion of the past hours suddenly snapped into absolute conviction. She looked back to the screen before her, and saw the way in.

CHAPTER 108

Emily's heart raced as she looked down at the computer screen with renewed focus. The online catalogue for Oriel's library was localized to the college's collection, but it formed part of the centralized interface for all of Oxford's libraries: the Oxford Libraries Interface System, or OLIS. Though Oxford had customized the system to suit its federated collection of over 95 independent college, faculty and departmental libraries, it was all based on a core software package called GEOWEB – a spectacularly hideous, cumbersome and counter-intuitive cataloguing system that Emily had used in countless libraries all over the world. Even her home institution, Carleton College, used it, though they had recently packaged it under a new shell called 'The Bridge', meant to symbolize the connection between the bibliographic collections of Carlton and its rival institution that sat just over the river on the opposite side of the small town. The technology behind the brushed-up interfaces, however, remained the same.

Arno's words, in that conversation they had had so many months ago, Emily now knew had been offered in preparation. '*Have you ever observed how so many universities, all over the world, use this same archaic software? One version here, one version there, but at its core, it's all the same . . . This very system, Emily. Everywhere.*' The comment had seemed to be simply friendly, frustrated banter at the time. But with all that Emily had learned since, it was now clear that Arno had been telling her something. Something specific.

He was showing me the way in.

Emily pulled her wooden chair closer to the desk, setting her left hand to the computer's keyboard and taking the mouse in her right. The familiar blue and white interface of the OLIS catalogue appeared on the screen, awaiting instruction as it did every hour of every day and every night. And, as Athanasius had noted of the Keeper's ability to access the library, the catalogue was accessible anywhere and at any time. Any computer, any phone, any iPad. It was universal access in its fullest form.

Emily rubbed her hands together, suddenly aware that her fingers were shaking so severely that she didn't know if she would be able to type.

Calm down, she reprimanded herself. *One step at a time.*

With that, she went through a routine that had become second nature during her days as a graduate student. She selected the main database for the whole of the university collection, ancient as well as modern, then clicked the 'Search for Keywords' tab to call up the advanced search interface.

Three search fields appeared, allowing her to tailor her query however she wished.

Somehow, she thought, *this gets me to the door. To the real network. To the library.* The question was how. GEOWEB's interface was bare-boned and simple: just a few search fields and a 'submit search' button on a white page. There was no room for hidden tabs or concealed links. *It has to be something I type*, Emily thought. *Some sequence of terms – basically an extended set of passwords.*

She closed her eyes and tried to focus. There were three fields on the page. Arno's first set of clues had contained three phrases. The Council's henchmen now had his handwritten sheet of paper, but its contents were burnt into Emily's memory. Typing slowly, recalling each phrase precisely, word for word, she entered them into the three fields:

1. University's Church, oldest of them all
2. To pray, between two Queens
3. Fifteen, if by morning

She stared at the three phrases in the small text entry fields on the monitor. These words had sent her around the globe, and now they were assembled again in one place. The way in, Emily reassured herself, hoping that the only three phrases that leapt to mind would do the trick. She rolled the mouse and clicked firmly on 'Submit Search'.

Her hopes were immediately dashed.

The page that resulted contained nothing, and Emily's heart sank. More precisely, the screen before her announced

'0 Records Found', spitting back her phrases in the form of a complex search query at the top of the screen. But it was a technological version of the same thing. Nothing at all.

A desperate longing to find the right set of keywords filled Emily's mind.

I need another set of three terms.

She no longer merely thought to herself, but in her excitement spoke aloud. 'Three . . . three . . .' Her mind flashed back to the first clue she had discovered for herself, etched into the altar screen of the University College chapel, not far down the road from her present location.

'Glass, sand and light,' she reiterated, recalling how the terms had proven themselves a map for her way downward, to the halls beneath the Bibliotheca Alexandrina. Now she navigated her way back to the new search interface on the computer and entered the three terms in the blank fields.

Glass. Sand. Light. She again clicked 'Submit Search' with an almost uncontrollable anticipation, and this time her pulse increased at the result. A few records appeared on the results display, the more general keywords registering a few hits in the University's 10-million strong collection; but as she looked over the listings, she quickly realized the volumes were innocuous. Unrelated. None of the results bore any relation to her search, or to what she really aimed to find. She clicked through to the more detailed entries of a few, but the process only reaffirmed that the volumes bore no connection to the library.

She made her way back to the main search screen. She had travelled to three cities in the course of her journey –

the solution might lie there. Feverishly, she entered their names: Oxford, Alexandria, Istanbul. Once more, the search yielded no meaningful results, only a listing of volumes that clearly had nothing to do with the library. She tried changing 'Istanbul' to 'Constantinople', but the alteration produced no useful changes.

I need something else in threes!

Every failed attempt caused Emily to edge yet further forward in her chair, to the point where she was now close to sliding off it entirely – but the frustration of dead-end combination after dead-end combination did not sway her from the firm belief that she was on the right track. Arno had highlighted to her this interface months ago. The past four days had helped her to see what it was she was searching for, and why it needed to be found. Now she simply needed the key that would unlock the door that was, one way or another, sitting right before her.

'The three groups,' she spurted aloud. Thumping her fingers loudly on the keys, she typed in her three new phrases: the Library of Alexandria, the Society, the Council.

The screen went blank and seemed to take an interminable length of time to load the results page, and Emily tensed. Was this it? Had she found the right combination?

But when the page finally loaded, it contained only the familiar indication of a small set of standard results, which Emily scanned and again determined were unrelated. The network connection had simply been slow.

Emily's frustration mounted by the second, and she realized her own anticipation was getting the better of her.

Calm yourself, she scolded. *This isn't a race. Don't just frantically enter whatever comes to mind.*

She withdrew her hands from the keyboard and interlaced her fingers, cracking her knuckles and realigning herself on the hard, wooden chair.

You've got to set yourself to this with focus. Like someone who means it.

And for the second time that morning, a single phrase evoked a potent memory. Emily's earlier thought on electronic catalogues had sent her mind racing back to her brief encounter with Arno Holmstrand in the library stacks in Minnesota, and her own self-scolding caricature at this moment, '*Like someone who means it*', now sent her mind back to another encounter with Arno that had always remained etched in her memory. She had re-lived the memory only four days ago, on her drive to the airport with her college colleague as she grappled with the news of Holmstrand's murder. It was a saying that seemed to characterize the eccentricity and quirkiness of the distinguished academic, and Emily's mind now returned to it with singular focus.

'*Say a thing three times*,' Arno had often pontificated, whenever caught out on his tendency towards threefold repetition, '*and people know you mean it. Once, it might have been an accident. Twice, it could be a coincidence. But when a man says something thrice, he says it for certain.*'

Emily closed her eyes and relived the first speech in which she had heard Holmstrand utter his famous quip. *Thrice.* Emily had smiled at the archaism when it was delivered. Now, as she sat before the terminal interface in the Oriel

College library, it caused her whole world to stop and go silent.

Three times. Could it be so simple? Could it be that this comment, which Arno had uttered in Emily's hearing at least a half-dozen times, was meant specifically for her? Another preparation – an instruction for things to come?

She opened her eyes and stared long at the three blank search fields on the catalogue interface before her. Where moments ago she had raced to enter every combination of terms and phrases her mind could concoct, she now looked at the waiting page before her with a kind of terror. If the thought forming in her mind was right, then Arno Holmstrand had been preparing Emily for this moment since their first encounters, seemingly countless months ago, embedding every 'chance' meeting, every 'spontaneous' phrase with a meaning he meant Emily to decipher, decode and use when the time was right. It might normally have taken five years to recruit a new candidate to the Society, but Holmstrand had managed to embed a tremendous amount into Emily's preparations in only a little over one. Their off-hand conversations, even the turns of phrase he had used in public lectures when Emily was in attendance, had all been aimed at providing her with the tools she would need, when the moment was come, to succeed in the quest on which Arno intended to send her. A quest that had since led her around the world. A quest meeting its fulfilment in this very moment.

It was an impossibly elaborate plan, one that suggested almost unfathomable pre-planning, investigation, preparation and worldwide coordination.

It sounds inconceivably elaborate, she thought. *And exactly like what one would expect of the Keeper of the Library of Alexandria.*

With terrified resolve, Emily unfolded her hands and set them on the keyboard. In the first field, for 'Author', she typed what it was she meant to find: the Library of Alexandria. Clicking the mouse to the 'Title' field, she entered the same phrase again, and followed it with identical wording for the third and final 'Publisher' field.

Thrice, because I mean it.

Emily Wess clicked the button for the search. The screen went blank, and then to a familiar white as the next page started to load. But as the browser's progress indicator neared the halfway mark, the whole terminal went black. For a long moment it remained entirely dark. And then, at the top of the screen, there appeared a familiar symbol – no longer etched in stone, but as familiar as it had been in Arno's letter, on the wooden screen in University College, on the door in Alexandria and on a divan in Istanbul, now pixel-perfect for a digital age.

And beneath it, the front page to an online collection like none other Emily had ever seen.

CHAPTER 109

'Hello, Oxford 518 219.' Peter Wexler answered the telephone in the traditional manner, leaving off the dialling codes and sounding suitably old-fashioned in his greeting.

'Professor, it's Emily.'

'Dr Wess, I've been waiting.'

The professor was relieved to hear from Emily.

'Tell me, have you got it? Have you found your way in?' He, like Emily, recognized the urgency of the situation.

There was only a brief hesitation in Emily's voice.

'I've found it.'

'Thank God.' Wexler's exclamation was followed by a lengthy, reflective pause. While the immediate need – the ability to expose the conspiracy in Washington DC might now be in their hands – he still couldn't entirely fathom what Emily had just discovered. The Library of Alexandria. Found.

'I'm looking at it right now. The whole collection. Electronic, just like Athanasius said. The interface is spectacular. And the things I can call up . . . Professor, you simply can't imagine.'

Wexler struggled to absorb what his former student was saying.

'How – how did you find it?'

Emily walked Wexler through the progress of her past hours: her frustration on the Internet, her memory of Arno's strangely insistent comments about library catalogue interfaces, his emphasis on three-fold repetition.

She spoke, knowing the Council would be listening.

'The front door to the library,' Emily continued, 'was hidden behind the simple belief that no one would be so daft as to enter "The Library of Alexandria" in every search field on a page. GEOWEB is one of the most widely used cataloguing interfaces in the world, and its advanced search defaults to three fields, all for different search criteria. Who's going to enter the same phrase in each one?'

Wexler was dumbfounded.

'And that got you in?'

'It got me to the door,' Emily corrected. 'To a blank screen with the library's symbol and a password field. Nothing else.'

The interface had been concealed beneath the immense unlikelihood of anyone entering search terms in the repetitious combination Emily had finally tried. But beyond that concealment, it still remained secretive. Should anyone have chanced upon it, they would have had no idea what they were looking at: just a strange symbol and a request for a password. Even so, Emily was unsure whether this was the way the interface was always concealed, or whether it was simply a tool for access that Arno had left behind for her – Emily's own unique 'front door' to the library that Holmstrand had accessed in his own way.

'How did you get past the password?' Wexler asked.

'Trial and error. I tried every combination of clues, words, comments from the materials Arno left for me. When none of these worked, I tried phrases I remembered him uttering, titles of his books. Everything I could think of.'

'What was it, in the end?'

The ears she knew were listening shaped Emily's response.

'Let's just say it was something I knew well. But not something I'm prepared to tell you over the phone.' Emily smiled as she remembered the moment she entered the correct phrase: the title of her doctoral thesis. Arno Holmstrand had set up every detail of the path to discovering the library with Emily in mind. It was her own experience, her own history, her own memories and work that had provided her with the key to unlocking the puzzles set before her at every turn. And they had, in the end, got her precisely where Holmstrand had wanted her to go.

Wexler had gone silent at Emily's hesitation. Was she afraid others might be listening? Might be after her? Yet she seemed not to hesitate at sharing other details over the line.

Emily continued with the course of their dialogue she had plotted before picking up the phone.

'Listen, Professor, you were right. Not only is the listing of people involved in the Washington plot contained in the library, but so are details about every aspect of its working.

There are more than enough concrete details to expose it fully.'

'And we still have time,' Wexler added, looking at his watch. It was only a little after 9.20 a.m. Across the pond, Washington DC was still a few hours from coming fully to life for the new day.

There was a slight pause as Emily thought over her next words carefully. She'd developed her plan in the long moments of wonder after she'd discovered her way into the library, and it had crystallized as she'd read the full details of just what the Council was doing in Washington. The details came to her with startling speed, and Emily knew precisely what it was she had to do. The way to the library had been complex, but the way forward, to her surprise, came simply and with a comforting sense of calm and responsibility.

'I'm going to a different location to assemble the necessary information from the library. Go to your office in an hour and a half, at eleven. I'll meet you there, and we can phone up the BBC with the scoop of the century.'

'Are you sure?' Wexler asked. His own suspicions were rising. Something didn't feel right, and nothing at all felt safe. He found himself anxiously worried for his former pupil.

'Absolutely. Just meet me there at eleven. If I'm a few minutes late, stay put. I'll get there as soon as I can.'

With that, Emily hung up the phone. She would not be late. In fact, she would be at the office in under ten minutes. That would give her a little over an hour to do what she needed to do.

CHAPTER 110

Oriel College, Oxford
An hour and a half later – 10.50 a.m. GMT

Emily sat at Peter Wexler's desk in his Oxford office. She had arrived only minutes after her phone call to the professor, cleverly got herself past his cunning leave-the-key-on-the-doorframe security system, and had been at work ever since. If her plan was to succeed, speed was of the essence. She knew the Council's Friends would come for her, but she hoped her conversation with Wexler – which included her intention to work from another location until their meeting time – would keep them from arriving until her work was done.

Her intention was simple. The only necessary ingredient was time. If she could finish before she was interrupted, before she was stopped, then everything would be in place and accomplished.

Even as she had booted up Wexler's office computer and set about her plan, Emily had been aware that her actions would amount to a break with centuries, millennia, of tradition. She wondered what Athanasius would think of her plan, given all the attention to secrecy that had pervaded the Society of Librarians since it had first been founded. She wondered what Arno Holmstrand would think. The Keeper had brought her to the door of the library itself, had guided her in, but he had provided little – no, nothing – in the way of instruction as to what she was to do with the information once it was at her fingertips, as it was now. What she was to do with her new responsibility.

You left it to me, Emily had muttered to herself as she had traced her steps back to the library's interface and logged in from Wexler's office. *And now I have to act.*

The absence of instruction only reinforced Emily's course of action. Holmstrand had carefully crafted every movement to bring her here. He had made his intentions elaborate and extensive. Emily had been guided, led, almost manhandled by the man's designs – until now. Arno had provided the approach, but he had left Emily to walk into the library's history of her own accord, to determine her own path.

Ever the professor, Emily thought. *Ever the teacher.* He had given his student tools. What Emily did with them was for her alone to determine.

She had thought through the ramifications of her plan a dozen times in the short period that had elapsed since it had first been conceived. Everything would change. The Society would never look the same. The Council could never again operate as it had. There were risks, and dangers, but they were necessary in bringing down a plot that would have ramifications for every nation in the modern world. Besides, Emily would never feel comfortable simply being absorbed into an organization that had functioned the way the Society had for so long. It may have had noble aims, but it had spent history skirting the edge of morality: gathering, preserving, cherishing, but also censoring, manipulating, controlling. Emily knew she could not play a part in such activities. She was now the only person alive who had access to information governments the world over would kill to obtain, to possess in the dark corners where they manufactured their own plots and schemes. She knew she could never determine what to share, what to conceal. More, she was not sure any person could, or should, be given the power and ability to make such choices.

No, her plan was the right one. The only one. The light that had for so long been buried under the Egyptian sands, hidden away in corners of empires and secret vaults, would again see the full force of day.

Emily brought her focus back to the computer. 45 minutes into its progress, her work advanced on schedule. She had only to watch it come to completion, then share the news – both of her discovery, and of her actions – with Wexler when he arrived. She did not know whether the professor would praise or condemn her choice. But he would live with it. More importantly, Emily would be able to live with it.

When, a moment later, the door to Peter Wexler's office burst open, torn away from its old hinges by the force mounted against it, it was not the professor who stood before Emily

Wess. As Jason Westerberg charged into the room, ensuring that, apart from the presence of Emily it was empty, Ewan Westerberg appeared in the doorframe, levelling a gun at Emily's forehead.

CHAPTER 111

'Dr Wess,' Ewan announced. 'We meet at long last.' He spoke in a professional American accent, silver hair perfectly combed, black suit tailored precisely to his form. He reeked of business, power and authority, and held the gun before him without any hint of discomfort at its ominous suggestion.

Emily did not recognize the man, but his companion she recognized as the more commanding of the two men who had attacked her in Istanbul. Two and two quickly came together.

'You must be the Secretary,' Emily answered, looking across Wexler's desk to the two men. The computer to her left continued to carry out her instructions.

'One fact, among many,' Ewan answered, 'that you should not know. The Keeper was mistaken to have involved you.' His eyes bored into Emily's. 'But all mistakes can be corrected.' The gun maintained its aim at the moist patch of skin between Emily's eyes.

Emily, however, did not cower at the gesture. Her life had changed in the past twenty-four hours, and somewhere in that period she had found a resolve she had not possessed before. As she looked up at the man who almost certainly planned to kill her, Emily felt a certain peace. Maybe this was to be the end. But this man would not defeat her.

'I apologize if I'm not the face you expected to see,' Ewan continued. 'By the time Peter Wexler arrives, this will all be over.' He nodded towards the phone lying beside the keyboard on Wexler's desk. The naiveté of Emily Wess almost disappointed the Secretary. 'We listened in on your discovery. We've followed your steps, found the same interface. The only missing ingredient is the password.'

Emily allowed her eyes to glance quickly at the monitor before flashing them back to the Secretary and his gun.

Almost. It's not quite done.

Ewan took a step forward, annoyed at the young woman's silent obstinacy. Drawing back the hammer of his cherished Army revolver, he said threateningly, 'I promise you, Dr Wess, you are going to tell me that password. And then you are going to die. These are simply facts, which you can either accept or try to deny. But there is no way I am leaving this room without access to the library, and final assurance that my work in Washington will not be undone by an amateurish, insignificant nobody like yourself.'

Jason, standing to his father's side, watched Emily's eyes widen at his father's commanding threat. He also took note of the computer on the desk. Emily had been working on it when they'd entered the room.

'Are you logged in now?' he asked, interrupting the Secretary's measured, threatening silence. The sheer potential of what was present on the small desktop computer, the fact that it was all here, now, washed away his usual restraint.

Emily considered stalling, hesitating in her response. But she had had the time she required. The process was now at its completion, and there was little purpose in hiding it. It was time for secrecy to come to an end.

'Yes,' she finally answered, turning in her chair to face Jason. 'With no one else left alive who knows how to access it, I guess the past few days have fulfilled Holmstrand's wish and turned me into the library's new Keeper.'

Ewan and Jason both cringed at her audacity. To believe herself worthy of possessing, by default, information the Council had worked for over a millennium to obtain – it was unthinkable. Ewan's finger tightened around the trigger.

'I was just performing a little update, in keeping with my new role,' Emily continued. Her heart sped faster than she had ever known it to beat, but she forced herself to maintain a controlled composure. 'You know, entering in a few details to do with this whole adventure of ours.' She reached out and turned the monitor to face across the desk, coming into the Secretary's line of sight. Ewan glanced at the screen, keeping his gun levelled on Emily. A progress indicator showed Emily's updates being saved – a traditional sliding bar edging from left to right to show the percentage of the update completed. A number beside the indicator showed '97.5%', and Ewan watched it tick over to 98 before he cast his gaze back to Emily.

A. M. DEAN

'A dedicated, if pointless, activity, Dr Wess. I am far less interested in putting material into the library than I am in getting it out.'

Emily sat back in the old desk chair.

'If only you knew what is in there,' she said. 'You might be a little more carefu—'

'Don't you lecture me on the library!' Ewan boomed.

Emily froze; the sight of the Secretary losing his composure was a fearful one.

'Don't you dare presume to tell me one thing about this library!' Ewan continued, his face turning a vicious red. 'You, who know about it only from storybooks and the scraps of history that were left for you and the rest of this ignorant world. What could you possibly know? My whole life has been this library, as was my father's life, and his before him. I can recite more about its contents in my sleep than you ever knew in the whole of your pitiful life.' He forced the gun closer to Emily's head as he spoke of her in the past tense, as a person already dead. 'And you, you have the audacity to tell me to be careful! To stand in awe of what I don't know! When you, like our Council, have worked for over a thousand years to seek out the truth, to obtain what is yours; when you have fought empires and states to keep your sights honed in on the truth; when you have made the sacrifices we have made to get what we need – *then* you can speak to me about what is in there.' He waved the gun towards the monitor, its progress indicator continuing to move towards its finishing mark.

'The Society of Librarians has believed itself noble all

496

these centuries,' Ewan continued, furiously, 'believed itself
sacred and humanitarian. But what is it other than another
version of us, seeking and keeping power for itself? What has
given them the right, since the time of the great kings and
empires, to see themselves as guardians of mankind's wisdom
and truth?'

'It may surprise you to learn I don't disagree with you, not
entirely,' Emily answered, stomping down her nerves. The
words threw Ewan slightly off pace. 'I agree that having such
power in an unlimited, concealed way is dangerous, for anyone.
But at least the Society has been lofty in its aims.'

'No, they've shown themselves only to be cowards, hiding
in the dark,' Ewan answered, 'shovelling knowledge into dark
vaults, burying it in the earth. We, *we* – ' he indicated Jason,
and by him the whole of the Council ' – we have learned
to *act*. To *do*. Even with the library hidden from us, we have
gained power. Strength. We have controlled governments,
scientists, technologies. We have forged a network of power
that knows no international or cultural boundaries, which
accomplishes its aims in the face of every obstacle. Just look
at the American government: the strongest in the world, and
yet we have brought it to its knees. A few years of promoting
the right people to the right offices, then a few strategic assassinations, a handful of carefully crafted documents leaked to
just the right hands, and we have brought down a president,
putting our own man in his place. A council member, one
of my men, will be president of the United States, surrounded
in office by his fellow Councilmen. And yet the cowardly
animals who make up the Society call themselves the rightful

A. M. DEAN

guardians of the library's knowledge! Imagine what we could have done, had we had their resources at our fingertips!' Ewan's rage filled the office, and he spat out the words with a hatred that had been brewing since his youth.

Emily now sat completely still, and even Jason remained frozen in the corner, his still-swollen eyes entranced by his father's renewed anger.

At long last, Emily spoke.

'I have to admit, I never would have thought you could reach so far into Washington as you have. I've seen your list of who is involved. Imagine what the world will say when it finds out Vice President Hines has been a member of your Council for over fifteen years. You must have had this plot in mind for decades.' She didn't have to pretend to be awe-struck by the Council's remarkable scheme.

'No one outside this room and my Council chambers will ever know,' Ewan answered, his anger still fierce.

'But even then,' Emily continued, unabated, 'that would only be the first shock. What will they say when they learn that the man you have organized to depose President Tratham, to arrest him in the Oval Office itself, has been a member of your Council even longer. Mark Huskins, a four-star General in the US Army, on your payroll since before he ever enlisted.'

'I told you, no one will ever kn—'

'Or Ashton Davis,' Emily's momentum kept her words rolling, despite the Secretary's interruption. 'The US secretary of defence, the man to whom the whole nation's security is entrusted, a third-generation Council member. Tell me, Mr Westerberg, how many of his military decisions during this president's administration haven't been simply the public front for your own designs?' Charged up with the knowledge of events she had gained from the library, Emily now rose to her feet, coming face to face with the Secretary.

'Once this becomes public knowledge, do you honestly believe there will be any place on earth where you and your Council can hide? Do you believe there is any nation that won't feel the betrayal of your decades and centuries of political manoeuvring, your undermining of governments.' She leaned forward towards Westerberg. 'Do you think you, Mr Secretary, will live through this catastrophe?'

Ewan had listened to enough of the imbecilic threats of Emily Wess, and hatred now coursed through every vein in his body. He took two long, deep breaths, regaining his commanding composure. With his free hand he straightened his suit and wiped the spittle from the edges of his mouth and chin.

'It is not me who should be worried about living through this moment,' he said, his voice all at once back to its smooth, business-like tone. 'Your prophecies of doom are all well and good, Dr Wess, but the hair-brained plan you and Peter Wexler concocted to share these details with the world will go no further than the phone call wasted to plan it.

'And now,' he continued with icy resolve, 'now you will give the library to me. I will ask only this once. If your response isn't to cooperate immediately, I will pick up the phone, and within minutes your fiancé will be dead – and I will make you listen as my men kill him, right there at the campground hideout where the two of you had your romantic weekend together.' He watched Emily's expression as he spoke, pleased to see surprise and fear at the fact that the Council had discovered where Michael was hiding. 'And then I will kill your parents,' he continued, 'and your friends. And I will carry on with everyone you know, every one you hold dear – whatever it takes. Mark my words well: you *will* give me the library.'

Emily swallowed hard. The Secretary was right. She had no choice. She straightened her own posture, attempting to mirror Ewan's own professional demeanour.

'That won't be necessary,' she said, with all the boldness she could force. 'I fully intend to give it to you. You, and everyone else, will have it in about – ' she looked down at the monitor, its progress indicator at 99% ' – about twelve seconds.'

At first, Ewan didn't understand; and then his faced blanched.

'What are you talking about?' He kept his gun trained on Emily, but glanced at the computer screen.

Jason, however, understood perfectly.

'Oh, hell,' he said, stepping forward to the monitor. He took it in both his hands and turned it fully towards him. As he looked closely at the sliding graph, moving towards its mark, he felt his skin go cold.

'What is it!' Ewan demanded, flashing his glance back and forth between the son at his side and the professor at the end of his gun.

'She's not updating the library,' Jason answered, the words sticking in his throat. 'She's *uploading* it.'

Ewan's enraged eyes snapped back to Emily.

'Uploading? To where? To what!'

Emily stared back.

'To everyone. To the Internet. The *public* Internet. I have found the library, and you have found it through me; but in a matter of seconds, its entire contents will be available to the world at large. To everyone. As it should be.'

Ewan felt a tearing pain in his chest as he listened to Emily's words. The progress indicator on the monitor slid to 99.9%.

'Including,' Emily added, 'everything it contains on your Council, your activities in Washington, your crimes. I've taken the liberty of highlighting these, so they're easily accessible. Every name, every date, every detail. You will come out of the dark, along with everything else.'

Ewan spun to his son.

'Stop this! Cancel it. Destroy it. Do something. *Anything*!'

Jason frantically reached across the desk for the keyboard, pulling it towards him. But as he situated it beneath his hands and made ready to type, the glowing blue line of the indicator completely filled the bar, and the number beside it changed before his eyes.

100%. Upload Complete.

CHAPTER 112

11.10 a.m.

'No!' Ewan Westerberg let out a cry that was almost bestial in its force, his eyes wide and pinned on the screen. He seethed with the frustrated anger of a lifetime.

He snapped his head back to Emily. In his rage, in his defeat, there was only one thing left to do to the woman. She would pay with her life for the countless lives she had just destroyed. In a single motion, Ewan raised his right arm back to the level of Emily's face and moved his finger to the trigger.

A gunshot echoed in the small office with deafening force. Emily's body seemed to contract and go rigid. Whatever pain a gunshot inflicted, she did not feel it. She only heard the thundering noise, saw the startled rage of her attacker's face, and wondered how it would look to watch the world disappear.

But when the body slumped downward and fell across the desk, it was not Emily's. Ewan Westerberg, pierced in the back of the head by a bullet hole, fell with a thud. Behind the Secretary, in the doorway, Peter Wexler stood flanked by two armed police, their firearms still drawn and levelled at Ewan's body. A third moved into the room and cornered Jason Westerberg, whose eyes did not move from his father's fallen form even as the officer pinned him to the wall and cuffed his hands.

Emily couldn't speak. As she felt the symptoms of shock start to well within her, Wexler pushed his way through the officers and stepped around his desk. Emily turned to take in his focused expression.

'Your phone call,' Wexler explained. 'I may be a curmudg-eonly old man, but even I know when something foul is afoot. You feared others might be listening to our call. I feared you were right, and that the members of this Council would try to stop you, so I brought reinforcements. The more I pondered your worry, and the dimensions of the group you had described to me, the more I knew we weren't going to be left alone here.' He looked down at the dead body slumped over his desk. 'It seems both our fears were justified.'

Emily Wess looked into the face of her mentor. Somehow, through it all, a grateful smile came. She embraced the older man who had just saved her life.

When the moment had passed, Wexler looked down on the scene.

'So, it's all over?'

Emily gazed at the computer, its 'Upload Complete' notice still flashing on the screen.

'No,' she said. 'It's just beginning.'

EPILOGUE

The sky was a clear blue as Emily stepped out of an unmarked building at the heart of the nation's capital. She had been interrogated by the FBI for almost a day and a half, probed for any information she knew about what was being reported the world over as a plot the vice president had concocted to claim the power of the Oval Office for himself and his men. Never before had the country faced such a long-running and far-reaching conspiracy with so many of its pivotal leaders part of the treason.

Two days after his attempted coup, it was the vice president who sat in a jail cell, not the president. Samuel Tratham, vindicated in his denial of any involvement in illegal dealings abroad, sat again behind his desk in the Oval Office, his power and reputation intact. A cache of documents had been released that proved the earlier materials to be forgeries and inventions, even down to the Afghan video calling for retaliation. The plot was vast, international and extensive.

Already the FBI had arrested – in addition to the vice president himself – the secretary of defence, Ashton Davis, and the chief general of the US Army, Mark Huskins. Of the core figures that had been part of the 'tactical response team' assembled by Secretary Davis, only the director of the Secret Service, Brad Whitley, had been found to be guiltless. Even so, when he learned how he had been played by Davis and Huskins, it had taken him less than an hour to tender his resignation to the president. Tratham, knowing a good and duty-bound man when he saw one, had already refused to accept it.

Emily had shared everything she knew about the coup with the interrogators. The release of the materials that had exposed the plot and exonerated the president – including a list of all the 'Friends' the Society had stationed as operatives throughout the country – had been anonymous, but they had quickly traced the release to Wexler's office, and through it to Wess. It made her something of a heroine of the hour, even among her interrogators, but she had been explicit in her sessions with the FBI: she did not wish to be named. And they had thus far honoured her request. Every media outlet in the world was covering the story, and each was crediting the exposure to 'an anonymous leak containing an untold wealth of information'.

That anonymity was what Emily wanted. As she stared around her at the surprisingly peaceful Washington landscape, she mused over the long hours of questioning that had just concluded. She'd told them everything – within reason, and with a certain twist on the details. She had told them of the plot, of being contacted by a man in Egypt, about being given access to a vast collection of intelligence she had then published onto the Internet. Everything they needed to know. But as to the source, as to the nature of the library's existence and the centuries-old operation of the Society, she chose to keep these matters to herself. As far as the government and the public would know, a vast store of previously private knowledge was now public. As to how it had been gathered, as to the expansive network of Librarians that still straddled the globe, still gathered data, the world would have to remain in ignorance.

Some things still needed to remain hidden. The work of the library had prevented a crisis. Faced with its future, Emily knew it could prevent others – but only if its ability to observe, collect, consolidate and expose information remained active, and remained secret. She was not willing to pick-and-choose the truths to share in the way her predecessors had been; but she had seen into the darker side of human manipulation in the past week, and was no longer willing simply to stand back and let such forces exist unchallenged.

The new Keeper had work still to do, and though its contours may have changed, there was still a role for the Society to play.

An hour later, Emily stood outside the domestic arrivals gate at Dulles International Airport. In the past 48 hours she had seen into the heart of ancient vaults of wisdom and power, she had stared into a gun barrel and witnessed an evil empire's fall, she had been interrogated in the belly of a Washington governmental complex and shaken the hand of a grateful president; but in the mix of all this, she had come to realize that there was only one sight, one face, she really wanted to see. The knowledge of millennia might now be hers, but without this person, it meant nothing.

She looked up, and saw the face she longed for, beaming from the gate.

'Why hello there, Mrs Keeper,' Michael said, approaching, his expression a warm smile. He gazed into her eyes a moment before throwing his arms around her. They shared a long, profound embrace.

'I've missed you,' Emily finally said. Michael said nothing, only pulled her more fully into his arms.

'You owe me,' he finally muttered into her ear, teasingly, 'for running off like that without me.'

'What do you say I make it up to you,' Emily offered. 'We could go on a trip.'

Michael raised a wry eyebrow at the suggestion of travel by the woman who had just journeyed around the world without him.

'*Together*,' she added, laughing. 'Sit on a beach somewhere. Read a good book.'

'You have something in mind?' Michael asked.

'Whatever you want,' Emily answered. 'I've got access to a pretty good library.'

AUTHOR'S NOTE

The plot of *The Lost Library* is constructed on the bedrock
of genuine history, and plays with authentic historical
mysteries that are often interesting enough to captivate in
their own right.

The ancient Royal Library of Alexandria.

The details provided in the book on this once-great miracle
of the ancient world are accurate, as is the general sense of
mystery over the ultimate fate of Egypt's remarkable literary
legacy. Founded at the behest of Ptolemy II Philadelphus
some time in the early third century BC, its endowment and
rapid expansion appear to have been part of the new regime's
intention to create a glory and legacy for Egypt that even
the earlier Pharaohs had not managed. Linking ancient religion, philosophy, science and the arts, the Library became a
storehouse for wisdom the world over – and the charter,
perhaps dating to the reign of Ptolemy III, for its librarians
to confiscate the written works of all visitors to the city so

that they could be copied and entered into the collection, is a genuine part of the Library's remarkable history.

The translation work of the librarians attained renown in their own day, and that reputation remains even in ours. The translation of the Hebrew scriptures into Greek, commissioned for the Library by Ptolemy II and, by tradition, carried out by seventy translator-scribes, came quickly to be known as the *Septuaginta* (which translates as 'of the seventy') and was the standard version of the scriptures known throughout the world within two generations. It is the version quoted by Christ and his disciples, and it remains even today the version of the Old Testament employed by many of the world's Christians.

The Royal Library became the ancient world's great centre of learning, with its librarians including men whose names continue to inspire historians and scholars (e.g. Apollonius of Rhodes, Eratosthenes, Aristophanes of Byzantium). The assertion in the novel, that no one knows how large the Library eventually became, is accurate – as is the note that it assuredly quickly surpassed the initial aim of 500,000 scrolls. Mark Antony's sacking of Pergamum in the first century BC, donating the entire contents of its library's 200,000-scroll collection to the Royal Library in Alexandria, would have seen to that rather quickly.

The various theories discussed by Kyle, Emily and Wexler regarding the destruction and disappearance of the Library are all genuine hypotheses entertained by scholars today. The once-popular belief that the Library burned during the attack by Caesar in 48 BC is, as Emily notes, impossible, given that ancient documents give evidence of its on-going existence much later. The two possibilities explored in the novel – namely, the sack of the city by Amr ibn al'Aas around AD 642, and the destruction of Pagan centres of learning in Alexandria by Patriarch Theophilus in the fourth century AD – are the most popular hypotheses amongst scholars today; but the disappearance of the once-great Library does, indeed, remain one of the great mysteries of antiquity. All that can be known for certain is that by the sixth century, it is simply a non-entity in the historical record.

The new Bibliotheca Alexandrina in modern-day Egypt.

The details provided in *The Lost Library* on this impressive building's history and dimensions are, remarkably, true. Dedicated in 2002, this $220-million structure is almost as impressive as its ancient namesake. Though its 8-million-volume capacity is impressive, its physical dimensions are perhaps its most impacting features. The brain-child of Norwegian architectural firm Snøhetta, whom UNESCO appointed to create the new monument to Egyptian history and culture, its 160-metre diameter granite disk of a roof is meant to represent the rising Sun, and its facade contains text in 120 of the world's languages and scripts. Designed at an angle and sloping into a pool of water meant to symbolize the sea, its main reading room alone contains 70,000 square metres of floor space. As Emily's guide relates, the Bibliotheca Alexandrina is home to a separate collection of ancient and modern maps, a wing of dedicated multimedia materials, a scientifically advanced book- and manuscript-restoration department, and even an extensive Braille collection. There really is a planetarium in the complex, as well as eight separate museum halls with more than 30 special collections.

What may surprise some readers is that the guide's claim in the book, that the Bibliotheca Alexandrina is home to the only complete copy of the Internet Archive, is also true (though since 2002 the Archive also now has other main hubs). The new library was donated a databank of over 200 computers with more than 100 terabytes of storage, valued then at over $5 million USD, containing a complete 'snapshot' of every page on the internet from 1996-2001, taken every two months. Since that time, the Internet Archive project continues to create a running archive of the whole internet, and to make this publicly available to posterity. The Bibliotheca Alexandrina remains one of its principal data centres.

It was, in part, this confluence of the ancient Royal Library's history with the future-leaning digital work of the new library, that was the inspiration for one of the main currents in this book.

The royal palaces of Topkapi and Dolmabahce
in Istanbul.

These two magnificent testimonies to the reign of the Sultans in Turkey are faithfully described in *The Lost Library*, and are just as distinct and different from one another as Emily's perception relates. While both are major tourist attractions today, and while Topkapi Palace is by far the more authentic reflection of true Ottoman royal culture, it is nevertheless the much later, nineteenth-century Dolmabahce Palace that is the more visually stunning. Architecturally grotesque, playing chiefly to the desire to impress Western European visitors without maintaining any distinct style of its own, it is an overwhelming building in every sense of the word: 110,000 square metres of floor space contain the famous Baccarat Crystal Staircase, as well as a grand hall in which hangs the world's largest chandelier – a 750-lamp behemoth that was the gift of England's Queen Victoria.

Contained within the palace is the bedroom of Mustafa Kemal Ataturk, the founding father of modern Turkey. The clock on the table is still stopped at 9:05 a.m., marking the precise moment of his death on November 10th, 1938 – as all the clocks in the Palace were for many years. Devotees of history will be happy to know that, so far as I am aware, no furniture in the room has actually been defaced.

The University Church of St Mary the Virgin
and the Bodleian Library in Oxford.

I am happy to say that the University Church of St Mary the Virgin in Oxford has not actually been destroyed, and stands proudly in that city's centre today, as it has since the thirteenth century. A spectacular sight with a tower that offers some of the best views of the city, the University Church has a remarkable history and has been a central monument in much of the religious history of Britain and post-Reformation development. Cardinal Newman preached from its pulpit before stirring unrest by leaving Anglicanism for the Roman Catholic Church; and John Wesley, a key figure in the history of Methodism, also preached there before being banned for his too-provocative tone. The Church was also used as a courtroom, and notches in its interior pillars can still be seen, where once a platform was erected for the trial of Latimer, Ridley and Cranmer (now known as the 'Oxford Martyrs'), who were burnt in the middle of Oxford's Broad Street for refusing to bow to the nation's new Roman Catholic leanings. Those sad moments of its history aside, the stained glass and carvings in the Church are wonders in their own right.

The Bodleian Library – the central library of the University of Oxford – is one of the great institutions of scholarship in the Western world. There really are miles of underground library tunnels and chambers running beneath it and beneath most of central Oxford, even if they might not be used for quite the things I've described in the book.

ACKNOWLEDGEMENTS

The Lost Library would never have come about without the assistance of various individuals who have offered invaluable support throughout the writing and production process. A close friend and brilliant writer, E.F., provided a series of careful readings and detailed comments in the early stages of writing, without which this book would have been very different.

Especially at the middle stages of writing, I benefited from the careful comment, criticism and editorial evolution provided by Paul McCarthy, a talented creative editor. But I owe the most to Thomas Stofer and Luigi Bonomi at LBA, who, amidst the hundreds of submissions and hopeful queries that come across their desks as two of the finest literary agents in the business, saw in an early manuscript of *The Lost Library* the potential for a powerful novel, and helped me bring it to the reader in the form you hold in your hands today. I realize that investing time and energy in a first-time novelist is always a risk, and for taking that risk and for putting so much energy and enthusiasm into turning risk into reality, I shall forever be grateful.

And, as a capstone, to the whole team at Pan Macmillan: most especially Wayne Brookes, Publishing Director, together with my superb editorial team of Eli Dryden, Donna Condon and Louise Buckley, amongst so many others involved in this project. These are the women and men who took what started as scraps of paper on my office desk and brought it to printing presses all across the globe, working with almost unreal energy and enthusiasm to bring this book to light. My sincere thanks to all.

extracts reading groups
competitions books new
discounts extracts
competitions
books
new
events books
extracts
new titles reading groups
interviews
events extracts
discounts
new books events
events new
discounts extracts discounts
www.panmacmillan.com
extracts events reading groups
competitions books extracts new